# The Three Ju

Edgar Wallace

**Alpha Editions**

This edition published in 2023

ISBN : 9789357933452

Design and Setting By
**Alpha Editions**
www.alphaedis.com
Email - info@alphaedis.com

# Chapter I                The Firm of Oberzohn

"£520 p.a. Wanted at once, Laboratory Secretary (lady). Young; no previous experience required, but must have passed recognized examination which included physics and inorganic (elementary) chemistry. Preference will be given to one whose family has some record in the world of science. Apply by letter, Box 9754, *Daily Megaphone*. If applicant is asked to interview advertiser, fare will be paid from any station within a hundred and fifty miles of London."

A GOOD friend sent one of the issues containing this advertisement to Heavytree Farm and circled the announcement with a blue pencil.

Mirabelle Leicester found the newspaper on the hall settee when she came in from feeding the chickens, and thought that it had been sent by the Alington land agent who was so constantly calling her attention to the advertisers who wished to buy cheap farms. It was a practice of his. She had the feeling that he resented her presence in the country, and was anxious to replace her with a proprietor less poverty-stricken.

Splitting the wrapper with a dusty thumb, she turned naturally to the advertisement pages, having the agent in mind. Her eyes went rapidly down the "Wanted to Buy" column. There were several "gentlemen requiring small farm in good district," but none that made any appeal to her, and she was wondering why the parsimonious man had spent tuppence-ha'penny on postage and paper when the circled paragraph caught her eye.

"Glory!" said Mirabelle, her red lips parted in excited wonder.

Aunt Alma looked up from her press-cutting book, startled as Mirabelle dashed in.

"Me!" she said dramatically, and pointed a finger at the advertisement. "I am young—I have no experience—I have my higher certificate—and daddy was something in the world of science. And, Alma, we are exactly a hundred and forty miles from London town!"

"Dear me!" said Aunt Alma, a lady whose gaunt and terrifying appearance was the terror of tradesmen and farm hands, though a milder woman never knitted stockings.

"Isn't it wonderful? This solves all our problems. We'll leave the farm to Mark, open the flat in Bloomsbury . . . we can afford one or even two theatres a week . . ."

Alma read the announcement for the second time.

"It seems good," she said with conventional caution, "though I don't like the idea of your working, my dear. Your dear father . . ."

"Would have whisked me up to town and I should have had the job by to-night," said Mirabelle definitely.

But Alma wasn't sure. London was full of pitfalls and villainy untold lurked in its alleys and dark passages. She herself never went to London except under protest.

"I was there years ago when those horrible Four Just Men were about, my dear," she said, and Mirabelle, who loved her, listened to the oft-told story. "They terrorized London. One couldn't go out at night with the certainty that one would come back again alive . . . and to think that they have had a free pardon! It is simply encouraging crime."

"My dear," said Mirabelle (and this was her inevitable rejoinder), "they weren't criminals at all. They were very rich men who gave up their lives to punishing those whom the law let slip through its greasy old fingers. And they were pardoned for the intelligence work they did in the war—one worked for three months in the German War Office—and there aren't four at all: there are only three. I'd love to meet them—they must be dears!"

When Aunt Alma made a grimace, she was hideous. Mirabelle averted her eyes.

"Anyway, they are not in London now, darling," she said, "and you will be able to sleep soundly at nights."

"What about the snake?" asked Miss Alma Goddard ominously.

Now if there was one thing which no person contemplating a visit to London wished to be reminded about, it was the snake.

Six million people rose from their beds every morning, opened their newspapers and looked for news of the snake. Eighteen daily newspapers never passed a day without telling their readers that the scare was childish and a shocking commentary on the neurotic tendencies of the age; they also published, at regular intervals, intimate particulars of the black *mamba*, its habits and its peculiar deadliness, and maintained quite a large staff of earnest reporters to "work up the story."

The black mamba, most deadly of all the African snakes, had escaped from the Zoo one cold and foggy night in March. And there should have been the end of him—a three-line paragraph, followed the next day by another three-line paragraph detailing how the snake was found dead on the frozen ground—no mamba could live under a temperature of 75° Fahrenheit. But the second paragraph never appeared. On the 2nd of April a policeman found a man huddled up in a doorway in Orme Place. He proved to be a well known and apparently wealthy stockbroker, named Emmett. He was dead. In his swollen face were found two tiny punctured wounds, and the eminent scientist who was called into consultation gave his opinion that the man had died from snake-bite: an especially deadly snake. The night was chilly; the man had been to a theatre alone. His chauffeur stated that he had left his master in the best of spirits on the doorstep. The key found in the dead man's hand showed that he was struck before the car had turned. When his affairs were investigated he was found to be hopelessly insolvent. Huge sums drawn from his bank six months before had disappeared.

London had scarcely recovered from this shocking surprise when the snake struck again. This time in the crowded street, and choosing a humble victim, though by no means a blameless one. An ex-convict named Sirk, a homeless down-and-out, was seen to fall by a park-keeper near the Achilles statue in Hyde Park. By the time the keeper reached him he was dead. There was no sign of a snake—nobody was near him. This time the snake had made his mark on the wrist—two little punctured wounds near together.

A month later the third man fell a victim. He was a clerk of the Bank of England, a reputable man who was seen to fall forward in a subway train, and, on being removed to hospital, was discovered to have died—again from snake-bite.

So that the snake became a daily figure of fear, and its sinister fame spread even so far afield as Heavytree Farm.

"Stuff!" said Mirabelle, yet with a shiver. "Alma, I wish you wouldn't keep these horrors in your scrap-book."

"They are Life," said Alma soberly, and then: "When will you take up your appointment?" she asked, and the girl laughed.

"We will make a beginning right away—by applying for the job," she said practically. "And you needn't start packing your boxes for a very long time!"

An hour later she intercepted the village postman and handed him a letter.

And that was the beginning of the adventure which involved so many lives and fortunes, which brought the Three Just Men to the verge of dissolution, and one day was to turn the heart of London into a battle-field.

Two days after the letter was dispatched came the answer, typewritten, surprisingly personal, and in places curiously worded. There was an excuse for that, for the heading on the note-paper was

On the third day Mirabelle Leicester stepped down from a 'bus in the City Road and entered the unimposing door of Romance, and an inquisitive chauffeur who saw her enter followed and overtook her in the lobby.

"Excuse me, madame—are you Mrs. Carter?"

Mirabelle did not look like Mrs. Anybody.

"No," she said, and gave her name.

"But you're the lady from Hereford . . . you live with your mother at Telford Park . . . ?"

The man was so agitated that she was not annoyed by his insistence. Evidently he had instructions to meet a stranger and was fearful of missing her.

"You have made a mistake—I live at Heavytree Farm, Daynham—with my aunt."

"Is she called Carter?"

She laughed.

"Miss Alma Goddard—now are you satisfied?"

"Then you're not the lady, miss; I'm waiting to pick her up."

The chauffeur withdrew apologetically.

The girl waited in the ornate ante-room for ten minutes before the pale youth with the stiff, upstanding hair and the huge rimless spectacles returned. His face was large, expressionless, unhealthy. Mirabelle had noted as a curious circumstance that every man she had seen in the office was of the same type. Big heavy men who gave the impression that they had been called away from some very urgent work to deal with the triviality of her inquiries. They were speechless men who glared solemnly at her through thick lenses and nodded or shook their heads according to the requirements of the moment. She expected to meet foreigners in the offices of Oberzohn & Smitts; Germans, she imagined, and was surprised later to discover that both principals and staff were in the main Swedish.

The pale youth, true to the traditions of the house, said nothing: he beckoned her with a little jerk of his head, and she went into a larger room, where half a dozen men were sitting at half a dozen desks and writing furiously, their noses glued short-sightedly to the books and papers which engaged their attention. Nobody looked up as she passed through the waist-high gate which separated the caller from the staff. Hanging upon the wall between two windows was a map of Africa with great green patches. In one corner of the room were stacked a dozen massive ivory tusks, each bearing a hanging label. There was the model of a steamship in a case on a window-ledge, and on another a crudely carved wooden idol of native origin.

The youth stopped before a heavy rosewood door and knocked. When a deep voice answered, he pushed open the door and stood aside to let her pass. It was a gigantic room—that was the word which occurred to her as most fitting, and the vast space of it was emphasized by the almost complete lack of furniture. A very small ebony writing-table, two very small chairs and a long and narrow black cupboard fitted into a recess were all the furnishings she could see. The high walls were covered with a golden paper. Four bright-red rafters ran across the black ceiling—the floor was completely covered with a deep purple carpet. It seemed that there was a rolled map above the fire-place—a long thin cord came down from the cornice and ended in a tassel within reach.

The room, with its lack of appointments, was so unexpected a vision that the girl stood staring from walls to roof, until she observed her guide making urgent signs, and then she advanced towards the man who stood with his back to the tiny fire that burnt in the silver fire-place.

He was tall and grey; her first impression was of an enormously high forehead. The sallow face was long, and nearer at hand, she saw, covered by innumerable lines and furrows. She judged him to be about fifty until he spoke, and then she realized that he was much older.

"Miss Mirabelle Leicester?"

His English was not altogether perfect; the delivery was queerly deliberate and he lisped slightly.

"Pray be seated. I am Dr. Eruc Oberzohn. I am not German. I admire the Germans, but I am Swedish. You are convinced?"

She laughed, and when Mirabelle Leicester laughed, less susceptible men than Dr. Eruc Oberzohn had forgotten all other business. She was not very tall—her slimness and her symmetrical figure made her appear so. She had in her face and in her clear grey eyes something of the country-side; she belonged to the orchards where the apple-blossom lay like heavy snow upon the bare branches; to the cold brooks that ran noisily under hawthorn hedges. The

April sunlight was in her eyes and the springy velvet of meadows everlastingly under her feet.

To Dr. Oberzohn she was a girl in a blue tailor-made costume. He saw that she wore a little hat with a straight brim that framed her face just above the lift of her curved eyebrows. A German would have seen these things, being a hopeless sentimentalist. The doctor was not German; he loathed their sentimentality.

"Will you be seated? You have a scientific training?"

Mirabelle shook her head.

"I haven't," she confessed ruefully, "but I've passed in the subjects you mentioned in your advertisement."

"But your father—he was a scientist?"

She nodded gravely.

"But not a great scientist," he stated. "England and America do not produce such men. Ah, tell me not of your Kelvins, Edisons, and Newtons! They were incomplete, dull men, ponderous men—the fire was not there."

She was somewhat taken aback, but she was amused as well. His calm dismissal of men who were honoured in the scientific world was so obviously sincere.

"Now talk to me of yourself." He seated himself in the hard, straight-backed chair by the little desk.

"I'm afraid there is very little I can tell you, Dr. Oberzohn. I live with my aunt at Heavytree Farm in Gloucester, and we have a flat in Doughty Court. My aunt and I have a small income—and I think that is all."

"Go on, please," he commanded. "Tell me of your sensations when you had my letter—I desire to know your mind. That is how I form all opinions; that is how I made my immense fortune. By the analysis of the mind."

She had expected many tests; an examination in elementary science; a typewriting test possibly (she dreaded this most); but she never for one moment dreamt that the flowery letter asking her to call at the City Road offices of Oberzohn & Smitts would lead to an experiment in psycho-analysis.

"I can only tell you that I was surprised," she said, and the tightening line of her mouth would have told him a great deal if he were the student of human nature he claimed to be. "Naturally the salary appeals to me—ten pounds a week is such a high rate of pay that I cannot think I am qualified——"

"You are qualified." His harsh voice grew more strident as he impressed this upon her. "I need a laboratory secretary. You are qualified"—he hesitated, and then went on—"by reason of distinguished parentage. Also"—he hesitated again for a fraction of a second—"also because of general education. Your duties shall commence soon!" He waved a long, thin hand to the door in the corner of the room. "You will take your position at once," he said.

The long face, the grotesquely high forehead, the bulbous nose and wide, crooked mouth all seemed to work together when he spoke. At one moment the forehead was full of pleats and furrows—at the next, comparatively smooth. The point of his nose dipped up and down at every word, only his small, deep-set eyes remained steadfast, unwinking. She had seen eyes like those before, brown and pathetic. Of what did they remind her? His last words brought her to the verge of panic.

"Oh, I could not possibly start to-day," she said in trepidation.

"To-day, or it shall be never," he said with an air of finality.

She had to face a crisis. The salary was more than desirable; it was necessary. The farm scarcely paid its way, for Alma was not the best of managers. And the income grew more and more attenuated. Last year the company in which her meagre fortune was invested had passed a dividend and she had to give up her Swiss holiday.

"I'll start now." She had to set her teeth to make this resolve.

"Very good; that is my wish."

He was still addressing her as though she were a public meeting. Rising from his chair, he opened the little door and she went into a smaller room. She had seen laboratories, but none quite so beautifully fitted as this—shelf upon shelf of white porcelain jars, of cut-glass bottles, their contents engraved in frosted letters; a bench that ran the length of the room, on which apparatus of every kind was arranged in order. In the centre of the room ran a long, glass-topped table, and here, in dustproof glass, were delicate instruments, ranging from scales which she knew could be influenced by a grain of dust, to electrical machines, so complicated that her heart sank at the sight of them.

"What must I do?" she asked dismally.

Everything was so beautifully new; she was sure she would drop one of those lovely jars . . . all the science of the school laboratory had suddenly drained out of her mind, leaving it a blank.

"You will do." Remarkably enough, the doctor for the moment seemed as much at a loss as the girl. "First—quantities. In every jar or bottle there is a quantity. How much? Who knows? The last secretary was careless, stupid. She kept no book. Sometimes I go for something—it is not there! All gone. That is very regrettable."

"You wish me to take stock?" she asked, her hopes reviving at the simplicity of her task.

There were measures and scales enough. The latter stood in a line like a platoon of soldiers ranged according to their size. Everything was very new, very neat. There was a smell of drying enamel in the room as though the place had been newly painted.

"That is all," said the long-faced man.

He put his hand in the pocket of his frock-coat and took out a large wallet. From this he withdrew two crisp notes.

"Ten pounds," he said briefly. "We pay already in advance. There is one more thing I desire to know," he said. "It is of the aunt. She is in London?"

Mirabelle shook her head.

"No, she is in the country. I expected to go back this afternoon, and if I was—successful, we were coming to town to-morrow."

He pursed his thickish lips; she gazed fascinated at his long forehead rippled in thought.

"It will be a nervous matter for her if you stay in London to-night—no?"

She smiled and shook her head.

"No. I will stay at the flat; I have often stayed there alone, but even that will not be necessary. I will wire asking her to come up by the first train."

"Wait." He raised a pompous hand and darted back to his room. He returned with a packet of telegraph forms. "Write your telegram," he commanded. "A clerk shall dispatch it at once."

Gratefully she took the blanks and wrote her news and request.

"Thank you," she said.

Mr. Oberzohn bowed, went to the door, bowed again, and the door closed behind him.

Fortunately for her peace of mind, Mirabelle Leicester had no occasion to consult her employer or attempt to open the door. Had she done so, she would have discovered that it was locked. As for the telegram she had written, that was a curl of black ash in his fire.

# Chapter II      The Three Men of Curzon Street

NO. 233, Curzon Street, was a small house. Even the most enthusiastic of agents would not, if he had any regard to his soul's salvation, describe its dimensions with any enthusiasm. He might enlarge upon its bijou beauties, refer reverently to its historical association, speak truthfully of its central heating and electric installation, but he would, being an honest man, convey the impression that No. 233 was on the small side.

The house was flanked by two modern mansions, stone-fronted, with metal and glass doors that gave out a blur of light by night. Both overtopped the modest roof of their neighbour by many stories—No. 233 had the appearance of a little man crushed in a crowd and unable to escape, and there was in its mild frontage the illusion of patient resignation and humility.

To that section of Curzon Street wherein it had its place, the house was an offence and was, in every but a legal sense, a nuisance. A learned Chancery judge to whom application had been made on behalf of neighbouring property owners, ground landlords and the like, had refused to grant the injunction for which they had pleaded, "prohibiting the said George Manfred from carrying on a business, to wit the Triangle Detective Agency, situate at the aforesaid number two hundred and thirty-three Curzon Street in the City of Westminster in the County of Middlesex."

In a judgment which occupied a third of a column of *The Times* he laid down the dictum that a private detective might be a professional rather than a business man—a dictum which has been, and will be, disputed to the end of time.

So the little silver triangle remained fixed to the door, and he continued to interview his clients—few in number, for he was most careful to accept only those who offered scope for his genius.

A tall, strikingly handsome man, with the face of a patrician and the shoulders of an athlete, Curzon Street—or such of the street as took the slightest notice of anything—observed him to be extremely well dressed on all occasions. He was a walking advertisement for a Hanover Street tailor who was so fashionable that he would have died with horror at the very thought of advertising at all. Car folk held up at busy crossings glanced into his limousine, saw the clean-cut profile and the tanned, virile face, and guessed him for a Harley Street specialist. Very few people knew him socially. Dr. Elver, the Scotland Yard surgeon, used to come up to Curzon Street at times and give his fantastic views on the snake and its appearances, George Manfred and his friends listening in silence and offering no help. But apart from Elver and an Assistant Commissioner of Police, a secretive man, who dropped in at odd moments to smoke a pipe and talk of old times, the social callers were few and far between.

His chauffeur-footman was really better known than he. At the mews where he garaged his car, they called him "Lightning," and it was generally agreed that this thin-faced, eager-eyed man would sooner or later meet the end which inevitably awaits all chauffeurs who take sharp corners on two wheels at sixty miles an hour: some of the critics had met the big Spanz on the road and had reproached him afterwards, gently or violently, according to the degree of their scare.

Few knew Mr. Manfred's butler, a dark-browed foreigner, rather stout and somewhat saturnine. He was a man who talked very little even to the cook and the two housemaids who came every morning at eight and left the house punctually at six, for Mr. Manfred dined out most nights.

He advertised only in the more exclusive newspapers, and not in his own name; no interviews were granted except by appointment, so that the arrival of Mr. Sam Barberton was in every sense an irregularity.

He knocked at the door just as the maids were leaving, and since they knew little about Manfred and his ways except that he liked poached eggs and spinach for breakfast, the stranger was allowed to drift into the hall, and here the taciturn butler, hastily summoned from his room, found him.

The visitor was a stubby, thick-set man with a brick-red face and a head that was both grey and bald. His dress and his speech were equally rough. The butler saw that he was no ordinary artisan because his boots were of a kind known as *veldtschoons*. They were of undressed leather, patchily bleached by the sun.

"I want to see the boss of this Triangle," he said in a loud voice, and, diving into his waistcoat pocket, brought out a soiled newspaper cutting.

The butler took it from him without a word. It was the *Cape Times*—he would have known by the type and the spacing even if on the back there had not been printed the bisected notice of a church bazaar at Wynberg. The butler studied such things.

"I am afraid that you cannot see Mr. Manfred without an appointment," he said. His voice and manner were most unexpectedly gentle in such a forbidding man.

"I've got to see him, if I sit here all night," said the man stubbornly, and symbolized his immovability by squatting down in the hall chair.

Not a muscle of the servant's face moved. It was impossible to tell whether he was angry or amused.

"I got this cutting out of a paper I found on the *Benguella*—she docked at Tilbury this afternoon—and I came straight here. I should never have dreamt of coming at all, only I want fair play for all concerned. That Portuguese feller with a name like a cigar—Villa, that's it!—he said, 'What's the good of going to London when we can settle everything on board ship?' But half-breed Portuguese! My God, I'd rather deal with bushmen! Bushmen are civilized—look here."

Before the butler realized what the man was doing, he had slipped off one of his ugly shoes. He wore no sock or stocking underneath, and he upturned the sole of his bare foot for inspection. The flesh was seamed and puckered into red weals, and the butler knew the cause.

"Portuguese," said the visitor tersely as he resumed his shoe. "Not niggers—Portugooses—half-bred, I'll admit. They burnt me to make me talk, and they'd have killed me only one of those hell-fire American traders came along—full of fight and fire-water. He brought me into the town."

"Where was this?" asked the butler.

"Mosamades: I went ashore to look round, like a fool. I was on a Woerman boat that was going up to Boma. The skipper was a Hun, but white—he warned me."

"And what did they want to know from you?"

The caller shot a suspicious glance at his interrogator.

"Are you the boss?" he demanded.

"No—I'm Mr. Manfred's butler. What name shall I tell him?"

"Barberton—Mister Samuel Barberton. Tell him I want certain things found out. The address of a young lady by the name of Miss Mirabelle Leicester. And I'll tell your governor something too. This Portugoose got drunk one night, and spilled it about the fort they've got in England. Looks like a house but it's a fort: he went there. . . ."

No, he was not drunk; stooping to pick up an imaginary match-stalk, the butler's head had come near the visitor; there was a strong aroma of tobacco but not of drink.

"Would you very kindly wait?" he asked, and disappeared up the stairs.

He was not gone long before he returned to the first landing and beckoned Mr. Barberton to come. The visitor was ushered into a room at the front of the house, a small room, which was made smaller by the long grey velvet curtains that hung behind the empire desk where Manfred was standing.

"This is Mr. Barberton, sir," said the butler, bowed, and went out, closing the door.

"Sit down, Mr. Barberton." He indicated a chair and seated himself. "My butler tells me you have quite an exciting story to tell me—you are from the Cape?"

"No, I'm not," said Mr. Barberton. "I've never been at the Cape in my life."

The man behind the desk nodded.

"Now, if you will tell me——"

"I'm not going to tell you much," was the surprisingly blunt reply. "It's not likely that I'm going to tell a stranger what I wouldn't even tell Elijah Washington—and he saved my life!"

Manfred betrayed no resentment at this cautious attitude. In that room he had met many clients who had shown the same reluctance to accept him as their confidant. Yet he had at the back of his mind the feeling that this man, unlike the rest, might remain adamant to the end: he was curious to discover the real object of the visit.

Barberton drew his chair nearer the writing-table and rested his elbows on the edge.

"It's like this, Mr. What's-your-name. There's a certain secret which doesn't belong to me, and yet does in a way. It is worth a lot of money. Mr. Elijah Washington knew that and tried to pump me, and Villa got a gang of Kroomen to burn my feet, but I've not told yet. What I want you to do is to find Miss Mirabelle Leicester; and I want to get her quick, because there's only about two weeks, if you understand me, before this other crowd gets busy—Villa is certain to have cabled 'em, and according to him they're hot!"

Mr. Manfred leant back in his padded chair, the glint of an amused smile in his grey eyes.

"I take it that what you want us to do is to find Miss Leicester?"

The man nodded energetically.

"Have you the slightest idea as to where she is to be found? Has she any relations in England?"

"I don't know," interrupted the man. "All I know is that she lives here somewhere, and that her father died three years ago, on the twenty-ninth of May—make a note of that: he died in England on the twenty-ninth of May."

That was an important piece of information, and it made the search easy, thought Manfred.

"And you're going to tell me about the fort, aren't you?" he said, as he looked up from his notes.

Barberton hesitated.

"I was," he admitted, "but I'm not so sure that I will now, until I've found this young lady. And don't forget"—he rapped the table to emphasize his words—"that crowd is hot!"

"Which crowd?" asked Manfred good-humouredly. He knew many "crowds," and wondered if it was about one which was in his mind that the caller was speaking.

"The crowd I'm talking about," said Mr. Barberton, who spoke with great deliberation and was evidently weighing every word he uttered for fear that he should involuntarily betray his secret.

That seemed to be an end of his requirements, for he rose and stood a little awkwardly, fumbling in his inside pocket.

"There is nothing to pay," said Manfred, guessing his intention. "Perhaps, when we have located your Miss Mirabelle Leicester, we shall ask you to refund our out-of-pocket expenses."

"I can afford to pay——" began the man.

"And we can afford to wait." Again the gleam of amusement in the deep eyes.

Still Mr. Barberton did not move.

"There's another thing I meant to ask you. You know all that's happening in this country?"

"Not quite everything," said the other with perfect gravity.

"Have you ever heard of the Four Just Men?"

It was a surprising question. Manfred bent forward as though he had not heard aright.

"The Four——?"

"The Four Just Men—three, as a matter of fact. I'd like to get in touch with those birds."

Manfred nodded.

"I think I have heard of them," he said.

"They're in England now somewhere. They've got a pardon: I saw that in the *Cape Times*—the bit I tore the advertisement from."

"The last I heard of them, they were in Spain," said Manfred, and walked round the table and opened the door. "Why do you wish to get in touch with them?"

"Because," said Mr. Barberton impressively, "the crowd are scared of 'em—that's why."

Manfred walked with his visitor to the landing.

"You have omitted one important piece of information," he said with a smile, "but I did not intend your going until you told me. What is your address?"

"Petworth Hotel, Norfolk Street."

Barberton went down the stairs; the butler was waiting in the hall to show him out, and Mr. Barberton, having a vague idea that something of the sort was usual in the houses of the aristocracy, slipped a silver coin in his hand. The dark-faced man murmured his thanks: his bow was perhaps a little lower, his attitude just a trifle more deferential.

He closed and locked the front door and went slowly up the stairs to the office room. Manfred was sitting on the empire table, lighting a cigarette. The chauffeur-valet had come through the grey curtains to take the chair which had been vacated by Mr. Barberton.

"He gave me half a crown—generous fellow," said Poiccart, the butler. "I like him, George."

"I wish I could have seen his feet," said the chauffeur, whose veritable name was Leon Gonsalez. He spoke with regret. "He comes from West Sussex, and there is insanity in his family. The left parietal is slightly recessed and the face is asymmetrical."

"Poor soul!" murmured Manfred, blowing a cloud of smoke to the ceiling. "It's a great trial introducing one's friends to you, Leon."

"Fortunately, you have no friends," said Leon, reaching out and taking a cigarette from the open gold case on the table. "Well, what do you think of our Mr. Barberton's mystery?"

George Manfred shook his head.

"He was vague, and, in his desire to be diplomatic, a little incoherent. What about your own mystery, Leon? You have been out all day . . . have you found a solution?"

Gonsalez nodded.

"Barberton is afraid of something," said Poiccart, a slow and sure analyst. "He carried a gun between his trousers and his waistcoat—you saw that?"

George nodded.

"The question is, who or which is the crowd? Question two is, where and who is Miss Mirabelle Leicester? Question three is, why did they burn Barberton's feet . . . and I think that is all."

The keen face of Gonsalez was thrust forward through a cloud of smoke.

"I will answer most of them and propound two more," he said. "Mirabelle Leicester took a job to-day at Oberzohn's—laboratory secretary!"

George Manfred frowned.

"Laboratory? I didn't know that he had one."

"He hadn't till three days ago—it was fitted in seventy-two hours by experts who worked day and night; the cost of its installation was sixteen hundred pounds—and it came into existence to give Oberzohn an excuse for engaging Mirabelle Leicester. You sent me out to clear up that queer advertisement which puzzled us all on Monday—I have cleared it up. It was designed to bring our Miss Leicester into the Oberzohn establishment. We all agreed when we discovered who was the advertiser, that Oberzohn was working for something—I watched his office for two days, and she was the only applicant for the job—hers the only letter they answered. Oberzohn lunched with her at the Ritz-Carlton—she sleeps to-night in Chester Square."

There was a silence which was broken by Poiccart.

"And what is the question you have to propound?" he asked mildly.

"I think I know," said Manfred, and nodded. "The question is: how long has Mr. Samuel Barberton to live?"

"Exactly," said Gonsalez with satisfaction. "You are beginning to understand the mentality of Oberzohn!"

# Chapter III                    The Vendetta

THE man who that morning walked without announcement into Dr. Oberzohn's office might have stepped from the pages of a catalogue of men's fashions. He was, to the initiated eye, painfully new. His lemon gloves, his dazzling shoes, the splendour of his silk hat, the very correctness of his handkerchief display, would have been remarkable even in the Ascot paddock on Cup day. He was good-looking, smooth, if a trifle plump, of face, and he wore a tawny little moustache and a monocle. People who did not like Captain Monty Newton—and their names were many—said of him that he aimed at achieving the housemaid's conception of a guardsman. They did not say this openly, because he was a man to be propitiated rather than offended. He had money, a place in the country, a house in Chester Square, and an assortment of cars. He was a member of several good clubs, the committees of which never discussed him without offering the excuse of war-time courtesies for his election. Nobody knew how he made his money, or, if it were inherited, whose heir he was. He gave extravagant parties, played cards well, and enjoyed exceptional luck, especially when he was the host and held the bank after one of the splendid dinners he gave in his Chester Square mansion.

"Good morning, Oberzohn—how is Smitts?"

It was his favourite jest, for there was no Smitts, and had been no Smitts in the firm since '96.

The doctor, peering down at the telegram he was writing, looked up.

"Good morning, Captain Newton," he said precisely.

Newton passed to the back of him and read the message he was writing. It was addressed to "Miss Alma Goddard, Heavytree Farm, Daynham, Gloucester," and the wire ran:

> "Have got the fine situation. Cannot expeditiously return to-night. I am sleeping at our pretty flat in Doughty Court. Do not come up until I send for you.—MISS MIRABELLE LEICESTER."

"She's here, is she?" Captain Newton glanced at the laboratory door. "You're not going to send that wire? 'Miss Mirabelle Leicester!' 'Expeditiously return!' She'd tumble it in a minute. Who is Alma Goddard?"

"The aunt," said Oberzohn. "I did not intend the dispatching until you had seen it. My English is too correct."

He made way for Captain Newton, who, having taken a sheet of paper from the rack on which to deposit with great care his silk hat, and having stripped his gloves and deposited them in his hat, sat down in the chair from which the older man had risen, pulled up the knees of his immaculate trousers, tore off the top telegraph form, and wrote under the address:

> "Have got the job. Hooray! Don't bother to come up, darling, until I am settled. Shall sleep at the flat as usual. Too busy to write. Keep my letters.—MIRABELLE."

"That's real," said Captain Newton, surveying his work with satisfaction. "Push it off."

He got up and straddled his legs before the fire.

"The hard part of the job may be to persuade the lady to come to Chester Square," he said.

"My own little house——" began Oberzohn.

"Would scare her to death," said Newton with a loud laugh. "That dog-kennel! No, it is Chester Square or nothing. I'll get Joan or one of the girls to drop in this afternoon and chum up with her. When does the *Benguella* arrive?"

"This afternoon: the person has booked rooms by radio at the Petworth Hotel."

"Norfolk Street . . . humph! One of your men can pick him up and keep an eye on him. Lisa? So much the better. That kind of trash will talk for a woman. I don't suppose he has seen a white woman in years. You ought to fire Villa—crude beast! Naturally the man is on his guard now."

"Villa is the best of my men on the coast," barked Oberzohn fiercely. Nothing so quickly touched the raw places of his amazing vanity as a reflection upon his organizing qualities.

"How is trade?"

Captain Newton took a long ebony holder from his tail pocket, flicked out a thin platinum case and lit a cigarette in one uninterrupted motion.

"Bat!" When Dr. Oberzohn was annoyed the purity of his pronunciation suffered. "There is nothing but expense!"

Oberzohn & Smitts had once made an enormous income from the sale of synthetic alcohol. They were, amongst other things, coast traders. They bought rubber and ivory, paying in cloth and liquor. They sold arms secretly, organized tribal wars for their greater profit, and had financed at least two Portuguese revolutions nearer at home. And with the growth of their fortune, the activities of the firm had extended. Guns and more guns went out of Belgian and French workshops. To Kurdish insurrectionaries, to ambitious Chinese generals, to South American politicians, planning to carry their convictions into more active fields. There was no country in the world that did not act as host to an O. & S. agent—and agents can be very expensive. Just now the world was alarmingly peaceful. A revolution had failed most dismally in Venezuela, and Oberzohn & Smitts had not been paid for two ship-loads of lethal weapons ordered by a general who, two days after the armaments were landed, had been placed against an *adobe* wall and incontinently shot to rags by the soldiers of the Government against which he was in rebellion.

"But that shall not matter." Oberzohn waved bad trade from the considerable factors of life. "This shall succeed: and then I shall be free to well punish——"

"To punish well," corrected the purist, stroking his moustache. "Don't split your infinitives, Eruc—it's silly. You're thinking of Manfred and Gonsalez and Poiccart? Leave them alone. They are nothing!"

"Nothing!" roared the doctor, his sallow face instantly distorted with fury. "To leave them alone, is it? Of my brother what? Of my brother in heaven, sainted martyr . . . !"

He spun round, gripped the silken tassel of the cord above the fire-place, and pulled down, not a map, but a picture. It had been painted from a photograph by an artist who specialized in the gaudy banners which hang before every booth at every country fair. In this setting the daub was a shrieking incongruity; yet to Dr. Oberzohn it surpassed in beauty the masterpieces of the Prado. A full-length portrait of a man in a frock-coat. He leaned on a pedestal in the attitude which cheap photographers believe is the acme of grace. His big face, idealized as it was by the artist, was brutal and stupid. The carmine lips were parted in a simper. In one hand he held a scroll of paper, in the other a Derby hat which was considerably out of drawing.

"My brother!" Dr. Oberzohn choked. "My sainted Adolph . . . murdered! By the so-called Three Just Men . . . my brother!"

"Very interesting," murmured Captain Newton, who had not even troubled to look up. He flicked the ash from his cigarette into the fire-place and said no more.

Adolph Oberzohn had certainly been shot dead by Leon Gonsalez: there was no disputing the fact. That Adolph, at the moment of his death, was attempting to earn the generous profits which come to those who engage in a certain obnoxious trade between Europe and the South American states, was less open to question. There was a girl in it: Leon followed his man to Porto Rico, and in the Café of the Seven Virtues they had met. Adolph was by training a gunman and drew first—and died first. That was the story of Adolph Oberzohn: the story of a girl whom Leon Gonsalez smuggled back to Europe belongs elsewhere. She fell in love with her rescuer and frightened him sick.

Dr. Oberzohn let the portrait roll up with a snap, blew his nose vigorously, and blinked the tears from his pale eyes.

"Yes, very sad, very sad," said the captain cheerfully. "Now what about this girl? There is to be nothing rough or raw, you understand, Eruc? I want the thing done sweetly. Get that bug of the Just Men out of your mind—they are out of business. When a man lowers himself to run a detective agency he's a back number. If they start anything we'll deal with them scientifically, eh? Scientifically!"

He chuckled with laughter at this good joke. It was obvious that Captain Newton was no dependant on the firm of Oberzohn & Smitts. If he was not the dominant partner, he dominated that branch which he had once served in a minor capacity. He owed much to the death of Adolph—he never regretted the passing of that unsavoury man.

"I'll get one of the girls to look her over this afternoon—where is your telephone pad—the one you write messages received?"

The doctor opened a drawer of his desk and took out a little memo pad, and Newton found a pencil and wrote:

> "To Mirabelle Leicester, care Oberzohn (Phone) London. Sorry
> I can't come up to-night. Don't sleep at flat alone. Have wired
> Joan Newton to put you up for night. She will call.—ALMA."

"There you are," said the gallant captain, handing the pad to the other. "That message came this afternoon. All telegrams to Oberzohn come by 'phone—never forget it!"

"Ingenious creature!" Dr. Oberzohn's admiration was almost reverential.

"Take her out to lunch . . . after lunch, the message. At four o'clock, Joan or one of the girls. A select dinner. To-morrow the office . . . gently, gently. Bull-rush these schemes and your plans die the death of a dog."

He glanced at the door once more.

"She won't come out, I suppose?" he suggested. "Deuced awkward if she came out and saw Miss Newton's brother!"

"I have locked the door," said Dr. Oberzohn proudly.

Captain Newton's attitude changed: his face went red with sudden fury.

"Then you're a—you're a fool! Unlock the door when I've gone—and keep it unlocked! Want to frighten her?"

"It was my idea to risk nothing," pleaded the long-faced Swede.

"Do as I tell you."

Captain Newton brushed his speckless coat with the tips of his fingers. He pulled on his gloves, fitted his hat with the aid of a small pocket-mirror he took from his inside pocket, took up his clouded cane and strolled from the room.

"Ingenious creature," murmured Dr. Oberzohn again, and went in to offer the startled Mirabelle an invitation to lunch.

# Chapter IV                    The Snake Strikes

THE great restaurant, with its atmosphere of luxury and wealth, had been a little overpowering. The crowded tables, the soft lights, the very capability and nonchalance of the waiters, were impressive. When her new employer had told her that it was his practice to take the laboratory secretary to lunch, "for I have no other time to speak of business things," she accepted uncomfortably. She knew little of office routine, but she felt that it was not customary for principals to drive their secretaries from the City Road to the Ritz-Carlton to lunch expensively at that resort of fashion and the epicure. It added nothing to her self-possession that her companion was an object of interest to all who saw him. The gay luncheon-parties forgot their dishes and twisted round to stare at the extraordinary-looking man with the high forehead.

At a little table alone she saw a man whose face was tantalizingly familiar. A keen, thin face with eager, amused eyes. Where had she seen him before? Then she remembered: the chauffeur had such a face—the man who had followed her into Oberzohn's when she arrived that morning. It was absurd, of course; this man was one of the leisured class, to whom lunching at the Ritz-Carlton was a normal event. And yet the likeness was extraordinary.

She was glad when the meal was over. Dr. Oberzohn did not talk of "business things." He did not talk at all, but spent his time shovelling incredible quantities of food through his wide slit of a mouth. He ate intently, noisily— Mirabelle was glad the band was playing, and she went red with suppressed laughter at the whimsical thought; and after that she felt less embarrassed.

No word was spoken as the big car sped citywards. The doctor had his thoughts and ignored her presence. The only reference he made to the lunch was as they were leaving the hotel, when he had condescended to grunt a bitter complaint about the quality of English-made coffee.

He allowed her to go back to her weighing and measuring without displaying the slightest interest in her progress.

And then came the crowning surprise of the afternoon—it followed the arrival of a puzzling telegram from her aunt. She was weighing an evil-smelling mass of powder when the door opened and there floated into the room a delicate-looking girl, beautifully dressed. A small face framed in a mass of little golden-brown curls smiled a greeting.

"You're Mirabelle Leicester, aren't you? I'm Joan Newton—your aunt wired me to call on you."

"Do you know my aunt?" asked Mirabelle in astonishment. She had never heard Alma speak of the Newtons, but then, Aunt Alma had queer reticences. Mirabelle had expected a middle-aged dowd—it was amazing that her unprepossessing relative could claim acquaintance with this society butterfly.

"Oh, yes—we know Alma very well," replied the visitor. "Of course, I haven't seen her since I was *quite* a little girl—she's a dear."

She looked round the laboratory with curious interest.

"What a nasty-smelling place!" she said, her nose upturned. "And how do you like old—er—Mr. Oberzohn?"

"Do you know him?" asked Mirabelle, astounded at the possibility of this coincidence.

"My brother knows him—we live together, my brother and I, and he knows everybody. A man about town has to, hasn't he, dear?"

"Man about town" was an expression that grated a little; Mirabelle was not of the "dearing" kind. The combination of errors in taste made her scrutinize the caller more closely. Joan Newton was dressed beautifully but not well. There was something . . . Had Mirabelle a larger knowledge of life, she might have thought that the girl had been dressed to play the part of a lady by somebody who wasn't quite sure of the constituents of the part. Captain Newton she did not know at the time, or she would have guessed the dress authority.

"I'm going to take you back to Chester Square after Mr. Oberzohn—such a funny name, isn't it?—has done with you. Monty insisted upon my bringing the Rolls. Monty is my brother; he's rather classical."

Mirabelle wondered whether this indicated a love of the Greek poets or a passion for the less tuneful operas. Joan (which was her real name) meant no more than classy: it was a favourite word of hers; another was "morbid."

Half an hour later the inquisitive chauffeur put his foot on the starter and sent his car on the trail of the Rolls, wondering what Mirabelle Leicester had in common with Joan Alice Murphy, who had brought so many rich young men to the green board in Captain Newton's beautiful drawing-room, where stakes ran high and the captain played with such phenomenal luck.

───────────

"And there you are," said Gonsalez complacently. "I've done a very good day's work. Oberzohn has gone back to his rabbit-hutch to think up new revolutions—Miss Mirabelle Leicester is to be found at 307, Chester Square. Now the point is, what do we do to save the valuable life of Mr. Sam Barberton?"

Manfred looked grave.

"I hardly like the thought of the girl spending the night in Newton's house," he said.

"Why allow her to remain there?" asked Poiccart in his heavy way.

"Exactly!" Leon nodded.

George Manfred looked at his watch.

"Obviously the first person to see is friend Barberton," he said. "If we can prevail on him to spend the evening with us, the rest is a simple matter——"

The telephone bell rang shrilly and Leon Gonsalez monopolized the instrument.

"Gloucester? Yes." He covered the receiver with his hand. "I took the liberty of asking Miss Alma Goddard to ring me up . . . her address I discovered very early in the day: Heavytree Farm, Daynham, near Gloucester . . . yes, yes, it is Mr. Johnson speaking. I wanted to ask you if you would take a message to Miss Leicester . . . oh, she isn't at home?" Leon listened attentively, and, after a few minutes: "Thank you very much. She is staying at Doughty Court? She wired you . . . oh, nothing very important. I—er—am her old science master and I saw an advertisement . . . oh, she has seen it, has she?"

He hung up the receiver.

"Nothing to go on," he said. "The girl has wired to say she is delighted with her job. The aunt is not to come up until she is settled, and Mirabelle is sleeping at Doughty Court."

"And a very excellent place too," said Manfred. "When we've seen Mr. Barberton I shouldn't be surprised if she didn't sleep there after all."

Petworth Hotel in Norfolk Street was a sedate residential hostel, greatly favoured by overseas visitors, especially South Africans. The reception clerk thought Mr. Barberton was out: the hall porter was sure.

"He went down to the Embankment—he said he'd like to see the river before it was dark," said that confidant of so many visitors.

Manfred stepped into the car by Leon's side—Poiccart seldom went abroad, but sat at home piecing together the little jigsaw puzzles of life that came to Curzon Street for solution. He was the greatest of all the strategists: even Scotland Yard brought some of its problems for his inspection.

"On the Embankment?" Manfred looked up at the blue and pink sky. The sun had gone down, but the light of day remained. "If it were darker I should be worried . . . stop, there's Dr. Elver."

The little police surgeon who had passed them with a cheery wave of his hand turned and walked back.

"Well, Children of the Law"—he was inclined to be dramatic—"on what dread errand of vengeance are you bound?"

"We are looking for a man named Barberton to ask him to dinner," said Manfred, shaking hands.

"Sounds tame to me: has he any peculiarities which would appeal to me?"

"Burnt feet," said Leon promptly. "If you would like to learn how the coastal intelligence department extract information from unwilling victims, come along."

Elver hesitated. He was a man burnt up by the Indian suns, wizened like a dried yellow apple, and he had no interest in the world beyond his work.

"I'll go with you," he said, stepping into the car. "And if your Barberton man fails you, you can have me as a guest. I like to hear you talking. One cannot know too much of the criminal mind! And life is dull since the snake stopped biting!"

The car made towards Blackfriars Bridge, and Manfred kept watch of the sidewalk. There was no sign of Barberton, and he signalled Leon to turn and come back. This brought the machine to the Embankment side of the broad boulevard. They had passed under Waterloo Bridge and were nearing Cleopatra's Needle when Gonsalez saw the man they were seeking.

He was leaning against the parapet, his elbows on the coping and his head sunk forward as though he were studying the rush of the tide below. The car pulled up near a policeman who was observing the lounger thoughtfully. The officer recognized the police surgeon and saluted.

"Can't understand that bird, sir," he said. "He's been standing there for ten minutes—I'm keeping an eye on him because he looks to me like a suicide who's thinkin' it over!"

Manfred approached the man, and suddenly, with a shock, saw his face. It was set in a grin—the eyes were wide open, the skin a coppery red.

"Elver! Leon!"

As Leon sprang from the car, Manfred touched the man's shoulder and he fell limply to the ground. In a second the doctor was on his knees by the side of the still figure.

"Dead," he said laconically, and then: "Good God!"

He pointed to the neck, where a red patch showed.

"What is that?" asked Manfred steadily.

"The snake!" said the doctor.

# Chapter V                    The Golden Woman

BARBERTON had been stricken down in the heart of London, under the very eyes of the policeman, it proved.

"Yes, sir, I've had him under observation for a quarter of an hour. I saw him walking along the Embankment, admiring the view, long before he stopped here."

"Did anybody go near him or speak to him?" asked Dr. Elver, looking up.

"No, sir, he stood by himself. I'll swear that nobody was within two yards of him. Of course, people have been passing to and fro, but I have been looking at him all the time, and I've not seen man or woman within yards of him, and my eyes were never off him."

A second policeman had appeared on the scene, and he was sent across to Scotland Yard in Manfred's car, for the ambulance and the police reserves necessary to clear and keep in circulation the gathering crowd. These returned simultaneously, and the two friends watched the pitiable thing lifted into a stretcher, and waited until the white-bodied vehicle had disappeared with its sad load before they returned to their machine.

Gonsalez took his place at the wheel; George got in by his side. No word was spoken until they were back at Curzon Street. Manfred went in alone, whilst his companion drove the machine to the garage. When he returned, he found Poiccart and George deep in discussion.

"You were right, Raymond." Leon Gonsalez stripped his thin coat and threw it on a chair. "The accuracy of your forecasts is almost depressing. I am waiting all the time for the inevitable mistake, and I am irritated when this doesn't occur. You said the snake would reappear, and the snake has reappeared. Prophesy now for me, O seer!"

Poiccart's heavy face was gloomy; his dark eyes almost hidden under the frown that brought his bushy eyebrows lower.

"One hasn't to be a seer to know that our association with Barberton will send the snake wriggling towards Curzon Street," he said. "Was it Gurther or Pfeiffer?"

Manfred considered.

"Pfeiffer, I think. He is the steadier of the two. Gurther has brain-storms; he is on the neurotic side. And that nine-thonged whip of yours, Leon, cannot have added to his mental stability. No, it was Pfeiffer, I'm sure."

"I suppose the whip unbalanced him a little," said Leon. He thought over this aspect as though it were one worth consideration. "Gurther is a sort of Jekyll and Hyde, except that there is no virtue to him at all. It is difficult to believe, seeing him dropping languidly into his seat at the opera, that this exquisite young man in his private moments would not change his linen more often than once a month, and would shudder at the sound of a running bathtap! That almost sounds as though he were a morphia fiend. I remember a case in '99 . . . but I am interrupting you?"

"What precautions shall you take, Leon?" asked George Manfred.

"Against the snake?" Leon shrugged his shoulders. "The old military precaution against Zeppelin raids; the precaution the farmer takes against a plague of wasps. You cannot kneel on the chest of the *vespa vulgaris* and extract his sting with an anæsthetic. You destroy his nest—you bomb his hangar. Personally, I have never feared dissolution in any form, but I have a childish objection to being bitten by a snake."

Poiccart's saturnine face creased for a moment in a smile.

"You've no objection to stealing my theories," he said dryly, and the other doubled up in silent laughter.

Manfred was pacing the little room, his hands behind him, a thick Egyptian cigarette between his lips.

"There's a train leaves Paddington for Gloucester at ten forty-five," he said. "Will you telegraph to Miss Goddard, Heavytree Farm, and ask her to meet the train with a cab? After that I shall want two men to patrol the vicinity of the farm day and night."

Poiccart pulled open a drawer of the desk, took out a small book and ran his finger down the index.

"I can get this service in Gloucester," he said. "Gordon, Williams, Thompson and Elfred—they're reliable people and have worked for us before."

Manfred nodded.

"Send them the usual instructions by letter. I wonder who will be in charge of this Barberton case. If it's Meadows, I can work with him. On the other hand, if it's Arbuthnot, we shall have to get our information by subterranean methods."

"Call Elver," suggested Leon, and George pulled the telephone towards him.

It was some time before he could get into touch with Dr. Elver, and then he learnt, to his relief, that the redoubtable Inspector Meadows had complete charge.

"He's coming up to see you," said Elver. "As a matter of fact, the chief was here when I arrived at the Yard, and he particularly asked Meadows to consult with you. There's going to be an awful kick at the Home Secretary's office about this murder. We had practically assured the Home Office that there would be no repetition of the mysterious deaths and that the snake had gone dead for good."

Manfred asked a few questions and then hung up.

"They are worried about the public—you never know what masses will do in given circumstances. But you can gamble that the English mass does the same thing—Governments hate intelligent crowds. This may cost the Home Secretary his job, poor soul! And he's doing his best."

A strident shout in the street made him turn his head with a smile.

"The late editions have got it—naturally. It might have been committed on their doorstep."

"But why?" asked Poiccart. "What was Barberton's offence?"

"His first offence," said Leon promptly, without waiting for Manfred to reply, "was to go in search of Miss Mirabelle Leicester. His second and greatest was to consult with us. He was a dead man when he left the house."

The faint sound of a bell ringing sent Poiccart down to the hall to admit an unobtrusive, middle-aged man, who might have been anything but what he was: one of the cleverest trackers of criminals that Scotland Yard had known in thirty years. A sandy-haired, thin-faced man, who wore pince-nez and looked like an actor, he had been a visitor to Curzon Street before, and now received a warm welcome. With little preliminary he came to the object of his call, and Manfred told him briefly what had happened, and the gist of his conversation with Barberton.

"Miss Mirabelle Leicester is——" began Manfred.

"Employed by Oberzohn—I know," was the surprising reply. "She came up to London this morning and took a job as laboratory assistant. I had no idea that Oberzohn & Smitts had a laboratory on the premises."

"They hadn't until a couple of days ago," interrupted Leon. "The laboratory was staged especially for her."

Meadows nodded, then turned to Manfred.

"He didn't give you any idea at all why he wanted to meet Miss Leicester?"

George shook his head.

"No, he was very mysterious indeed on that subject," he said.

"He arrived by the *Benguella*, eh?" said Meadows, making a note. "We ought to get something from the ship before they pay off their stewards. If a man isn't communicative on board ship, he'll never talk at all! And we may find something in his belongings. Would you like to come along, Manfred?"

"I'll come with pleasure," said George gravely. "I may help you a little—you will not object to my making my own interpretation of what we see?"

Meadows smiled.

"You will be allowed your private mystery," he said.

A taxi set them down at the Petworth Hotel in Norfolk Street, and they were immediately shown up to the room which the dead man had hired but had not as yet occupied. His trunk, still strapped and locked, stood on a small wooden trestle, his overcoat was hanging behind the door; in one corner of the room was a thick hold-all, tightly strapped, and containing, as they subsequently discovered, a weather-stained mackintosh, two well-worn blankets and an air pillow, together with a collapsible canvas chair, also showing considerable signs of usage. This was the object of their preliminary search.

The lock of the trunk yielded to the third key which the detective tried. Beyond changes of linen and two suits, one of which was practically new and bore the tab of a store in St. Paul de Loanda, there was very little to enlighten them. They found an envelope full of papers, and sorted them out one by one on the bed. Barberton was evidently a careful man: he had preserved his hotel bills, writing on their backs brief but pungent comments about the accommodation he had enjoyed or suffered. There was an hotel in Lobuo which was full of vermin; there was one at Mossamedes of which he had written: "Rats ate one boot. Landlord made no allowance. Took three towels and pillow-slip."

"One of the Four Just Men in embryo," said Meadows dryly.

Manfred smiled.

On the back of one bill were closely written columns of figures: "12/6, 13/15, 10/7, 17/12, about 24," etc. Against a number of these figures the word "about" appeared, and Manfred observed that invariably this qualification marked one of the higher numbers. Against the 10/7 was a thick pencil mark.

There were amongst the papers several other receipts. In St. Paul he had bought a "pistol automatic of precision" and ammunition for the same. The "pistol automatic of precision" was not in the trunk.

"We found it in his pocket," said Meadows briefly. "That fellow was expecting trouble, and was entitled to, if it is true that they tortured him at Mosamodes."

"Moss-*am*-o-dees," Manfred corrected the mispronunciation. It almost amounted to a fad in him that to hear a place miscalled gave him a little pain.

Meadows was reading a letter, turning the pages slowly.

"This is from his sister: she lives at Brightlingsea, and there's nothing in it except . . ." He read a portion of the letter aloud:

> ". . . thank you for the books. The children will appreciate them. It must have been like old times writing them—but I can understand how it helped pass the time. Mr. Lee came over and asked if I had heard from you. He is wonderful."

The letter was in an educated hand.

"He didn't strike me as a man who wrote books," said Meadows, and continued his search.

Presently he unfolded a dilapidated map, evidently of Angola. It was rather on the small scale, so much so that it took in a portion of the Kalahari Desert in the south, and showed in the north the undulations of the rolling Congo.

"No marks of any kind," said Meadows, carrying the chart to the window to examine it more carefully. "And that, I think, is about all—unless this is something."

"This" was wrapped in a piece of cloth, and was fastened to the bottom and the sides of the trunk by two improvised canvas straps. Meadows tried to pull it loose and whistled.

"Gold," he said. "Nothing else can weigh quite as heavily as this."

He lifted out the bundle eventually, unwrapped the covering, and gazed in amazement on the object that lay under his eyes. It was an African *bête*, a nude, squat idol, rudely shaped, the figure of a native woman.

"Gold?" said Manfred incredulously, and tried to lift it with his finger and thumb. He took a firmer grip and examined the discovery closely.

There was no doubt that it was gold, and fine gold. His thumb-nail made a deep scratch in the base of the statuette. He could see the marks where the knife of the inartistic sculptor had sliced and carved.

Meadows knew the coast fairly well: he had made many trips to Africa and had stopped off at various ports en route.

"I've never seen anything exactly like it before," he said, "and it isn't recent workmanship either. When you see this"—he pointed to a physical peculiarity of the figure—"you can bet that you've got something that's been made at least a couple of hundred years, and probably before then. The natives of West and Central Africa have not worn toe-rings, for example, since the days of the Cæsars."

He weighed the idol in his hand.

"Roughly ten pounds," he said. "In other words, eight hundred pounds' worth of gold."

He was examining the cloth in which the idol had been wrapped, and uttered an exclamation.

"Look at this," he said.

Written on one corner, in indelible pencil, were the words:

"Second shelf up left Gods lobby sixth."

Suddenly Manfred remembered.

"Would you have this figure put on the scales right away?" he said. "I'm curious to know the exact weight."

"Why?" asked Meadows in surprise, as he rang the bell.

The proprietor himself, who was aware that a police search was in progress, answered the call, and, at the detective's request, hurried down to the kitchen and returned in a few minutes with a pair of scales, which he placed on the table. He was obviously curious to know the purpose for which they were intended, but Inspector Meadows did not enlighten him, standing pointedly by the door until the gentleman had gone.

The figure was taken from under the cloth where it had been hidden whilst the scales were being placed, and put in one shallow pan on the machine.

"Ten pounds seven ounces," nodded Manfred triumphantly. "I thought that was the one!"

"One what?" asked the puzzled Meadows.

"Look at this list."

Manfred found the hotel bill with the rows of figures and pointed to the one which had a black cross against it.

"10/7," he said. "That is our little fellow, and the explanation is fairly plain. Barberton found some treasure-house filled with these statues. He took away the lightest. Look at the figures! He weighed them with a spring balance, one of those which register up to 21 lbs. Above that he had to guess—he puts 'about 24,' 'about 22.'"

Meadows looked at his companion blankly, but Manfred was not deceived. That clever brain of the detective was working.

"Not for robbery—the trunk is untouched. They did not even burn his feet to find the idol or the treasure-house: they must have known nothing of that. It was easy to rob him—or, if they knew of his gold idol, they considered it too small loot to bother with."

He looked slowly round the apartment. On the mantelshelf was a slip of brown paper like a pipe-spill.

He picked it up, looked at both sides, and, finding the paper blank, put it back where he had found it. Manfred took it down and absently drew the strip between his sensitive finger-tips.

"The thing to do," said Meadows, taking one final look round, "is to find Miss Leicester."

Manfred nodded.

"That is one of the things," he said slowly. "The other, of course, is to find Johnny."

"Johnny?" Meadows frowned suspiciously. "Who is Johnny?" he asked.

"Johnny is my private mystery." George Manfred was smiling. "You promised me that I might have one!"

# Chapter VI In Chester Square

WHEN Mirabelle Leicester went to Chester Square, her emotions were a curious discord of wonder, curiosity and embarrassment. The latter was founded on the extraordinary effusiveness of her companion, who had suddenly, and with no justification, assumed the position of dearest friend and lifelong acquaintance. Mirabelle thought the girl was an actress: a profession in which sudden and violent friendships are not of rare occurrence. She wondered why Aunt Alma had not made an effort to come to town, and wondered more that she had known of Alma's friendship with the Newtons. That the elder woman had her secrets was true, but there was no reason why she should have refrained from speaking of a family who were close enough friends to be asked to chaperon her in town.

She had time for thought, for Joan Newton chattered away all the time, and if she asked a question, she either did not wait for approval, or the question was answered to her own satisfaction before it was put.

Chester Square, that dignified patch of Belgravia, is an imposing quarter. The big house into which the girl was admitted by a footman had that air of luxurious comfort which would have appealed to a character less responsive to refinement than Mirabelle Leicester's. She was ushered into a big drawing-room which ran from the front to the back of the house, and did not terminate even there, for a large, cool conservatory, bright with flowers, extended a considerable distance.

"Monty isn't back from the City yet," Joan rattled on. "My dear! He's awfully busy just now, what with stocks and shares and things like that."

She spoke as though "stocks and shares and things like that" were phenomena which had come into existence the day before yesterday for the occupation of Monty Newton.

"Is there a boom?" asked Mirabelle with a smile, and the term seemed to puzzle the girl.

"Ye-es, I suppose there is. You know what the Stock Exchange is, my dear? Everybody connected with it is wealthy beyond the dreams of avarice. The money they make is simply wicked! And they can give a girl an awfully good time—theatres, parties, dresses, pearls—why, Monty would think nothing of giving a string of pearls to a girl if he took a liking to her!"

In truth Joan was walking on very uncertain ground. Her instructions had been simple and to the point. "Get her to Chester Gardens, make friends with her, and don't mention the fact that I know Oberzohn." What was the object of bringing Mirabelle Leicester to the house, what was behind this move of Monty's, she did not know. She was merely playing for safety, baiting the ground, as it were, with her talk of good times and vast riches, in case that was required of her. For she, no less than many of her friends, entertained a wholesome dread of Monty Newton's disapproval, which usually took a definitely unpleasant shape.

Mirabelle was laughing softly.

"I didn't know that stockbrokers were so rich," she said dryly, "and I can assure you that some of them aren't!"

She passed tactfully over the *gaucherie* of the pearls that Monty would give to any girl who took his fancy. By this time she had placed Joan: knew something of her upbringing, guessed pretty well the extent of her intelligence, and marvelled a little that a man of the unknown Mr. Newton's position should have allowed his sister to come through the world without the benefit of a reasonably good education.

"Come up to your room, my dear," said Joan. "We've got a perfectly topping little suite for you, and I'm sure you'll be comfortable. It's at the front of the house, and if you can get used to the milkmen yowling about the streets before they're aired, you'll have a perfectly topping time."

When Mirabelle inspected the apartment she was enchanted. It fulfilled Joan's vague description. Here was luxury beyond her wildest dreams. She admired the silver bed and the thick blue carpet, the silken panelled walls, the exquisite fittings, and stood in rapture before the entrance of a little bathroom, with its silver and glass, its shaded lights and marble walls.

"I'll have a cup of tea sent up to you, my dear. You'll want to rest after your horrible day at that perfectly terrible factory, and I wonder you can stand Oberzohn, though they tell me he's quite a nice man. . . ."

She seemed anxious to go, and Mirabelle was no less desirous of being alone.

"Come down when you feel like it," said Joan at parting, and ran down the stairs, reaching the hall in time to meet Mr. Newton, who was handing his hat and gloves to his valet.

"Well, is she here?"

"She's here all right," said Joan, who was not at all embarrassed by the presence of the footman. "Monty, isn't she a bit of a fool? She couldn't say boo to a goose. What is the general scheme?"

He was brushing his hair delicately in the mirror above the hall-stand.

"What's what scheme?" he asked, after the servant had gone, as he strolled into the drawing-room before her.

"Bringing her here—is she sitting into a game?"

"Don't be stupid," said Monty without heat, as he dropped wearily to a low divan and drew a silken cushion behind him. "Nor inquisitive," he added. "You haven't scared her, have you?"

"I like that!" she said indignantly.

She was one of those ladies who speak more volubly and with the most assurance when there is a mirror in view, and she had her eyes fixed upon herself all the time she was talking, patting a strand of hair here and there, twisting her head this way and that to get a better effect, and never once looking at the man until he drew attention to himself.

"Scared! I'll bet she's never been to such a beautiful house in her life! What is she, Monty? A typist or something? I don't understand her."

"She's a lady," said Monty offensively. "That's the type that'll always seem like a foreign language to you."

She lifted one shoulder delicately.

"I don't pretend to be a lady, and what I am, you've made me," she said, and the reproach was mechanical. He had heard it before, not only from her but from others similarly placed. "I don't think it's very kind to throw my education up in my face, considering the money I've made for you."

"And for yourself." He yawned. "Get me some tea."

"You might say 'please' now and again," she said resentfully, and he smiled as he took up the evening paper, paying her no more attention, until she had rung the bell with a vicious jerk and the silver tray came in and was deposited on a table near him.

"Where are you going to-night?"

His interest in her movements was unusual, and she was flattered.

"You know very well, Monty, where I'm going to-night," she said reproachfully. "You promised to take me too. I think you'd look wonderful as a Crusader—one of them—those old knights in armour."

He nodded, but not to her comment.

"I remember, of course—the Arts Ball."

His surprise was so well simulated that she was deceived.

"Fancy your forgetting! I'm going as Cinderella, and Minnie Gray is going as a pierrette——"

"Minnie Gray isn't going as anything," said Monty, sipping his tea. "I've already telephoned to her to say that the engagement is off. Miss Leicester is going with you."

"But, Monty——" protested the girl.

"Don't 'but Monty' me," he ordered. "I'm telling you! Go up and see this girl, and put it to her that you've got a spare ticket for the dance."

"But her costume, Monty! The girl hasn't got a fancy dress. And Minnie———"

"Forget Minnie, will you? Mirabelle Leicester is going to the Arts Ball to-night." He tapped the tray before him to emphasize every word. "You have a ticket to spare, and you simply can't go alone because I have a very important business engagement and your friend has failed you. Her dress will be here in a few minutes: it is a bright green domino with a bright-red hood."

"How perfectly hideous!" She forgot for the moment her disappointment in this outrage. "Bright green! Nobody has a complexion to stand that!"

Yet he ignored her.

"You will explain to Miss Leicester that the dress came from a friend who, through illness or any cause you like to invent, is unable to go to the dance—she'll jump at the chance. It is one of the events of the year and tickets are selling at a premium."

She asked him what that meant, and he explained patiently.

"Maybe she'll want to spend a quiet evening—have one of those headaches," he went on. "If that is so, you can tell her that I've got a party coming to the house to-night, and they will be a little noisy. Did she want to know anything about me?"

"No, she didn't," snapped Joan promptly. "She didn't want to know about anything. I couldn't get her to talk. She's like a dumb oyster."

Mirabelle was sitting by the window, looking down into the square, when there was a gentle tap at the door and Joan came in.

"I've got wonderful news for you," she said.

"For me?" said Mirabelle in surprise.

Joan ran across the room, giving what she deemed to be a surprisingly life-like representation of a young thing full of innocent joy.

"I've got an extra ticket for the Arts Ball to-night. They're selling at a—they're very expensive. Aren't you a lucky girl!"

"I?" said Mirabelle in surprise. "Why am I the lucky girl?"

Joan rose from the bed and drew back from her reproachfully.

"You surely will come with me? If you don't, I shan't be able to go at all. Lady Mary and I were going together, and now she's sick!"

Mirabelle opened her eyes wider.

"But I can't go, surely. It is a fancy dress ball, isn't it? I read something about it in the papers. And I'm awfully tired to-night."

Joan pouted prettily.

"My dear, if you lay down for an hour you'd be fit. Besides, you couldn't sleep here early to-night: Monty's having one of his men parties, and they're a noisy lot of people—though thoroughly respectable," she added hastily.

Poor Joan had a mission outside her usual range.

"I'd love to go,"—Mirabelle was anxious not to be a kill-joy,—"if I could get a dress."

"I've got one," said the girl promptly, and ran out of the room.

She returned very quickly, and threw the domino on the bed.

"It's not pretty to look at, but it's got this advantage, that you can wear almost anything underneath."

"What time does the ball start?" Mirabelle, examining her mind, found that she was not averse to going; she was very human, and a fancy dress ball would be a new experience.

"Ten o'clock," said Joan. "We can have dinner before Monty's friends arrive. You'd like to see Monty, wouldn't you? He's downstairs—such a gentleman, my dear!"

The girl could have laughed.

A little later she was introduced to the redoubtable Monty, and found his suave and easy manner a relief after the jerky efforts of the girl to be entertaining. Monty had seen most parts of the world and could talk entertainingly about them all. Mirabelle rather liked him, though she thought he was something of a fop, yet was not sorry when she learned that, so far from having friends to dinner, he did not expect them to arrive until after she and Joan had left.

The meal put her more at her ease. He was a polished man of the world, courteous to the point of pomposity; he neither said nor suggested one thing that could offend her; they were half-way through dinner when the cry of a newsboy was heard in the street. Through the dining-room window she saw the footman go down the steps and buy a newspaper. He glanced at the stop-press space and came back slowly up the stairs reading. A little later he came into the room, and must have signalled to her host, for Monty went out immediately and she heard their voices in the passage. Joan was uneasy.

"I wonder what's the matter?" she asked, a little irritably. "It's very bad manners to leave ladies in the middle of dinner——"

At that moment Monty came back. Was it imagination on her part, or had he gone suddenly pale? Joan saw it, and her brows met, but she was too wise to make a comment upon his appearance.

Mr. Newton seated himself in his place with a word of apology and poured out a glass of champagne. Only for a second did his hand tremble, and then, with a smile, he was his old self.

"What is wrong, Monty?"

"Wrong? Nothing," he said curtly, and took up the topic of conversation where he had laid it down before leaving the room.

"It isn't that old snake, is it?" asked Joan with a shiver. "Lord! that unnerves me! I never go to bed at night without looking under, or turning the clothes right down to the foot! They ought to have found it months ago if the police——"

At this point she caught Monty Newton's eye, cold, menacing, malevolent, and the rest of her speech died on her lips.

Mirabelle went upstairs to dress, and Joan would have followed but the man beckoned her.

"You're a little too talkative, Joan," he said, more mildly than she had expected. "The snake is not a subject we wish to discuss at dinner. And listen!" He walked into the passage and looked round, then came back and closed the door. "Keep that girl near you."

"Who is going to dance with me?" she asked petulantly. "I look like having a hell of a lively night!"

"Benton will be there to look after you, and one of the 'Old Guard'——"

He saw the frightened look in her face and chuckled.

"What's the matter, you fool?" he asked good-humouredly. "He'll dance with the girl."

"I wish those fellows weren't going to be there," she said uneasily, but he went on, without noticing her:

"I shall arrive at half-past eleven. You had better meet me near the entrance to the American bar. My party didn't turn up, you understand. You'll get back here at midnight."

"So soon?" she said in dismay. "Why, it doesn't end till——"

"You'll be back here at midnight," he said evenly. "Go into her room, clear up everything she may have left behind. You understand? Nothing is to be left."

"But when she comes back she'll——"

"She'll not come back," said Monty Newton, and the girl's blood ran cold.

# Chapter VII        "Moral Suasion"

"THERE'S a man wants to see you, governor."

It was a quarter-past nine. The girls had been gone ten minutes, and Montague Newton had settled himself down to pass the hours of waiting before he had to dress. He put down the patience cards he was shuffling.

"A man to see me? Who is he, Fred?"

"I don't know: I've never seen him before. Looks to me like a 'busy.'"

A detective! Monty's eyebrows rose, but not in trepidation. He had met many detectives in the course of his chequered career and had long since lost his awe of them.

"Show him in," he said with a nod.

The slim man in evening dress who came softly into the room was a stranger to Monty, who knew most of the prominent figures in the world of criminal detection. And yet his face was in some way familiar.

"Captain Newton?" he asked.

"That is my name." Newton rose with a smile.

The visitor looked slowly round towards the door through which the footman had gone.

"Do your servants always listen at the keyhole?" he asked, in a quiet, measured tone, and Newton's face went a dusky red.

In two strides he was at the door and had flung it open, just in time to see the disappearing heels of the footman.

"Here, you!" He called the man back, a scowl on his face. "If you want to know anything, will you come in and ask?" he roared. "If I catch you listening at my door, I'll murder you!"

The man with a muttered excuse made a hurried escape.

"How did you know?" growled Newton, as he came back into the room and slammed the door behind him.

"I have an instinct for espionage," said the stranger, and went on, without a break: "I have called for Miss Mirabelle Leicester."

Newton's eyes narrowed.

"Oh, you have, have you?" he said softly. "Miss Leicester is not in the house. She left a quarter of an hour ago."

"I did not see her come out of the house?"

"No, the fact is, she went out by way of the mews. My—er"—he was going to say "sister" but thought better of it—"my young friend——"

"Flash Jane Smith," said the stranger. "Yes?"

Newton's colour deepened. He was rapidly reaching the point when his sang-froid, nine-tenths of his moral assets, was in danger of deserting him.

"Who are you, anyway?" he asked.

The stranger wetted his lips with the tip of his tongue, a curiously irritating action of his, for some inexplicable reason.

"My name is Leon Gonsalez," he said simply.

Instinctively the man drew back. Of course! Now he remembered, and the colour had left his cheeks, leaving him grey. With an effort he forced a smile.

"One of the redoubtable Four Just Men? What extraordinary birds you are!" he said. "I remember ten-fifteen years ago, being scared out of my life by the very mention of your name—you came to punish where the law failed, eh?"

"You must put that in your reminiscences," said Leon gently. "For the moment I am not in an autobiographical mood."

But Newton could not be silenced.

"I know a man"—he was speaking slowly, with quiet vehemence—"who will one day cause you a great deal of inconvenience, Mr. Leon Gonsalez: a man who never forgets you in his prayers. I won't tell you who he is."

"It is unnecessary. You are referring to the admirable Oberzohn. Did I not kill his brother . . . ? Yes, I thought I was right. He was the man with the oxycephalic head and the queerly prognathic jaw. An interesting case: I would like to have had his measurements, but I was in rather a hurry."

He spoke almost apologetically for his haste.

"But we're getting away from the subject, Mr. Newton. You say this young lady has left your house by the mews, and you were about to suggest she left in the care of Miss—I don't know what you call her. Why did she leave that way?"

Leon Gonsalez had something more than an instinct for espionage: he had an instinct for truth, and he knew two things immediately: first, that Newton was not lying when he said the girl had left the house; secondly, that there was an excellent, but not necessarily a sinister, reason for the furtive departure.

"Where has she gone?"

"Home," said the other laconically. "Where else should she go?"

"She came to dinner . . . intending to stay the night?"

"Look here, Gonsalez," interrupted Monty Newton savagely. "You and your gang were wonderful people twenty years ago, but a lot has happened since then—and we don't shiver at the name of the Three Just Men. I'm not a child—do you get that? And you're not so very terrible at close range. If you want to complain to the police——"

"Meadows is outside. I persuaded him to let me see you first," said Leon, and Newton started.

"Outside?" incredulously.

In two strides he was at the window and had pulled aside the blind. On the other side of the street a man was standing on the edge of the sidewalk, intently surveying the gutter. He knew him at once.

"Well, bring him in," he said.

"Where has this young lady gone? That is all I want to know."

"She has gone home, I tell you."

Leon went to the door and beckoned Meadows; they spoke together in low tones, and then Meadows entered the room and was greeted with a stiff nod from the owner of the house.

"What's the idea of this, Meadows—sending this bird to cross-examine me?"

"This bird came on his own," said Meadows coldly, "if you mean Mr. Gonsalez? I have no right to prevent any person from cross-examining you. Where is the young lady?"

"I tell you she has gone home. If you don't believe me, search the house—either of you."

He was not bluffing: Leon was sure of that. He turned to the detective.

"I personally have no wish to trouble this gentleman any more."

He was leaving the room when, from over his shoulder:

"That snake is busy again, Newton."

"What snake are you talking about?"

"He killed a man to-night on the Thames Embankment. I hope it will not spoil Lisa Marthon's evening."

Meadows, watching the man, saw him change colour.

"I don't know what you mean," he said loudly.

"You arranged with Lisa to pick up Barberton to-night and get him talking. And there she is, poor girl, all dressed to kill, and only a dead man to vamp—only a murdered man." He turned suddenly, and his voice grew hard. "That is a good word, isn't it, Newton—murder?"

"I didn't know anything about it."

As Newton's hand came towards the bell:

"We can show ourselves out," said Leon.

He shut the door behind him, and presently there was a slam of the outer door. Monty got to the window too late to see his unwelcome guests depart, and went up to his room to change, more than a little perturbed in mind.

The footman called him from the hall.

"I'm sorry about that affair, sir. I thought it was a 'busy' . . ."

"You think too much, Fred"—Newton threw the words down at his servitor with a snarl. "Go back to your place, which is the servants' hall. I'll ring you if I want you."

He resumed his progress up the stairs and the man turned sullenly away.

He opened the door of his room, switched on the light, had closed the door and was half-way to his dressing-table, when an arm like steel closed round his neck, he was jerked suddenly backward on to the floor, and looked up into the inscrutable face of Gonsalez.

"Shout and you die!" whispered a voice in his ear.

Newton lay quiet.

"I'll fix you for this," he stammered.

The other shook his head.

"I think not, if by 'fixing' me you mean you're going to complain to the police. You've been under my watchful eye for quite a long time, Monty Newton, and you'll be amazed to learn that I've made several visits to your house. There is a little wall safe behind that curtain"—he nodded towards the corner of the room—"would you be surprised to learn that I've had the door open and every one of its documentary contents photographed?"

He saw the fear in the man's eyes as he snapped a pair of aluminium handcuffs of curious design about Monty's wrists. With hardly an effort he lifted him, heavy as he was, threw him on the bed, and, having locked the door, returned, and, sitting on the bed, proceeded first to strap his ankles and then leisurely to take off his prisoner's shoes.

"What are you going to do?" asked Monty in alarm.

"I intend finding out where Miss Leicester has been taken," said Gonsalez, who had stripped one shoe and, pulling off the silken sock, was examining the man's bare foot critically. "Ordinary and strictly legal inquiries take time and fail at the end—unfortunately for you, I have not a minute to spare."

"I tell you she's gone home."

Leon did not reply. He pulled open a drawer of the bureau, searched for some time, and presently found what he sought: a thin silken scarf. This, despite the struggles of the man on the bed, he fastened about his mouth.

"In Mosamodes," he said—"and if you ever say that before my friend George Manfred, be careful to give its correct pronunciation: he is rather touchy on the point—some friends of yours took a man named Barberton, whom they subsequently murdered, and tried to make him talk by burning his feet. He was a hero. I'm going to see how heroic you are."

"For God's sake don't do it!" said the muffled voice of Newton.

Gonsalez was holding a flat metal case which he had taken from his pocket, and the prisoner watched him, fascinated, as he removed the lid, and snapped a cigar-lighter close to its blackened surface. A blue flame rose and swayed in the draught.

"The police force is a most excellent institution," said Leon. He had found a silver shoe-horn on the table and was calmly heating it in the light of the flame, holding the rapidly warming hook with a silk handkerchief. "But unfortunately, when you are dealing with crimes of violence, moral suasion and gentle treatment produce nothing more poignant in the bosom of your adversary than a sensation of amused and derisive contempt. The English, who make a god of the law, gave up imprisoning thugs and flogged them, and there are few thugs left. When the Russian gunmen came to London, the authorities did the only intelligent thing—they held back the police and brought up the artillery, having only one desire, which was to kill the gunmen at any expense. Violence fears violence. The gunman lives in the terror of the gun—by the way, I understand the old guard is back in full strength?"

When Leon started in this strain he could continue for hours.

"I don't know what you mean," mumbled Monty.

"You wouldn't." The intruder lifted the blackened, smoking shoe-horn, brought it as near to his face as he dared.

"Yes, I think that will do," he said, and came slowly towards the bed.

The man drew up his feet in anticipation of pain, but a long hand caught him by the ankles and drew them straight again.

"They've gone to the Arts Ball." Even through the handkerchief the voice sounded hoarse.

"The Arts Ball?" Gonsalez looked down at him, and then, throwing the hot shoe-horn into the fire-place, he removed the gag. "Why have they gone to the Arts Ball?"

"I wanted them out of the way to-night."

"Is—Oberzohn likely to be at the Arts Ball?"

"Oberzohn!" The man's laugh bordered on the hysterical.

"Or Gurther?"

This time Mr. Newton did not laugh.

"I don't know who you mean," he said.

"We'll go into that later," replied Leon lightly, pulling the knot of the handkerchief about the ankles. "You may get up now. What time do you expect them back?"

"I don't know. I told Joan not to hurry, as I was meeting somebody here to-night."

Which sounded plausible. Leon remembered that the Arts Ball was a fancy dress affair, and there was some reason for the departure from the mews instead of from the front of the house. As though he were reading his thoughts, Newton said:

"It was Miss Leicester's idea, going through the back. She was rather shy . . . she was wearing a domino."

"Colour?"

"Green, with a reddish hood."

Leon looked at him quickly.

"Rather distinctive. Was that the idea?"

"I don't know what the idea was," growled Newton, sitting on the edge of the bed and pulling on a sock. "But I do know this, Gonsalez," he said, with an outburst of anger which was half fear: "that you'll be sorry you did this to me!"

Leon walked to the door, turned the key and opened it.

"I only hope that you will not be sorry I did not kill you," he said, and was gone.

Monty Newton waited until from his raised window he saw the slim figure pass along the sidewalk and disappear round a corner, and then he hurried down, with one shoe on and one off, to call New Cross 93.

# Chapter VIII        The House of Oberzohn

IN a triangle two sides of which were expressed by the viaducts of converging railroads and the base by the dark and sluggish waters of the Grand Surrey Canal, stood the gaunt ruins of a store in which had once been housed the merchandise of the O. & S. Company. A Zeppelin in passing had dropped an incendiary bomb at random, and torn a great ugly gap in the roof. The fire that followed left the iron frames of the windows twisted and split; the roof by some miracle remained untouched except for the blackened edges about the hole through which the flames had rushed to the height of a hundred feet.

The store was flush with the canal towing-path; barges had moored here, discharging rubber in bales, palm nut, nitrates even, and had restocked with Manchester cloth and case upon case of Birmingham-made geegaws of brass and lacquer.

Mr. Oberzohn invariably shipped his spirituous cargoes from Hamburg, since Germany is the home of synthesis. In the centre of the triangle was a red-brick villa, more unlovely than the factory, missing as it did that ineffable grandeur, made up of tragedy and pathos, attaching to a burnt-out building, however ugly it may have been in its prime.

The villa was built from a design in Mr. Oberzohn's possession, and was the exact replica of the house in Sweden where he was born. It had high, gabled ends at odd and unexpected places. The roof was shingled with grey tiles; there were glass panels in the curious-looking door, and iron ornaments in the shape of cranes and dogs flanking the narrow path through the rank nettle and dock which constituted his garden.

Here he dwelt, in solitude, yet not in solitude, for two men lived in the house, and there was a stout Swedish cook and a very plain Danish maid, a girl of vacant countenance, who worked from sun-up to midnight without complaint, who seldom spoke and never smiled. The two men were somewhere in the region of thirty. They occupied the turret rooms at each end of the building, and had little community of interest. They sometimes played cards together with an old and greasy pack, but neither spoke more than was necessary. They were lean, hollow-faced men, with a certain physiognomical resemblance. Both had thin, straight lips; both had round, staring, dark eyes filled with a bright but terrifying curiosity.

"They look," reported Leon Gonsalez, when he went to examine the ground, "as if they are watching pigs being killed and enjoying every minute of it.

Iwan Pfeiffer is one, Sven Gurther is the other. Both have escaped the gallows or the axe in Germany; both have convictions against them. They are typical German-trained criminals—as pitiless as wolves. Dehumanized."

The "Three," as was usual, set the machinery of the law in motion, and found that the hands of the police were tied. Only by stretching the law could the men be deported, and the law is difficult to stretch. To all appearance they offended in no respect. A woman, by no means the most desirable of citizens, laid a complaint against one. There was an investigation—proof was absent; the very character of the complainant precluded a conviction, and the matter was dropped—by the police.

Somebody else moved swiftly.

One morning, just before daybreak, a policeman patrolling the tow-path heard a savage snarl and looked round for the dog. He found instead, up one of those narrow entries leading to the canal bank, a man. He was tied to the stout sleeper fence, and his bare back showed marks of a whip. Somebody had held him up at night as he prowled the bank in search of amusement, had tied and flogged him. Twenty-five lashes: an expert thought the whip used was the official cat-o'-nine-tails.

Scotland Yard, curious, suspicious, sought out the Three Just Men. They had alibis so complete as to be unbreakable. Sven Gurther went unavenged—but he kept from the tow-path thereafter.

In this house of his there were rooms which only Dr. Oberzohn visited. The Danish maid complained to the cook that when she had passed the door of one as the doctor came out, a blast of warm, tainted air had rushed out and made her cough for an hour. There was another room in which from time to time the doctor had installed a hotchpotch of apparatus. Vulcanizing machines, electrical machines (older and more used than Mirabelle had seen in her brief stay in the City Road), a liquid air plant, not the most up-to-date but serviceable.

He was not, curiously enough, a doctor in the medical sense. He was not even a doctor of chemistry. His doctorate was in Literature and Law. These experiments of his were hobbies—hobbies that he had pursued from his childhood.

On this evening he was sitting in his stuffy parlour reading a close-printed and closer-reasoned volume of German philosophy, and thinking of something else. Though the sun had only just set, the blinds and curtains were drawn; a wood fire crackled in the grate, and the bright lights of three half-watt lamps made glaring radiance.

An interruption came in the shape of a telephone call. He listened, grunting replies.

"So!" he said at last, and spoke a dozen words in his strange English.

Putting aside his book, he hobbled in his velvet slippers across the room and pressed twice upon the bell-push by the side of the fire-place. Gurther came in noiselessly and stood waiting.

He was grimy, unshaven. The pointed chin and short upper lip were blue. The V of his shirt visible above the waistcoat was soiled and almost black at the edges. He stood at attention, smiling vacantly, his eyes fixed at a point above the doctor's head.

Dr. Oberzohn lifted his eyes from his book.

"I wish you to be a gentleman of club manner to-night," he said. He spoke in that hard North-German tongue which the Swede so readily acquires.

"Ja, Herr Doktor!"

The man melted from the room.

Dr. Oberzohn for some reason hated Germans. So, for the matter of that, did Gurther and Pfeiffer, the latter being Polish by extraction and Russian by birth. Gurther hated Germans because they stormed the little jail at Altostadt to kill him after the dogs found Frau Siedlitz's body. He would have died then but for the green police, who scented a Communist rising, scattered the crowd and sent Gurther by-road to the nearest big town under escort. The two escorting policemen were never seen again. Gurther reappeared mysteriously in England two years after, bearing a veritable passport. There was no proof even that he was Gurther. Leon knew, Manfred knew, Poiccart knew.

There had been an alternative to the whipping.

"It would be a simple matter to hold his head under water until he was drowned," said Leon.

They debated the matter, decided against this for no sentimental or moral reason—none save expediency. Gurther had his whipping and never knew how near to the black and greasy water of the canal he had been.

Dr. Oberzohn resumed his book—a fascinating book that was all about the human soul and immortality and time. He was in the very heart of an analysis of eternity when Gurther reappeared dressed in the "gentleman-club manner." His dress-coat fitted perfectly; shirt and waistcoat were exactly the right cut. The snowy shirt, the braided trousers, the butterfly bow, and winged collar. . . .

"That is good." Dr. Oberzohn went slowly over the figure. "But the studs should be pearl—not enamel. And the watch-chain is demode—it is not worn. The gentleman-club manner does not allow of visible ornament. Also I think a moustache . . . ?"

"Ja, Herr Doktor!"

Gurther, who was once an actor, disappeared again. When he returned the enamel studs had gone: there were small pearls in their place, and his white waistcoat had no chain across. And on his upper lip had sprouted a small brown moustache, so natural that even Oberzohn, scrutinizing closely, could find no fault with it. The doctor took a case from his pocket, fingered out three crisp notes.

"Your hands, please?"

Gurther took three paces to the old man, halted, clicked his heels and held out his hands for inspection.

"Good! You know Leon Gonsalez? He will be at the Arts Ball. He wears no fancy dress. He was the man who whipped you."

"He was the man who whipped me," said Gurther without heat.

There was a silence, Dr. Oberzohn pursing his lips.

"Also, he did that which brands him as an infamous assassin . . . I think . . . yes, I think my dear Gurther . . . there will be a girl also, but the men of my police will be there to arrange such matters. Benton will give you instructions. For you, only Gonsalez."

Gurther bowed stiffly.

"I have implored the order," he said, bowed again and withdrew. Later, Dr. Oberzohn heard the drone of the little car as it bumped and slithered across the grass to the road. He resumed his book: this matter of eternity was fascinating.

---

The Arts Ball at the Corinthian Hall was one of the events of the season, and the tickets, issued exclusively to the members of three clubs, were eagerly sought by society people who could not be remotely associated with any but the art of living.

When the girl came into the crowded hall, she looked around in wonder. The balconies, outlined in soft lights and half-hidden with flowers, had been converted into boxes; the roof had been draped with blue and gold tissue; at one end of the big hall was a veritable bower of roses, behind which one of the two bands was playing. Masks in every conceivable guise were swinging rhythmically across the polished floor. To the blasé, there was little difference between the Indians, the pierrots and the cavaliers to be seen here and those they had seen a hundred times on a hundred different floors.

As the girl gazed round in wonder and delight, forgetting all her misgivings, two men, one in evening dress, the other in the costume of a brigand, came from under the shadow of the balcony towards them.

"Here are our partners," said Joan, with sudden vivacity. "Mirabelle, I want you to know Lord Evington."

The man in evening dress stroked his little moustache, clicked his heels and bent forward in a stiff bow. He was thin-faced, a little pallid, unsmiling. His round, dark eyes surveyed her for a second, and then:

"I'm glad to meet you, Miss Leicester," he said, in a high, harsh voice, that had just the trace of a foreign accent.

This struck the girl with as much surprise as the cold kiss he had implanted upon her hand, and, as if he read her thoughts, he went on quickly:

"I have lived so long abroad that England and English manners are strange to me. Won't you dance? And had you not better mask? I must apologize to you for my costume." He shrugged his shoulders. "But there was no gala dress available."

She fixed the red mask, and in another second she was gliding through the crowd and was presently lost to view.

"I don't understand it all, Benton."

Joan was worried and frightened. She had begun to realize that the game she played was something different . . . her part more sinister than any rôle she had yet filled. To jolly along the gilded youth to the green tables of Captain Monty Newton was one thing; but never before had she seen the gang working against a woman.

"I don't know," grumbled the brigand, who was not inaptly arrayed. "There's been a hurry call for everybody." He glanced round uneasily as though he feared his words might be overheard. "All the guns are here—Defson, Cuccini, Jewy Stubbs . . ."

"The guns?" she whispered in horror, paling under her rouge. "You mean . . . ?"

"The guns are out: that's all I know," he said doggedly. "They started drifting in half an hour before you came."

Joan was silent, her heart racing furiously. Then Monty had told her the truth. She knew that somewhere behind Oberzohn, behind Monty Newton, was a force perfectly dovetailed into the machine, only one cog of which she had seen working. These card parties of Monty's were profitable enough, but for a long time she had had a suspicion that they were the merest side-line. The organization maintained a regular corps of gunmen, recruited from every quarter of the globe. Monty Newton talked sometimes in his less sober moments of what he facetiously described as the "Old Guard." How they were employed, on what excuse, for what purpose, she had never troubled to think. They came and went from England in batches. Once Monty had told her that Oberzohn's people had gone to Smyrna, and he talked vaguely of unfair competition that had come to the traders of the O. & S. outfit. Afterwards she read in the paper of a "religious riot" which resulted in the destruction by fire of a great block of business premises. After that Monty spoke no more of competition. The Old Guard returned to England, minus one of its number, who had been shot in the stomach in the course of this "religious riot." What particular faith he possessed in such a degree as to induce him to take up arms for the cause, she never learned. She knew he was dead, because Monty had written to the widow, who lived in the Bronx.

Joan knew a lot about Monty's business, for an excellent reason. She was with him most of the time; and whether she posed as his niece or daughter, his sister, or some closer relationship, she was undoubtedly the nearest to a confidante he possessed.

"Who is that man with the moustache—is he one?" she asked.

"No; he's Oberzohn's man—for God's sake don't tell Monty I told you all this! I got orders to-night to put him wise about the girl."

"What about her . . . what are they doing with her?" she gasped in terror.

"Let us dance," said Benton, and half guided, half carried her into the throng.

They had reached the centre of the floor when, with no warning, every light in the hall went out.

# Chapter IX          Before the Lights Went Out

THE band had stopped, a rustle of hand-clapping came from the hot dancers, and almost before the applause had started the second band struck up "Kulloo."

Mirabelle was not especially happy. Her partner was the most correct of dancers, but they lacked just that unity of purpose, that oneness of interest which makes all the difference between the ill- and the well-matched.

"May we sit down?" she begged. "I am rather hot."

"Will the gracious lady come to the little hall?" he asked. "It is cooler there, and the chairs are comfortable."

She looked at him oddly.

" 'Gracious lady' is a German expression—why do you use it, Lord Evington? I think it is very pretty," she hastened to assure him.

"I lived for many years in Germany," said Mr. Gurther. "I do not like the German people—they are so stupid."

If he had said "German police" he would have been nearer to the truth; and had he added that the dislike was mutual, he might have gained credit for his frankness.

At the end of the room, concealed by the floral decorations of the bandstand, was a door which led to a smaller room, ordinarily separated from the main hall by folding doors which were seldom opened. To-night the annexe was to be used as a conservatory. Palms and banked flowers were everywhere. Arbours had been artificially created, and there were cosy nooks, half-hidden by shrubs, secluded seats and tables, all that ingenuity could design to meet the wishes of sitters-out.

He stood invitingly at the entrance of a little grotto, dimly illuminated by one Chinese lantern.

"I think we will sit in the open," said Mirabelle, and pulled out a chair.

"Excuse me."

Instantly he was by her side, the chair arranged, a cushion found, and she sank down with a sigh of relief. It was early yet for the loungers: looking round, she saw that, but for a solitary waiter fastening his apron with one eye upon possible customers, they were alone.

"You will drinke wine . . . no? An orangeade? Good!" He beckoned the waiter and gave his order. "You must excuse me if I am a little strange. I have been in Germany for many years—except during the war, when I was in France."

Mr. Gurther had certainly been in Germany for many years, but he had never been in France. Nor had he heard a shot fired in the war. It is true that an aerial bomb had exploded perilously near the prison at Mainz in which he was serving ten years for murder, but that represented his sole warlike experience.

"You live in the country, of course?"

"In London: I am working with Mr. Oberzohn."

"So: he is a good fellow. A gentleman."

She had not been very greatly impressed by the doctor's breeding, but it was satisfying to hear a stranger speak with such heartiness of her new employer. Her mind at the moment was on Heavytree Farm: the cool parlour with its chintzes—a room, at this hour, fragrant with the night scents of flowers which came stealing through the open casement. There was a fox-terrier, Jim by name, who would be wandering disconsolately from room to room, sniffing unhappily at the hall door. A lump came up into her throat. She felt very far from home and very lonely. She wanted to get up and run back to where she had left Joan and tell her that she had changed her mind and must go back to Gloucester that night . . . she looked impatiently for the waiter. Mr. Gurther was fiddling with some straws he had taken from the glass container in the centre of the table. One end of the straws showed above the edge of the table, the others were thrust deep in the wide-necked little bottle he had in the other hand. The hollow straws held half an inch of the red powder that filled the bottle.

"Excuse!"

The waiter put the orangeades on the table and went away to get change. Mirabelle's eyes were wistfully fixed on a little door at the end of the room. It gave to the street, and there were taxicabs which could get her to Paddington in ten minutes.

When she looked round he was stirring the amber contents of her glass with a spoon. Two straws were invitingly protruding from the foaming orangeade. She smiled and lifted the glass as he fitted a cigarette into his long black holder.

"I may smoke—yes?"

The first taste she had through the straws was one of extreme bitterness. She made a wry face and put down the glass.

"How horrid!"

"Did it taste badly . . . ?" he began, but she was pouring out water from a bottle.

"It was most unpleasant——"

"Will you try mine, please?" He offered the glass to her and she drank. "It may have been something in the straw." Here he was telling her the fact.

"It was . . ."

The room was going round and round, the floor rising up and down like the deck of a ship in a stormy sea. She rose, swayed, and caught him by the arm.

"Open the little door, waiter, please—the lady is faint."

The waiter turned to the door and threw it open. A man stood there—just outside the door. He wore over his dinner dress a long cloak in the Spanish style. Gurther stood staring, a picture of amused dismay, his cigarette still unlit. He did not move his hands. Gonsalez was waiting there, alert . . . death grinning at him . . . and then the room went inky black. Somebody had turned the main switch.

# Chapter X          When the Lights Went Out

FIVE, ten minutes passed before the hall-keeper tripped and stumbled and cursed his way to the smaller room and, smashing down the hired flowers, he passed through the wreckage of earthen pots and tumbled mould to the control. Another second and the rooms were brilliantly lit again—the band struck up a two-step and fainting ladies were escorted to the decent obscurity of their retiring rooms.

The manager of the hall came flying into the annexe.

"What happened—main fuse gone?"

"No," said the hall-keeper sourly, "some fool turned over the switch."

The agitated waiter protested that nobody had been near the switch-box.

"There was a lady and gentleman here, and another gentleman outside." He pointed to the open door.

"Where are they now?"

"I don't know. The lady was faint."

The three had disappeared when the manager went out into a small courtyard that led round the corner of the building to a side street. Then he came back on a tour of inspection.

"Somebody did it from the yard. There's a window open—you can reach the switch easily."

The window was fastened and locked.

"There is no lady or gentleman in the yard," he said. "Are you sure they did not go into the big hall?"

"In the dark—maybe."

The waiter's nervousness was understandable. Mr. Gurther had given him a five-pound note and the man had not as yet delivered the change. Never would he return to claim it if all that his keen ears heard was true.

Four men had appeared in the annexe: one shut the door and stood by it. The three others were accompanied by the manager, who called Phillips, the waiter.

"This man served them," he said, troubled. Even the most innocent do not like police visitations.

"What was the gentleman like?"

Phillips gave a brief and not inaccurate description.

"That is your man, I think, Herr Fluen?"

The third of the party was bearded and plump; he wore a Derby hat with evening dress.

"That is Gurther," he nodded. "It will be a great pleasure to meet him. For eight months the Embassy has been striving for his extradition. But our people at home . . . !"

He shrugged his shoulders. All properly constituted officials behave in such a manner when they talk of governments.

"The lady now"—Inspector Meadows was patently worried—"she was faint, you say. Had she drunk anything?"

"Orangeade—there is the glass. She said there was something nasty in the straws. These."

Phillips handed them to the detective. He wetted his finger from them, touched his tongue and spat out quickly.

"Yes," he said, and went out by the little door.

Gonsalez, of course: but where had he gone, and how, with a drugged girl on his hands and the Child of the Snake? Gurther was immensely quick to strike, and an icy-hearted man: the presence of a woman would not save Leon.

"When the light went out——" began the waiter, and the trouble cleared from Mr. Meadows' face.

"Of course—I had forgotten that," he said softly. "The lights went out!"

All the way back to the Yard he was trying to bring something from the back of his mind—something that was there, the smooth tip of it tantalizingly displayed, yet eluding every grasp. It had nothing to do with the lights—nor Gonsalez, nor yet the girl. Gurther? No. Nor Manfred? What was it? A name had been mentioned to him that day—it had a mysterious significance. A golden idol! He picked up the end of the thought . . . Johnny! Manfred's one mystery. That was the dust which lay on all thought. And now that he remembered, he was disappointed. It was so ridiculously unimportant a matter to baffle him.

He left his companions at the corner of Curzon Street and went alone to the house. There was a streak of light showing between the curtains in the upstairs room. The passage was illuminated—Poiccart answered his ring at once.

"Yes, George and Leon were here a little time back—the girl? No, they said nothing about a girl. They looked rather worried, I thought. Miss Leicester, I suppose? Won't you come in?"

"No, I can't wait. There's a light in Manfred's room."

The ghost of a smile lit the heavy face and faded as instantly.

"My room also," he said. "Butlers take vast liberties in the absence of their masters. Shall I give a message to George?"

"Ask him to call me at the Yard."

Poiccart closed the door on him; stopped in the passage to arrange a salver on the table and hung up a hat. All this Meadows saw through the fanlight and walking-stick periscope which is so easily fitted and can be of such value. And seeing, his doubts evaporated.

Poiccart went slowly up the stairs into the little office room, pulled back the curtains and opened the window at the top. The next second, the watching detective saw the light go out and went away.

"I'm sorry to keep you in the dark," said Poiccart.

The men who were in the room waited until the shutters were fast and the curtains pulled across, and then the light flashed on. White of face, her eyes closed, her breast scarcely moving, Mirabelle Leicester lay on the long settee. Her domino was a heap of shimmering green and scarlet on the floor, and Leon was gently sponging her face, George Manfred watching from the back of the settee, his brows wrinkled.

"Will she die?" he asked bluntly.

"I don't know: they sometimes die of that stuff," replied Leon cold-bloodedly. "She must have had it pretty raw. Gurther is a crude person."

"What was it?" asked George.

Gonsalez spread out his disengaged hand in a gesture of uncertainty.

"If you can imagine morphia with a kick in it, it was that. I don't know. I hope she doesn't die: she is rather young—it would be the worst of bad luck."

Poiccart stirred uneasily. He alone had within his soul what Leon would call "a trace" of sentiment.

"Could we get Elver?" he asked anxiously, and Leon looked up with his boyish smile.

"Growing onions in Seville has softened you, Raymondo mio!" He never failed in moments of great strain to taunt the heavy man with his two years of agricultural experiment, and they knew that the gibes were deliberately designed to steady his mind. "Onions are sentimental things—they make you cry: a vegetable *muchos simpatico*! This woman is alive!"

Her eyelids had fluttered twice. Leon lifted the bare arm, inserted the needle of a tiny hypodermic and pressed home the plunger.

"To-morrow she will feel exactly as if she had been drunk," he said calmly, "and in her mouth will be the taste of ten rank cigars. Oh, senorinetta, open thy beautiful eyes and look upon thy friends!"

The last sentence was in Spanish. She heard: the lids fluttered and rose.

"You're a long way from Heavytree Farm, Miss Leicester."

She looked up wonderingly into the kindly face of George Manfred.

"Where am I?" she asked faintly, and closed her eyes again with a grimace of pain.

"They always ask that—just as they do in books," said Leon oracularly. "If they don't say 'Where am I?' they ask for their mothers. She's quite out of danger."

One hand was on her wrist, another at the side of her neck.

"Remarkably regular. She has a good head—mathematical probably."

"She is very beautiful," said Poiccart in a hushed voice.

"All people are beautiful—just as all onions are beautiful. What is the difference between a lovely maid and the ugliest of duennas—what but a matter of pigmentation and activity of tissue? Beneath that, an astounding similarity of the circulatory, sustentacular, motorvascular———"

"How long have we got?" Manfred interrupted him, and Leon shook his head.

"I don't know—not long, I should think. Of course, we could have told Meadows and he'd have turned out police reserves, but I should like to keep them out of it."

"The Old Guard was there?"

"Every man jack of them—those tough lads! They will be here just as soon as the Herr Doktor discovers what is going forward. Now, I think you can travel. I want her out of the way."

Stooping, he put his hands under her and lifted her. The strength in his frail body was a never-ending source of wonder to his two friends.

They followed him down the stairs and along the short passage, down another flight to the kitchen. Manfred opened a door and went out into the paved yard. There was a heavier door in the boundary wall. He opened this slowly and peeped out. Here was the inevitable mews. The sound of an engine running came from a garage near by. Evidently somebody was on the look out for them. A long-bodied car drew up noiselessly and a woman got out. Beside the driver at the wheel sat two men.

"I think you'll just miss the real excitement," said Gonsalez, and then to the nurse he gave a few words of instruction and closed the door on her.

"Take the direct road," he said to the driver. "Swindon—Gloucester. Good night."

"Good night, sir."

He watched anxiously as the machine swung into the main road. Still he waited, his head bent. Two minutes went by, and the faint sound of a motor-horn, a long blast and a short, and he sighed.

"They're clear of the danger zone," he said.

*Plop!*

He saw the flash, heard the smack of the bullet as it struck the door, and his hand stiffened. There was a thudding sound—a scream of pain from a dark corner of the mews and the sound of voices. Leon drew back into the yard and bolted the door.

"He had a new kind of silencer. Oberzohn is rather a clever old bird. But my air pistol against their gun for noiselessness."

"I didn't expect the attack from that end of the mews." Manfred was slipping a Browning back to his pocket.

"If they had come from the other end the car would not have passed—I'd like to get one of those silencers."

They went into the house. Poiccart had already extinguished the passage light.

"You hit your man—does that thing kill?"

"By accident—it is possible. I aimed at his stomach: I fear that I hit him in the head. He would not have squealed for a stomach wound. I fear he is alive."

He felt his way up the stairs and took up the telephone. Immediately a voice said, "Number?"

"Give me 8877 Treasury."

He waited, and then a different voice asked:

"Yes—Scotland Yard speaking."

"Can you give me Mr. Meadows?"

Manfred was watching him frowningly.

"That you, Meadows? . . . They have shot Leon Gonsalez—can you send police reserves and an ambulance?"

"At once."

Leon hung up the receiver, hugging himself.

"The idea being——?" said Poiccart.

"These people are clever." Leon's voice was charged with admiration. "They haven't cut the wires—they've simply tapped it at one end and thrown it out of order on the exchange side."

"Phew!" Manfred whistled. "You deceived me—you were talking to Oberzohn?"

"Captain Monty and Lew Cuccini. They may or may not be deceived, but if they aren't, we shall know all about it."

He stopped dead. There was a knock on the front door, a single, heavy knock. Leon grinned delightedly.

"One of us is now supposed to open an upper window cautiously and look out, whereupon he is instantly gunned. I'm going to give these fellows a scare."

He ran up the stairs to the top floor, and on the landing, outside an attic door, pulled at a rope. A fire ladder lying flat against the ceiling came down, and at the same time a small skylight opened. Leon went into the room, and his pocket-lamp located what he needed: a small papier-mâché cylinder, not unlike a seven-pound shell. With this on his arm, he climbed up the ladder on to the roof, fixed the cylinder on a flat surface, and, striking a match, lit a touch-paper. The paper sizzled and spluttered, there was a sudden flash and "boom!" a dull explosion, and a white ball shot up into the sky, described a graceful curve and burst into a shower of brilliant crimson stars. He waited till the last died out; then, with the hot cylinder under his arm, descended the ladder, released the rope that held it in place, and returned to his two friends.

"They will imagine a secret arrangement of signals with the police," he said; "unless my knowledge of their psychology is at fault, we shall not be bothered again."

Ten minutes later there was another knock at the door, peremptory, almost official in its character.

"This," said Leon, "is a policeman to summon us for discharging fireworks in the public street!"

He ran lightly down into the hall and without hesitation pulled open the door. A tall, helmeted figure stood on the doorstep, notebook in hand.

"Are you the gentleman that let off that rocket——" he began.

Leon walked past him, and looked up and down Curzon Street. As he had expected, the Old Guard had vanished.

# Chapter XI                    Gurther

MONTY NEWTON dragged himself home, a weary, angry man, and let himself in with his key. He found the footman lying on the floor of the hall asleep, his greatcoat pulled over him, and stirred him to wakefulness with the toe of his boot.

"Get up," he growled. "Anybody been here?"

Fred rose, a little dazed, rubbing his eyes.

"The old man's in the drawing-room," he said, and his employer passed on without another word.

As he opened the door, he saw that all the lights in the drawing-room were lit. Dr. Oberzohn had pulled a small table near the fire, and before this he sat bolt upright, a tiny chess-board before him, immersed in a problem. He looked across to the new-comer for a second and then resumed his study of the board, made a move . . .

"Ach!" he said in tones of satisfaction. "Leskina was wrong! It is possible to mate in five moves!"

He pushed the chess-men into confusion and turned squarely to face Newton.

"Well, have you concluded these matters satisfactorily?"

"He brought up the reserves," said Monty, unlocking a tantalus on a side table and helping himself liberally to whisky. "They got Cuccini through the jaw. Nothing serious."

Dr. Oberzohn laid his bony hands on his knees.

"Gurther must be disciplined," he said. "Obviously he has lost his nerve; and when a man loses his nerve also he loses his sense of time. And his timing— how deplorable! The car had not arrived; my excellent police had not taken position . . . deplorable!"

"The police are after him: I suppose you know that?" Newton looked over his glass.

Dr. Oberzohn nodded.

"The extradition so cleverly avoided is now accomplished. But Gurther is too good a man to be lost. I have arranged a hiding-place for him. He is of many uses."

"Where did he go?"

Dr. Oberzohn's eyebrows wrinkled up and down.

"Who knows?" he said. "He has the little machine. Maybe he has gone to the house—the green light in the top window will warn him and he will move carefully."

Newton walked to the window and looked out. Chester Square looked ghostly in the grey light of dawn. And then, out of the shadows, he saw a figure move and walk slowly towards the south side of the square.

"They're watching this house," he said, and laughed.

"Where is my young lady?" asked Oberzohn, who was staring glumly into the fire.

"I don't know . . . there was a car pulled out of the mews as one of our men 'closed' the entrance. She has probably gone back to Heavytree Farm, and you can sell that laboratory of yours. There is only one way now, and that's the rough way. We have time—we can do a lot in six weeks. Villa is coming this morning—I wish we'd taken that idol from the trunk. That may put the police on to the right track."

Dr. Oberzohn pursed his lips as though he were going to whistle, but he was guilty of no such frivolity.

"I am glad they found him," he said precisely. "To them it will be a scent. What shall they think, but that the unfortunate Barberton had come upon an old native treasure-house? No, I do not fear that." He shook his head. "Mostly I fear Mr. Johnson Lee and the American, Elijah Washington."

He put his hand into his jacket pocket and took out a thin pad of letters.

"Johnson Lee is for me difficult to understand. For what should a gentleman have to do with this boor that he writes so friendly letters to him?"

"How did you get these?"

"Villa took them: it was one of the intelligent actions also to leave the statue."

He passed one of the letters across to Newton. It was addressed "Await arrival, Poste Restante, Mosamedes." The letter was written in a curiously round, boyish hand. Another remarkable fact was that it was perforated across the page at regular intervals, and upon the lines formed by this perforation Mr. Johnson Lee wrote.

"Dear B.," the letter ran, "I have instructed my banker to cable you £500. I hope this will carry you through and leave enough to pay your fare home. You may be sure that I shall not breathe a

- 64 -

word, and your letters, of course, nobody in the house can read but me. Your story is amazing, and I advise you to come home at once and see Miss Leicester.

"Your friend,

"JOHNSON LEE."

The note-paper was headed "Rath Hall, January 13th."

"They came to me to-day. If I had seen them before, there would have been no need for the regrettable happening."

He looked thoughtfully at his friend.

"They will be difficult: I had that expectation," he said, and Monty knew that he referred to the Three Just Men. "Yet they are mortal also—remember that, my Newton: they are mortal also."

"As we are," said Newton gloomily.

"That is a question," said Oberzohn, "so far as I am concerned."

Dr. Oberzohn never jested; he spoke with the greatest calm and assurance. The other man could only stare at him.

Although it was light, a green lamp showed clearly in the turret room of the doctor's house as he came within sight of the ugly place. And, seeing that warning, he did not expect to be met in the passage by Gurther. The man had changed from his resplendent kit and was again in the soiled and shabby garments he had discarded the night before.

"You have come, Gurther?"

"Ja, Herr Doktor."

"To my parlour!" barked Dr. Oberzohn, and marched ahead.

Gurther followed him and stood with his back to the door, erect, his chin raised, his bright, curious eyes fixed on a point a few inches above his master's head.

"Tell me now." The doctor's ungainly face was working ludicrously.

"I saw the man and struck, Herr Doktor, and then the lights went out and I went to the floor, expecting him to shoot. . . . I think he must have taken the gracious lady. I did not see, for there was a palm between us. I returned at once to the greater hall, and walked through the people on the floor. They were very frightened."

"You saw them?"

"Yes, Herr Doktor," said Gurther. "It is not difficult for me to see in the dark. After that I ran to the other entrance, but they were gone."

"Come here."

The man took two stilted paces towards the doctor and Oberzohn struck him twice in the face with the flat of his hand. Not a muscle of the man's face moved: he stood erect, his lips framed in a half-grin, his curious eyes staring straight ahead.

"That is for bad time, Gurther. Nobody saw you return?"

"No, Herr Doktor, I came on foot."

"You saw the light?"

"Yes, Herr Doktor, and I thought it best to be here."

"You were right," said Oberzohn. "March!"

He went into the forbidden room, turned the key, and passed into the super-heated atmosphere. Gurther stood attentively at the door. Presently the doctor came out, carrying a long case covered with baize under his arm. He handed it to the waiting man, went into the room, and, after a few minutes' absence, returned with a second case, a little larger.

"March!" he said.

Gurther followed him out of the house and across the rank, weed-grown "garden" towards the factory. A white mist had rolled up from the canal, and factory and grounds lay under the veil.

He led the way through an oblong gap in the wall where once a door had stood, and followed a tortuous course through the blackened beams and twisted girders that littered the floor. Only a half-hearted attempt had been made to clear up the wreckage after the fire, and the floor was ankle-deep in the charred shreds of burnt cloth. Near the far end of the building, Oberzohn stopped, put down his box and pushed aside the ashes with his foot until he had cleared a space about three feet square. Stooping, he grasped an iron ring and pulled, and a flagstone came up with scarcely an effort, for it was well counter-weighted. He took up the box again and descended the stone stairs, stopping only to turn on a light.

The vaults of the store had been practically untouched by the fire. There were shelves that still carried dusty bales of cotton goods. Oberzohn was in a hurry. He crossed the stone floor in two strides, pulled down the bar of another door, and, walking into the darkness, deposited his box on the floor.

The electric power of the factory had, in the old days, been carried on two distinct circuits, and the connection with the vaults was practically untouched by the explosion.

They were in a smaller room now, fairly comfortably furnished. Gurther knew it well, for it was here that he had spent the greater part of his first six months in England. Ventilation came through three small gratings near the roof. There was a furnace, and, as Gurther knew, an ample supply of fuel in one of the three cellars that opened into the vault.

"Here will you stay until I send for you," said Oberzohn. "To-night, perhaps, after they have searched. You have a pistol?"

"Ja, Herr Doktor."

"Food, water, bedding—all you need." Oberzohn jerked open another of the cellars and took stock of the larder. "To-night I may come for you—to-morrow night—who knows? You will light the fire at once." He pointed to the two baize-covered boxes. "Good morning, Gurther."

"Good morning, Herr Doktor."

Oberzohn went up to the factory level, dropped the trap and his foot pushed back the ashes which hid its presence, and with a cautious look round he crossed the field to his house. He was hardly in his study before the first police car came bumping along the lane.

# Chapter XII    Leon Theorizes

MAKING inquiries, Detective-Inspector Meadows discovered that, on the previous evening at eight o'clock, two men had called upon Barberton. The first of these was described as tall and rather aristocratic in appearance. He wore dark, horn-rimmed spectacles. The hotel manager thought he might have been an invalid, for he walked with a stick. The second man seemed to have been a servant of some kind, for he spoke respectfully to the visitor.

"No, he gave no name, Mr. Meadows," said the manager. "I told him of the terrible thing which had happened to Mr. Barberton, and he was so upset that I didn't like to press the question."

Meadows was on his circuitous way to Curzon Street when he heard this, and he arrived in time for breakfast. Manfred's servants regarded it as the one eccentricity of an otherwise normal gentleman that he invariably breakfasted with his butler and chauffeur. This matter had been discussed threadbare in the tiny servants' hall, and it no longer excited comment when Manfred telephoned down to the lower regions and asked for another plate.

The Triangle were in cheerful mood. Leon Gonsalez was especially bright and amusing, as he invariably was after such a night as he had spent.

"We searched Oberzohn's house from cellar to attic," said Meadows when the plate had been laid.

"And of course you found nothing. The elegant Gurther?"

"He wasn't there. That fellow will keep at a distance if he knows that there's a warrant out for him. I suspect some sort of signal. There was a very bright green light burning in one of those ridiculous Gothic turrets."

Manfred stifled a yawn.

"Gurther went back soon after midnight," he said, "and was there until Oberzohn's return."

"Are you sure?" asked the astonished detective.

Leon nodded, his eyes twinkling.

"After that, one of those infernal river mists blotted out observation," he said, "but I should imagine Herr Gurther is not far away. Did you see his companion, Pfeiffer?"

Meadows nodded.

"Yes, he was cleaning boots when I arrived."

"How picturesque!" said Gonsalez. "I think he will have a valet the next time he goes to prison, unless the system has altered since your days, George?"

George Manfred, who had once occupied the condemned cell in Chelmsford Prison, smiled.

"An interesting man, Gurther," mused Gonsalez. "I have a feeling that he will escape hanging. So you could not find him? I found him last night. But for the lady, who was both an impediment and an interest, we might have put a period to his activities." He caught Meadows' eye. "I should have handed him to you, of course."

"Of course," said the detective dryly.

"A remarkable man, but nervous. You are going to see Mr. Johnson Lee?"

"What made you say that?" asked the detective in astonishment, for he had not as yet confided his intention to the three men.

"He will surprise you," said Leon. "Tell me, Mr. Meadows: when you and George so thoroughly and carefully searched Barberton's box, did you find anything that was suggestive of his being a cobbler, let us say—or a bookbinder?"

"I think in his sister's letter there was a reference to the books he had made. I found nothing particular except an awl and a long oblong of wood which was covered with pinpricks. As a matter of fact, when I saw it my first thought was that, living the kind of life he must have done in the wilderness, it was rather handy to be able to repair his own shoes. The idea of bookbinding is a new one."

"I should say he never bound a book in his life, in the ordinary sense of the word," remarked Manfred; "and as Leon says, you will find Johnson Lee a very surprising man."

"Do you know him?"

Manfred nodded gravely.

"I have just been on the telephone to him," he said. "You'll have to be careful of Mr. Lee, Meadows. Our friend the snake may be biting his way, and will, if he hears a breath of suspicion that he was in Barberton's confidence."

The detective put down his knife and fork.

"I wish you fellows would stop being mysterious," he said, half annoyed, half amused. "What is behind this business? You talk of the snake as though you could lay your hands on him."

"And we could," they said in unison.

"Who is he?" challenged the detective.

"The Herr Doktor," smiled Gonsalez.

"Oberzohn?"

Leon nodded.

"I thought you would have discovered that by connecting the original three murders together—and murders they were. First"—he ticked the names off on his fingers—"we have a stockbroker. This gentleman was a wealthy speculator who occasionally financed highly questionable deals. Six months before his death he drew from the bank a very large sum of money in notes. By an odd coincidence the bank clerk, going out to luncheon, saw his client and Oberzohn driving past in a taxicab, and as they came abreast he saw a large blue envelope go into Oberzohn's pocket. The money had been put into a blue envelope when it was drawn. The broker had financed the doctor, and when the scheme failed and the money was lost, he not unnaturally asked for its return. He trusted Oberzohn not at all; carried his receipt about in his pocket, and never went anywhere unless he was armed—that fact did not emerge at the inquest, but you know it is true."

Meadows nodded.

"He threatened Oberzohn with exposure at a meeting they had in Winchester Street, on the day of his death. That night he returns from a theatre or from his club, and is found dead on the doorstep. No receipt is found. What follows?

"A man, a notorious blackmailer, homeless and penniless, was walking along the Bayswater Road, probably looking for easy money, when he saw the broker's car going into Orme Place. He followed on the off-chance of begging a few coppers. The chauffeur saw him. The tramp, on the other hand, must have seen something else. He slept the next night at Rowton House, told a friend, who had been in prison with him, that he had a million pounds as good as in his hand. . . ."

Meadows laughed helplessly.

"Your system of investigation is evidently more thorough than ours."

"It is complementary to yours," said George quietly. "Go on, Leon."

"Now what happened to our friend the burglar? He evidently saw somebody in Orme Place whom he either recognized or trailed to his home. For the next day or two he was in and out of public telephone booths, though no number has been traced. He goes to Hyde Park, obviously by appointment—and the snake-bites!

"There was another danger to the confederacy. The bank clerk, learning of the death of the client, is troubled. I have proof that he called Oberzohn on the 'phone. If you remember, when the broker's affairs were gone into, it was found that he was almost insolvent. A large sum of money had been drawn out of the bank and paid to 'X.' The certainty that he knew who 'X.' was, worried this decent bank clerk, and he called Oberzohn, probably to ask him why he had not made a statement. On the day he telephoned the snake man, that day he died."

The detective was listening in silent wonder.

"It sounds like a page out of a sensational novel," he said, "yet it hangs together."

"It hangs together because it is true." Poiccart's deep voice broke into the conversation. "This has been Oberzohn's method all his life. He is strong for logic, and there is no more logical action in the world than the destruction of those who threaten your safety and life."

Meadows pushed away his plate, his breakfast half eaten.

"Proof," he said briefly.

"What proof can you have, my dear fellow?" scoffed Leon.

"The proof is the snake," persisted Meadows. "Show me how he could educate a deadly snake to strike, as he did, when the victim was under close observation, as in the case of Barberton, and I will believe you."

The Three looked at one another and smiled together.

"One of these days I will show you," said Leon. "They have certainly tamed their snake! He can move so quickly that the human eye cannot follow him. Always he bites on the most vital part, and at the most favourable time. He struck at me last night, but missed me. The next time he strikes"—he was speaking slowly and looking at the detective through the veriest slits of his half-closed eyelids—"the next time he strikes, not all Scotland Yard on the one side, nor his agreeable company of gunmen on the other, will save him!"

Poiccart rose suddenly. His keen ears had heard the ring of a bell, and he went noiselessly down the stairs.

"The whole thing sounds like a romance to me." Meadows was rubbing his chin irritably. "I am staring at the covers of a book whilst you are reading the pages. I suppose you devils have the A and Z of the story?"

Leon nodded.

"Why don't you tell me?"

"Because I value your life," said Leon simply. "Because I wish—we all wish—to keep the snake's attention upon ourselves."

Poiccart came back at that moment and put his head in the door.

"Would you like to see Mr. Elijah Washington?" he asked, and they saw by the gleam in his eyes that Mr. Elijah Washington was well worth meeting.

He arrived a second or two later, a tall, broad-shouldered man with a reddish face. He wore pince-nez, and behind the rimless glasses his eyes were alive and full of bubbling laughter. From head to foot he was dressed in white; the cravat which flowed over the soft silk shirt was a bright yellow; the belt about his waist as bright as scarlet.

He stood beaming upon the company, his white panama crushed under his arm, both huge hands thrust into his trousers pockets.

"Glad to know you folks," he greeted them in a deep boom of a voice. "I guess Mr. Barberton told you all about me. That poor little guy! Listen: he was a he-man all right, but kinder mysterious. They told me I'd find the police chief here—Captain Meadows?"

"Mister," said the inspector, "I'm that man."

Washington put out his huge paw and caught the detective's hand with a grip that would have been notable in a boa constrictor.

"Glad to know you. My name is Elijah Washington—the Natural History Syndicate, Chicago."

"Sit down, Mr. Washington." Poiccart pushed forward a chair.

"I want to tell you gentlemen that this Barberton was murdered. Snake? Listen, I know snakes—brought up with 'um! Snakes are my hobby: I know 'um from egg-eaters to 'tigers'—*notechis sentatus*, moccasins, copperheads, corals, mamba, *fer de lance*—gosh! snakes are just common objects like flies. An' I tell you boys right here and now, that there ain't a snake in this or the next world that can climb up a parapet, bite a man and get away with it with a copper looking on."

He beamed from one to the other: he was almost paternal.

"I'd like to have shown you folks a worse-than-mamba," he said regretfully, "but carrying round snakes in your pocket is just hot dog: it's like a millionaire wearin' diamond ear-rings just to show he can afford 'em. I liked that little fellow; I'm mighty sorry he's dead, but if any man tells you that a snake bit him, go right up to him, hit him on the nose, and say 'Liar!' "

"You will have some coffee?" Manfred had rung the bell.

"Sure I will: never have got used to this tea-drinking habit. I'm on the wagon too: got scared up there in the backlands of Angola———"

"What were you doing there?" asked Leon.

"Snakes," said the other briefly. "I represent an organization that supplies specimens to zoos and museums. I was looking for a flying snake—there ain't such a thing, though the natives say there is. I got a new kinder cobra—*viperidæ crotalinæ*—and yet not!"

He scratched his head, bringing his scientific perplexity into the room. Leon's heart went out to him.

He had met Barberton by accident. Without shame he confessed that he had gone to a village in the interior for a real solitary jag, and returning to such degree of civilization as Mossamedes represented, he found a group of Portuguese breeds squatting about a fire at which the man's feet were toasting.

"I don't know what he was—a prospector, I guess. He was one of those what-is-its you meet along that coast. I've met his kind most everywhere— as far south as Port Nottosh. In Angola there are scores: they go native at the end."

"You can tell us nothing about Barberton?"

Mr. Elijah Washington shook his head.

"No, sir: I know him same as I might know you. It got me curious when I found out the why of the torturing: he wouldn't tell where it was."

"Where what was?" asked Manfred quickly, and Mr. Washington was surprised.

"Why, the writing they wanted to get. I thought maybe he'd told you. He said he was coming right along to spill all that part of it. It was a letter he'd found in a tin box—that was all he'd say."

They looked at one another.

"I know no more about it than that," Mr. Washington added, when he saw Gonsalez' lips move. "It was just a letter. Who it was from, why, what it was about, he never told me. My first idea was that he'd been flirting round about here, but divorce laws are mighty generous and they wouldn't trouble to get evidence that way. A man doesn't want any documents to get rid of his wife. I dare say you folks wonder why I've come along." Mr. Washington raised his steaming cup of coffee, which must have been nearly boiling, and drank it at one gulp. "That's fine," he said, "the nearest to coffee I've had since I left home."

He wiped his lips with a large and vivid silk handkerchief.

"I've come along, gentlemen, because I've got a pretty good idea that I'd be useful to anybody who's snake-hunting in this little dorp."

"It's rather a dangerous occupation, isn't it?" said Manfred quietly.

Washington nodded.

"To you, but not to me," he said. "I am snake-proof."

He pulled up his sleeve: the forearm was scarred and pitted with old wounds.

"Snakes," he said briefly. "That's cobra." He pointed proudly. "When that snake struck, my boys didn't wait for anything, they started dividing my kit. Sort of appointed themselves a board of executors and joint heirs of the family estate."

"But you were very ill?" said Gonsalez.

Mr. Washington shook his head.

"No, sir, not more than if a bee bit me, and not so much as if a wasp had got in first punch. Some people can eat arsenic, some people can make a meal of enough morphia to decimate a province. I'm snake-proof—been bitten ever since I was five."

He bent over towards them, and his jolly face went suddenly serious.

"I'm the man you want," he said.

"I think you are," said Manfred slowly.

"Because this old snake ain't finished biting. There's a graft in it somewhere, and I want to find it. But first I want to vindicate the snake. Anybody who says a snake's naturally vicious doesn't understand. Snakes are timid, quiet, respectful things, and don't want no trouble with nobody. If a snake sees you coming, he naturally lights out for home. When momma snake's running around with her family, she's naturally touchy for fear you'd tread on any of her boys and girls, but she's a lady, and if you give her time she'll Maggie 'um and get 'um into the parlour where the foot of white man never trod."

Leon was looking at him with a speculative eye.

"It is queer to think," he said, speaking half to himself, "that you may be the only one of us who will be alive this day week!"

Meadows, not easily shocked, felt a cold shiver run down his spine.

# Chapter XIII　　　　Mirabelle Goes Home

THE prediction that Leon Gonsalez had made was not wholly fulfilled, though he himself had helped to prevent the supreme distress he prophesied. When Mirabelle Leicester awoke in the morning, her head was thick and dull, and for a long time she lay between sleeping and waking, trying to bring order to the confusion of her thoughts, her eyes on the ceiling towards a gnarled oak beam which she had seen before somewhere; and when at last she summoned sufficient energy to raise herself on her elbow, she looked upon the very familiar surroundings of her own pretty little room.

Heavytree Farm! What a curious dream she had had! A dream filled with fleeting visions of old men with elongated heads, of dance music and a crowded ball-room, of a slightly over-dressed man who had been very polite to her at dinner. Where did she dine? She sat up in bed, holding her throbbing head.

Again she looked round the room and slowly, out of her dreams, emerged a few tangible facts. She was still in a state of bewilderment when the door opened and Aunt Alma came in, and the unprepossessing face of her relative was accentuated by her look of anxiety.

"Hullo, Alma!" said Mirabelle dully. "I've had such a queer dream."

Alma pressed her lips tightly together as she placed a tray on a table by the side of the bed.

"I think it was about that advertisement I saw." And then, with a gasp: "How did I come here?"

"They brought you," said Alma. "The nurse is downstairs having her breakfast. She's a nice woman and keeps press-cuttings."

"The nurse?" asked Mirabelle in bewilderment.

"You arrived here at three o'clock in the morning in a motor-car. You had a nurse with you." Alma enumerated the circumstances in chronological order. "And two men. First one of the men got out and knocked at the door. I was worried to death. In fact, I'd been worried all the afternoon, ever since I had your wire telling me not to come up to London."

"But I didn't send any such wire," replied the girl.

"After I came down, the man—he was really a gentleman and very pleasantly spoken—told me that you'd been taken ill and a nurse had brought you home. They then carried you, the two men and the nurse, upstairs and laid you on the bed, and nurse and I undressed you. I simply couldn't get you to wake up: all you did was to talk about the orangeade."

"I remember! It was so bitter, and Lord Evington let me drink some of his. And then I . . . I don't know what happened after that," she said, with a little grimace.

"Mr. Gonsalez ordered the car, got the nurse from a nursing home," explained Alma.

"Gonsalez! Not my Gonsalez—the—the Four Just Men Gonsalez?" she asked in amazement.

"I'm sure it was Gonsalez: they made no secret about it. You can see the gentlemen who brought you: he's about the house somewhere. I saw him in Heavytree Lane not five minutes ago, strolling up and down and smoking. A pipe," added Alma.

The girl got out of bed; her knees were curiously weak under her, but she managed to stagger to the window, and, pushing open the casement still farther, looked out across the patchwork quilt of colour. The summer flowers were in bloom; the delicate scents came up on the warm morning air, and she stood for a moment, drinking in great draughts of the exquisite perfume, and then, with a sigh, turned back to the waiting Alma.

"I don't know how it all happened and what it's about, but my word, Alma, I'm glad to be back! That dreadful man . . . ! We lunched at the Ritz-Carlton. . . . I never want to see another restaurant or a ball-room or Chester Square, or anything but old Heavytree!"

She took the cup of tea from Alma's hand, drank greedily, and put it down with a little gasp.

"That was wonderful! Yes, the tea was too, but I'm thinking about Gonsalez. If it should be he!"

"I don't see why you should get excited over a man who's committed I don't know how many murders."

"Don't be silly, Alma!" scoffed the girl. "The Just Men have never murdered, any more than a judge and jury murder."

The room was still inclined to go round, and it was with the greatest difficulty that she could condense the two Almas who stood before her into one tangible individual.

"There's a gentleman downstairs: he's been waiting since twelve."

And when she asked, she was to learn, to her dismay, that it was half-past one.

"I'll be down in a quarter of an hour," she said recklessly. "Who is it?"

"I've never heard of him before, but he's a gentleman," was the unsatisfactory reply. "They didn't want to let him come in."

"Who didn't?"

"The gentlemen who brought you here in the night."

Mirabelle stared at her.

"You mean . . . they're guarding the house?"

"That's how it strikes me," said Alma bitterly. "Why they should interfere with us, I don't know. Anyway, they let him in. Mr. Johnson Lee."

The girl frowned.

"I don't know the name," she said.

Alma walked to the window.

"There's his car," she said, and pointed.

It was just visible, standing at the side of the road beyond the box hedge, a long-bodied Rolls, white with dust. The chauffeur was talking to a strange man, and from the fact that he was smoking a pipe Mirabelle guessed that this was one of her self-appointed custodians.

She had her bath, and with the assistance of the nurse, dressed and came shakily down the stairs. Alma was waiting in the brick-floored hall.

"He wants to see you alone," she said in a stage whisper. "I don't know whether I ought to allow it, but there's evidently something wrong. These men prowling about the house have got thoroughly on my nerves."

Mirabelle laughed softly as she opened the door and walked in. At the sound of the door closing, the man who was sitting stiffly on a deep settee in a window recess got up. He was tall and bent, and his dark face was lined. His eyes she could not see; they were hidden behind dark green glasses, which were turned in her direction as she came across the room to greet him.

"Miss Mirabelle Leicester?" he asked, in the quiet, modulated voice of an educated man.

He took her hand in his.

"Won't you sit down?" she said, for he remained standing after she had seated herself.

"Thank you." He sat down gingerly, holding between his knees the handle of the umbrella he had brought into the drawing-room. "I'm afraid my visit may be inopportune, Miss Leicester," he said. "Have you by any chance heard about Mr. Barberton?"

Her brows wrinkled in thought.

"Barberton? I seem to have heard the name."

"He was killed yesterday on the Thames Embankment."

Then she recollected.

"The man who was bitten by the snake?" she asked in horror.

The visitor nodded.

"It was a great shock to me, because I have been a friend of his for many years, and had arranged to call at his hotel on the night of his death." And then abruptly he turned the conversation in another and a surprising direction. "Your father was a scientist, Miss Leicester?"

She nodded.

"Yes, he was an astronomer, an authority upon meteors."

"Exactly. I thought that was the gentleman. I have only recently had his book read to me. He was in Africa for some years?"

"Yes," she said quietly, "he died there. He was studying meteors for three years in Angola. You probably know that a very large number of shooting stars fall in that country. My father's theory was that it was due to the ironstone mountains which attract them—so he set up a little observatory in the interior." Her lips trembled for a second. "He was killed in a native rising," she said.

"Do you know the part of Angola where he had his observatory?"

She shook her head.

"I'm not sure. I have never been in Africa, but perhaps Aunt Alma may know."

She went out to find Alma waiting in the passage, in conversation with the pipe-smoker. The man withdrew hastily at the sight of her.

"Alma, do you remember what part of Angola father had his observatory?" she asked.

Alma did not know off-hand, but one of her invaluable scrap-books contained all the information that the girl wanted, and she carried the book to Mr. Lee.

"Here are the particulars," she said, and laid the book open before them.

"Would you read it for me?" he requested gently, and she read to him the three short paragraphs which noted that Professor Leicester had taken up his residence in Bishaka.

"That is the place," interrupted the visitor. "Bishaka! You are sure that Mr. Barberton did not communicate with you?"

"With me?" she said in amazement. "No—why should he?"

He did not answer, but sat for a long time, turning the matter over in his mind.

"You're perfectly certain that nobody sent you a document, probably in the Portuguese language, concerning"—he hesitated—"Bishaka?"

She shook her head, and then, as though he had not seen the gesture, he asked the question again.

"I'm certain," she said. "We have very little correspondence at the farm, and it isn't possible that I could overlook anything so remarkable."

Again he turned the problem over in his mind.

"Have you any documents in Portuguese or in English . . . any letters from your father about Angola?"

"None," she said. "The only reference my father ever made to Bishaka was that he was getting a lot of information which he thought would be valuable, and that he was a little troubled because his cameras, which he had fixed in various parts of the country to cover every sector of the skies, were being disturbed by wandering prospectors."

"He said that, did he?" asked Mr. Lee eagerly. "Come now, that explains a great deal!"

In spite of herself she laughed.

"It doesn't explain much to me, Mr. Lee," she said frankly. And then, in a more serious tone: "Did Barberton come from Angola?"

"Yes, Barberton came from that country," he said in a lower voice. "I should like to tell you"—he hesitated—"but I am rather afraid."

"Afraid to tell me? Why?"

He shook his head.

"So many dreadful things have happened recently to poor Barberton and others, that knowledge seems a most dangerous thing. I wish I could believe that it would not be dangerous to you," he added kindly, "and then I could speak what is in my mind and relieve myself of a great deal of anxiety." He rose slowly. "I think the best thing I can do is to consult my lawyer. I was foolish to keep it from him so long. He is the only man I can trust to search my documents."

She could only look at him in astonishment.

"But surely you can search your own documents?" she said good-humouredly.

"No, I'm afraid I can't. Because"—he spoke with the simplicity of a child—"I am blind."

"Blind?" gasped Mirabelle, and the man laughed gently.

"I am pretty capable for a blind man, am I not? I can walk across a room and avoid all the furniture. The only thing I cannot do is to read—at least, read the ordinary print. I can read Braille: poor Barberton taught me. He was a schoolmaster," he explained, "at a blind school near Brightlingsea. Not a particularly well-educated man, but a marvellously quick writer of Braille. We have corresponded for years through that medium. He could write a Braille letter almost as quickly as you can with pen and ink."

Her heart was full of pity for the man: he was so cheery, so confident, and withal so proud of his own accomplishments, that pity turned to admiration. He had the ineffable air of obstinacy which is the possession of so many men similarly stricken, and she began to realize that self-pity, that greatest of all afflictions which attends blindness, had been eliminated from his philosophy.

"I should like to tell you more," he said, as he held out his hand. "Probably I will dictate a long letter to you to-morrow, or else my lawyer will do so, putting all the facts before you. For the moment, however, I must be sure of my ground. I have no desire to raise in your heart either fear or—hope. Do you know a Mr. Manfred?"

"I don't know him personally," she said quickly. "George Manfred?"

He nodded.

"Have you met him?" she asked eagerly. "And Mr. Poiccart, the Frenchman?"

"No, not Mr. Poiccart. Manfred was on the telephone to me very early this morning. He seemed to know all about my relationships with my poor friend. He knew also of my blindness. A remarkable man, very gentle and courteous. It was he who gave me your address. Perhaps," he mused, "it would be advisable if I first consulted him."

"I'm sure it would!" she said enthusiastically. "They are wonderful. You have heard of them, of course, Mr. Lee—the Four Just Men?"

He smiled.

"That sounds as though you admire them," he said. "Yes, I have heard of them. They are the men who, many years ago, set out to regularize the inconsistencies of the English law, to punish where no punishment is provided by the code. Strange I never associated them. . . ."

He meditated upon the matter in silence for a long while, and then:

"I wonder," he said, but did not tell her what he was wondering.

She walked down the garden path with him into the roadway and stood chatting about the country and the flowers that he had never seen, and the weather and such trivialities as people talk about when their minds are occupied with more serious thoughts which they cannot share, until the big limousine pulled up and he stepped into its cool interior. He had the independence which comes to the educated blind and gently refused the offer of her guidance, an offer she did not attempt to repeat, sensing the satisfaction he must have had in making his way without help. She waved her hand to the car as it moved off, and so naturally did his hand go up in salute that for a moment she thought he had seen her.

So he passed out of her sight, and might well have passed out of her life, for Mr. Oberzohn had decreed that the remaining hours of blind Johnson Lee were to be few.

But it happened that the Three Men had reached the same decision in regard to Mr. Oberzohn, only there was some indecision as to the manner of his passing. Leon Gonsalez had original views.

# Chapter XIV          The Pedlar

THE man with the pipe was standing within half a dozen paces of her. She was going back through the gate, when she remembered Aunt Alma's views on the guardianship.

"Are you waiting here all day?" she asked.

"Till this evening, miss. We're to be relieved by some men from Gloucester—we came from town, and we're going back with the nurse, if you can do without her?"

"Who placed you here?" she asked.

"Mr. Gonsalez. He thought it would be wise to have somebody around."

"But why?"

The big man grinned.

"I've known Mr. Gonsalez many years," he said. "I'm a police pensioner, and I can remember the time when I'd have given a lot of money to lay my hands on him—but I've never asked him why, miss. There is generally a good reason for everything he does."

Mirabelle went back into the farmhouse, very thoughtful. Happily, Alma was not inquisitive; she was left alone in the drawing-room to reconstruct her exciting yesterday.

Mirabelle harboured very few illusions. She had read much, guessed much, and in the days of her childhood had been in the habit of linking cause to effect. The advertisement was designed especially for her: that was her first conclusion. It was designed to bring her into the charge of Oberzohn. For now she recognized this significant circumstance: never once, since she had entered the offices of Oberzohn & Smitts, until the episode of the orangeade, had she been free to come and go as she wished. He had taken her to lunch, he had brought her back; Joan Newton had been her companion in the drive from the house, and from the house to the hall; and from then on she did not doubt that Oberzohn's surveillance had continued, until . . .

Dimly she remembered the man in the cloak who had stood in the rocking doorway. Was that Gonsalez? Somehow she thought it must have been.

Gonsalez, watchful, alert—why? She had been in danger—was still in danger. Though why anybody should have picked unimportant her, was the greatest of all mysteries.

In some inexplicable way the death of Barberton had been associated with that advertisement and the attention she had received from Dr. Oberzohn and his creatures. Who was Lord Evington? She remembered his German accent and his "gracious lady," the curious click of his heels and his stiff bow. That was a clumsy subterfuge which she ought to have seen through from the first. He was another of her watchers. And the drugged orangeade was his work. She shuddered. Suppose Leon Gonsalez, or whoever it was, had not arrived so providentially, where would she be at this moment?

Walking to the window, she looked out, and the sight of the two men just inside the gate gave her a sense of infinite relief and calm; and the knowledge that she, for some reason, was under the care and protection of this strange organization about which she had read, thrilled her.

She walked into the vaulted kitchen, to find the kitchen table covered with fat volumes, and Aunt Alma explaining to the interested nurse her system of filing. Two subjects interested that hard-featured lady: crime and family records. She had two books filled with snippings from country newspapers relating to the family of a distant cousin who had been raised to a peerage during the war. She had another devoted to the social triumphs of a distant woman, Goddard, who had finally made a sensational appearance as petitioner in the most celebrated divorce suit of the age. But crime, generally speaking, was Aunt Alma's chief preoccupation. It was from these voluminous cuttings that Mirabelle had gained her complete knowledge of the Four Just Men and their operations. There were books packed with the story of the Ramon murder, arranged with loving care in order of time, for chronology was almost a vice in Alma Goddard. Only one public sensation was missing from her collection, and she was explaining the reason to the nurse as Mirabelle came into the kitchen.

"No, my dear," she was saying, "there is nothing about The Snake. I won't have anything to do with that: it gives me the creeps. In fact, I haven't read anything that has the slightest reference to it."

"I've got every line," said the nurse enthusiastically. "My brother is a reporter on the *Megaphone*, and he says this is the best story they've had for years——"

Mirabelle interrupted this somewhat gruesome conversation to make inquiries about luncheon. Her head was steady now and she had developed an appetite.

The front door stood open, and as she turned to go into the dining-room to get her writing materials, she heard an altercation at the gate. A third man had appeared: a grimy-looking pedlar who carried a tray before him, packed with all manner of cheap buttons and laces. He was a middle-aged man with a ragged beard, and despite the warmth of the day, was wearing a long overcoat that almost reached to his heels.

"You may or you may not be," the man with the pipe was saying, "but you're not going in here."

"I've served this house for years," snarled the pedlar. "What do you mean by interfering with me? You're not a policeman."

"Whether I'm a policeman or a dustman or a postman," said the patient guard, "you don't pass through this gate—do you understand that?"

At this moment the pedlar caught sight of the girl at the door and raised his battered hat with a grin. He was unknown to the girl; she did not remember having seen him at the house before. Nor did Alma, who came out at that moment.

"He's a stranger here, but we're always getting new people up from Gloucester," she said. "What does he want to sell?"

She stalked out into the garden, and at the sight of her the grin left the pedlar's face.

"I've got some things I'd like to sell to the young lady, ma'am," he said.

"I'm not so old, and I'm a lady," replied Alma sharply. "And how long is it since you started picking and choosing your customers?"

The man grumbled something under his breath, and without waiting even to display his wares, shuffled off along the dusty road, and they watched him until he was out of sight.

Heavytree Farm was rather grandly named for so small a property. The little estate followed the road to Heavytree Lane, which formed the southern boundary of the property. The lane itself ran at an angle to behind the house, where the third boundary was formed by a hedge dividing the farmland from the more pretentious estate of a local magnate. It was down the lane the pedlar turned.

"Excuse me, ma'am," said the companion of the man with the pipe.

He opened the gate, walked in, and, making a circuit of the house, reached the orchard behind. Here a few outhouses were scattered, and, clearing these, he came to the meadow, where Mirabelle's one cow ruminated in the lazy manner of her kind. Half hidden by a thick-boled apple-tree, the watcher waited, and presently, as he expected, he saw a head appear through the boundary hedge. After an observation the pedlar sprang into the meadow and stood, taking stock of his ground. He had left his tray and his bag, and, running with surprising swiftness for a man of his age, he gained a little wooden barn, and, pulling open the door, disappeared into its interior. By this time the guard had been joined by his companion and they had a short consultation, the man with the pipe going back to his post before the house, whilst the other walked slowly across the meadow until he came to the closed door of the barn.

Wise in his generation, he first made a circuit of the building, and discovered there were no exits through the blackened gates. Then, pulling both doors open wide:

"Come out, bo'!" he said.

The barn was empty, except for a heap of hay that lay in one corner and some old and wheelless farm-wagons propped up on three trestles awaiting the wheelwright's attention.

A ladder led to a loft, and the guard climbed slowly. His head was on a level with the dark opening, when:

"Put up your hands!"

He was looking into the adequate muzzle of an automatic pistol.

"Come down, bo'!"

"Put up your hands," hissed the voice in the darkness, "or you're a dead man!"

The watcher obeyed, cursing his folly that he had come alone.

"Now climb up."

With some difficulty the guard brought himself up to the floor level.

"Step this way, and step lively," said the pedlar. "Hold your hands out."

He felt the touch of cold steel on his wrist, heard a click.

"Now the other hand."

The moment he was manacled, the pedlar began a rapid search.

"Carry a gun, do you?" he sneered, as he drew a pistol from the man's hip pocket. "Now sit down."

In a few seconds the discomfited guard was bound and gagged. The pedlar, crawling to the entrance of the loft, looked out between a crevice in the boards. He was watching not the house, but the hedge through which he had climbed. Two other men had appeared there, and he grunted his satisfaction. Descending into the barn, he pulled away the ladder and let it fall on the floor, before he came out into the open and made a signal.

The second guard had made his way back by the shortest cut to the front of the house, passing through the garden and in through the kitchen door. He stopped to shoot the bolts, and the girl, coming into the kitchen, saw him.

"Is anything wrong?" she asked anxiously.

"I don't know, miss." He was looking at the kitchen windows: they were heavily barred. "My mate has just seen that pedlar go into the barn."

She followed him to the front door. He had turned to go, but, changing his mind, came back, and she saw him put his hand into his hip pocket and was staggered to see him produce a long-barrelled Browning.

"Can you use a pistol, miss?"

She nodded, too surprised to speak, and watched him as he jerked back the jacket and put up the safety catch.

"I want to be on the safe side, and I'd feel happier if you were armed."

There was a gun hanging on the wall and he took it down.

"Have you any shells for this?" he asked.

She pulled open the drawer of the hall-stand and took out a cardboard carton.

"They may be useful," he said.

"But surely, Mr.——"

"Digby." He supplied his name.

"Surely you're exaggerating? I don't mean that you're doing it with any intention of frightening me, but there isn't any danger to us?"

"I don't know. I've got a queer feeling—had it all morning. How far is the nearest house from here?"

"Not half a mile away," she said.

"You're on the 'phone?"

She nodded.

"I'm scared, maybe. I'll just go out into the road and have a look round. I wish that fellow would come back," he added fretfully.

He walked slowly up the garden path and stood for a moment leaning over the gate. As he did so, he heard the rattle and asthmatic wheezing of an ancient car, and saw a tradesman's trolley come round a corner of Heavytree Lane. Its pace grew slower as it got nearer to the house, and opposite the gate it stopped altogether. The driver getting down with a curse, lifted up the battered tin bonnet, and, groping under the seat, brought out a long spanner. Then, swift as thought, he half turned and struck at Digby's head. The girl heard the sickening impact, saw the watcher drop limply to the path, and in another second she had slammed the door and thrust home the bolts.

She was calm; the hand that took the revolver from the hall-table did not tremble.

"Alma!" she called, and Alma came running downstairs.

"What on earth——?" she began, and then saw the pistol in Mirabelle's hands.

"They are attacking the house," said the girl quickly. "I don't know who 'they' are, but they've just struck down one of the men who was protecting us. Take the gun, Alma."

Alma's face was contorted, and might have expressed fear or anger or both. Mirabelle afterwards learnt that the dominant emotion was one of satisfaction to find herself in so warlike an environment.

Running into the drawing-room, the girl pushed open the window, which commanded a view of the road. The gate was unfastened and two men, who had evidently been concealed inside the trolley, were lifting the unconscious man, and she watched, with a calm she could not understand in herself, as they threw him into the interior and fastened the tailboard. She counted four in all, including the driver, who was climbing back to his seat. One of the new-comers, evidently the leader, was pointing down the road towards the lane, and she guessed that he was giving directions as to where the car should wait, for it began to go backwards almost immediately and with surprising smoothness, remembering the exhibition it had given of decrepitude a few minutes before.

The man who had given instructions came striding down the path towards the door.

"Stop!"

He looked round with a start into the levelled muzzle of a Browning, and his surprise would, in any other circumstances, have been comical.

"It's all right, miss——" he began.

"Put yourself outside that gate," said Mirabelle coolly.

"I wanted to see you . . . very important——"

*Bang!*

Mirabelle fired a shot, aimed above his head, towards the old poplar. The man ducked and ran. Clear of the gate he dropped to the cover of a hedge, where his men already were, and she heard the murmur of their voices distinctly, for the day was still, and the far-off chugging of the trolley's engine sounded close at hand. Presently she saw a head peep round the hedge.

"Can I have five minutes' talk with you?" asked the leader loudly.

He was a thick-set, bronzed man, with a patch of lint plastered to his face, and she noted unconsciously that he wore gold ear-rings.

"There's no trouble coming to you," he said, opening the gate as he spoke. "You oughtn't to have fired, anyway. Nobody's going to hurt you——"

He had advanced a yard into the garden as he spoke.

*Bang, bang!*

In her haste she had pressed butt and trigger just a fraction too long, and, startled by the knowledge that another shot was coming, her hand jerked round, and the second shot missed his head by the fraction of an inch. He disappeared in a flash, and a second later she saw their hats moving swiftly above the box. They were running towards the waiting car.

"Stay here, Alma!"

Alma Goddard nodded grimly, and the girl flew up the stairs to her room. From this elevation she commanded a better view. She saw them climb into the van, and in another second the limp body of the guard was thrown out into the hedge; then, after a brief space of time, the machine began moving and, gathering speed, disappeared in a cloud of dust on the Highcombe Road.

Mirabelle came down the stairs at a run, pulled back the bolts and flew out and along the road towards the still figure of the detective. He was lying by the side of the ditch, his head a mass of blood, and she saw that he was still breathing. She tried to lift him, but it was too great a task. She ran back to the house. The telephone was in the hall: an old-fashioned instrument with a handle that had to be turned, and she had not made two revolutions before she realized that the wire had been cut.

Alma was still in the parlour, the gun gripped tight in her hand, a look of fiendish resolution on her face.

"You must help me to get Digby into the house," she said.

"Where is he?"

Mirabelle pointed, and the two women, returning to the man, half lifted, half dragged him back to the hall. Laying him down on the brick floor, the girl went in search of clean linen. The kitchen, which was also the drying place for Alma's more intimate laundry, supplied all that she needed. Whilst Alma watched unmoved the destruction of her wardrobe, the girl bathed the wound and the frightened nurse (who had disappeared at the first shot) applied a rough dressing. The wound was an ugly one, and the man showed no signs of recovering consciousness.

"We shall have to send Mary into Gloucester for an ambulance," said Mirabelle. "We can't send nurse—she doesn't know the way."

"Mary," said Alma calmly, "is at this moment having hysterics in the larder. I'll harness the dog-cart and go myself. But where is the other man?"

Mirabelle shook her head.

"I don't like to think what has happened to him," she said. "Now, Alma, do you think we can get him into the drawing-room?"

Together they lifted the heavy figure and staggered with it into the pretty little room, laying him at last upon the settee under the window.

"He can rest there till we get the ambulance," began Mirabelle, and a chuckle behind her made her turn with a gasp.

It was the pedlar, and in his hand he held the pistol which she had discarded.

"I only want you"—he nodded to the girl. "You other two women can come out here." He jerked his head to the passage. Under the stairs was a big cupboard and he pulled the door open invitingly. "Get in here. If you make a noise, you'll be sorry for yourselves."

Alma's eyes wandered longingly to the gun she had left in the corner, but before she could make a move he had placed himself between her and the weapon.

"Get inside," said the pedlar, and Mirabelle was not much surprised when Aunt Alma meekly obeyed.

He shut the door on the two women and fastened the hatch.

"Now, young lady, put on your hat and be lively!"

He followed her up the stairs into her room and watched her while she found a hat and a cloak. She knew only too well that it was a waste of time even to temporize with him. He, for his part, was so exultant at his success that he grew almost loquacious.

"I suppose you saw the boys driving away and you didn't remember that I was somewhere around? Was that you doing the shooting?"

She did not answer.

"It couldn't have been Lew, or you'd have been dead," he said. He was examining the muzzle of the pistol. "It was you all right." He chuckled. "Ain't you the game one! Sister, you ought to be——"

He stopped dead, staring through the window. He was paralysed with amazement at the sight of a bare-headed Aunt Alma flying along the Gloucester Road. With an oath he turned to the girl.

"How did she get out? Have you got anybody here? Now speak up."

"The cupboard under the stairs leads to the wine cellar," said Mirabelle coolly, "and there are two ways out of the wine cellar. I think Aunt Alma found one of them."

With an oath, he took a step towards her, gripped her by the arm and jerked her towards the door.

"Lively!" he said, and dragged her down the stairs through the hall, into the kitchen.

He shot back the bolts, but the lock of the kitchen door had been turned.

"This way." He swore cold-bloodedly, and, her arm still in his powerful grip, he hurried along the passage and pulled open the door.

It was an unpropitious moment. A man was walking down the path, a half-smile on his face, as though he was thinking over a remembered jest. At the sight of him the pedlar dropped the girl's arm and his hand went like lightning to his pocket.

"When will you die?" said Leon Gonsalez softly. "Make a choice, and make it quick!"

And the gun in his hand seemed to quiver with homicidal eagerness.

# Chapter XV                    Two "Accidents"

THE pedlar, his face twitching, put up his shaking hands.

Leon walked to him, took the Browning from his moist grip and dropped it into his pocket.

"Your friends are waiting, of course?" he said pleasantly.

The pedlar did not answer.

"Cuccini too? I thought I had incapacitated him for a long time."

"They've gone," growled the pedlar.

Gonsalez looked round in perplexity.

"I don't want to take you into the house. At the same time, I don't want to leave you here," he said. "I almost wish you'd drawn that gun of yours," he added regretfully. "It would have solved so many immediate problems."

This particular problem was solved by the return of the dishevelled Alma and the restoration to her of her gun.

"I would so much rather you shot him than I," said Leon earnestly. "The police are very suspicious of my shootings, and they never wholly believe that they are done in self-defence."

With a rope he tied the man, and tied him uncomfortably, wrists to ankles. That done, he made a few inquiries and went swiftly out to the barn, returning in a few minutes with the unhappy guard.

"It can't be helped," said Leon, cutting short the man's apologies. "The question is, where are the rest of the brethren?"

Something zipped past him: it had the intensified hum of an angry wasp, and a second later he heard a muffled "Plop!" In a second he was lying flat on the ground, his Browning covering the hedge that hid Heavytree Lane.

"Run to the house," he called urgently. "They won't bother about you." And the guard, nothing loth, sprinted for the cover of walls.

Presently Leon located the enemy, and at a little distance off he saw the flat top of the covered trolley. A man walked slowly and invitingly across the gap in the hedge, but Gonsalez held his fire, and presently the manœuvre was repeated. Obviously they were trying to concentrate his mind upon the gap whilst they were moving elsewhere. His eyes swept the meadow boundary—

running parallel, he guessed, was a brook or ditch which would make excellent cover.

Again the man passed leisurely across the gap. Leon steadied his elbow, and glanced along the sight. As he did so, the man reappeared.

*Crack!*

Gonsalez aimed a foot behind him. The man saw the flash and jumped back, as he had expected. In another second he was writhing on the ground with a bullet through his leg.

Leon showed his teeth in a smile and switched his body round to face the new point of attack. It came from the spot that he had expected: a little rise of ground that commanded his position.

The first bullet struck the turf to his right with an angry buzz, sent a divot flying heavenward, and ricochetted with a smack against a tree. Before the raised head could drop to cover, Gonsalez fired; fired another shot to left and right, then, rising, raced for the shelter of the tree, and reached it in time to see three heads bobbing back to the road. He waited, covering the gap, but the people who drew the wounded man out of sight did not show themselves, and a minute later he saw the trolley moving swiftly down the by-road, and knew that danger was past.

The firing had attracted attention. He had not been back in the house a few minutes before a mounted policeman, his horse in a lather, came galloping up to the gate and dismounted. A neighbouring farm had heard the shots and telephoned to constabulary head-quarters. For half an hour the mounted policeman took notes, and by this time half the farmers in the neighbourhood, their guns under their arms, had assembled in Mirabelle's parlour.

She had not seen as much of the redoubtable Leon as she could have wished, and when they had a few moments to themselves she seized the opportunity to tell him of the call which Lee had made that morning. Apparently he knew all about it, for he expressed no surprise, and was only embarrassed when she showed a personal interest in himself and his friends.

It was not a very usual experience for him, and he was rather annoyed with himself at this unexpected glimpse of enthusiasm and hero-worship, sane as it was, and based, as he realized, upon her keen sense of justice.

"I'm not so sure that we've been very admirable really," he said. "But the difficulty is to produce at the moment a judgment which would be given from a distance of years. We have sacrificed everything which to most men would make life worth living, in our desire to see the scales held fairly."

"You are not married, Mr. Gonsalez?"

He stared into the frank eyes.

"Married? Why, no," he said, and she laughed.

"You talk as though that were a possibility that had never occurred to you."

"It hasn't," he admitted. "By the very nature of our work we are debarred from that experience. And is it an offensive thing to say that I have never felt my singleness to be a deprivation?"

"It is very rude," she said severely, and Leon was laughing to himself all the way back to town as at a great joke that improved upon repetition.

"I think we can safely leave her for a week," he reported, on his return to Curzon Street. "No, nothing happened. I was held up in a police trap near Newbury for exceeding the speed limit. They said I was doing fifty, but I should imagine it was nearer eighty. Meadows will get me out of that. Otherwise, I must send the inevitable letter to the magistrate and pay the inevitable fine. Have you done anything about Johnson Lee?"

Manfred nodded.

"Meadows and the enthusiastic Mr. Washington have gone round to see him. I have asked Washington to go because"—he hesitated—"the snake is a real danger, so far as he is concerned. Elijah Washington promises to be a very real help. He is afraid of nothing, and has undertaken to stay with Lee and to apply such remedies for snake-bites as he knows."

He was putting on his gloves as he spoke, and Leon Gonsalez looked at him with a critical admiration.

"Are you being presented at Court, or are you taking tea with a duchess?"

"Neither. I'm calling upon friend Oberzohn."

"The devil you are!" said Leon, his eyebrows rising.

"I have taken the precaution of sending him a note, asking him to keep his snakes locked up," said Manfred, "and as I have pointedly forwarded the carbon copy of the letter, to impress the fact that another exists and may be brought in evidence against him, I think I shall leave Oberzohn & Smitts' main office without hurt. If you are not too tired, Leon, I would rather prefer the Buick to the Spanz."

"Give me a quarter of an hour," said Leon, and went up to his room to make himself tidy.

It was fifteen minutes exactly when the Buick stopped at the door, and Manfred got into the saloon. There was no partition between driver and passenger, and conversation was possible.

"It would have been as well if you'd had Brother Newton there," he suggested.

"Brother Newton will be on the spot: I took the precaution of sending him a similar note," said Manfred. "I shouldn't imagine they'll bring out their gunmen."

"I know two, and possibly three, they won't bring out." Gonsalez grinned at the traffic policeman who waved him into Oxford Street. "That Browning of mine throws high, Manfred: I've always had a suspicion it did. Pistols are queer things, but this may wear into my hand." He talked arms and ammunition until the square block of Oberzohn & Smitts came into sight. "Good hunting!" he said, as he got out, opened the saloon door and touched his hat to Manfred as he alighted.

He got back into his seat, swung the little car round in a circle, and sat on the opposite side of the road, his eyes alternately on the entrance and on the mirror which gave him a view of the traffic approaching him from the rear.

Manfred was not kept in the waiting-room for more than two minutes. At the end of that time, a solemn youth in spectacles, with a little bow, led him across the incurious office into the presence of the illustrious doctor.

The old man was at his desk. Behind him, his debonair self, Monty Newton, a large yellow flower in his buttonhole, a smile on his face. Oberzohn got up like a man standing to attention.

"Mr. Manfred, this is a great honour," he said, and held out his hand stiffly.

An additional chair had been placed for the visitor: a rich-looking tapestried chair, to which the doctor waved the hand which Manfred did not take.

"Good morning, Manfred." Newton removed his cigar and nodded genially. "Were you at the dance last night?"

"I was there, but I didn't come in," said Manfred, seating himself. "You did not turn up till late, they tell me?"

"It was of all occurrences the most unfortunate," said Dr. Oberzohn, and Newton laughed.

"I've lost his laboratory secretary and he hasn't forgiven me," he said almost jovially. "The girl he took on yesterday. Rather a stunner in the way of looks. She didn't wish to go back to the country where she came from, so my sister offered to put her up for the night in Chester Square. I'm blessed if she didn't lose herself at the dance, and we haven't seen her since!"

"It was a terrible thing," said Oberzohn sadly. "I regard her as in my charge. For her safety I am responsible. You, I trust, Mr. Newton——"

"I don't think I should have another uneasy moment if I were you, doctor," said Manfred easily. "The young lady is back at Heavytree Farm. I thought that would surprise you. And she is still there: that will surprise you more, if you have not already heard by telephone that your Old Guard failed dismally to—er—bring her back to work. I presume that was their object?"

"My old guard, Mr. Manfred?" Oberzohn shook his head in bewilderment. "This is beyond my comprehension."

"Is your sister well?" asked Manfred blandly.

Newton shrugged his shoulders.

"She is naturally upset. And who wouldn't be? Joan is a very tender-hearted girl."

"She has been that way for years," said Manfred offensively. "May I smoke?"

"Will you have one of my cigarettes?"

Manfred's grave eyes fixed the doctor in a stare that held the older man against his will.

"I have had just one too many of your cigarettes," he said. His words came like a cold wind. "I do not want any more, Herr Doktor, or there will be vacancies in your family circle. Who knows that, long before you compound your wonderful elixir, you may be called to normal immortality?"

The yellow face of Oberzohn had turned to a dull red.

"You seem to know so much about me, Mr. Manfred, as myself," he said in a husky whisper.

Manfred nodded.

"More. For whilst you are racing against time to avoid the end of a life which does not seem especially worthy of preservation, and whilst you know not what day or hour that end may come, I can tell you to the minute." The finger of his gloved hand pointed the threat.

All trace of a smile had vanished from Monty Newton's face. His eyes did not leave the caller's.

"Perhaps you shall tell me." Oberzohn found a difficulty in speaking. Rage possessed him, and only his iron will choked down the flames from view.

"The day that injury comes to Mirabelle Leicester, that day you go out—you and those who are with you!"

"Look here, Manfred, there's a law in this country——" began Monty Newton hotly.

"I am the law." The words rang like a knell of fate. "In this matter I am judge, jury, hangman. Old or young, I will not spare," he said evenly.

"Are you immortal too?" sneered Monty.

Only for a second did Manfred's eyes leave the old man's face.

"The law is immortal," he said. "If you dream that, by some cleverly concerted coup, you can sweep me from your path before I grow dangerous, be sure that your sweep is clean."

"You haven't asked me to come here to listen to this stuff, have you?" asked Newton, and though his words were bold, his manner aggressive, there were shadows on his face which were not there when Manfred had come into the room—shadows under his eyes and in his cheeks where plumpness had been.

"I've come here to tell you to let up on Miss Leicester. You're after something that you cannot get, and nobody is in a position to give you. I don't know what it is—I will make you a present of that piece of information. But it's big—bigger than any prize you've ever gone after in your wicked lives. And to get that, you're prepared to sacrifice innocent lives with the recklessness of spendthrifts who think there is no bottom to their purse. The end is near!"

He rose slowly and stood by the table, towering over the stiff-backed doctor.

"I cannot say what action the police will take over this providential snake-bite, Oberzohn, but I'll make you this offer: I and my friends will stand out of the game and leave Meadows to get you in his own way. You think that means you'll go scot-free? But it doesn't. These police are like bulldogs: once they've got a grip of you, they'll never let go."

"What is the price you ask for this interesting service?" Newton was puffing steadily at his cigar, his hands clasped behind him, his feet apart, a picture of comfort and well-being.

"Leave Miss Leicester alone. Find a new way of getting the money you need so badly."

Newton laughed.

"My dear fellow, that's a stupid thing to say. Neither Oberzohn nor I are exactly poor."

"You're bankrupt, both of you," said Manfred quietly. "You are in the position of gamblers when the cards have run against you for a long time. You have no reserve, and your expenses are enormous. Find another way, Newton—and tell your sister"—he paused by the door, looking down into the white lining of his silk hat—"I'd like to see her at Curzon Street to-morrow morning at ten o'clock."

"Is that an order?" asked Newton sarcastically.

Manfred nodded.

"Then let me tell you," roared the man, white with passion, "that I take no orders for her or for me. Got swollen heads since you've had your pardon, haven't you? You look out for me, Manfred. I'm not exactly harmless."

He felt the pressure of the doctor's foot upon his and curbed his temper.

"All right," he growled, "but don't expect to see Joan."

He added a coarse jest, and Manfred raised his eyes slowly and met his.

"You will be hanged by the State or murdered by Oberzohn—I am not sure which," he said simply, and he spoke with such perfect confidence that the heart of Monty Newton turned to water.

Manfred stood in the sidewalk and signalled, and the little car came swiftly and noiselessly across. Leon's eyes were on the entrance. A tall man standing in the shadow of the hall was watching. He was leaning against the wall in a negligent attitude, and for a second Leon was startled.

"Get in quickly!"

Leon almost shouted the words back, and Manfred jumped into the machine, as the chauffeur sent the car forward, with a jerk that strained every gear.

"What on——?" began Manfred, but the rest of his words were lost in the terrific crash which followed.

The leather hood of the machine was ripped down at the back, a splinter of glass struck Leon's cap and sliced a half-moon neatly. He jammed on the brakes, threw open the door of the saloon and leaped out. Behind the car was a mass of wreckage; a great iron casting lay split into three pieces amidst a tangle of broken packing-case. Leon looked up; immediately above the entrance to Oberzohn & Smitts' was a crane, which had swung out with a heavy load just before Manfred came out. The steel wire hung loosely from the derrick. He heard excited voices speaking from the open doorway three floors above, and two men in large glasses were looking down and gabbling in a language he did not understand.

"A very pretty accident. We might have filled half a column in the evening newspapers if we had not moved."

"And the gentleman in the hall—what was he doing?"

Leon walked back through the entrance: the man had disappeared, but near where he had been standing was a small bell-push which, it was obvious, had recently been fixed, for the wires ran loosely on the surface of the wall and were new.

He came back in time to see a policeman crossing the road.

"I wish to find out how this accident occurred, constable," he said. "My master was nearly killed."

The policeman looked at the ton of debris lying half on the sidewalk, half on the road, then up at the slackened hawser.

"The cable has run off the drum, I should think."

"I should think so," said Leon gravely.

He did not wait for the policeman to finish his investigations, but went home at a steady pace, and made no reference to the "accident" until he had put away his car and had returned to Curzon Street.

"The man in the hall was put there to signal when you were under the load—certain things must not happen," he said. "I am going out to make a few inquiries."

Gonsalez knew one of Oberzohn's staff: a clean young Swede, with that knowledge of English which is normal in Scandinavian countries; and at nine o'clock that night he drifted into a Swedish restaurant in Dean Street and found the young man at the end of his meal. It was an acquaintance—one of many—that Leon had assiduously cultivated. The young man, who knew him as Mr. Heinz—Leon spoke German remarkably well—was glad to have a companion with whom he could discuss the inexplicable accident of the afternoon.

"The cable was not fixed to the drum," he said. "It might have been terrible: there was a gentleman in a motor-car outside, and he had only moved away a few inches when the case fell. There is bad luck in that house. I am glad that I am leaving at the end of the week."

Leon had some important questions to put, but he did not hurry, having the gift of patience to a marked degree. It was nearly ten when they parted, and Gonsalez went back to his garage, where he spent a quarter of an hour.

At midnight, Manfred had just finished a long conversation with the Scotland Yard man who was still at Brightlingsea, when Leon came in, looking very pleased with himself. Poiccart had gone to bed, and Manfred had switched out one circuit of lights when his friend arrived.

"Thank you, my dear George," said Gonsalez briskly. "It was very good of you, and I did not like troubling you, but——"

"It was a small thing," said Manfred with a smile, "and involved merely the changing of my shoes. But why? I am not curious, but why did you wish me to telephone the night watchman at Oberzohn's to be waiting at the door at eleven o'clock for a message from the doctor?"

"Because," said Leon cheerfully, rubbing his hands, "the night watchman is an honest man; he has a wife and six children, and I was particularly wishful not to hurt anybody. The building doesn't matter: it stands, or stood, isolated from all others. The only worry in my mind was the night watchman. He was at the door—I saw him."

Manfred asked no further questions. Early the next morning he took up the paper and turned to the middle page, read the account of the "Big Fire in City Road" which had completely gutted the premises of Messrs. Oberzohn & Smitts; and, what is more, he expected to read it before he had seen the paper.

"Accidents are accidents," said Leon the philosopher that morning at breakfast. "And that talk I had with the clerk last night told me a lot: Oberzohn has allowed his fire insurance to lapse!"

IN one of the forbidden rooms that was filled with the apparatus which Dr. Oberzohn had accumulated for his pleasure and benefit, was a small electrical furnace which was the centre of many of his most interesting experiments. There were, in certain known drugs, constituents which it was his desire to eliminate. Dr. Oberzohn believed absolutely in many things that the modern chemist would dismiss as fantastical. He believed in the philosopher's stone, in the transmutation of base metals to rare; he had made diamonds, of no great commercial value, it is true; but his supreme faith was that somewhere in the materia medica was an infallible elixir which would prolong life far beyond the normal span. It was to all other known properties as radium is to pitch-blende. It was something that only the metaphysician could discover, only the patient chemist could materialize. Every hour he could spare he devoted himself to his obsession; and he was in the midst of one of his experiments when the telephone bell called him back to his study. He listened, every muscle of his face moving, to the tale of disaster that Monty Newton wailed.

"It is burning still? Have you no fire-extinguishing machinery in London?"

"Is the place insured or is it not?" asked Monty for the second time.

Dr. Oberzohn considered.

"It is not," he said. "But this matter is of such small importance compared with the great thing which is coming, that I shall not give it a thought."

"It was incendiary," said Newton angrily. "The fire brigade people are certain of it. That cursed crowd are getting back on us for what happened this afternoon."

"I know of nothing that happened this afternoon," said Dr. Oberzohn coldly. "You know of nothing either. It was an accident which we all deplored. As to this man . . . we shall see."

He hung up the telephone receiver very carefully, went along the passage, down a steep flight of dark stairs, and into a basement kitchen. Before he opened the door he heard the sound of furious voices, and he stood for a moment surveying the scene with every feeling of satisfaction. Except for two men, the room was empty. The servants used the actual kitchen at the front of the house, and this place was little better than a scullery. On one side of the deal table stood Gurther, white as death, his round eyes red with rage. On the other, the short, stout Russian Pole, with his heavy pasty face and baggy eyes; his little moustache and beard bristling with anger. The cards scattered on the table and the floor told the Herr Doktor that this was a repetition of the quarrel which was so frequent between them.

"Schweinhund!" hissed Gurther. "I saw you palm the King as you dealt. Thief and robber of the blind——"

"You German dog! You——"

They were both speaking in German. Then the doctor saw the hand of Gurther steal down and back.

"Gurther!" he called, and the man spun round. "To my parlour—march!"

Without a word, the man strode past him, and the doctor was left with the panting Russian.

"Herr Doktor, this Gurther is beyond endurance!" His voice trembled with rage. "I would sooner live with a pig than this man, who is never normal unless he is drugged."

"Silence!" shouted Oberzohn, and pointed to the chair. "You shall wait till I come," he said.

When he came back to his room, he found Gurther standing stiffly to attention.

"Now, Gurther," he said—he was almost benevolent as he patted the man on the shoulder—"this matter of Gonsalez must end. Can I have my Gurther hiding like a worm in the ground? No, that cannot be. To-night I will send you to this man, and you are so clever that you cannot fail. He whipped you, Gurther—tied you up and cruelly beat you. Always remember that, my brave fellow—he beat you till you bled. Now you shall see the man again. You will go in a dress for-every-occasion," he said. "The city-clerk manner. You will watch him in your so clever way, and you shall strike—it is permitted."

"Ja, Herr Doktor."

He turned on his heels and disappeared through the door. The doctor waited till he heard him going up the stairs, and then he rang for Pfeiffer. The man came in sullenly. He lacked all the precision of the military Gurther; yet, as Oberzohn knew, of the two he was the more alert, the more cunning.

"Pfeiffer, it has come to me that you are in some danger. The police wish to take you back to Warsaw, where certain unpleasant things happened, as you well know. And I am told"—he lowered his voice—"that a friend of ours would be glad to see you go, hein?"

The man did not raise his sulky eyes from the floor, did not answer, or by any gesture or movement of body suggest that he had heard what the older man had said.

"Gurther goes to-morrow, perhaps on our good work, perhaps to speak secretly to his friends in the police—who knows? He has work to do: let him do it, Pfeiffer. All my men will be there—at a place called Brightlingsea. You also shall go. Gurther would rob a blind man? Good! You shall rob one also. As for Gurther, I do not wish him back. I am tired of him: he is a madman. All men are mad who sniff that white snuff up their foolish noses—eh, Pfeiffer?"

Still the awkward-looking man made no reply.

"Let him do his work: you shall not interfere, until—it is done."

Pfeiffer was looking at him now, a cold sneer on his face.

"If he comes back, I do not," he said. "This man is frightening me. Twice the police have been here—three times . . . you remember the woman. The man is a danger, Herr Doktor. I told you he was the day you brought him here."

"He can dress in the gentleman-club manner," said the doctor gently.

"Pshaw!" said the other scornfully. "Is he not an actor who has postured and painted his face and thrown about his legs for so many marks a week?"

"If he does not come back I shall be relieved," murmured the doctor. "Though it would be a mistake to leave him so that these cunning men could pry into our affairs."

Pfeiffer said nothing: he understood his instructions; there was nothing to be said.

"When does he go?"

"Early to-morrow, before daylight. You will see him, of course."

He said something in a low tone, that only Pfeiffer heard. The shadow who stood in stockinged feet listening at the door only heard two words. Gurther grinned in the darkness; his bright eyes grew luminous. He heard his companion move towards the door and sped up the stairs without a sound.

———————

Rath Hall was a rambling white building of two stories, set in the midst of a little park, so thickly wooded that the house was invisible from the road; and since the main entrance to the estate was a very commonplace gate, without lodge or visible drive beyond, Gonsalez would have missed the place had he not recognized the man who was sitting on the moss-grown and broken wall who jumped down as Leon stopped his car.

"Mr. Meadows is at the house, sir. He said he expected you."

"And where on earth is the house?" asked Leon Gonsalez, as he went into reverse.

For answer the detective opened the gate wide and Leon sent his car winding between the trees, for close at hand he recognized where a gravel drive had once been, and, moreover, saw the tracks of cars in the soft earth. He arrived just as Mr. Johnson Lee was taking his two guests in to dinner, and Meadows was obviously glad to see him. He excused himself and took Leon aside into the hall, where they could not be overheard.

"I have had your message," he said. "The only thing that has happened out of the ordinary is that the servants have an invitation to a big concert at Brightlingsea. You expected that?"

Leon nodded.

"Yes: I hope Lee will let them go. I prefer that they should be out of the way. A crude scheme—but Oberzohn does these things. Has anything else happened?"

"Nothing. There have been one or two queer people around."

"Has he showed you the letters he had from Barberton?"

To his surprise the inspector answered in the affirmative.

"Yes, but they are worse than Greek to me. A series of tiny protuberances on thick brown paper. He keeps them in his safe. He read some of the letters to me: they were not very illuminating."

"But the letter of letters?" asked Leon anxiously. "That which Lee answered—by the way, you know that Mr. Lee wrote all his letters between perforated lines?"

"I've seen the paper," nodded the detective. "No, I asked him about that, but apparently he is not anxious to talk until he has seen his lawyer, who is coming down to-night. He should have been here, in fact, in time for dinner."

They passed into the dining-room together. The blind man was waiting patiently at the head of the table, and with an apology Leon took the place that had been reserved for him. He sat with his back to the wall, facing one of the three long windows that looked out upon the park. It was a warm night and the blinds were up, as also was the middle window that faced him. He made a motion to Mr. Washington, who sat opposite him, to draw a little aside, and the American realized that he wished an uninterrupted view of the park.

"Would you like the window closed?" asked Mr. Lee, leaning forward and addressing the table in general. "I know it is open," he said with a little laugh, "because I opened it! I am a lover of fresh air."

They murmured their agreement and the meal went on without any extraordinary incident. Mr. Washington was one of those adaptable people who dovetail into any environment in which they find themselves. He was as much at home at Rath Hall as though he had been born and bred in the neighbourhood. Moreover, he had a special reason for jubilation: he had found a rare adder when walking in the woods that morning, and spent ten minutes explaining in what respect it differed from every other English adder.

"Is it dead?" asked Meadows nervously.

"Kill it?" said the indignant Mr. Washington. "Why should I kill it? I saw a whole lot of doves out on the lawn this morning—should I kill 'em? No, sir! I've got none of those mean feelings towards snakes. I guess the Lord sent snakes into this world for some other purpose than to be chased and killed every time they're seen. I sent him up to London to-day by train to a friend of mine at the Zoological Gardens. He'll keep him until I'm ready to take him back home."

Meadows drew a long sigh.

"As long as he's not in your pocket," he said.

"Do you mind?"

Leon's voice was urgent as he signalled Washington to move yet farther to the left, and when the big man moved his chair, Leon nodded his thanks. His eyes were on the window and the darkening lawn. Not once did he remove his gaze.

"It's an extraordinary thing about Poole, my lawyer," Mr. Lee was saying. "He promised faithfully he'd be at Rath by seven o'clock. What is the time?"

Meadows looked at his watch.

"Half-past eight," he said. He saw the cloud that came over the face of the blind owner of Rath Hall.

"It is extraordinary! I wonder if you would mind——"

His foot touched a bell beneath the table and his butler came in.

"Will you telephone to Mr. Poole's house and ask if he has left?"

The butler returned in a short time.

"Yes, sir, Mr. Poole left the house by car at half-past six."

Johnson Lee sat back in his chair.

"Half-past six? He should have been here by now."

"How far away does he live?"

"About fifteen miles. I thought he might have come down from London rather late. That is extraordinary."

"He may have had tyre trouble," said Leon, not shifting his fixed stare.

"He could have telephoned."

"Did anybody know he was coming—anybody outside your own household?" asked Gonsalez.

The blind man hesitated.

"Yes, I mentioned the fact to the post office this morning. I went in to get my letters, and found that one I had written to Mr. Poole had been returned through a stupid mistake on my part. I told the postmaster that he was coming this evening and that there was no need to forward it."

"You were in the public part of the post office?"

"I believe I was."

"You said nothing else, Mr. Lee—nothing that would give any idea of the object of this visit?"

Again his host hesitated.

"I don't know. I'm almost afraid that I did," he confessed. "I remember telling the postmaster that I was going to talk to Mr. Poole about poor Barberton—Mr. Barberton was very well known in this neighbourhood."

"That is extremely unfortunate," said Leon.

He was thinking of two things at the same time: the whereabouts of the missing lawyer, and the wonderful cover that the wall between the window and the floor gave to any man who might creep along out of sight until he got back suddenly to send the snake on its errand of death.

"How many men have you got in the grounds, by the way, Meadows?"

"One, and he's not in the grounds but outside on the road. I pull him in at night, or rather in the evening, to patrol the grounds, and he is armed." He said this with a certain importance. An armed English policeman is a tremendous phenomenon, that few have seen.

"Which means that he has a revolver that he hasn't fired except at target practice," said Leon. "Excuse me—I thought I heard a car."

He got up noiselessly from the table, went round the back of Mr. Lee, and, darting to the window, looked out. A flower-bed ran close to the wall, and beyond that was a broad gravel drive. Between gravel and flowers was a wide strip of turf. The drive continued some fifty feet to the right before it turned under an arch of rambler roses. To the left it extended for less than a dozen feet, and from this point a path parallel to the side of the house ran into the drive.

"Do you hear it?" asked Lee.

"No, sir, I was mistaken."

Leon dipped his hand into his side pocket, took out a handful of something that looked like tiny candies wrapped in coloured paper. Only Meadows saw him scatter them left and right, and he was too discreet to ask why. Leon saw the inquiring lift of his eyebrows as he came back to his seat, but was wilfully dense. Thereafter, he ate his dinner with only an occasional glance towards the window.

"I'm not relying entirely upon my own lawyer's advice," said Mr. Lee. "I have telegraphed to Lisbon to ask Dr. Pinto Caillao to come to England, and he may be of greater service even than Poole, though where——"

The butler came in at this moment.

"Mrs. Poole has just telephoned, sir. Her husband has had a bad accident: his car ran into a tree trunk which was lying across the road near Lawley. It was on the other side of the bend, and he did not see it until too late."

"Is he very badly hurt?"

"No, sir, but he is in the Cottage Hospital. Mrs. Poole says he is fit to travel home."

The blind man sat open-mouthed.

"What a terrible thing to have happened!" he began.

"A very lucky thing for Mr. Poole," said Leon cheerfully. "I feared worse than that——"

From somewhere outside the window came a "snap!"—the sound that a Christmas cracker makes when it is exploded. Leon got up from the table, walked swiftly to the side of the window and jumped out. As he struck the earth, he trod on one of the little bon-bons he had scattered and it cracked viciously under his foot.

There was nobody in sight. He ran swiftly along the grass-plot, slowing his pace as he came to the end of the wall, and then jerked round, gun extended stiffly. Still nobody. Before him was a close-growing box hedge, in which had been cut an opening. He heard the crack of a signal behind him, guessed that it was Meadows, and presently the detective joined him. Leon put his fingers to his lips, leapt the path to the grass on the other side, and dodged behind a tree until he could see straight through the opening in the box hedge. Beyond was a rose-garden, a mass of pink and red and golden blooms.

Leon put his hand in his pocket and took out a black cylinder, fitting it, without taking his eyes from the hedge opening, to the muzzle of his pistol. Meadows heard the dull thud of the explosion before he saw the pistol go up. There was a scatter of leaves and twigs and the sound of hurrying feet. Leon dashed through the opening in time to see a man plunge into a plantation.

"*Plop!*"

The bullet struck a tree not a foot from the fugitive.

"That's that!" said Leon, and took off his silencer. "I hope none of the servants heard it, and most of all that Lee, whose hearing is unfortunately most acute, mistook the shot for something else."

He went back to the window, stopping to pick up such of his crackers as had not exploded.

"They are useful things to put on the floor of your room when you're expecting to have your throat cut in the middle of the night," he said pleasantly. "They cost exactly two dollars a hundred, and they've saved my life more often than I can count. Have you ever waited in the dark to have your throat cut?" he asked. "It happened to me three times, and I will admit that it is not an experience that I am anxious to repeat. Once in Bohemia, in the city of Prague; once in New Orleans, and once in Ortona."

"What happened to the assassins?" asked Meadows with a shiver.

"That is a question for the theologian, if you will forgive the well-worn jest," said Leon. "I think they are in hell, but then I'm prejudiced."

Mr. Lee had left the dining-table and was standing at the front door, leaning on his stick; and with him an interested Mr. Washington.

"What was the trouble?" asked the old man in a worried voice. "It is a great handicap not being able to see things. But I thought I heard a shot fired."

"Two," said Leon promptly. "I hoped you hadn't heard them. I don't know who the man was, Mr. Lee, but he certainly had no right in the grounds, and I scared him off."

"You must have used a silencer: I did not hear the shots fully. Did you catch a view of the man's face?"

"No, I saw his back," he said. Leon thought it was unnecessary to add that a man's back was as familiar to him as his face. For when he studied his enemies, his study was a very thorough and complete one. Moreover, Gurther ran with a peculiar swing of his shoulder.

He turned suddenly to the master of Rath Hall.

"May I speak with you privately for a few minutes, Mr. Lee?" he asked. He had taken a sudden resolution.

"Certainly," said the other courteously, and tapped his way into the hall and into his private study.

For ten minutes Leon was closeted with him. When he came out, Meadows had gone down to his man at the gate, and Washington was standing disconsolately alone. Leon took him by the arm and led him on to the lawn.

"There's going to be real trouble here to-night," he said, and told him the arrangement he had made with Mr. Johnson Lee. "I've tried to persuade him to let me see the letter which is in his safe, but he is like rock on that matter, and I'd hate to burgle the safe of a friend. Listen."

Elijah Washington listened and whistled.

"They stopped the lawyer coming," Gonsalez went on, "and now they're mortally scared if, in his absence, the old man tells us what he intended keeping for his lawyer."

"Meadows is going to London, isn't he?"

Leon nodded slowly.

"Yes, he is going to London—by car. Did you know all the servants were going out to-night?"

Mr. Washington stared at him.

"The women, you mean?"

"The women and the men," said Leon calmly. "There is an excellent concert at Brightlingsea to-night, and though they will be late for the first half of the performance, they will thoroughly enjoy the latter portion of the programme. The invitation is not mine, but it is one I thoroughly approve."

"But does Meadows want to go away when the fun is starting?"

Apparently Inspector Meadows was not averse from leaving at this critical moment. He was, in fact, quite happy to go. Mr. Washington's views on police intelligence underwent a change for the worse.

"But surely he had better stay?" said the American. "If you're expecting an attack . . . they are certain to marshal the whole of their forces?"

"Absolutely certain," said the calm Gonsalez. "Here is the car."

The Rolls came out from the back of the house at that moment and drew up before the door.

"I don't like leaving you," said Meadows, as he swung himself up by the driver's side and put his bag on the seat.

"Tell the driver to avoid Lawley like the plague," said Leon. "There's a tree down, unless the local authorities have removed it—which is very unlikely."

He waited until the tail lights of the machine had disappeared into the gloom, then he went back to the hall.

"Excuse me, sir," said the butler, struggling into his greatcoat as he spoke. "Will you be all right—there is nobody left in the house to look after Mr. Lee. I could stay——"

"It was Mr. Lee's suggestion you should all go," said Gonsalez briefly. "Just go outside and tell me when the lights of the char-à-banc come into view. I want to speak to Mr. Lee before you go."

He went into the library and shut the door behind him. The waiting butler heard the murmur of his voice and had some qualms of conscience. The tickets had come from a local agency; he had never dreamt that, with guests in the house, his employer would allow the staff to go in its entirety.

It was not a char-à-banc but a big closed bus that came lumbering up the apology for a drive, and swept round to the back of the house, to the annoyance of the servants, who were gathered in the hall.

"Don't bother, I will tell him," said Leon. He seemed to have taken full charge of the house, an unpardonable offence in the eyes of well-regulated servants.

He disappeared through a long passage leading into the mysterious domestic regions, and returned to announce that the driver had rectified his error and was coming to the front entrance: an unnecessary explanation, since the big vehicle drew up as he was telling the company.

"There goes the most uneasy bunch of festive souls it has ever been my misfortune to see," he said, as the bus, its brakes squeaking, went down the declivity towards the unimposing gate. "And yet they'll have the time of their

- 109 -

lives. I've arranged supper for them at the Beech Hotel, and although they are not aware of it, I am removing them to a place where they'd give a lot of money to be—if they hadn't gone!"

"That leaves you and me alone," said Mr. Washington glumly, but brightened up almost at once. "I can't say that I mind a rough house, with or without gun-play," he said. He looked round the dark hall a little apprehensively. "What about fastening the doors behind?" he asked.

"They're all right," said Leon. "It isn't from the back that danger will come. Come out and enjoy the night air . . . it is a little too soon for the real trouble."

But here, for once, he was mistaken.

Elijah Washington followed him into the park, took two paces, and suddenly Leon saw him stagger. In a second he was by the man's side, bent and peering, his glasses discarded on the grass.

"Get me inside," said Washington's voice. He was leaning heavily upon his companion.

With his arm round his waist, taking half his weight, Leon pushed the man into the hall but did not close the door. Instead, as the American sat down with a thud upon a hall seat, Leon fell to the ground, and peered along the artificial skyline he had created. There was no movement, no sign of any attacker. Then and only then did he shut the door and drop the bar, and pushing the study door wide, carried the man into the room and switched on the lights.

"I guess something got me then," muttered Washington.

His right cheek was red and swollen, and Leon saw the tell-tale bite; saw something else. He put his hand to the cheek and examined his finger-tips.

"Get me some whisky, will you?—about a gallon of it."

He was obviously in great pain and sat rocking himself to and fro.

"Gosh! This is awful!" he groaned. "Never had any snake that bit like this!"

"You're alive, my friend, and I didn't believe you when you said you were snake-proof."

Leon poured out a tumbler of neat whisky and held it to the American's lips.

"Down with Prohibition!" murmured Washington, and did not take the glass from his lips until it was empty. "You can give me another dose of that—I shan't get pickled," he said.

He put his hand up to his face and touched the tiny wound gingerly.

"It is wet," he said in surprise.

"What did it feel like?"

"Like nothing so much as a snake-bite," confessed the expert.

Already his face was puffed beneath the eyes, and the skin was discoloured black and blue.

Leon crossed to the fire-place and pushed the bell, and Washington watched him in amazement.

"Say, what's the good of ringing? The servants have gone."

There was a patter of feet in the hall, the door was flung open and George Manfred came in, and behind him the startled visitor saw Meadows and a dozen men.

"For the Lord's sake!" he said sleepily.

"They came in the char-à-banc, lying on the floor," explained Leon, "and the only excuse for bringing a char-à-banc here was to send the servants to that concert."

"You got Lee away?" asked Manfred.

Leon nodded.

"He was in the car that took friend Meadows, who transferred to the char-à-banc somewhere out of sight of the house."

Washington had taken a small cardboard box from his pocket and was rubbing a red powder gingerly upon the two white-edged marks, groaning the while.

"This is certainly a snake that's got the cobra skinned to death and a rattlesnake's bite ain't worse than a dog nip," he said. "Mamba nothing! I know the mamba; he is pretty fatal, but not so bad as this."

Manfred looked across to Leon.

"Gurther?" he asked simply, and Gonsalez nodded.

"It was intended for me obviously, but, as I've said before, Gurther is nervous. And it didn't help him any to be shot up."

"Do you fellows mind not talking so loud?" He glanced at the heavy curtains that covered the windows. Behind these the shutters had been fastened, and Dr. Oberzohn was an ingenious man.

Leon took a swift survey of the visitor's feet; they wore felt slippers.

"I don't think I can improve upon the tactics of the admirable Miss Leicester," he said, and went up to Mr. Lee's bedroom, which was in the centre of the house and had a small balcony, the floor of which was formed by the top of the porch.

The long French windows were open and Leon crawled out into the darkness and took observation through the pillars of the balustrade. They were in the open now, making no attempt to conceal their presence. He counted seven, until he saw the cigarette of another near the end of the drive. What were they waiting for? he wondered. None of them moved; they were not even closing on the house. And this inactivity puzzled him. They were awaiting a signal. What was it to be? Whence would it come?

He saw a man come stealthily across the lawn . . . one or two? His eyes were playing tricks. If there were two, one was Gurther. There was no mistaking him. For a second he passed out of view behind a pillar of the balcony. Leon moved his head . . . Gurther had fallen! He saw him stumble to his knees and tumble flat upon the ground. What did that mean?

He was still wondering when he heard a soft scraping, and a deep-drawn breath, and tried to locate the noise. Suddenly, within a few inches of his face, a hand came up out of the darkness and gripped the lower edge of the balcony.

Swiftly, noiselessly, Gonsalez wriggled back to the room, drew erect in the cover of the curtains and waited. His hand touched something; it was a long silken cord by which the curtains were drawn. Leon grinned in the darkness and made a scientific loop.

The intruder drew himself up on to the parapet, stepped quietly across, then tiptoed to the open window. He was not even suspicious, for the French windows had been open all the evening. Without a sound, he stepped into the room and was momentarily silhouetted against the starlight reflected in the window.

"Hatless," thought Leon. That made things easier. As the man took another stealthy step, the noose dropped over his neck, jerked tight and strangled the cry in his throat. In an instant he was lying flat on the ground with a knee in his back. He struggled to rise, but Leon's fist came down with the precision of a piston-rod, and he went suddenly quiet.

Gonsalez loosened the slip-knot, and, flinging the man over his shoulder, carried him out of the room and down the stairs. He could only guess that this would be the only intruder, but left nothing to chance, and after he had handed his prisoner to the men who were waiting in the hall, he ran back to the room, to find, as he had expected, that no other adventurer had followed the lead. They were still standing at irregular intervals where he had seen them last. The signal was to come from the house. What was it to be? he wondered.

He left one of his men on guard in the room and went back to the study, to find that the startled burglar was an old friend. Lew Cuccini was looking from one of his captors to the other, a picture of dumbfounded chagrin. But the most extraordinary discovery that Leon made on his return to the study was that the American snake-charmer was his old cheerful self, and, except for his unsightly appearance, seemed to be none the worse for an ordeal which would have promptly ended the lives of ninety-nine men out of a hundred.

"Snake-proof—that's me. Is this the guy that did it?" He pointed to Cuccini.

"Where is Gurther?" asked Manfred.

Cuccini grinned up into his face.

"You'd better find out, boss," he said. "He'll fix you. As soon as I shout——"

"Cuccini——" Leon's voice was gentle. The point of the long-bladed knife that he held to the man's neck was indubitably sharp. Cuccini shrank back. "You will not shout. If you do, I shall cut your throat and spoil all these beautiful carpets—that is a genuine silken Bokhara, George. I haven't seen one in ten years." He nodded to the soft-hued rug on which George Manfred was standing. "What is the signal, Cuccini?" turning his attention again to the prisoner. "And what happens when you give the signal?"

"Listen," said Cuccini, "that throat-cutting stuff don't mean anything to me. There's no third degree in this country, and don't forget it."

"You have never seen my ninety-ninth degree." Leon smiled like a delighted boy. "Put something in his mouth, will you?"

One of the men tied a woollen scarf round Cuccini's head.

"Lay him on the sofa."

He was already bound hand and foot and helpless.

"Have you any wax matches? Yes, here are some." Leon emptied a cut-glass container into the palm of his hand and looked blandly round at the curious company. "Now, gentlemen, if you will leave me alone for exactly five minutes, I will give Mr. Cuccini an excellent imitation of the persuasive methods of Gian Visconti, an excellent countryman of his, and the inventor of the system I am about to apply."

Cuccini was shaking his head furiously. A mumble of unintelligible sounds came from behind the scarf.

"Our friend is not unintelligent. Any of you who say that Signor Cuccini is unintelligent will incur my severest displeasure," said Leon.

They sat the man up and he talked brokenly, hesitatingly.

"Splendid," said Leon, when he had finished. "Take him into the kitchen and give him a drink—you'll find a tap above the kitchen sink."

"I've often wondered, Leon," said George, when they were alone together, "whether you would ever carry out these horrific threats of yours of torture and malignant savagery?"

"Half the torture of torture is anticipation," said Leon easily, lighting a cigarette with one of the matches he had taken from the table, and carefully guiding the rest back into the glass bowl. "Any man versed in the art of suggestive description can dispense with thumbscrews and branding irons, little maidens and all the ghastly apparatus of criminal justice ever employed by our ancestors. I, too, wonder," he mused, blowing a ring of smoke to the ceiling, "whether I could carry my threats into execution—I must try one day." He nodded pleasantly, as though he were promising himself a great treat.

Manfred looked at his watch.

"What do you intend doing—giving the signal?"

Gonsalez nodded.

"And then?"

"Letting them come in. We may take refuge in the kitchen. I think it would be wiser."

George Manfred nodded.

"You're going to allow them to open the safe?"

"Exactly," said Leon. "I particularly wish that safe to be opened, and since Mr. Lee demurs, I think this is the best method. I had that in my mind all the time. Have you seen the safe, George? I have. Nobody but an expert could smash it. I have no tools. I did not provide against such a contingency, and I have scruples. Our friends have the tools—and no scruples!"

"And the snake—is there any danger?"

Leon snapped his fingers.

"The snake has struck for the night, and will strike no more! As for Gurther——"

"He owes you something."

Leon sent another ring up and did not speak until it broke on the ceiling.

"Gurther is dead," he said simply. "He has been lying on the lawn in front of the house for the past ten minutes."

# Chapter XVII                    Written in Braille

LEON briefly related the scene he had witnessed from the balcony.

"It was undoubtedly Gurther," he said. "I could not mistake him. He passed out of view for a second behind one of the pillars, and when I looked round he was lying flat on the ground."

He threw his cigarette into the fire-place.

"I think it is nearly time," he said. He waited until Manfred had gone, and, going to the door, moved the bar and pulled it open wide.

Stooping down, he saw that the opening of the door had been observed, for one of the men was moving across the lawn in the direction of the house. From his pocket he took a small electric lamp and sent three flickering beams into the darkness. To his surprise, only two men walked forward to the house. Evidently Cuccini was expected to deal with any resistance before the raid occurred.

The house had been built in the fifteenth century, and the entrance hall was a broad, high barn of a place. Some Georgian architect, in the peculiar manner of his kind, had built a small minstrel gallery over the dining-room entrance and immediately facing the study. Leon had already explored the house and had found the tiny staircase that led to this architectural monstrosity. He had no sooner given the signal than he dived into the dining-room, through the tall door, and was behind the thick curtains at the back of the narrow gallery when the first two men came in. He saw them go straight into the study and push open the door. At the same time a third man appeared under the porch, though he made no attempt to enter the hall.

Presently one of those who had gone into the study came out and called Cuccini by name. When no answer came, he went grumbling back to his task. What that task was, Leon could guess, before the peculiarly acrid smell of hot steel was wafted to his sensitive nostrils.

By crouching down he could see the legs of the men who were working at the safe. They had turned on all the lights, and apparently expected no interruption. The man at the door was joined by another man.

"Where is Lew?"

In the stillness of the house the words, though spoken in a low tone, were audible.

"I don't know—inside somewhere. He had to fix that dago."

Leon grinned. This description of himself never failed to tickle him.

One of the workers in the library came out at this point.

"Have you seen Cuccini?"

"No," said the man at the door.

"Go in and find him. He ought to be here."

Cuccini's absence evidently made him uneasy, for though he returned to the room he was out again in a minute, asking if the messenger had come back. Then, from the back of the passage, came the searcher's voice:

"The kitchen's locked."

The safe-cutter uttered an expression of amazement.

"Locked? What's the idea?"

He came to the foot of the stairs and bellowed up:

"Cuccini!"

Only the echo answered him.

"That's queer." He poked his head in the door of the study. "Rush that job, Mike. There's some funny business here." And over his shoulder, "Tell the boys to get ready to jump."

The man went out into the night and was absent some minutes, to return with an alarming piece of news.

"They've gone, boss. I can't see one of them."

The "boss" cursed him, and himself went into the grounds on a visit of inspection. He came back in a hurry, ran into the study, and Leon heard his voice:

"Stand ready to clear."

"What about Cuccini?"

"Cuccini will have to look after himself . . . got it, Mike?"

The deep voice said something. There followed the sound of a crack, as though something of iron had broken. It was the psychological moment. Leon parted the curtains and dropped lightly to the floor.

The man at the door turned in a flash at the sound.

"Put 'em up!" he said sharply.

"Don't shoot." Leon's voice was almost conversational in its calmness. "The house is surrounded by police."

With an oath the man darted out of the door, and at that instant came the sound of the first shot, followed by desultory firing from the direction of the road. The second guard had been the first to go. Leon ran to the door, slammed it tight and switched on the lights as the two men came from the study. Under the arm of one was a thick pad of square brown sheets. He dropped his load and put up his hands at the sight of the gun; but his companion was made of harder material, and, with a yell, he leapt at the man who stood between him and freedom. Leon twisted aside, advanced his shoulder to meet the furious drive of the man's fist; then, dropping his pistol, he stooped swiftly and tackled him below the knees. The man swayed, sought to recover his balance and fell with a crash on the stone floor. All the time his companion stood dazed and staring, his hands waving in the air.

There was a knock at the outer door. Without turning his back upon his prisoners, Leon reached for the bar and pulled it up. Manfred came in.

"The gentleman who shouted 'Cuccini' scared them. I think they've got away. There were two cars parked on the road."

His eyes fell upon the brown sheets scattered on the floor and he nodded.

"I think you have all you want, Leon," he said.

The detectives came crowding in at that moment and secured their prisoners whilst Leon Gonsalez and his friend went out on to the lawn to search for Gurther.

The man lay as he had fallen, on his face, and as Leon flashed his lamp upon the figure, he saw that the snake had struck behind the ear.

"Gurther?" frowned Leon.

He turned the figure on its back and gave a little gasp of surprise, for there looked up to the starry skies the heavy face of Pfeiffer.

"Pfeiffer! I could have sworn it was the other! There has been some double-crossing here. Let me think." He stood for fully a minute, his chin on his hand. "I could have understood Gurther; he was becoming a nuisance and a danger to the old man. Pfeiffer, the more reliable of the two, hated him. My first theory was that Gurther had been put out by order of Oberzohn."

"Suppose Gurther heard that order, or came to know of it?" asked Manfred quietly.

Leon snapped his fingers.

"That is it! We had a similar case a few years ago, you will remember, George? The old man gave the 'out' order to Pfeiffer—and Gurther got his blow in first. Shrewd fellow!"

When they returned to the house, the three were seated in a row in Johnson Lee's library. Cuccini, of course, was an old acquaintance. Of the other two men, Leon recognized one, a notorious gunman whose photograph had embellished the pages of *Hue and Cry* for months.

The third, and evidently the skilled workman of the party, for he it was whom they had addressed as "Mike" and who had burnt out the lock of Lee's safe, was identified by Meadows as Mike Selwyn, a skilful burglar and bank-smasher, who had, according to his statement, only arrived from the Continent that afternoon in answer to a flattering invitation which promised considerable profit to himself.

"And why I left Milan," he said bitterly, "where the graft is easy and the money's good, I'd like you to tell me!"

The prisoners were removed to the nearest secure lock-up, and by the time Lee's servants returned from their dance, all evidence of an exciting hour had disappeared, except that the blackened and twisted door of the safe testified to the sinister character of the visitation.

Meadows returned as they were gathering together the scattered sheets. There were hundreds of them, all written in Braille characters, and Manfred's sensitive fingers were skimming their surface.

"Oh, yes," he said, in answer to a question that was put to him, "I knew Lee was blind, the day we searched Barberton's effects. That was my mystery." He laughed. "Barberton expected a call from his old friend and had left a message for him on the mantelpiece. Do you remember that strip of paper? It ran: 'Dear Johnny, I will be back in an hour.' These are letters,"—he indicated the papers.

"The folds tell me that," said Meadows. "You may not get a conviction against Cuccini; the two burglars will come up before a judge, but to charge Cuccini means the whole story of the snake coming out, and that means a bigger kick than I'm prepared to laugh away—I am inclined to let Cuccini go for the moment."

Manfred nodded. He sat with the embossed sheets on his knee.

"Written from various places," he went on.

It was curious to see him, his fingers running swiftly along the embossed lines, his eyes fixed on vacancy.

"So far I've learnt nothing, except that in his spare time Barberton amused himself by translating native fairy stories into English and putting them into Braille for use in the blind school. I knew, of course, that he did that, because I'd already interviewed his sister, who is the mistress of the girls' section."

He had gone through half a dozen letters when he rose from the table and walked across to the safe.

"I have a notion that the thing we're seeking is not here," he said. "It is hardly likely that he would allow a communication of that character to be jumbled up with the rest of the correspondence."

The safe door was open and the steel drawer at the back had been pulled out. Evidently it was from this receptacle that the letters had been taken. Now the drawer was empty. Manfred took it out and measured the depth of it with his finger.

"Let me see," said Gonsalez suddenly.

He groped along the floor of the safe, and presently he began to feel carefully along the sides.

"Nothing here," he said. He drew out half a dozen account books and a bundle of documents which at first glance Manfred had put aside as being personal to the owner of Rath Hall. These were lying on the floor amidst the mass of molten metal that had burnt deep holes in the carpet. Leon examined the books one by one, opening them and running his nail along the edge of the pages. The fourth, a weighty ledger, did not open so easily—did not, indeed, open at all. He carried it to the table and tried to pull back the cover.

"Now, how does this open?"

The ledger covers were of leather; to all appearance a very ordinary book, and Leon was anxious not to disturb so artistic a camouflage. Examining the edge carefully, he saw a place where the edges had been forced apart. Taking out a knife, he slipped the thin blade into the aperture. There was a click and the cover sprang up like the lid of a box.

"And this, I think, is what we are looking for," said Gonsalez.

The interior of the book had been hollowed out, the edges being left were gummed tight, and the receptacle thus formed was packed close with brown papers; brown, except for one, which was written on a large sheet of foolscap, headed: "Bureau of the Ministry of Colonies, Lisbon."

Barberton had superimposed upon this long document his Braille writing, and now one of the mysteries was cleared up.

"Lee said he had never received any important documents," said Manfred, "and, of course, he hadn't, so far as he knew. To him this was merely a sheet of paper on which Braille characters were inscribed. Read this, Leon."

Leon scanned the letter. It was dated "July 21st, 1912," and bore, in the lower left-hand corner, the seal of the Portuguese Colonial Office. He read it through rapidly and at the end looked up with a sigh of satisfaction.

"And this settles Oberzohn and Co., and robs them of a fortune, the extent of which I think we shall discover when we read Barberton's letter."

He lit a cigarette and scanned the writing again, whilst Meadows, who did not understand Leon's passion for drama, waited with growing impatience.

> "Illustrious Senhor," began Leon, reading. "I have this day had the honour of placing before His Excellency the President, and the Ministers of the Cabinet, your letter dated May 15th, 1912. By a letter dated January 8th, 1911, the lands marked Ex. 275 on the Survey Map of the Biskara district, were conceded to you, Illustrious Senhor, in order to further the cause of science—a cause which is very dear to the heart of His Excellency the President. Your further letter, in which you complain, Illustrious Senhor, that the incursion of prospectors upon your land is hampering your scientific work, and your request that an end may be put to these annoyances by the granting to you of an extension of the concession, so as to give you title to all minerals found in the aforesaid area, Ex. 275 on the Survey Map of Biskara, and thus making the intrusion of prospectors illegal, has been considered by the Council, and the extending concession is hereby granted, on the following conditions: The term of the concession shall be for twelve years, as from the 14th day of June, 1912, and shall be renewable by you, your heirs or nominees, every twelfth year, on payment of a nominal sum of 1,000 milreis. In the event of the concessionnaire, his heirs or nominees, failing to apply for a renewal on the 14th day of June, 1924, the mineral rights of the said area, Ex. 275 on the Survey Map of Biskara, shall be open to claim in accordance with the laws of Angola——"

Leon sat back.

"Fourteenth of June?" he said, and looked up. "Why, that is next week—five days! We've cut it rather fine, George."

"Barberton said there were six weeks," said Manfred. "Obviously he made the mistake of timing the concession from July 21st—the date of the letter. He must have been the most honest man in the world; there was no other reason why he should have communicated with Miss Leicester. He could have kept quiet and claimed the rights for himself. Go on, Leon."

"That is about all," said Leon, glancing at the tail of the letter. "The rest is more or less flowery and complimentary and has reference to the scientific work in which Professor Leicester was engaged. Five days—phew!" he whistled.

"We may now find something in Barberton's long narrative to give us an idea of the value of this property." Manfred turned the numerous pages. "Do any of you gentlemen write shorthand?"

Meadows went out into the hall and brought back an officer. Waiting until he had found pencil and paper, Leon began the extraordinary story of William Barberton—most extraordinary because every word had been patiently and industriously punched in the Braille characters.

# Chapter XVIII
# The Story of Mont d'Or

"DEAR FRIEND JOHNNY,—

"I have such a lot to tell you that I hardly know where to begin. I've struck rich at last, and the dream I've often talked over with you has come true. First of all, let me tell you that I have come upon nearly £50,000 worth of wrought gold. We've been troubled round here with lions, one of which took away a carrier of mine, and at last I decided to go out and settle accounts with this fellow. I found him six miles from the camp and planted a couple of bullets into him without killing him, and decided to follow up his spoor. It was a mad thing to do, trailing a wounded lion in the jungle, and I didn't realize how mad until we got out of the bush into the hills and I found Mrs. Lion waiting for me. She nearly got me too. More by accident than anything else, I managed to shoot her dead at the first shot, and got another pot at her husband as he was slinking into a cave which was near our tent.

"As I had gone so far, I thought I might as well go the whole hog, especially as I'd seen two lion cubs playing round the mouth of the cave, and bringing up my boys, who were scared to death, I crawled in, to find, as I expected, that the old lion was nearly gone, and a shot finished him. I had to kill the cubs; they were too young to be left alone, and too much of a nuisance to bring back to camp. This cave had been used as a lair for years; it was full of bones, human amongst them.

"But what struck me was the appearance of the roof, which, I was almost certain, had been cut out by hand. It was like a house, and there was a cut door in the rock at the back. I made a torch and went through on a tour of inspection, and you can imagine my surprise when I found myself in a little room with a line of stone niches or shelves. There were three lines of them on each side. Standing on these at intervals there were little statuettes. They were so covered with dust that I thought they were stone, until I tried to take one down to examine it; then I knew by its weight that it was gold, as they all were.

"I didn't want my boys to know about my find, because they are a treacherous lot, so I took the lightest, after weighing them all with a spring balance, and made a note where I'd taken it from. You might think that was enough of a find for one man in a lifetime, but my luck had set in. I sent the boys back and ordered them to break camp and join me on top of the Thaba. I called it the Thaba, because it is rather like a hill I know in Basutoland, and is one of two.

- 123 -

"The camp was moved up that night; it was a better pitch than any we had had. There was water, plenty of small game, and no mosquitoes. The worst part of it was the terrific thunderstorms which come up from nowhere, and until you've seen one in this ironstone country you don't know what a thunderstorm is like! The hill opposite was slightly smaller than the one I had taken as a camp, and between was a shallow valley, through which ran a small shallow river—rapids would be a better word.

"Early the next morning I was looking round through my glasses, and saw what I thought was a house on the opposite hill. I asked my head-man who lived there, and he told me that it was once the house of the Star Chief; and I remembered that somebody told me, down in Mossamedes, that an astronomer had settled in this neighbourhood and had been murdered by the natives. I thought I would go over and have a look at the place. The day being cloudy and not too hot, I took my gun and a couple of boys and we crossed the river and began climbing the hill. The house was, of course, in ruins; it had only been a wattle hut at the best of times. Part of it was covered with vegetation, but out of curiosity I searched round, hoping to pick up a few things that might be useful to me, more particularly kettles, for my boys had burnt holes in every one I had. I found a kettle, and then, turning over a heap of rubbish which I think must have been his bed, I found a little rusty tin box and broke it open with my stick. There were a few letters which were so faded that I could only read a word here and there, and in a green oilskin, a long letter from the Portuguese Government."

(It was at this point, either by coincidence or design, that the narrative continued on the actual paper to which he referred.)

"I speak Portuguese and can read it as easily as English, and the only thing that worried me about it was that the concession gave Professor Leicester all rights to my cave. My first idea was to burn it, but then I began to realize what a scoundrelly business that would be, and I took the letters out into the sun and tried to find if he had any relations, hoping that I'd be able to fix it up with them to take at any rate 50 per cent. of my find. There was only one letter that helped me. It was written in a child's hand and was evidently from his daughter. It had no address, but there was the name—'Mirabelle Leicester.'

"I put it in my pocket with the concession and went on searching, but found nothing more. I was going down the hill towards the valley when it struck me that perhaps this man had found gold, and the excuse for getting the concession was a bit of artfulness. I sent a boy back to the camp for a pick, a hammer and a spade, and when he returned I began to make a cutting in the side of the hill. There was nothing to guide me—no outcrop, such as you usually find near a true reef—but I hadn't been digging for an hour before I struck the richest bed of conglomerate I've ever seen. I was either dreaming, or my good angel had at last led me to the one place in the hill where gold could be found. I had previously sent the boys back to the camp and told them to wait for me, because, if I did strike metal, I did not want the fact advertised all over Angola, where they've been looking for gold for years.

"Understand, it was not a reef in the ordinary sense of the word, it was all conglomerate, and the wider I made my cutting, the wider the bed appeared. I took the pick to another part of the hill and dug again, with the same result—conglomerate. It was as though nature had thrown up a huge golden hump on the earth. I covered both cuttings late that night and went back to camp. (I was stalked by a leopard in the low bush, but managed to get him.)

"Early next morning, I started off and tried another spot, and with the same result; first three feet of earth, then about six inches of shale, and then conglomerate. I tried to work through the bed, thinking that it might be just a skin, but I was saved much exertion by coming upon a deep rift in the hill about twenty feet wide at the top and tapering down to about fifty feet below the ground level. This gave me a section to work on, and as near as I can judge, the conglomerate bed is something over fifty feet thick and I'm not so sure that it doesn't occur again after an interval of twenty feet or more, for I dug more shale and had a showing of conglomerate at the very bottom of the ravine.

"What does this mean, Johnny? It means that we have found a hill of gold; not solid gold, as in the story-books, but gold that pays ounces and probably pounds to the ton. How the prospectors have missed it all these years I can't understand, unless it is that they've made their cuttings on the north side of the hill, where they have found nothing but slate and sandstone. The little river in the valley must be feet deep in alluvial, for I panned the bed and got eight ounces of pure gold in an hour—and that was by rough and ready methods. I had to be careful not to make the boys too curious, and I am breaking camp to-morrow, and I want you to cable or send me £500 to Mossamedes. The statuette I'm bringing home is worth all that. I would bring more, only I can't trust these Angola boys; a lot of them are mission boys and can read Portuguese, and they're too friendly with a half-breed called Villa, who is an agent of Oberzohn & Smitts; the traders and I know these people to be the most unscrupulous scoundrels on the coast.

"I shall be at Mossamedes about three weeks after you get this letter, but I don't want to get back to the coast in a hurry, otherwise people are going to suspect I have made a strike."

Leon put the letter down.

"There is the story in a nutshell, gentlemen," he said. "I don't, for one moment, believe that Mr. Barberton showed Villa the letter. It is more likely that one of the educated natives he speaks about saw it and reported it to Oberzohn's agent. Portuguese is the lingua franca of that part of the coast. Barberton was killed to prevent his meeting the girl and telling her of his find—incidentally, of warning her to apply for a renewal of the concession. It wasn't even necessary that they should search his belongings to recover the letter, because once they knew of its existence and the date which Barberton had apparently confounded with the date the letter was written, their work was simply to present an application to the Colonial Office at Lisbon. It was quite different after Barberton was killed, when they learnt or guessed that the letter was in Mr. Lee's possession."

Meadows agreed.

"That was the idea behind Oberzohn's engagement of Mirabelle Leicester?"

"Exactly, and it was also behind the attack upon Heavytree Farm. To secure this property they must get her away and keep her hidden either until it is too late for her to apply for a renewal, or until she has been bullied or forced into appointing a nominee."

"Or married," said Leon briskly. "Did that idea occur to you? Our tailor-made friend, Monty Newton, may have had matrimonial intentions. It would have been quite a good stroke of business to secure a wife and a large and auriferous hill at the same time. This, I think, puts a period to the ambitions of Herr Doktor Oberzohn."

He got up from the table and handed the papers to the custody of the detective, and turned with a quizzical smile to his friend.

"George, do you look forward with any pleasure to a two hundred and fifty miles' drive?"

"Are you the chauffeur?" asked George.

"I am the chauffeur," said Leon cheerfully. "I have driven a car for many years and I have not been killed yet. It is unlikely that I shall risk my precious life and yours to-night. Come with me and I promise never to hit her up above sixty except on the real speedways."

Manfred nodded.

"We will stop at Oxley and try to get a 'phone call through to Gloucester," said Leon. "This line is, of course, out of order. They would do nothing so stupid as to neglect the elementary precaution of disconnecting Rath Hall."

At Oxley the big Spanz pulled up before the dark and silent exterior of an inn, and Leon, getting down, brought the half-clad landlord to the door and explained his mission, and also learned that two big cars had passed through half an hour before, going in the direction of London.

"That was the gang. I wonder how they'll explain to their paymaster their second failure?"

His first call was to the house in Curzon Street, but there was no reply.

"Ring them again," said Leon. "You left Poiccart there?"

Manfred nodded.

They waited for five minutes; still there was no reply.

"How queer!" said Manfred. "It isn't like Poiccart to leave the house. Get Gloucester."

At this hour of the night the lines are comparatively clear, and in a very short time he heard the Gloucester operator's voice, and in a few seconds later the click that told them they were connected with Heavytree Farm. Here there was some delay before the call was answered.

It was not Mirabelle Leicester nor her aunt who spoke. Nor did he recognize the voice of Digby, who had recovered sufficiently to return to duty.

"Who is that?" asked the voice sharply. "Is that you, sergeant?"

"No, it is Mr. Meadows," said Leon mendaciously.

"The Scotland Yard gentleman?" It was an eager inquiry. "I'm Constable Kirk, of the Gloucester Police. My sergeant's been trying to get in touch with you, sir."

"What is the matter?" asked Leon, a cold feeling at his heart.

"I don't know, sir. About half an hour ago, I was riding past here—I'm one of the mounted men—and I saw the door wide open and all the lights on, and when I came in there was nobody up. I woke Miss Goddard and Mr. Digby, but the young lady was not in the house."

"Lights everywhere?" asked Leon quickly.

"Yes, sir—in the parlour at any rate."

"No sign of a struggle?"

"No, sir, but a car passed me three miles from the house and it was going at a tremendous rate. I think she may have been in that. Mr. Digby and Miss Goddard have just gone into Gloucester."

"All right, officer. I am sending Mr. Gonsalez down to see you," said Leon, and hung up the receiver.

"What is it?" asked George Manfred, who knew that something was wrong by his friend's face.

"They've got Mirabelle Leicester after all," said Leon. "I'm afraid I shall have to break my promise to you, George. That machine of mine is going to travel before daybreak!"

# Chapter XIX                    At Heavytree Farm

IT had been agreed that, having failed in their attack, and their energies for the moment being directed to Rath Hall, an immediate return of the Old Guard to Heavytree Farm was unlikely. This had been Meadows' view, and Leon and his friend were of the same mind. Only Poiccart, that master strategist, working surely with a queer knowledge of his enemies' psychology, had demurred from this reasoning; but as he had not insisted upon his point of view, Heavytree Farm and its occupants had been left to the care of the local police and the shaken Digby.

Aunt Alma offered to give up her room to the wounded man, but he would not hear of this, and took the spare bedroom; an excellent position for a defender, since it separated Mirabelle's apartment from the pretty little room which Aunt Alma used as a study and sleeping-place.

The staff of Heavytree Farm consisted of an ancient cowman, a cook and a maid, the latter of whom had already given notice and left on the afternoon of the attack. She had, as she told Mirabelle in all seriousness, a weak heart.

"And a weak head too!" snapped Alma. "I should not worry about your heart, my girl, if I were you."

"I was top of my class at school," bridled the maid, touched to the raw by this reflection upon her intelligence.

"It must have been a pretty small class," retorted Alma.

A new maid had been found, a girl who had been thrilled by the likelihood that the humdrum of daily labour would be relieved by exciting events out of the ordinary, and before evening the household had settled down to normality. Mirabelle was feeling the reaction and went to bed early that night, waking as the first slant of sunlight poured through her window. She got up, feeling, she told herself, as well as she had felt in her life. Pulling back the chintz curtains, she looked out upon a still world with a sense of happiness and relief beyond measure. There was nobody in sight. Pools of mist lay in the hollows, and from one white farmstead, far away on the slope of the hill, she saw the blue smoke was rising. It was a morning to remember, and, to catch its spirit the better, she dressed hastily and went down into the garden. As she walked along the path she heard a window pulled open and the bandaged head of Mr. Digby appeared.

"Oh, it's you, is it, miss?" he said with relief, and she laughed.

"There is nothing more terrible in sight than a big spider," she said, and pointed to a big flat fellow, who was already spinning his web between the tall hollyhocks. And the first of the bees was abroad.

"If anybody had come last night I shouldn't have heard them," he confessed. "I slept like a dead man." He touched his head gingerly. "It smarts, but the ache is gone," he said, not loth to discuss his infirmities. "The doctor said I had a narrow escape; he thought there was a fracture. Would you like me to make you some tea, miss, or shall I call the servant?"

She shook her head, but he had already disappeared, and came seeking her in the garden ten minutes later, with a cup of tea in his hand. He told her for the second time that he was a police pensioner and had been in the employ of Gonsalez for three years. The Three paid well, and had, she learned to her surprise, considerable private resources.

"Does it pay them—this private detective business?"

"Lord bless your heart, no, miss!" He scoffed at the idea. "They are very rich men. I thought everybody knew that. They say Mr. Gonsalez was worth a million even before the war."

This was astonishing news.

"But why do they do this"—she hesitated—"this sort of thing?"

"It is a hobby, miss," said the man vaguely. "Some people run race-horses, some own yachts—these gentlemen get a lot of pleasure out of their work and they pay well," he added.

Men in the regular employ of the Three Just Men not only received a good wage, but frequently a bonus which could only be described as colossal. Once, after they had rounded up and destroyed a gang of Spanish bank robbers, they had distributed £1,000 to every man who was actively employed.

He hinted rather than stated that this money had formed part of the loot which the Three had recovered, and did not seem to think that there was anything improper in this distribution of illicit gains.

"After all, miss," he said philosophically, "when you collect money like that, it's impossible to give it back to the people it came from. This Diego had been holding up banks for years, and banks are not like people—they don't feel the loss of money."

"That's a thoroughly immoral view," said Mirabelle, intent upon her flower-picking.

"It may be, miss," agreed Digby, who had evidently been one of the recipients of bounty, and took a complacent and a tolerant view. "But a thousand pounds is a lot of money."

The day passed without event. From the early evening papers that came from Gloucester she learned of the fire at Oberzohn's, and did not connect the disaster with anything but an accident. She was not sorry. The fire had licked out one ugly chapter from the past. Incidentally it had destroyed a crude painting which was, to Dr. Oberzohn, more precious than any that Leonardo had painted or Raphael conceived, but this she did not know.

It was just before the dinner hour that there came the first unusual incident of the day. Mirabelle was standing by the garden gate, intent upon the glories of the evening sky, which was piled high with red and slate-coloured cumuli. The glass was falling and a wet night was promised. But the loveliness of that lavish colouring held her. And then she became dimly aware that a man was coming towards the house from the direction of Gloucester. He walked in the middle of the road slowly, as though he, too, were admiring the view and there was no need to hurry. His hands were behind him, his soft felt hat at the back of his head. A stocky-looking man, but his face was curiously familiar. He turned his unsmiling eyes in her direction, and, looking again at his strong features, at the tiny grey-black moustache under his aquiline nose, she was certain she had seen him before. Perhaps she had passed him in the street, and had retained a subconscious mental picture of him.

He slowed his step until, when he came abreast of her, he stopped.

"This is Heavytree Lane?" he asked, in a deep, musical voice.

"No—the lane is the first break in the hedge," she smiled. "I'm afraid it isn't much of a road—generally it is ankle-deep in mud."

He looked past her to the house; his eyes ranged the windows, dropped for a moment upon a climbing clematis, and came back to her.

"I don't know Gloucestershire very well," he said, and added: "You have a very nice house."

"Yes," she said in surprise.

"And a garden." And then, innocently: "Do you grow onions?"

She stared at him and laughed.

"I think we do—I am not sure. My aunt looks after the kitchen garden."

His sad eyes wandered over the house again.

"It is a very nice place," he said, and, lifting his hat, went on.

Digby was out: he had gone for a gentle walk, and, looking up the road after the stranger, she saw the guard appear round a bend in the road, saw him stop and speak to the stranger. Apparently they knew one another, for they shook hands at meeting, and after a while Digby pointed down the road to where she was standing, and she saw the man nod. Soon after the stranger went on out of view. Who could he be? Was it an additional guard that the three men had put to protect her? When Digby came up to her, she asked him.

"That gentleman, miss? He is Mr. Poiccart."

"Poiccart?" she said, delighted. "Oh, I wish I had known!"

"I was surprised to see him," said the guard. "As a matter of fact, he's the one of the three gentlemen I've met the most. He's generally in Curzon Street, even when the others are away."

Digby had nothing to say about Poiccart except that he was a very quiet gentleman and took no active part in the operations of the Just Men.

"I wonder why he wanted to know about onions?" asked the girl thoughtfully. "That sounded awfully mysterious."

It would not have been so mysterious to Leon.

The house retired to bed soon after ten, Alma going the rounds, and examining the new bolts and locks which had been attached that morning to every door which gave ingress to the house.

Mirabelle was unaccountably tired, and was asleep almost as soon as her head touched the pillow.

She heard in her dreams the swish of the rain beating against her window, lay for a long time trying to energize herself to rise and shut the one open window where the curtains were blowing in. Then came a heavier patter against a closed pane, and something rattled on the floor of her room. She sat up. It could not be hail, although there was a rumble of thunder in the distance.

She got out of bed, pulled on her dressing-gown, went to the window, and had all her work to stifle a scream. Somebody was standing on the path below . . . a woman! She leaned out.

"Who is it?" she asked.

"It is me—I—Joan!" There was a sob in the voice of the girl. Even in that light Mirabelle could see that the girl was drenched. "Don't wake anybody. Come down—I want you."

"What is wrong?" asked Mirabelle in a low voice.

"Everything . . . everything!"

She was on the verge of hysteria. Mirabelle lit a candle and crossed the room, went downstairs softly, so that Alma should not be disturbed. Putting the candle on the table, she unbarred and unbolted the door, opened it, and, as she did so, a man slipped through the half-opened door, his big hands smothering the scream that rose to her lips.

Another man followed and, lifting the struggling girl, carried her into the drawing-room. One of the men took a small iron bottle from his pocket, to which ran a flexible rubber tube ending in a large red cap. Her captor removed his hands just as long as it took to fix the cap over her face. A tiny faucet was turned. Mirabelle felt a puff on her face, a strangely sweet taste, and then her heart began to beat thunderously. She thought she was dying, and writhed desperately to free herself.

"She's all right," said Monty Newton, lifting an eyelid for a second. "Get a blanket." He turned fiercely to the whimpering girl behind him. "Shut up, you!" he said savagely. "Do you want to rouse the whole house?"

A woebegone Joan was whimpering softly, tears running down her face, her hands clasping and unclasping in the agony of her mind.

"You told me you weren't going to hurt her!" she sobbed.

"Get out," he hissed, and pointed to the door. She went meekly.

A heavy blanket was wrapped round the unconscious girl, and, lifting her between them, the two men went out into the rain, where the old trolley was waiting, and slid her along the straw-covered floor. In another second the trolley moved off, gathering speed.

By this time the effect of the gas had worn off and Mirabelle had regained consciousness. She put out a hand and touched a woman's knee.

"Who is that—Alma?"

"No," said a miserable voice, "it's Joan."

"Joan? Oh, yes, of course . . . why did you do it?—how wicked!"

"Shut up!" Monty snarled. "Wait until you get to—where you're going, before you start these 'whys' and 'wherefores.'"

Mirabelle was deathly sick and bemused, and for the next hour she was too ill to feel even alarmed. Her head was going round and round, and ached terribly, and the jolting of the truck did not improve matters in this respect.

Monty, who was sitting with his back to the truck's side, was smoking. He cursed now and then, as some unusually heavy jolt flung him forward. They passed through the heart of the storm: the flicker of lightning was almost incessant and the thunder was deafening. Rain was streaming down the hood of the trolley, rendering it like a drum.

Mirabelle fell into a little sleep and woke feeling better. It was still dark, and she would not have known the direction they were taking, only the driver took the wrong turning coming through a country town, and by the help of the lightning she saw what was indubitably the stand of a race-track, and a little later saw the word "Newbury." They were going towards London, she realized.

At this hour of the morning there was little or no traffic, and when they turned on to the new Great West Road a big car went whizzing past at seventy miles an hour and the roar of it woke the girl. Now she could feel the trolley wheels skidding on tram-lines. Lights appeared with greater frequency. She saw a store window brilliantly illuminated, the night watchman having evidently forgotten to turn off the lights at the appointed hour.

Soon they were crossing the Thames. She saw the red and green lights of a tug, and black upon near black a string of barges in mid-stream. She dozed again and was jerked wide awake when the trolley swayed and skidded over a surface more uneven than any. Once its wheels went into a pothole and she was flung violently against the side. Another time it skidded and was brought up with a crash against some obstacle. The bumping grew more gentle, and then the machine stopped, and Monty jumped down and called to her sharply.

Her head was clear now, despite its throbbing. She saw a queer-shaped house, all gables and turrets, extraordinarily narrow for its height. It seemed to stand in the middle of a field. And yet it was in London: she could see the glow of furnace fires and hear the deep boom of a ship's siren as it made its way down the river on the tide.

She had not time to take observations, for Monty fastened to her arm and she squelched through the mud up a flight of stone steps into a dimly lit hall. She had a confused idea that she had seen little dogs standing on the side of the steps, and a big bird with a long bill, but these probably belonged to the smoke of dreams which the gas had left.

Monty opened a door and pushed her in before him, and she stared into the face of Dr. Oberzohn.

He wore a black velvet dressing-gown that had once been a regal garment but was now greasy and stained. On his egg-shaped head he had an embroidered smoking-cap. His feet were encased in warm velvet slippers. He put down the book he had been reading, rubbed his glasses on one velvet sleeve, and then:

"So!" he said.

He pointed to the remains of a fire.

"Sit down, Mirabelle Leicester, and warm yourself. You have come quickly, my friend,"—he addressed Monty.

"I'm black and blue all over," growled Newton. "Why couldn't we have a car?"

"Because the cars were engaged, as I told you."

"Did you——" began Newton quickly, but the old man glanced significantly at the girl, shivering before the fire and warming her hands mechanically.

"I will answer, but you need not ask, in good time. This is not of all moments the most propitious. Where is your woman?"

He had forgotten Joan, and went out to find her shivering in the passage.

"Do you want her?" he asked, poking his head in the door.

"She shall go with this girl. You will explain."

"Where are you going to put her?"

Oberzohn pointed to the floor.

"Here? But——"

"No, no. My friend, you are too quick to see what is not meant. The gracious lady shall live in a palace—I have a certain friend who will no longer need it."

His face twitched in the nearest he ever approached to a smile. Groping under the table, he produced a pair of muddy Wellingtons, kicked off his slippers and pulled on the boots with many gasps and jerks.

"All that they need is there: I have seen to it. March!"

He led the way out of the room, pulling the girl to her feet, and Newton followed, Joan bringing up the rear. Inside the factory, Oberzohn produced a small hand torch from his pocket and guided them through the debris till he came to that part of the floor where the trap was. With his foot he moved the covering of rubbish, pulled up the trap and went down.

"I can't go down there, Monty, I can't!" said Joan's agitated voice. "What are you going to do with us? My God! if I'd known——"

"Don't be a fool," said Newton roughly. "What have you got to be afraid of? There's nothing here. We want you to look after her for a day or two. You don't want her to go down by herself: she'd be frightened to death."

Her teeth chattering, Joan stumbled down the steps behind him. Certainly the first view of her new quarters was reassuring. Two little trestle beds had been made; the underground room had been swept clean, and a new carpet laid on the floor. Moreover, the apartment was brilliantly lit, and a furnace gave almost an uncomfortable warmth which was nevertheless very welcome, for the temperature had dropped 20° since noon.

"In this box there are clothes of all varieties, and expensive to purchase," said Oberzohn, pointing to a brand-new trunk at the foot of one of the beds. "Food you will have in plenty—bread and milk newly every day. By night you shall keep the curtain over the ventilator." On the wall was a small black curtain about ten inches square.

Monty took her into the next apartment and showed her the wash-place. There was even a bath, a compulsory fixture under the English Factory Act in a store of this description, where, in the old days, men had to handle certain insanitary products of the Coast.

"But how do we get out, Monty? Where do we get exercise?"

"You'll come out to-morrow night: I'll see to that," he said, dropping his voice. "Now listen, Joan: you've got to be a sensible girl and help me. There's money in this—bigger money than you have ever dreamed of. And when we've got this unpleasant business over, I'm taking you away for a trip round the world."

It was the old promise, given before, never fulfilled, always hoped for. But this time it did not wholly remove her uneasiness.

"But what are you going to do with the girl?" she asked.

"Nothing; she will be kept here for a week. I'll swear to you that nothing will happen to her. At the end of a week she's to be released without a hair of her head being harmed."

She looked at him searchingly. As far as she was able to judge, he was speaking the truth. And yet——

"I can't understand it,"—she shook her head, and for once Monty Newton was patient with her.

"She's the owner of a big property in Africa, and that we shall get, if things work out right," he said. "The point is that she must claim within a few days. If she doesn't, the property is ours."

Her face cleared.

"Is that all?" She believed him, knew him well enough to detect his rare sincerity. "That's taken a load off my mind, Monty. Of course I'll stay and look after her for you—it makes it easier to know that nothing will happen. What are those baize things behind the furnace—they look like boxes?"

He turned on her quickly.

"I was going to tell you about those," he said. "You're not to touch them under any circumstances. They belong to the old man and he's very stuffy about such things. Leave them just as they are. Let him touch them and nobody else. Do you understand?"

She nodded, and, to his surprise, pecked his cheek with her cold lips.

"I'll help you, boy," she said tremulously. "Maybe that trip will come off after all, if——"

"If what?"

"Those men—the men you were talking about—the Four Just Men, don't they call themselves? They scare me sick, Monty! They were the people who took her away before, and they'll kill us—even Oberzohn says that. They're after him. Has he"—she hesitated—"has he killed anybody? That snake stuff . . . you're not in it, are you, Monty?"

She looked more like a child than a sophisticated woman, clinging to his arm, her blue eyes looking pleadingly into his.

"Stuff! What do I know about snakes?" He disengaged himself and came back to where Oberzohn was waiting, a figure of patience.

The girl was lying on the bed, her face in the crook of her arm, and he was gazing at her, his expression inscrutable.

"That is all, then. Good night, gracious ladies."

He turned and marched back towards the step and waved his hand. Monty followed. The girl heard the thud of the trap fall, the scrape of the old man's boots, and then a rumbling sound, which she did not immediately understand. Later, when in a panic, she tried the trap, she found that a heavy barrel had been put on top, and that it was immovable.

# Chapter XX                    Gurther Reports

DR. OBERZHON had not been to bed for thirty-five years. It was his practice to sleep in a chair, and alternate his dozes with copious draughts from his favourite authors. Mostly the books were about the soul, and free will, and predestination, with an occasional dip into Nietzsche by way of light recreation. In ordinary circumstances he would have had need for all the philosophy he could master; for ruin had come. The destruction of his store, which, to all intents and purposes, was uninsured, would have been the crowning stroke of fate but for the golden vision ahead.

Villa, that handsome half-breed, had arrived in England and had been with the doctor all the evening. At that moment he was on his way to Liverpool to catch the Coast boat, and he had left with his master a record of the claims that had already been pegged out on Monte Doro, as he so picturesquely renamed the new mountain. There were millions there; uncountable wealth. And between the Herr Doktor and the achievement of this colossal fortune was a life which he had no immediate desire to take. The doctor was a bachelor; women bored him. Yet he was prepared to take the extreme step if by so doing he could doubly ensure his fortune. Mirabelle dead gave him one chance; Mirabelle alive and persuaded, multiplied that chance by a hundred.

He opened the book he was reading at the last page and took out the folded paper. It was a special licence to marry, and had been duly registered at the Greenwich Registrar's Office since the day before the girl had entered his employment. This was his second and most powerful weapon. He could have been legally married on this nearly a week ago. It was effective for two months at least, and only five days separated him from the necessity of a decision. If the time expired, Mirabelle could live. It was quite a different matter, killing in cold blood a woman for whom the police would be searching, and with whose disappearance his name would be connected, from that other form of slaying he favoured: the striking down of strange men in crowded thoroughfares. She was not for the snake—as yet.

He folded the paper carefully, put it back in the book and turned the page, when there was a gentle tap at the door and he sat up.

"Come in, Pfeiffer. March!"

The door opened slowly and a man sidled into the room, and at the sight of him Dr. Oberzohn gasped.

"Gurther!" he stammered, for once thrown out of his stride.

Gurther smiled and nodded, his round eyes fixed on the tassel of the Herr Doktor's smoking-cap.

"You have returned—and failed?"

"The American, I think, is dead, Herr Doktor," said the man in his staccato tone. "The so excellent Pfeiffer is also—dead!"

The doctor blinked twice.

"Dead?" he said gratingly. "Who told you this?"

"I saw him. Something happened . . . to the snake. Pfeiffer was bitten."

The old man's hard eyes fixed him.

"So!" he said softly.

"He died very quickly—in the usual manner," jerked Gurther, still with that stupid smile.

"So!" said the doctor again. "All then was failure, and out of it comes an American, who is nothing, and Pfeiffer, who is much—dead!"

"God have him in his keeping!" said Gurther, not lowering or raising his eyes. "And all the way back I thought this, Herr Doktor—how much better that it should be Pfeiffer and not me. Though my nerves are so bad."

"So!" said the doctor for the fourth time, and held out his hand.

Gurther slipped his fingers into his waistcoat pocket and took out a gold cigarette-case. The doctor opened it and looked at the five cigarettes that reposed, at the two halves of the long holder neatly lying in their proper place, closed the case with a snap and laid it on the table.

"What shall I do with you, Gurther? To-morrow the police will come and search this house."

"There is the cellar, Herr Doktor: it is very comfortable there. I would prefer it."

Dr. Oberzohn made a gesture like a boy wiping something from a slate.

"That is not possible: it is in occupation," he said. "I must find a new place for you." He stared and mused. "There is the boat," he said.

Gurther's smile did not fade.

The boat was a small barge, which had been drawn up into the private dock of the O. & S. factory, and had been rotting there for years, the playing-ground of rats, the doss-house of the homeless. The doctor saw what was in the man's mind.

"It may be comfortable. I will give you some gas to kill the rats, and it will only be for five-six days."

"Ja, Herr Doktor."

"For to-night you may sleep in the kitchen. One does not expect——"

There was a thunderous knock on the outer door. The two men looked at one another, but still Gurther grinned.

"I think it is the police," said the doctor calmly.

He got up to his feet, lifted the seat of a long hard-looking sofa, disclosing a deep cavity, and Gurther slipped in, and the seat was replaced. This done, the doctor waddled to the door and turned the key.

"Good morning, Inspector Meadows."

"May I come in?" said Meadows.

Behind him were two police officers, one in uniform.

"Do you wish to see me? Certainly." He held the door cautiously open and only Meadows came in, and preceded the doctor into his study.

"I want Mirabelle Leicester," said Meadows curtly. "She was abducted from her home in the early hours of this morning, and I have information that the car which took her away came to this house. There are tracks of wheels in the mud outside."

"If there are car tracks, they are mine," said the doctor calmly. He enumerated the makes of machines he possessed. "There is another matter: as to cars having come here in the night, I have a sense of hearing, Mr. Inspector Meadows, and I have heard many cars in Hangman's Lane—but not in my ground. Also, I'm sure you have not come to tell me of abducted girls, but to disclose to me the miscreant who burnt my store. That is what I expected of you."

"What you expect of me and what you get will be entirely different propositions," said Meadows unpleasantly. "Now come across, Oberzohn! We know why you want this girl—the whole plot has been blown. You think you'll prevent her from making a claim on the Portuguese Government for the renewal of a concession granted in June, 1912, to her father."

If Dr. Oberzohn was shocked to learn that his secret was out, he did not show it by his face. Not a muscle moved.

"Of such matters I know nothing. It is a fantasy, a story of fairies. Yet it must be true, Mr. Inspector Meadows, if you say it. No: I think you are deceived by the criminals of Curzon Street, W. Men of blood and murder, with records that are infamous. You desire to search my house? It is your privilege." He waved his hand. "I do not ask you for the ticket of search. From basement to attic the house is yours."

He was not surprised when Meadows took him at his word, and, going out into the hall, summoned his assistants. They visited each room separately, the old cook and the half-witted Danish girl accepting this visitation as a normal occurrence: they had every excuse to do so, for this was the second time in a fortnight that the house had been visited by the police.

"Now I'll take a look at your room, if you don't mind," said Meadows.

His quick eyes caught sight of the box ottoman against the wall, and the fact that the doctor was sitting thereon added to his suspicions.

"I will look in here, if you please," he said.

Oberzohn rose and the detective lifted the lid. It was empty. The ottoman had been placed against the wall, at the bottom of which was a deep recess. Gurther had long since rolled through the false back.

"You see—nothing," said Oberzohn. "Now perhaps you would like to search my factory? Perhaps amongst the rafters and the burnt girders I may conceal a something. Or the barge in my slipway? Who knows what I may place amongst the rats?"

"You're almost clever," said Meadows, "and I don't profess to be a match for you. But there are three men in this town who are! I'll be frank with you, Oberzohn. I want to put you where I can give you a fair trial, in accordance with the law of this country, and I shall resist, to the best of my ability, any man taking the law into his own hands. But whether you're innocent or guilty, I wouldn't stand in your shoes for all the money in Angola!"

"So?" said the doctor politely.

"Give up this girl, and I rather fancy that half your danger will be at an end. I tell you, you're too clever for me. It's a stupid thing for a police officer to say, but I can't get at the bottom of your snake. They have."

The old man's brows worked up and down.

"Indeed?" he said blandly. "And of which snake do you speak?"

Meadows said nothing more. He had given his warning: if Oberzohn did not profit thereby, he would be the loser.

Nobody doubted, least of all he, that, in defiance of all laws that man had made, independent of all the machinery of justice that human ingenuity had devised, inevitable punishment awaited Oberzohn and was near at hand.

# Chapter XXI          The Account Book

IT was five o'clock in the morning when the mud-spattered Spanz dropped down through the mist and driving rain of the Chiltern Hills and struck the main Gloucester Road, pulling up with a jerk before Heavytree Farm. Manfred sprang out, but before he could reach the door, Aunt Alma had opened it, and by the look of her face he saw that she had not slept that night.

"Where is Digby?" he asked.

"He's gone to interview the Chief Constable," said Alma. "Come in, Mr. Gonsalez."

Leon was wet from head to foot: there was not a dry square centimetre upon him. But he was his old cheerful self as he stamped into the hall, shaking himself free of his heavy mackintosh.

"Digby, of course, heard nothing, George."

"I'm the lightest sleeper in the world," said Aunt Alma, "but I heard not a sound. The first thing I knew was when a policeman came up and knocked at my door and told me that he'd found the front door open."

"No clue was left at all?"

"Yes," said Aunt Alma. They went into the drawing-room and she took up from the table a small black bottle with a tube and cap attached. "I found this behind the sofa. She'd been lying on the sofa; the cushions were thrown on the floor and she tore the tapestry in her struggle."

Leon turned the faucet, and, as the gas hissed out, sniffed.

"The new dental gas," he said. "But how did they get in? No window was open or forced?"

"They came in at the door: I'm sure of that. And they had a woman with them," said Aunt Alma proudly.

"How do you know?"

"There must have been a woman," said Aunt Alma. "Mirabelle would not have opened the door except to a woman, without waking either myself or Mr. Digby."

Leon nodded, his eyes gleaming.

"Obviously," he said.

"And I found the marks of a woman's foot in the passage. It is dried now, but you can still see it."

"I have already seen it," said Leon. "It is to the left of the door: a small pointed shoe and a rubber heel. Miss Leicester opened the door to the woman, the men came in, and the rest was easy. You can't blame Digby," he said appealingly to George.

He was the friend at court of every agent, but this time Manfred did not argue with him.

"I blame myself," he said. "Poiccart told me——"

"He was here," said Aunt Alma.

"Who—Poiccart?" asked Manfred, surprised, and Gonsalez slapped his knee.

"That's it, of course! What fools we are! We ought to have known why this wily old fox had left his post. What time was he here?"

Alma told him all the circumstances of the visit.

"He must have left the house immediately after us," said Leon, with a wide grin of amusement, "caught the five o'clock train for Gloucester, taxied across."

"And after that?" suggested Manfred.

Leon scratched his chin.

"I wonder if he's back?" He took up the telephone and put a trunk call through to London. "Somehow I don't think he is. Here's Digby, looking as if he expected to be summarily executed."

The police pensioner was indeed in a mournful and pathetic mood.

"I don't know what you'll think of me, Mr. Manfred——" he began.

"I've already expressed a view on that subject." George smiled faintly. "I'm not blaming you, Digby. To leave a man who has been knocked about as you have been without an opposite number, was the height of folly. I didn't expect them back so soon. As a matter of fact, I intended putting four men on from to-day. You've been making inquiries?"

"Yes, sir. The car went through Gloucester very early in the morning and took the Swindon road. It was seen by a cyclist policeman; he said there was a fat roll of tarpaulin lying on the tent of the trolley."

"No sign of anybody chasing it in a car, or on a motor-bicycle?" asked Manfred anxiously.

Poiccart had recently taken to motor-cycling.

"No, sir."

"You saw Mr. Poiccart?"

"Yes, he was just going back to London. He said he wanted to see the place with his own eyes."

George was disappointed. If it had been a visit of curiosity, Poiccart's absence from town was understandable. He would not have returned at the hour he was rung up.

Aunt Alma was cooking a hasty breakfast, and they had accepted her offer gratefully, for both men were famished; and they were in the midst of the meal when the London call came through.

"Is that you, Poiccart?"

"That is I," said Poiccart's voice. "Where are you speaking from?"

"Heavytree Farm. Did you see anything of Miss Leicester?"

There was a pause.

"Has she gone?"

"You didn't know?"

Another pause.

"Oh, yes, I knew; in fact, I accompanied her part of the way to London, and was bumped off when the trolley struck a refuge on the Great West Road. Meadows is here: he has just come from Oberzohn's. He says he has found nothing."

Manfred thought for a while.

"We will be back soon after nine," he said.

"Leon driving you?" was the dry response.

"Yes—in spite of which we shall be back at nine."

"That man has got a grudge against my driving," said Leon, when Manfred reported the conversation. "I knew it was he when Digby described the car and said there was a fat roll of mackintosh on the top. 'Fat roll' is not a bad description. Do you know whether Poiccart spoke to Miss Leicester?"

"Yes, he asked her if she grew onions"—a reply which sent Leon into fits of silent laughter.

Breakfast was over and they were making their preparations for departure, when Leon asked unexpectedly:

"Has Miss Leicester a writing-table of her own?"

"Yes, in her room," said Alma, and took him up to show him the old bureau.

He opened the drawers without apology, took out some old letters, turned them over, reading them shamelessly. Then he opened the blotter. There were several sheets of blank paper headed "Heavytree Farm," and two which bore her signature at the bottom. Alma explained that the bank account of the establishment was in Mirabelle's name, and, when it was necessary to draw cash, it was a rule of the bank that it should be accompanied by a covering letter—a practice which still exists in some of the old West-country banking establishments. She unlocked a drawer that he had not been able to open and showed him a cheque-book with three blank cheques signed with her name.

"That banker has known me since I was so high," said Alma scornfully. "You wouldn't think there'd be so much red-tape."

Leon nodded.

"Do you keep any account books?"

"Yes, I do," said Alma in surprise. "The household accounts, you mean?"

"Could I see one?"

She went out and returned with a thin ledger, and he made a brief examination of its contents. Wholly inadequate, thought Alma, considering the trouble she had taken and the interest he had shown.

"That's that," he said. "Now, George, *en voiture!*"

"Why did you want to see the account book?" asked Manfred as they bowled up the road.

"I am naturally commercial-minded," was the unsatisfactory reply. "And, George, we're short of juice. Pray like a knight in armour that we sight a filling station in the next ten minutes."

If George had prayed, the prayer would have been answered: just as the cylinders started to miss they pulled up the car before a garage, and took in a supply which was more than sufficient to carry them to their destination. It was nine o'clock exactly when the car stopped before the house. Poiccart, watching the arrival from George's room, smiled grimly at the impertinent gesture of the chauffeur.

Behind locked doors the three sat in conference.

"This has upset all my plans," said Leon at last. "If the girl was safe, I should settle with Oberzohn to-night."

George Manfred stroked his chin thoughtfully. He had once worn a trim little beard, and had never got out of that beard-stroking habit of his.

"We think exactly alike. I intended suggesting that course," he said gravely.

"The trouble is Meadows. I should like the case to have been settled one way or the other, and for Meadows to be out of it altogether. One doesn't wish to embarrass him. But the urgency is very obvious. It would have been very easy," said Leon, a note of regret in his gentle voice. "Now of course it is impossible until the girl is safe. But for that"—he shrugged his shoulders—"to-morrow friend Oberzohn would have experienced a sense of lassitude. No pain . . . just a little tiredness. Sleep, coma—death on the third day. He is an old man, and one has no desire to hurt the aged. There is no hurt like fear. As for Gurther, we will try a more violent method, unless Oberzohn gets him first. I sincerely hope he does."

"This is news to me. What is this about Gurther?" asked Poiccart.

Manfred told him.

"Leon is right now," Poiccart nodded. He rose from the table and unlocked the door. "If any of you men wish to sleep, your rooms are ready; the curtains are drawn, and I will wake you at such and such an hour."

But neither were inclined for sleep. George had to see a client that morning: a man with a curious story to tell. Leon wanted a carburetter adjusted. They would both sleep in the afternoon, they said.

The client arrived soon after. Poiccart admitted him and put him in the dining-room to wait before he reported his presence.

"I think this is your harem man," he said, and went downstairs to show up the caller.

He was a commonplace-looking man with a straggling, fair moustache and a weak chin.

"Debilitated or degenerate," he suggested.

"Probably a little of both," assented Manfred, when the butler had announced him.

He came nervously into the room and sat down opposite to Manfred.

"I tried to get you on the 'phone last night," he complained, "but I got no answer."

"My office hours are from ten till two," said George good-humouredly. "Now will you tell me again this story of your sister?"

The man leaned back in the chair and clasped his knees, and began in a sing-song voice, as though he were reciting something that he had learned by heart.

"We used to live in Turkey. My father was a merchant of Constantinople, and my sister, who went to school in England, got extraordinary ideas, and came back a most violent pro-Turk. She is a very pretty girl and she came to know some of the best Turkish families, although my father and I were dead against her going about with these people. One day she went to call on Hymar Pasha, and that night she didn't come back. We went to the Pasha's house and asked for her, but he told us she had left at four o'clock. We then consulted the police, and they told us, after they had made investigations, that she had been seen going on board a ship which left for Odessa the same night. I hadn't seen her for ten years, until I went down to the Gringo Club, which is a little place in the East End—not high class, you understand, but very well conducted. There was a cabaret show after midnight, and whilst I was sitting there, thinking about going home—very bored, you understand, because that sort of thing doesn't appeal to me—I saw a girl come out from behind a curtain dressed like a Turkish woman, and begin a dance. She was in the middle of the dance when her veil slipped off. It was Marie! She recognized me at once, and darted through the curtains. I tried to follow her, but they held me back."

"Did you go to the police?" asked Manfred.

The man shook his head.

"No, what is the use of the police?" he went on in a monotonous tone. "I had enough of them in Constantinople, and I made up my mind that I would get outside help. And then somebody told me of you, and I came along. Mr. Manfred, is it impossible for you to rescue my sister? I'm perfectly sure that she is being detained forcibly and against her will."

"At the Gringo Club?" asked Manfred.

"Yes," he nodded.

"I'll see what I can do," said George. "Perhaps my friends and I will come down and take a look round some evening. In the meantime will you go back to your friend Dr. Oberzohn and tell him that you have done your part and I will do mine? Your little story will go into my collection of Unplausible Inventions!"

He touched a bell and Poiccart came in.

"Show Mr. Liggins out, please. Don't hurt him—he may have a wife and children, though it is extremely unlikely."

The visitor slunk from the room as though he had been whipped.

The door had scarcely closed upon him when Poiccart called Leon down from his room.

"Son," he said, "George wants that man trailed."

Leon peeped out after the retiring victim of Turkish tyranny.

"Not a hard job," he said. "He has flat feet!"

Poiccart returned to the consulting-room.

"Who is he?" he asked.

"I don't know. He's been sent here either by Oberzohn or by friend Newton, the general idea being to bring us all together at the Gringo Club—which is fairly well known to me—on some agreeable evening. A bad actor! He has no tone. I shouldn't be surprised if Leon finds something very interesting about him."

"He's been before, hasn't he?"

Manfred nodded.

"Yes, he was here the day after Barberton came. At least, I had his letter the next morning and saw him for a few moments in the day. Queer devil, Oberzohn! And an industrious devil," he added. "He sets everybody moving at once, and of course he's right. A good general doesn't attack with a platoon, but with an army, with all his strength, knowing that if he fails to pierce the line at one point he may succeed at another. It's an interesting thought, Raymond, that at this moment there are probably some twenty separate and independent agencies working for our undoing. Most of them ignorant that their efforts are being duplicated. That is Oberzohn's way— always has been his way. It's the way he has started revolutions, the way he has organized religious riots."

After he had had his bath and changed, he announced his intention of calling at Chester Square.

"I'm rather keen on meeting Joan Newton again, even if she has returned to her normal state of Jane Smith."

Miss Newton was not at home, the maid told him when he called. Would he see Mr. Montague Newton, who was not only at home, but anxious for him to call, if the truth be told, for he had seen his enemy approaching.

"I shall be pleased," murmured Manfred, and was ushered into the splendour of Mr. Newton's drawing-room.

"Too bad about Joan," said Mr. Newton easily. "She left for the Continent this morning."

"Without a passport?" smiled Manfred.

A little slip on the part of Monty, but how was Manfred to know that the authorities had, only a week before, refused the renewal of her passport pending an inquiry into certain irregularities? The suggestion had been that other people than she had travelled to and from the Continent armed with this individual document.

"You don't need a passport for Belgium," he lied readily. "Anyway, this passport stuff's a bit overdone. We're not at war now."

"All the time we're at war," said Manfred. "May I sit down?"

"Do. Have a cigarette?"

"Let me see the brand before I accept," said Manfred cautiously, and the man guffawed as at a great joke.

The visitor declined the offer of the cigarette-case and took one from a box on the table.

"And is Jane making the grand tour?" he asked blandly.

"Jane's run down and wants a rest."

"What's the matter with Aylesbury?"

He saw the man flinch at the mention of the women's convict establishment, but he recovered instantly.

"It is not far enough out, and I'm told that there are all sorts of queer people living round there. No, she's going to Brussels and then on to Aix-la-Chapelle, then probably to Spa—I don't suppose I shall see her again for a month or two."

"She was at Heavytree Farm in the early hours of this morning," said Manfred, "and so were you. You were seen and recognized by a friend of mine—Mr. Raymond Poiccart. You travelled from Heavytree Farm to Oberzohn's house in a Ford trolley."

Not by a flicker of an eyelid did Monty Newton betray his dismay.

"That is bluff," he said. "I didn't leave this house last night. What happened at Heavytree Farm?"

"Miss Leicester was abducted. You are surprised, almost agitated, I notice."

"Do you think I had anything to do with it?" asked Monty steadily.

"Yes, and the police share my view. A provisional warrant was issued for your arrest this morning. I thought you ought to know."

Now the man drew back, his face went from red to white, and then to a deeper red again. Manfred laughed softly.

"You've got a guilty conscience, Newton," he said, "and that's half-way to being arrested. Where is Jane?"

"Gone abroad, I tell you."

He was thrown off his balance by this all too successful bluff and had lost some of his self-possession.

"She is with Mirabelle Leicester: of that I'm sure," said Manfred. "I've warned you twice, and it is not necessary to warn you a third time. I don't know how far deep you're in these snake murders: a jury will decide that sooner or later. But you're dead within six hours of my learning that Miss Leicester has been badly treated. You know that is true, don't you?"

Manfred was speaking very earnestly.

"You're more scared of us than you are of the law, and you're right, because we do not put our men to the hazard of a jury's intelligence. You get the same trial from us as you get from a judge who knows all the facts. You can't beat an English judge, Newton."

The smile returned and he left the room. Fred, near at hand, waiting in the passage but at a respectful distance from the door, let him out with some alacrity.

Monty Newton turned his head sideways, caught a fleeting glimpse of the man he hated—hated worse than he hated Leon Gonsalez—and then called harshly for his servant.

"Come here," he said, and Fred obeyed. "They'll be sending round to make inquiries, and I want you to know what to tell them," he said. "Miss Joan went away this morning to the Continent by the eight-fifteen. She's either in Brussels or Aix-la-Chapelle. You're not sure of the hotel, but you'll find out. Is that clear to you?"

"Yes, sir."

Fred was looking aimlessly about the room.

"What's the matter with you?"

"I was wondering where the clock is."

"Clock?" Now Monty Newton heard it himself. The tick-tick-tick of a cheap clock, and he went livid. "Find it," he said hoarsely, and even as he spoke his eyes fell upon the little black box that had been pushed beneath the desk, and he groped for the door with a scream of terror.

Passers-by in Chester Square saw the door flung open and two men rush headlong into the street. And the little American clock, which Manfred had purchased a few days before, went on ticking out the time, and was still ticking merrily when the police experts went in and opened the box. It was Manfred's oldest jest, and never failed.

# Chapter XXII　　　　In the Store Cellar

IT was impossible that Mirabelle Leicester could fail to realize the serious danger in which she stood. Why she had incurred the enmity of Oberzohn, for what purpose this man was anxious to keep her under his eye, she could not even guess. It was a relief to wake up in the early morning, as she did, and find Joan sleeping in the same room; for though she had many reasons for mistrusting her, there was something about this doll-faced girl that made an appeal to her.

Joan was lying on the bed fully dressed, and at the sound of the creaking bed she turned and got up, fastening her skirt.

"Well, how do you like your new home?" she asked, with an attempt at joviality, which she was far from feeling, in spite of Monty's assurances.

"I've seen better," said Mirabelle coolly.

"I'll bet you have!" Joan stretched and yawned; then, opening one of the cupboards, took a shovelful of coal and threw it into the furnace, clanging the iron door. "That's my job," she said humorously, "to keep you warm."

"How long am I going to be kept here?"

"Five days," was the surprising answer.

"Why five?" asked Mirabelle curiously.

"I don't know. Maybe they'll tell you," said Joan.

She fixed a plug in the wall and turned on the small electric fire. Disappearing, she came back with a kettle which she placed on top of the ring.

"The view's not grand, but the food's good," she said, with a gaiety that Mirabelle was now sure was forced.

"You're with these people, of course—Dr. Oberzohn and Newton?"

"Mister Newton," corrected Joan. "Yes, I'm his fiancée. We're going to be married when things get a little better," she said vaguely, "and there's no use in your getting sore with me because I helped to bring you here. Monty's told me all about it. They're going to do you no harm at all."

"Then why——" began Mirabelle.

"He'll tell you," interrupted Joan, "sooner or later. The old man, or—or— well, Monty isn't in this: he's only obliging Oberzohn."

With one thing Mirabelle agreed: it was a waste of time to indulge in recriminations or to reproach the girl for her supreme treachery. After all, Joan owed nothing to her, and had been from the first a tool employed for her detention. It would have been as logical for a convict to reproach the prison guard.

"How do you come to be doing this sort of thing?" she asked, watching the girl making tea.

"Where do you get 'this sort of thing' from?" demanded Joan. "If you suppose that I spend my life chaperoning females, you've got another guess coming. Scared, aren't you?"

She looked across at Mirabelle and the girl shook her head.

"Not really."

"I should be," confessed Joan. "Do you mind condensed milk? There's no other. Yes, I should be writhing under the table, knowing something about Oberzohn."

"If I were Oberzohn," said Mirabelle with spirit, "I should be hiding in a deep hole where the Four Just Men would not find me."

"Four Just Men!" sneered the girl, and then her face changed. "Were they the people who whipped Gurther?"

Mirabelle had not heard of this exploit, but she gave them credit with a nod.

"Is that so? Does Gurther know they're friends of yours?" she asked significantly.

"I don't know Gurther."

"He's the man who danced with you the other night—Lord—I forget what name we gave him. Because, if he does know, my dear," she said slowly, "you've got two people to be extremely careful with. Gurther's half mad. Monty has always said so. He dopes too, and there are times when he's not a man at all but a low-down wolf. I'm scared of *him*—I'll admit it. There aren't Four Just Men, anyway," she went off at a tangent. "There haven't been more than three for years. One of them was killed in Bordeaux. That's a town I'd hate to be killed in," said Joan irreverently.

An interval of silence followed whilst she opened an air-tight tin and took out a small cake, and, putting it on the table, cut it into slices.

"What are they like?" she asked.

Evidently the interval had been filled with thoughts of the men from Curzon Street.

"Monty says they're just bluff, but I'm not so sure that Monty tells me all he thinks. He's so scared that he told me to call and see them, just because they gave him an order—which isn't like Monty. They've killed people, haven't they?"

Mirabelle nodded.

"And got away with it? They must be clever." Joan's admiration was dragged from her. "Where do they get their money?"

That was always an interesting matter to Joan.

When the girl explained, she was really impressed. That they could kill and get away with it, was wonderful; that they were men of millions, placed them in a category apart.

"They'll never find you here," said Joan. "There's nobody living knows about this vault. There used to be eight men working here, sorting monkey hides, and every one of them's dead. Monty told me. He said this place is below the canal level, and Oberzohn can flood it in five minutes. Monty thinks the old man had an idea of running a slush factory here."

"What is a slush factory?" asked Mirabelle, open-mouthed.

"Phoney—snide—counterfeit. Not English, but Continental work. He was going to do that if things had gone really bad, but of course you make all the difference."

Mirabelle put down her cup.

"Does he expect to make money out of me?" she said, trying hard not to laugh.

The girl nodded solemnly.

"Does he think I have a great deal of money?"

"He's sure."

Joan was sure too. Her tone said that plainly enough.

Mirabelle sat down on the bed, for the moment too astonished to speak. Her own financial position was no mystery. She had been left sufficient to bring her in a small sum yearly, and with the produce of the farm had managed to make both ends meet. It was the failure of the farm as a source of profit which had brought her to her new job in London. Alma had also a small annuity; the farm was the girl's property, but beyond these revenues she had nothing. There was not even a possibility that she was an heiress. Her father had been a comparatively poor man, and had been supported in his numerous excursions to various parts of the world in search of knowledge by the scientific societies to which he was attached; his literary earnings were negligible; his books enjoyed only a very limited sale. She could trace her ancestry back for seven generations; knew of her uncles and aunts, and they did not include a single man or woman who, in the best traditions of the story-books, had gone to America and made an immense fortune.

"It is absurd," she said. "I have no money. If Mr. Oberzohn puts me up to ransom, it will have to be something under a hundred!"

"Put you up to ransom?" said Joan. "I don't get you there. But you're rich all right—I can tell you that. Monty says so, and Monty wouldn't lie to me."

Mirabelle was bewildered. It seemed almost impossible that a man of Oberzohn's intelligence and sources of information could make such a mistake. And yet Joan was earnest.

"They must have mistaken me for somebody else," she said, but Joan did not answer. She was sitting up in a listening attitude, and her eyes were directed towards the iron door which separated their sleeping apartment from the larger vault. She had heard the creak of the trap turning and the sound of feet coming down the stairs.

Mirabelle rose as Oberzohn came in. He wore his black dressing-gown, his smoking-cap was at the back of his head, and the muddy Wellington boots which he had pulled over his feet looked incongruous, and would at any other time have provoked her to laughter.

He favoured her with a stiff nod.

"You have slept well, gracious lady?" he said, and to her amazement took her cold hand in his and kissed it.

She felt the same feeling of revulsion and unreality as had overcome her that night at the dance when Gurther had similarly saluted her.

"It is a nice place, for young people and for old." He looked round the apartment with satisfaction. "Here I should be content to spend my life reading my books, and giving my mind to thought, but"—he spread his hands and shrugged—"what would you? I am a business man, with immense interests in every part of the world. I am rich, too, beyond your dreams! I have stores in every part of the world, and thousands of men and women on my pay-roll."

Why was he telling her all this, she wondered, reciting the facts in a monotonous voice. Surely he had not come down to emphasize the soundness of his financial position?

"I am not very much interested in your business, Mr. Oberzohn," she said, "but I want to know why I am being detained here. Surely, if you're so rich, you do not want to hold me to ransom?"

"To ransom?" His forehead went up and down. "That is foolish talk. Did she tell you?" He pointed at the girl, and his face went as black as thunder.

"No, I guessed," said Mirabelle quickly, not wishing to get her companion into bad odour.

"I do not hold you to ransom. I hold you, lovely lady, because you are good for my eyes. Did not Heine say, 'The beauty of women is a sedative to the soul'? You should read Heine: he is frivolous, but in his stupidity there are many clever thoughts. Now tell me, lovely lady, have you all you desire?"

"I want to go out," she said. "I can't stay in this underground room without danger to my health."

"Soon you shall go." He bowed stiffly again, and shuffled across the floor to the furnace. Behind this were the two baize-covered boxes, and one he lifted tenderly. "Here are secrets such as you should not pry into," he said in his awkward English. "The most potent of chemicals, colossal in power. The ignorant would touch them and they would explode—you understand?"

He addressed Mirabelle, who did not understand but made no answer.

"They must be kept warm for that reason. One I take, the other I leave. You shall not touch it—that is understood? My good friend has told you?" He brought his eyes to Joan.

"I understand all right," she said. "Listen, Oberzohn: when am I going out for a walk? This place is getting on my nerves already."

"To-night you shall have exercise with the lovely lady. I myself will accompany you."

"Why am I here, Mr. Oberzohn?" Mirabelle asked again.

"You are here because you are in danger," said Oberzohn, holding the green box under his arm. "You are in very great danger." He nodded with every word. "There are certain men, of all the most infamous, who have a design upon your life. They are criminal, cunning and wise—but not so cunning or wise as Dr. Oberzohn. Because I will not let you fall into their hands I keep you here, young miss. Good morning."

Again he bowed stiffly and went out, the iron door clanging behind him. They heard him climbing the stairs, the thud of the trap as it fell, and the rumble which Joan, at any rate, knew was made by the cement barrel being rolled to the top of the trap.

"Pleasant little fellow, isn't he?" said Joan bitterly. "Him and his chemicals!" She glared down at the remaining box. "If I were sure it wouldn't explode, I should smash it to smithereens!" she said.

Later she told the prisoner of Oberzohn's obsession; of how he spent time and money in his search for the vital elixir.

"Monty thinks he'll find it," she said seriously. "Do you know, that old man has had an ox stewed down to a pint? There used to be a king in Europe—I forget his name—who had the same stuff, but not so strong. Monty says that Oberzohn hardly ever takes a meal—just a teaspoonful of this dope and he's right for the day. And Monty says . . ."

For the rest of that dreary morning the girl listened without hearing to the wise sayings and clever acts of Monty; and every now and again her eyes strayed to the baize-covered box which contained "the most potent chemicals," and she wondered whether, in the direst extremity, she would be justified in employing these dread forces for her soul's salvation.

# Chapter XXIII                    The Courier

ELIJAH WASHINGTON came up to London for a consultation. With the exception of a blue contusion beneath his right eye, he was none the worse for his alarming experience.

Leon Gonsalez had driven him to town, and on the way up the big man had expressed views about snake-bite which were immensely interesting to the man at the wheel.

"I've figured it out this way: there is no snake at all. What happens is that these guys have extracted snake venom—and that's easy, by making a poison-snake bite on something soft—and have poisoned a dart or a burr with the venom. I've seen that done in Africa, particularly up in the Ituri country, and it's pretty common in South America. The fellow just throws or shoots it, and just where the dart hits, he gets snake-poisoning right away."

"That is an excellent theory," said Leon, "only—no dart or burr has ever been found. It is the first thing the police looked for in the case of the stockbroker. They had the ground searched for days. And it was just the same in the case of the tramp and the bank clerk, just the same in the case of Barberton. A dart would stick some time and would be found in the man's clothing or near the spot where he was struck down. How do you account for that?"

Mr. Washington very frankly admitted that he couldn't account for it at all, and Leon chuckled.

"*I* can," he said. "In fact, I know just how it's done."

"Great snakes!" gasped Washington in amazement. "Then why don't you tell the police?"

"The police know—now," said Leon. "It isn't snake-bite—it is nicotine poisoning."

"How's that?" asked the startled man, but Leon had his joke to himself.

After a consultation which had lasted most of the night they had brought Washington from Rath Hall, and on the way Leon hinted gently that the Three had a mission for him and hoped he would accept.

"You're much too good a fellow to be put into an unnecessarily dangerous position," he said; "and even if you weren't, we wouldn't lightly risk your blessed life; but the job we should ask you to do isn't exactly a picnic."

"Listen!" said Mr. Washington with sudden energy. "I don't want any more snakes—not that kind of snake! I've felt pain in my time, but nothing like this! I know it must have been snake venom, but I'd like to meet the little wriggler who brews the brand that was handed to me, and maybe I'd change my mind about collecting him—alive!"

Leon agreed silently, and for the next few moments was avoiding a street car on one side, a baker's cart on another, and a *blah* woman who was walking aimlessly in the road, apparently with no other intention than of courting an early death, this being the way of *blah* women.

"Phew!" said Mr. Washington, as the car skidded on the greasy road. "I don't know whether you're a good driver or just naturally under the protection of Providence."

"Both," said Leon, when he had straightened the machine. "All good drivers are that."

Presently he continued:

"It is snake venom all right, Mr. Washington; only snake venom that has been most carefully treated by a man who knows the art of concentration of its bad and the extraction of its harmless constituents. My theory is that certain alkaloids are added, and it is possible that there has been a blending of two different kinds of poison. But you're right when you say that no one animal carries in his poison sac that particular variety of death-juice. If it is any value to you, we are prepared to give you a snake-proof certificate!"

"I don't want another experience of that kind," Elijah Washington warned him; but Leon turned the conversation to the state of the road and the problems of traffic control.

There had been nothing seen or heard of Mirabelle, and Meadows' activities had for the moment been directed to the forthcoming inquest on Barberton. Nowadays, whenever he reached Scotland Yard, he moved in a crowd of reporters, all anxious for news of further developments. The Barberton death was still the livliest topic in the newspapers: the old scare of the snake had been revived and in some degree intensified. There was not a journal which did not carry columns of letters to the editor denouncing the inactivity of the police. Were they, asked one sarcastic correspondent, under the hypnotic influence of the snake's eyes? Could they not, demanded another, give up trapping speeders on the Lingfield road and bring their mighty brains to the elucidation of a mystery that was to cause every household in London the gravest concern? The Barberton murder was the peg on which every letter-writing faddist had a novel view to hang, and Mr. Meadows was not at that time the happiest officer in the force.

"Where is Lee?" asked Washington as they came into Curzon Street.

"He's in town for the moment, but we are moving him to the North of England, though I don't think there is any danger to him, now that Barberton's letters are in our possession. They would have killed him yesterday to prevent our handling the correspondence. To-day I should imagine he has no special importance in the eyes of Oberzohn and Company. And here we are!"

Mr. Washington got out stiffly and was immediately admitted by the butler. The three men went upstairs to where George Manfred was wrestling with a phase of the problem. He was not alone; Digby, his head swathed in bandages, sat, an unhappy man, on the edge of a chair and answered Leon's cheery greeting with a mournful smile.

"I'm sending Digby to keep observation on Oberzohn's house; and especially do I wish him to search that old boat of his."

He was referring to an ancient barge which lay on the mud at the bottom of Mr. Oberzohn's private dock. From the canal there was a narrow waterway into the little factory grounds. It was so long since the small cantilever bridge which covered the entrance had been raised, that locals regarded the bridge floor as part of the normal bank of the canal. But behind the green water-gates was a concrete dock large enough to hold one barge, and here for years a decrepit vessel had wallowed, the hunting-ground of rats and the sleeping-place of the desperately homeless.

"The barge is practically immovable: I've already reported on that," said Leon.

"It certainly has that appearance, and yet I would like a search," replied Manfred. "You understand that this is night duty, and I have asked Meadows to notify the local inspector that you will be on duty—I don't want to be pulled out of my bed to identify you at the Peckham police station. It isn't a cheerful job, but you might be able to make it interesting by finding your way into his grounds. I don't think the factory will yield much, but the house will certainly be a profitable study to an observer of human nature."

"I hope I do better this time, Mr. Manfred," said Digby, turning to go. "And, if you don't mind, I'll go by day and take a look at the place. I don't want to fall down this time!"

George smiled as he rose and shook the man's hand at parting.

"Even Mr. Gonsalez makes mistakes," he said maliciously, and Leon looked hurt.

Manfred tidied some papers on his desk and put them into a drawer, waiting for Poiccart's return. When he had come:

"Now, Mr. Washington, we will tell you what we wish you to do. We wish you to take a letter to Lisbon. Leon has probably hinted something to that effect, and it is now my duty to tell you that the errand is pretty certain to be an exceedingly dangerous one, but you are the only man I know to whom I could entrust this important document. I feel I cannot allow you to undertake this mission without telling you that the chances are heavily against your reaching Portugal."

"Bless you for those cheerful words," said Washington blankly. "The only thing I want to be certain about is, am I likely to meet Mr. Snake?"

Manfred nodded, and the American's face lengthened.

"I don't know that even that scares me," he said at last, "especially now that I know that the dope they use isn't honest snake-spit at all but a synthesized poison. It was having my confidence shaken in snakes that rattled me. When do you want me to go?"

"To-night."

Mr. Washington for the moment was perplexed, and Manfred continued:

"Not by the Dover-Calais route. We would prefer that you travelled by Newhaven-Dieppe. Our friends are less liable to be on the alert, though I can't even guarantee that. Oberzohn spends a lot of money in espionage. This house has been under observation for days. I will show you."

He walked to the window and drew aside the curtain.

"Do you see a spy?" he asked, with a twinkle in his eye.

Mr. Washington looked up and down the street.

"Sure!" he said. "That man at the corner smoking a cigar———"

"Is a detective officer from Scotland Yard," said Manfred. "Do you see anybody else?"

"Yes," said Washington after a while, "there's a man cleaning windows on the opposite side of the road: he keeps looking across here."

"A perfectly innocent citizen," said Manfred.

"Well, he can't be in any of those taxis, because they're empty." Mr. Washington nodded to a line of taxis drawn up on the rank in the centre of the road.

"On the contrary, he is in the first taxi on the rank—he is the driver! If you went out and called a cab, he would come to you. If anybody else called him, he would be engaged. His name is Clarke, he lives at 43, Portlington Mews; he is an ex-convict living apart from his wife, and he receives seven pounds a week for his services, ten pounds every time he drives Oberzohn's car, and all the money he makes out of his cab."

He smiled at the other's astonishment.

"So the chances are that your movements will be known; even though you do not call the cab, he will follow you. You must be prepared for that. I'm putting all my cards on the table, Mr. Washington, and asking you to do something which, if you cannot bring yourself to agree, must be done by either myself, Poiccart or Gonsalez. Frankly, none of us can be spared."

"I'll go," said the American. "Snake or no snake, I'm for Lisbon. What is my route?"

Poiccart took a folded paper from his pocket.

"Newhaven, Dieppe, Paris. You have a reserved compartment on the Sud Express; you reach Valladolid late to-morrow night, and change to the Portuguese mail. Unless I can fix an aeroplane to meet you at Irun. We are trying now. Otherwise, you should be in Lisbon at two o'clock on the following afternoon. He had better take the letter now, George."

Manfred unlocked the wall safe and took out a long envelope. It was addressed to "Senhor Alvaz Manuel y Cintra, Minister of Colonies," and was heavily sealed.

"I want you to place this in Senhor Cintra's hands. You'll have no difficulty there because you will be expected," he said. "Will you travel in that suit?"

The American thought.

"Yes, that's as good as any," he said.

"Will you take off your jacket?"

Mr. Washington obeyed, and with a small pair of scissors Manfred cut a slit in the lining and slipped the letter in. Then, to the American's astonishment, Leon produced a rolled housewife, threaded a needle with extraordinary dexterity, and for the next five minutes the snake-hunter watched the deft fingers stitching through paper and lining. So skilfully was the slit sewed that Elijah Washington had to look twice to make sure where the lining had been cut.

"Well, that beats the band!" he said. "Mr. Gonsalez, I'll send you my shirts for repair!"

"And here is something for you to carry." It was a black leather portfolio, well worn. To one end was attached a steel chain terminating in a leather belt. "I want you to put this round your waist, and from now on to carry this wallet. It contains nothing more important than a few envelopes imposingly sealed, and if you lose it no great harm will come."

"You think they'll go for the wallet?"

Manfred nodded.

"One cannot tell, of course, what Oberzohn will do, and he's as wily as one of his snakes. But my experience has been," he said, "that the cleverer the criminal, the bigger the fool and the more outrageous his mistakes. You will want money."

"Well, I'm not short of that," said the other with a smile. "Snakes are a mighty profitable proposition. Still, I'm a business man . . ."

For the next five minutes they discussed financial details, and he was more than surprised to discover the recklessness with which money was disbursed.

He went out, with a glance from the corner of his eye at the taximan, whose hand was raised inquiringly, but, ignoring the driver, he turned and walked towards Regent Street, and presently found a wandering taxi of an innocuous character, and ordered the man to drive to the Ritz-Carlton, where rooms had been taken for him.

He was in Regent Street before he looked round through the peep-hole, and, as Manfred had promised him, the taxi was following, its flag down to prevent chance hiring. Mr. Washington went up to his room, opened the window and looked out: the taxi had joined a near-by rank. The driver had left his box.

"He's on the 'phone," muttered Mr. Washington, and would have given a lot of money to have known the nature of the message.

# Chapter XXIV                           On the Night Mail

A MAN of habit, Mr. Oberzohn missed his daily journey to the City Road. In ordinary circumstances the loss would have been a paralysing one, but of late he had grown more and more wedded to his deep arm-chair and his ponderous volumes; and though the City Road had been a very useful establishment in many ways, and was ill replaced by the temporary building which his manager had secured, he felt he could almost dispense with that branch of his business altogether.

Oberzohn & Smitts was an institution which had grown out of nothing. The energy of the partners, and especially the knowledge of African trading conditions which the departed Smitts possessed, had produced a flourishing business which ten years before could have been floated for half a million pounds.

Orders still came in. There were up-country stores to be restocked; new, if unimportant, contracts to be fulfilled; there was even a tentative offer under consideration from one of the South American States for the armaments of a political faction. But Mr. Oberzohn was content to mark time, in the faith that the next week would see him superior to these minor considerations, and in a position, if he so wished, to liquidate his business and sell his stores and his trade. There were purchasers ready, but the half a million pounds had dwindled to a tenth of that sum, which outstanding bills would more than absorb. As Manfred had said, his running expenses were enormous. He had agents in every central Government office in Europe, and though they did not earn their salt, they certainly drew more than condiment for their services.

He had spent a busy morning in his little workshop-laboratory, and had settled himself down in his chair, when a telegraph messenger came trundling his bicycle across the rough ground, stopped to admire for a second the iron dogs which littered the untidy strip of lawn, and woke the echoes of this gaunt house with a thunderous knock. Mr. Oberzohn hurried to the door. A telegram to this address must necessarily be important. He took the telegram, slammed the door in the messenger's face and hurried back to his room, tearing open the envelope as he went.

There were three sheets of misspelt writing, for the wire was in Portuguese and telegraph operators are bad guessers. He read it through carefully, his lips moving silently, until he came to the end, then he started reading all over again, and, for a better understanding of its purport, he took a pencil and paper and translated the message into Swedish. He laid the telegram face downwards on the table and took up his book, but he was not reading. His busy mind slipped from Lisbon to London, from Curzon Street to the factory, and at last he shut his book with a bang, got up, and opening the door, barked Gurther's name. That strange man came downstairs in his stockinged feet, his hair hanging over his eyes, an unpleasant sight. Dr. Oberzohn pointed to the room and the man entered.

For an hour they talked behind locked doors, and then Gurther came out, still showing his teeth in a mechanical smile, and went up the stairs two at a time. The half-witted Danish maid, passing the door of the doctor's room, heard his gruff voice booming into the telephone, but since he spoke a language which, whilst it had some relation to her own, was subtly different, she could not have heard the instructions, admonitions, orders and suggestions which he fired in half a dozen different directions, even if she had heard him clearly.

This done, Dr. Oberzohn returned to his book and a midday refreshment, spooning his lunch from a small cup at his side containing a few fluid ounces of dark red liquid. One half of his mind was pursuing his well-read philosophers; the other worked at feverish speed, conjecturing and guessing, forestalling and baffling the minds that were working against him. He played a game of mental chess, all the time seeking for a check, and when at last he had discovered one that was adequate, he put down his book and went out into his garden, strolling up and down inside the wire fence, stopping now and again to pick a flower from a weed, or pausing to examine a rain-filled pothole as though it were the star object in a prize landscape.

He loved this ugly house, knew every brick of it, as a feudal lord might have known the castle he had built, the turret, the flat roof with its high parapet, that commanded a view of the canal bank on the one side and the railway arches left and right. They were railway arches which had a value to him. Most of them were blocked up, having been converted into lock-up garages and sheds, and through only a few could ingress be had. One, under which ran the muddy lane—why it was called Hangman's Lane nobody knew; another that gave to some allotments on the edge of his property; and a third through which he also could see daylight, but which spanned no road at all.

An express train roared past in a cloud of steam, and he scanned the viaduct with benignant interest. And then he performed his daily tour of inspection. Turning back into the house, he climbed the stairs to the third floor, opened a little door that revealed an extra flight of steps, and emerged on to the roof. At each corner was a square black shed, about the height of a man's chest. The doors were heavily padlocked, and near by each was a stout black box, equally weatherproof. There were other things here: great, clumsy wall-plugs at regular intervals. Seeing them, it might be thought that Mr. Oberzohn contemplated a night when, in the exultation of achievement, he would illuminate his ungainly premises. But up till now that night had not arrived, and in truth the only light usable was one which at the moment was dismantled in the larger of the four sheds.

From here he could look down upon the water cutting into the factory grounds; and the black bulk of the barge, which filled the entire width of the wharf, seemed so near that he could have thrown a stone upon it. His idle interest was in the sluggish black water that oozed through the gates. A slight mist lay upon the canal; a barge was passing down towards Deptford, and he contemplated the straining horse that tugged the barge rope with a mind set upon the time when he, too, might use the waterway in a swifter craft.

London lay around him, its spires and chimneys looming through the thin haze of smoke. Far away the sun caught the golden ball of St. Paul's and added a new star to the firmament. Mr. Oberzohn hated London—only this little patch of his had beauty in his eyes. Not the broad green parks and the flowering rhododendrons; not the majestic aisles of pleasure where the rich lounger rode or walked, nor the streets of stone-fronted stores, nor the pleasant green of suburban roads—he loved only these God-forgotten acres, this slimy wilderness in which he had set up his habitation.

He went downstairs, locking the roof door behind him, and, passing Gurther's room, knocked and was asked to enter. The man sat in his singlet; he had shaved once, but now the keen razor was going across his skin for the second time. He turned his face, shining with cream, and grinned round at the intruder, and with a grunt the doctor shut the door and went downstairs, knowing that the man was for the moment happy; for nothing pleased Gurther quite so much as "dressing up."

The doctor stood at the entrance of his own room, hesitating between books and laboratory, decided upon the latter, and was busy for the next two hours. Only once he came out, and that was to bring from the warm room the green baize box which contained "the most potent of chemicals, colossal in power."

---

The Newhaven-Dieppe route is spasmodically popular. There are nights when the trains to Paris are crowded; other nights when it is possible to obtain a carriage to yourself; and it happened that this evening, when Elijah Washington booked his seat, he might, if it had been physically possible, have sat in one compartment and put his feet on the seat in another.

Between the two great branches of the Anglo-Saxon race there is one notable difference. The Englishman prefers to travel in solitude and silence. His ideal journey is one from London to Constantinople in a compartment that is not invaded except by the ticket collector; and if it is humanly possible that he can reach his destination without having given utterance to anything more sensational than an agreement with some other passenger's comment on the weather, he is indeed a happy man. The American loves company; he has the acquisitiveness of the Latin, combined with the rhetorical virtues of the Teuton. Solitude makes him miserable; silence irritates him. He wants to talk about large and important things, such as the future of the country, the prospects of agriculture and the fluctuations of trade, about which the average Englishman knows nothing, and is less interested. The American has a town pride, can talk almost emotionally about a new drainage system and grow eloquent upon a municipal balance sheet. The Englishman does not cultivate his town pride until he reaches middle age, and then only in sufficient quantities to feel disappointed with the place of his birth after he has renewed its acquaintance.

Mr. Washington found himself in an empty compartment, and, grunting his dissatisfaction, walked along the corridor, peeping into one cell after another in the hope of discovering a fellow-countryman in a similar unhappy plight. His search was fruitless and he returned to the carriage in which his bag and overcoat were deposited, and settled down to the study of an English humorous newspaper and a vain search for something at which any intelligent man could laugh.

The doors of the coach were at either end, and most passengers entering had to pass the open entrance of Mr. Washington's compartment. At every click of the door he looked up, hoping to find a congenial soul. But disappointment awaited him, until a lady hesitated by the door. It was a smoking carriage, but Washington, who was a man of gallant character, would gladly have sacrificed his cigar for the pleasure of her society. Young, he guessed, and a widow. She was in black, an attractive face showed through a heavy veil.

"Is this compartment engaged?" she asked in a low voice that was almost a whisper.

"No, madam." Washington rose, hat in hand.

"Would you mind?" she asked in a soft voice.

"Why, surely! Sit down, ma'am," said the gallant American. "Would you like the corner seat by the window?"

She shook her head, and sat down near the door, turning her face from him.

"Do you mind my smoking?" asked Washington, after a while.

"Please smoke," she said, and again turned her face away.

"English," thought Mr. Washington in disgust, and hunched himself for an hour and a half of unrelieved silence.

A whistle blew, the train moved slowly from the platform, and Elijah Washington's adventurous journey had begun.

They were passing through Croydon when the girl rose, and, leaning out, closed the little glass-panelled door.

"You should let me do that," said Elijah reproachfully, and she murmured something about not wishing to trouble him, and he relapsed into his seat.

One or two of the men who passed looked in, and evidently this annoyed her, for she reached and pulled down the spring blind which partially hid her from outside observation, and after the ticket collector had been and had punched the slips, she lowered the second of the three blinds.

"Do you mind?" she asked.

"Sure not, ma'am," said Elijah, without any great heartiness. He had no desire to travel alone with a lady in a carriage so discreetly curtained. He had heard of cases . . . and by nature he was an extremely cautious man.

The speed of the train increased; the wandering passengers had settled down. The second of the ticket inspections came as they were rushing through Redhill, and Mr. Washington thought uncomfortably that there was a significant look in the inspector's face as he glanced first at the drawn blinds, then from the lady to himself.

She affected a perfume of a peculiarly pleasing kind. The carriage was filled with this subtle fragrance. Mr. Washington smelt it above the scent of his cigar. Her face was still averted; he wondered if she had gone to sleep, and, growing weary of his search for humour, he put down the paper, folded his hands and closed his eyes, and found himself gently drifting to that medley of the real and unreal which is the overture of dreams.

The lady moved; he looked at her out of the corner of his half-closed eyes. She had moved round so as to half face him. Her veil was still down, her white gloves were reflectively clasped on her knees. He shut his eyes again, until another movement brought him awake. She was feeling in her bag.

Mr. Washington was awake now—as wide awake as he had ever been in his life. In stretching out her hand, the lady had pulled short her sleeve, and there was a gap of flesh between the glove and the wrist of her blouse, and on her wrist was hair!

He shifted his position slightly, grunted as in his sleep, and dropped his hand to his pocket, and all the time those cold eyes were watching him through the veil.

Lifting the bottom of the veil, she put the ebony holder between her teeth and searched the bag for a match. Then she turned appealingly to him as though she had sensed his wakefulness. As she rose, Washington rose too, and suddenly he sprang at her and flung her back against the door. For a moment the veiled lady was taken by surprise, and then there was a flash of steel.

From nowhere a knife had come into her hand and Washington gripped the wrist and levered it over, pushing the palm of his hand under the chin. Even through the veil he could feel the bristles, and knew now, if he had not known before, that he had to deal with a man. A live, active man, rendered doubly strong by the knowledge of his danger. Gurther butted forward with his head, but Washington saw the attack coming, shortened his arm and jabbed full at the face behind the veil. The blow stopped the man, only for an instant, and again he came on, and this time the point of the knife caught the American's shoulder, and ripped the coat to the elbow. It needed this to bring forth Elijah Washington's mental and physical reserves. With a roar he gripped the throat of his assailant and threw him with such violence against the door that it gave, and the "widow in mourning" crashed against the panel of the outer corridor. Before he could reach the attacker, Gurther had turned and sped along the corridor to the door of the coach. In a second he had flung it open and had dropped to the footboard. The train was slowing to take Horsham Junction, and the cat eyes waited until he saw a good fall, and let go. Staring back into the darkness, Washington saw nothing, and then the train inspector came along.

"It was a man in woman's clothes," he said, a little breathlessly, and they went back to search the compartment, but Mr. Gurther had taken bag and everything with him, and the only souvenir of his presence was the heel of a shoe that had been torn off in the struggle.

# Chapter XXV　　　　　　　　Gurther Returns

THE train was going at thirty miles an hour when Gurther dropped on to a ridge of sand by the side of the track, and in the next second he was sliding forward on his face. Fortunately for him the veil, though torn, kept his eyes free. Stumbling to his feet, he looked round. The level-crossing gates should be somewhere here. He had intended jumping the train at this point, and Oberzohn had made arrangements accordingly. A signalman, perched high above the track, saw the figure and challenged.

"I've lost my way," said Gurther. "Where is the level-crossing?"

"A hundred yards farther on. Keep clear of those metals—the Eastbourne express is coming behind."

If Gurther had had his way, he would have stopped long enough to remove a rail for the sheer joy of watching a few hundred of the hated people plunged to destruction. But he guessed that the car was waiting, went sideways through the safety gates into a road which was fairly populous. There were people about who turned their heads and looked in amazement at the bedraggled woman in black, but he had got beyond worrying about his appearance.

He saw the car with the little green light which Oberzohn invariably used to mark his machines from others, and, climbing into the cab (as it was), sat down to recover his breath. The driver he knew as one of the three men employed by Oberzohn, one of whom Mr. Washington had seen that morning.

The journey back to town was a long one, though the machine, for a public vehicle, was faster than most. Gurther welcomed the ride. Once more he had failed, and he reasoned that this last failure was the most serious of all. The question of Oberzohn's displeasure did not really arise. He had travelled far beyond the point when the Swede's disapproval meant very much to him. But there might be a consequence more serious than any. He knew well with what instructions Pfeiffer had been primed on the night of the attack at Rath House—only Gurther had been quicker, and his snake had bitten first. Dr. Oberzohn had no illusions as to what had happened, and if he had tactfully refrained from making reference to the matter, he had his purpose and reasons. And this night journey with Elijah Washington was one of them.

There was no excuse; he had none to offer. His hand wandered beneath the dress to the long knife that was strapped to his side, and the touch of the worn handle was very reassuring. For the time being he was safe; until another man was found to take Pfeiffer's place Oberzohn was working single-handed and could not afford to dispense with the services of this, the last of his assassins.

It was past eleven when he dismissed the taxi at the end of the long lane, and, following the only safe path, came to the unpainted door that gave admission to Oberzohn's property. And the first words of his master told him that there was no necessity for explanation.

"So you did not get him, Gurther?"

"No, Herr Doktor."

"I should not have sent you." Oberzohn's voice was extraordinarily mild in all the circumstances. "That man you cannot kill—with the snake. I have learned since you went that he was bitten at the blind man's house, yet lives! That is extraordinary. I would give a lot of money to test his blood. You tried the knife?"

"Ja, Herr Doktor." He lifted his veil, stripped off hat and wig in one motion. The rouged and powdered face was bruised; from under the brown wig was a trickle of dried blood.

"Good! You have done as well as you could. Go to your room, Gurther—march!"

Gurther went upstairs and for a quarter of an hour was staring at his grinning face in the glass, as with cream and soiled towel he removed his make-up.

Oberzohn's very gentleness was a menace. What did it portend? Until that evening neither Gurther nor his dead companion had been taken into the confidence of the two men who directed their activities. He knew there were certain papers to be recovered; he knew there were men to be killed; but what value were the papers, or why death should be directed to this unfortunate or that, he neither knew nor cared. His duty had been to obey, and he had served a liberal paymaster well and loyally. That girl in the underground room? Gurther had many natural explanations for her imprisonment. And yet none of them fitted the conditions. His cogitations were wasted time. That night, for the first time, the doctor took him into his confidence.

He had finished dressing and was on his way to his kitchen when the doctor stood at the doorway and called him in.

"Sit down, Gurther." He was almost kind. "You will have a cigar? These are excellent."

He threw a long, thin, black cheroot, and Gurther caught it between his teeth and seemed absurdly pleased with his trick.

"The time has come when you must know something, Gurther," said the doctor. He took a fellow to the weed the man was smoking, and puffed huge clouds of rank smoke into the room. "I have for a friend—who? Heir Newton?" He shrugged his shoulders. "He is a very charming man, but he has no brains. He is the kind of man, Gurther, who would live in comfort, take all we gave him by our cleverness and industry, and never say thank you! And in trouble what will he do, Gurther? He will go to the police—yes, my dear friend, he will go to the police!"

He nodded. Gurther had heard the same story that night when he had crept soft-footed to the door and had heard the doctor discuss certain matters with the late Mr. Pfeiffer.

"He would, without a wink of his eyelash, without a snap of his hand, send you and me to death, and would read about our execution with a smile, and then go forth and eat his plum-pudding and roast beef! That is our friend Heir Newton! You have seen this with your own eyes?"

"*Ja, Herr Doktor!*" exclaimed the obedient Gurther.

"He is a danger for many reasons," Oberzohn proceeded deliberately. "Because of these three men who have so infamously set themselves out to ruin me, who burnt down my house, and who whipped you, Gurther—they tied you up to a post and whipped you with a whip of nine tails. You have not forgotten, Gurther?"

"*Nein, Herr Doktor.*" Indeed, Gurther had not forgotten, though the vacant smirk on his face might suggest that he had a pleasant memory of the happening.

"A fool in an organization," continued the doctor oracularly, "is like a bad plate on a ship, or a weak link in a chain. Let it snap, and what happens? You and I die, my dear Gurther. We go up before a stupid man in a white wig and a red cloak, and he hands us to another man who puts a rope around our necks, drops us through a hole in the ground—all because we have a stupid man like Herr Montague Newton to deal with."

"*Ja, Herr Doktor,*" said Gurther as his master stopped. He felt that this comment was required of him.

"Now, I will tell you the whole truth." The doctor carefully knocked off the ash of his cigar into the saucer of his cup. "There is a fortune for you and for me, and this girl that we have in the quiet place can give it to us. I can marry her, or I can wipe her out, so! If I marry her, it would be better, I think, and this I have arranged."

And then, in his own way, he told the story of the hill of gold, concealing nothing, reserving nothing—all that he knew, all that Villa had told him.

"For three-four days now she must be here. At the end of that time nothing matters. The letter to Lisbon—of what value is it? I was foolish when I tried to stop it. She has made no nominee, she has no heirs, she has known nothing of her fortune, and therefore is in no position to claim the renewal of the concession."

"Herr Doktor, will you graciously permit me to speak?"

The doctor nodded.

"Does the Newton know this?"

"The Newton knows all this," said the doctor.

"Will you graciously permit me to speak again, Herr Doktor? What was this letter I was to have taken, had I not been overcome by misfortune?"

Oberzohn examined the ceiling.

"I have thought this matter from every angle," he said, "and I have decided thus. It was a letter written by Gonsalez to the Secretary or the Minister of the Colonies, asking that the renewal of the concession should be postponed. The telegram from my friend at the Colonial Office in Lisbon was to this effect." He fixed his glasses, fumbled in his waistcoat and took out the three-page telegram. "I will read it to you in your own language—

" 'Application has been received from Leon Gonsalez, asking His Excellency to receive a very special letter which arrives in two days. The telegram does not state the contents of the letter, but the Minister has given orders for the messenger to be received. The present Minister is not favourable to concessions granted to England or Englishmen.' "

He folded the paper.

"Which means that there will be no postponement, my dear Gurther, and this enormous fortune will be ours."

Gurther considered this point and for a moment forgot to smile, and looked what he was in consequence: a hungry, discontented wolf of a man.

"Herr Doktor, graciously permit me to ask you a question?"

"Ask," said Oberzohn magnanimously.

"What share does Herr Newton get? And if you so graciously honoured me with a portion of your so justly deserved gains, to what extent would be that share?"

The other considered this, puffing away until the room was a mist of smoke.

"Ten thousand English pounds," he said at last.

"Gracious and learned doctor, that is a very small proportion of many millions," said Gurther gently.

"Newton will receive one half," said the doctor, his face working nervously, "if he is alive. If misfortune came to him, that share would be yours, Gurther, my brave fellow! And with so much money a man would not be hunted. The rich and the noble would fawn upon him; he would have his lovely yacht and steam about the summer seas everlastingly, huh?"

Gurther rose and clicked his heels.

"Do you desire me again this evening?"

"No, no, Gurther." The old man shook his head. "And pray remember that there is another day to-morrow, and yet another day after. We shall wait and hear what our friend has to say. Good night, Gurther."

"Good night, Herr Doktor."

The doctor looked at the door for a long time after his man had gone and took up his book. He was deep in the chapter which was headed, in the German tongue: "The Subconscious Activity of the Human Intellect in Relation to the Esoteric Emotions." To Dr. Oberzohn this was more thrilling than the most exciting novel.

# Chapter XXVI                    In Captivity

THE second day of captivity dawned unseen, in a world that lay outside the brick roof and glazed white walls of Mirabelle Leicester's prison-house. She had grown in strength and courage, but not so her companion. Joan, who had started her weary vigil with an almost cheerful gaiety, had sunk deeper and deeper into depression as the hours progressed, and Mirabelle woke to the sound of a woman's sobs, to find the girl sitting on the side of her bed, her head in her wet hands.

"I hate this place!" she sobbed. "Why does he keep me here? God! If I thought the hound was double-crossing me . . . ! I'll go mad if they keep me here any longer. I will, Leicester!" she screamed.

"I'll make some tea," said Mirabelle, getting out of bed and finding her slippers.

The girl sat throughout the operation huddled in a miserable heap, and by and by her whimpering got on Mirabelle's nerves.

"I don't know why *you* should be wretched," she said. "They're not after *your* money!"

"You can laugh—and how you can, I don't know," sobbed the girl, as she took the cup in her shaking hands. "I know I'm a fool, but I've never been locked up—like this before. I didn't dream he'd break his word. He swore he'd come yesterday. What time is it?"

"Six o'clock," said Mirabelle.

It might as well have been eight or midday, for all she knew to the contrary.

"This is a filthy place," said the hysterical girl. "I think they're going to drown us all . . . or that thing will explode"—she pointed to the green baize box— "I know it! I feel it in my blood. That beast Gurther is here somewhere, ugh! He's like a slimy snake. Have you ever seen him?"

"Gurther? You mean the man who danced with me?"

"That's he. I keep telling you who he is," said Joan impatiently. "I wish we could get out of here."

She jumped up suddenly.

"Come and see if you can help me lift the trap."

Mirabelle knew it was useless before she set forth on the quest for freedom. Their united efforts failed to move the stone, and Joan was on the point of collapse when they came back to their sleeping-room.

"I hope Gurther doesn't know that those men are friends of yours," she said, when she became calmer.

"You told me that yesterday. Would that make any difference?"

"A whole lot," said Joan vehemently. "He's got the blood of a fish, that man! There's nothing he wouldn't do. Monty ought to be flogged for leaving us here at his mercy. I'm not scared of Oberzohn—he's old. But the other fellow dopes, and goes stark, staring mad at times. Monty told me one night that he was" she choked—"a killer. He said that these German criminals who kill people are never satisfied with one murder, they go on and on until they've got twenty or thirty! He says that the German prisons are filled with men who have the murder habit."

"He was probably trying to frighten you."

"Why should he?" said the girl, with unreasonable anger. "And leave him alone! Monty is the best in the world. I adore the ground he walks on!"

Very wisely, Mirabelle did not attempt to traverse this view.

It was only when her companion had these hysterical fits that fear was communicated to her. Her faith was completely and whole-heartedly centred on the three men—upon Gonsalez. She wondered how old he was. Sometimes he looked quite young, at others an elderly man. It was difficult to remember his face; he owed so much to his expression, the smile in his eyes, to the strange, boyish eagerness of gesture and action which accompanied his speech. She could not quite understand herself; why was she always thinking of Gonsalez, as a maid might think of a lover? She went red at the thought. He seemed so apart, so aloof from the ordinary influences of women. Suppose she had committed some great crime and had escaped the vigilance of the law, would he hunt her down in the same remorseless, eager way, planning to cut off every avenue of her escape until he shepherded her into a prison cell? It was a horrible thought, and she screwed up her eyes tight to blot out the mental picture she had made.

It would have given her no ordinary satisfaction to have known how often Gonsalez's thoughts strayed to the girl who had so strangely come into his life. He spent a portion of his time that morning in his bedroom, fixing to the wall a large railway map which took in the south of England and the greater part of the Continent. A red-ink line marked the route from London to Lisbon, and he was fixing a little green flag on the line just south of Paris when Manfred strolled into the room and surveyed his work.

"The Sud Express is about there," he said, pointing to the last of the green flags, "and I think our friend will have a fairly pleasant and uneventful journey as far as Valladolid—where I have arranged for Miguel Garcia, an old friend of mine, to pick him up and shadow him on the westward journey—unless we get the 'plane. I'm expecting a wire any minute. By the way, the Dieppe police have arrested the gentleman who tried to bump him overboard in mid-Channel, but the man who snatched at his portfolio at the Gare St. Lazare is still at liberty."

"He must be getting quite used to it now," said Manfred coolly, and laughed to himself.

Leon turned.

"He's a good fellow," he said with quick earnestness. "We couldn't have chosen a better man. The woman on the train, of course, was Gurther. He is the only criminal I've ever known who is really efficient at disguising himself."

Manfred lit his pipe; he had lately taken to this form of smoking.

"The case grows more and more difficult every day. Do you realize that?"

Leon nodded.

"And more dangerous," he said. "By the laws of average, Gurther should get one of us the next time he makes an attempt. Have you seen the papers?"

Manfred smiled.

"They're crying for Meadows' blood, poor fellow! Which shows the extraordinary inconsistency of the public. Meadows has only been in one snake case. They credit him with having fallen down on the lot."

"They seem to be in remarkable agreement that the snake deaths come into the category of wilful murder," said Gonsalez as they went down the stairs together.

Meadows had been talking to the reporters. Indeed, that was his chief offence from the view-point of the official mind. For the first article in the code of every well-constituted policeman is, "Thou shalt not communicate to the Press."

Leon strolled aimlessly about the room. He was wearing his chauffeur's uniform, and his hands were thrust into the breeches pockets. Manfred, recognizing the symptoms, rang the bell for Poiccart, and that quiet man came from the lower regions.

"Leon is going to be mysterious," said Manfred dryly.

"I'm not really," protested Leon, but he went red. It was one of his most charming peculiarities that he had never forgotten how to blush. "I was merely going to suggest that there's a play running in London that we ought to see. I didn't know that 'The Ringer' was a play until this morning, when I saw one of Oberzohn's more genteel clerks go into the theatre, and, being naturally of an inquisitive turn of mind, followed him. A play that interests Oberzohn will interest me, and should interest you, George," he said severely, "and certainly should interest Meadows—it is full of thrilling situations! It is about a criminal who escapes from Dartmoor and comes back to murder his betrayer. There is one scene which is played in the dark, that ought to thrill you—I've been looking up the reviews of the dramatic critics, and as they are unanimous that it is not an artistic success, and is, moreover, wildly improbable, it ought to be worth seeing. I always choose an artistic success when I am suffering from insomnia," he added cruelly.

"Oberzohn is entitled to his amusements, however vulgar they may be."

"But this play isn't vulgar," protested Leon, "except in so far as it is popular. I found it most difficult to buy a seat. Even actors go to see the audience act."

"What seat did he buy?"

"Box A," said Leon promptly, "and paid for it with real money. It is the end box on the prompt side—and before you ask me whence I gained my amazing knowledge of theatrical technique, I will answer that even a child in arms knows that the prompt side is the left-hand side facing the audience."

"For to-night?"

Leon nodded.

"I have three stalls," he said and produced them from his pocket. "If you cannot go, will you give them to the cook? She looks like a woman who would enjoy a good cry over the sufferings of the tortured heroine. The seats are in the front row, which means that you can get in and out between the acts without walking on other people's knees."

"Must I go?" asked Poiccart plaintively. "I do not like detective plays, and I hate mystery plays. I know who the real murderer is before the curtain has been up ten minutes, and that naturally spoils my evening."

"Could you not take a girl?" asked Leon outrageously. "Do you know any who would go?"

"Why not take Aunt Alma?" suggested Manfred, and Leon accepted the name joyously.

Aunt Alma had come to town at the suggestion of the Three, and had opened up the Doughty Court flat.

"And really she is a remarkable woman, and shows a steadiness and a courage in face of the terrible position of our poor little friend, which is altogether praiseworthy. I don't think Mirabelle Leicester is in any immediate danger. I think I've said that before. Oberzohn merely wishes to keep her until the period of renewal has expired. How he will escape the consequences of imprisoning her, I cannot guess. He may not attempt to escape them, may accept the term of imprisonment which will certainly be handed out to him, as part of the payment he must pay for his millions."

"Suppose he kills her?" asked Poiccart.

For a second Leon's face twitched.

"He won't kill her," he said quietly. "Why should he? We know that he has got her—the police know. She is a different proposition from Barberton, an unknown man killed nobody knew how, in a public place. No, I don't think we need cross that bridge, only . . ." He rubbed his hands together irritably. "However, we shall see. And in the meantime I'm placing a lot of faith in Digby, a shrewd man with a sense of his previous shortcomings. You were wise there, George."

He was looking at the street through the curtains.

"Tittlemouse is at his post, the faithful hound!" he said, nodding towards the solitary taxicab that stood on the rank. "I wonder whether he expects——"

Manfred saw a light creep into his eyes.

"Will you want me for the next two hours?" Leon asked quickly, and was out of the room in a flash.

Ten minutes later, Poiccart and George were talking together when they heard the street door close, and saw Leon stroll to the edge of the pavement and wave his umbrella. The taxi-driver was suddenly a thing of quivering excitement. He leaned down, cranked his engine, climbed back into his seat and brought the car up quicker than any taxicab driver had ever moved before.

"New Scotland Yard," said Leon, and got into the machine.

The cab passed through the forbidding gates of the Yard and dropped him at the staff entrance.

"Wait here," said Leon, and the man shifted uncomfortably.

"I've got to be back at my garage——" he began.

"I shall not be five minutes," said Leon.

Meadows was in his room, fortunately.

"I want you to pull in this man and give him a dose of the third degree you keep in this country," said Leon. "He carries a gun; I saw that when he had to get down to crank up his cab in Piccadilly Circus. The engine stopped."

"What do you want to know?"

"All that there is to be known about Oberzohn. I may have missed one or two things. I've seen him outside the house. Oberzohn employs him for odd jobs and occasionally he acts as the old man's chauffeur. In fact, he drove the machine the day Miss Leicester lunched with Oberzohn at the Ritz-Carlton. He may not have a cabman's licence, and that will make it all the easier for you."

A few minutes later, a very surprised and wrathful man was marched into Cannon Row and scientifically searched. Leon had been right about the revolver; it was produced and found to be loaded, and his excuse that he carried the weapon as a protection following upon a recent murder of a cab-driver, had not the backing of the necessary permit. In addition—and this was a more serious offence—he held no permit from Scotland Yard to ply for hire on the streets, and his badge was the property of another man.

"Put him inside," said Meadows, and went back to report to the waiting Leon. "You've hit the bull's-eye first time. I don't know whether he will be of any use to us, but I don't despise even the smallest fish."

Whilst he was waiting, Leon had been engaged in some quick thinking.

"The man has been at Greenwich lately. One of my men saw him there twice, and I needn't say that he was driving Oberzohn."

"I'll talk to him later and telephone you," said Meadows, and Leon Gonsalez went back to Curzon Street, one large smile.

"You have merely exchanged a spy you know for a spy you don't know," said George Manfred, "though I never question these freakish acts of yours, Leon. So often they have a trick of turning up trumps. By the way, the police are raiding the Gringo Club in the Victoria Dock Road to-night, and they may be able to pick up a few of Mr. Oberzohn's young gentlemen who are certain to be regular users of the place."

The telephone bell rang shrilly, and Leon took up the receiver, and recognized Meadows' voice.

"I've got a queer story for you," said the inspector immediately.

"Did he talk?" asked the interested Leon.

"After a while. We took a finger-print impression, and found that he was on the register. More than that, he is a ticket-of-leave man. As an ex-convict we can send him back to finish his unexpired time. I promised to say a few words for him, and he spilt everything. The most interesting item is that Oberzohn is planning to be married."

"To be married? Who is this?" asked Manfred, in surprise. "Oberzohn?"

Leon nodded.

"Who is the unfortunate lady?" asked Leon.

There was a pause, and then:

"Miss Leicester."

Manfred saw the face of his friend change colour, and guessed.

"Does he know when?" asked Leon in a different voice.

"No. The licence was issued over a week ago, which means that Oberzohn can marry any morning he likes to bring along his bride. What's the idea, do you think?"

"Drop in this evening and either I or George will tell you," said Leon.

He put the telephone on the hook very carefully.

"That is a danger I had not foreseen, although it was obviously the only course Oberzohn could take. If he marries her, she cannot be called in evidence against him. May I see the book, George?"

Manfred unlocked the wall safe and brought back a small ledger. Leon Gonsalez turned the pages thoughtfully.

"Dennis—he has done good work for us, hasn't he?" he asked.

"Yes, he's a very reliable man. He owes us, amongst other things, his life. Do you remember, his wife was——"

"I remember." Leon scribbled the address of a man who had proved to be one of the most trustworthy of his agents.

"What are you going to do?" asked Manfred.

"I've put Dennis on the doorstep of the Greenwich registrar's office from nine o'clock in the morning until half-past three in the afternoon, and he will have instructions from me that, the moment he sees Oberzohn walk out of a cab with a lady, he must push him firmly but gently under the wheels of the cab and ask the driver politely to move up a yard."

Leon in his more extravagantly humorous moods was very often in deadly earnest.

# Chapter XXVII     Mr. Newton's Dilemma

THE most carefully guided streaks of luck may, in spite of all precautions, overflow into the wrong channel, and this had happened to Mr. Montague Newton, producing an evening that was financially disastrous and a night from which sleep was almost banished. He had had one of his little card parties; but whether it was the absence of Joan, and the inadequacy of her fluffy-haired substitute, or whether the wine had disagreed with one of the most promising victims, the result was the same. They had played *chemin de fer*, and the gilded pigeon, whose feathers seemed already to be ornamenting the head-dress of Monty Newton, had been successful, and when he should have been signing cheques for large amounts, he was cashing his counters with a reluctant host.

The night started wrong with Joan's substitute, whose name was Lisa. She had guided to the establishment, via an excellent dinner at Mero's, the son of an African millionaire. Joan, of course, would have brought him alone, but Lisa, less experienced, had allowed a young-looking friend of the victim to attach himself to the party, and she had even expected praise for her perspicacity and enterprise in producing two birds for the stone which Mr. Newton so effectively wielded, instead of one.

Monty did not resent the presence of the new-comer, and rather took the girl's view, until he learnt that Lisa's "find" was not, as she had believed, an officer of the Guards, but a sporting young lawyer with a large criminal practice, and one who had already, as a junior, conducted several prosecutions for the Crown. The moment his name was mentioned, Monty groaned in spirit. He was, moreover, painfully sober. His friend was not so favourably situated.

That was the first of the awkward things to happen. The second was the bad temper of the player, who, when the bank was considerably over £3,000, had first of all insisted upon the cards being reshuffled, and then had gone banquo—the game being baccarat. Even this contretemps might have been overcome, but after he had expressed his willingness to "give it," the card which Monty had so industriously palmed, slipped from his hand to the table, and though the fact was unnoticed by the players, the lawyer's attention being diverted at the moment, it was impossible to recover that very valuable piece of pasteboard. And Monty had done a silly thing. Instead of staging an artistic exhibition of annoyance at remarks which the millionaire's son had made, he decided to take a chance on the natural run of the cards. And he had lost. On top of that, the slightly inebriated player had decided that when a man had won a coup of £3,000 it was time to stop playing. So Monty experienced the mortification of paying out money, and accompanying his visitor to the door with a smile that was so genial and so full of good-fellowship that the young gentleman was compelled to apologize for his boorishness.

"Come along some other night and give me my revenge," said Monty.

"You bet I will! I'm going to South Africa to-morrow, but I shall be back early next year, and I'll look you up."

Monty watched him going down the steps and hoped he would break his neck.

He was worried about Joan—more worried than he thought it was possible for him to be about so light a girl. She was necessary to him in many ways. Lisa was a bungling fool, he decided, though he sent her home without hurting her feelings. She was a useful girl in many ways, and nothing spoils a tout quicker than constant nagging.

He felt very lonely in the house, and wandered from room to room, irritated with himself that the absence of this feather-brained girl, who had neither the education nor the breed of his own class, should make such a big difference. And it did; he had to admit as much to himself. He hated the thought of that underground room. He knew something of her temperament, and how soon her experience would get on her nerves. In many respects he wished he did not feel that way about her, because she had a big shock coming, and it was probably because he foresaw this hurt, that he was anxious to make the present as happy as he could for her.

After he had done what he was to do, there was no reason in the world why they should be bad friends, and he would give her a big present. Girls of that class soon forget their miseries if the present is large enough. Thus he argued, tossing from side to side in his bed, and all the time his thoughts playing about that infernal cellar. What she must be feeling! He did not worry at all about Mirabelle, because—well, she was a principal in the case. To him, Joan was the real victim.

Sleep did not come until daybreak, and he woke in his most irritable frame of mind. He had promised the girl he would call and see her, though he had privately arranged with Oberzohn not to go to the house until the expiry of the five days.

By lunch-time he could stand the worry no longer, and, ordering his car, drove to a point between New Cross and Bermondsey, walking on foot the remainder of the distance. Mr. Oberzohn expected the visit. He had a shrewd knowledge of his confederate's mental outfit, and when he saw this well-dressed man picking a dainty way across the littered ground, he strolled out on the steps to meet him.

"It is curious you should have come," he said.

"Why didn't you telephone?" growled Newton. This was his excuse for the visit.

"Because there are human machines at the end of every wire," said Oberzohn. "If they were automatic and none could listen, but you and I, we would talk and talk and then talk! All day long would I speak with you and find it a pleasure. But not with Miss This and Miss That saying, 'One moment, if you please,' and saying to the Scotland Yard man, 'Now you cut in'!"

"Is Gurther back?"

"Gurther is back," said the doctor soberly.

"Nothing happened to that bird? At least, I saw nothing in the evening papers."

"He has gone to Lisbon," replied the doctor indifferently. "Perhaps he will get there, perhaps he will not—what does it matter? I should like to see the letter, because it is data, and data has an irresistible charm for a poor old scientist. You will have a drink?"

Monty hesitated, as he always did when Oberzohn offered him refreshment. You could never be sure with Oberzohn.

"I'll have a whisky," he said at last, "a full bottle—one that hasn't been opened. I'll open it myself."

The doctor chuckled unevenly.

"You do not trust?" he said. "I think you are wise. For who is there in this world of whom a man can say, 'He is my friend. To the very end of my life I will have confidence in him'?"

Monty did not feel that the question called for an answer.

He took the whisky bottle to the light, examined the cork and drove in the corkscrew.

"The soda water—that also might be poisoned," said Dr. Oberzohn pleasantly.

At any other time he would not have made that observation. That he said it at all, betrayed a subtle but ominous change in their relationships. If Monty noticed this, he did not say a word, but filled his glass and sat down on the sofa to drink. And all the time the doctor was watching him interestedly.

"Yes, Gurther is back. He failed, but you must excuse failure in a good man. The perfect agent has yet to be found, and the perfect principal also. The American, Washington, had left Paris when I last heard of him. He is to be congratulated. If I myself lived in Paris I should always be leaving. It is a frivolous city."

Monty lit a cigar, and decided to arrive at the object of his visit by stages. For he had come to perform two important duties. He accounted as a duty a call upon Joan. No less was it a duty, and something of a relief also, to make his plan known to his partner.

"How are the girls?" he asked.

"They are very happy," said Dr. Oberzohn, who had not resumed his seat, but stood in an attitude somewhat reminiscent of Gurther, erect, staring, motionless. "Always my guests are happy."

"In that dog-hole?" said the other contemptuously. "I don't want Joan to be here."

The Herr Doktor shrugged.

"Then take her away, my friend," he said. "Why should she stay, if you are unhappy because this woman is not with you? She serves no purpose. Possibly she is fretting. By all means—I will bring her to you." He moved to the door.

"Wait a moment," said Monty. "I'll see her later and take her out perhaps, but I don't want her to be away permanently. Somebody ought to stay with that girl."

"Why? Am I not here?" asked Oberzohn blandly.

"You're here, and Gurther's here." Monty was looking out of the window and did not meet the doctor's eyes. "Especially Gurther. That's why I think that Mirabelle Leicester should have somebody to look after her. Has it ever struck you that the best way out of this little trouble is—marriage?"

"I have thought that," said the doctor. "You also have thought it? This is wonderful! You are beginning to think."

The change of tone was noticeable enough now. Monty snapped round at the man who had hitherto stood in apparent awe of him and his judgments.

"You can cut that sarcasm right out, Oberzohn," he said, and, without preamble: "I'm going to marry that girl."

Oberzohn said nothing to this.

"She's not engaged; she's got no love affairs at all. Joan told me, and Joan is a pretty shrewd girl. I don't know how I'm going to fix it, but I guess the best thing I can do is to pretend that I am a real friend and get her out of your cellar. She'll be so grateful that maybe she will agree to almost anything. Besides, I think I made an impression the first time I saw her. And I've got a position to offer her, Oberzohn: a house in the best part of London——"

"My house," interrupted Oberzohn's metallic voice.

"Your house? Well, *our* house, let us say. We're not going to quarrel about terms."

"I also have a position to offer her, and I do not offer her any other man's."

Oberzohn was looking at him wide-eyed, a comical figure; his elongated face seemed to stand out in the gloom like a pantomime mask.

"You?" Monty could hardly believe his ears.

"I, Baron Eruc Oberzohn."

"A baron, are you?" The room shook with Monty's laughter. "Why, you damned old fool, you don't imagine she'd marry you, do you?"

Oberzohn nodded.

"She would do anythings what I tell her." In his agitation his English was getting a little ragged. "A girl may not like a mans, but she might hate somethings worse—you understand? A woman says death is not'ing, but a woman is afeard of death, isn't it?"

"You're crazy," said Monty scornfully.

"I am crazy, am I? And a damned old fool also—yes? Yet I shall marry her."

There was a dead silence, and then Oberzohn continued the conversation, but on a much calmer note.

"Perhaps I am what you call me, but it is not a thing worthy for two friends to quarrel. To-morrow you shall come here, and we will discuss this matter like a business proposition, hein?"

Monty examined him as though he were a strange insect that had wandered into his ken.

"You're not a Swede, you're German," he said. "That baron stuff gave you away."

"I am from the Baltic, but I have lived many years in Sweden," said Oberzohn shortly. "I am not German: I do not like them."

More than this he would not say. Possibly he shared Gurther's repugnance towards his sometime neighbours.

"We shall not quarrel, anyway," he continued. "I am a fool, you are a fool, we are all fools. You wish to see your woman?"

"I wish to see Joan," said Monty gruffly. "I don't like that 'your woman' line of yours."

"I will go get her. You wait."

Again the long boots came from under the table, were dragged on to the doctor's awkward feet, and Monty watched him from the window as he crossed to the factory and disappeared.

He was gone five minutes before he came out again, alone. Monty frowned. What was the reason for this?

"My friend," panted Oberzohn, to whom these exertions were becoming more and more irksome, "it is not wise."

"I want to see her——" began Monty.

"Gently, gently; you shall see her. But on the canal bank Gurther has also seen a stranger, who has been walking up and down, pretending to fish. Who can fish in a canal, I ask you?"

"What is he to do with it?"

"Would it be wise to bring her in daylight, I ask you again? Do not the men think that your—that this girl is in Brussels?"

This had not occurred to Monty.

"I have an idea for you. It is a good idea. The brain of old fool Oberzohn sometimes works remarkably. This morning a friend sent to me a ticket for a theatre. Now you shall take her to-night. There is always a little fog when the sun is setting and you can leave the house in a car. Presently I will send a man to attract this watcher's attention, and then I will bring her to the house and you can call for her."

"I will wait for her." Monty was dogged on this point.

And wait he did, until an hour later a half-crazy girl came flying into the room and into his arms.

Dr. Oberzohn witnessed the reunion unmoved.

"That is a pretty scene for me," he said, "for one to be so soon married," and he left them alone.

"Monty, I can't possibly go back to that beastly place to-night. She'll have to stay by herself. And she's not a bad kid, Monty, but she doesn't know she's worth a lot of money."

"Have you been talking to her?" he asked angrily. "I told you——"

"No, I've only just asked her a few questions. You can't be in a poky hole like that, thrown together day and night, without talking, can you? Monty, you're absolutely sure nothing can happen to her?"

Monty cleared his throat.

"The worst thing that can happen to her," he said, "is to get married."

She opened her eyes at this.

"Does somebody want to marry her?"

"Oberzohn," he said.

"That old thing!" she scoffed.

Again he found a difficulty in speaking.

"I have been thinking it over, honey," he said. "Marriage doesn't mean a whole lot to anybody."

"It'll mean a lot to me," she said quietly.

"Suppose I married her?" he blurted.

"You!" She stepped back from him in horror.

"Only just a . . . well, this is the truth, Joan. It may be the only way to get her money. Now you're in on this graft, and you know what you are to me. A marriage—a formal marriage—for a year or two, and then a divorce, and we could go away together, man and wife."

"Is that what he meant?" She jerked her head to the door. "About 'married so soon'?"

"He wants to marry her himself."

"Let him," she said viciously. "Do you think I care about money? Isn't there any other way of getting it?"

He was silent. There were too many other ways of getting it for him to advance a direct negative.

"Oh, Monty, you're not going to do that?"

"I don't know what I'm going to do yet," he said.

"But not that?" she insisted, clinging to him by his coat.

"We'll talk about it to-night. The old man's got us tickets for the theatre. We'll have a bit of dinner up West and go on, and it really doesn't matter if anybody sees us, because they know very well you're not in Brussels. What is that queer scent you've got?"

Joan laughed, forgetting for the moment the serious problem which faced her.

"Joss-sticks," she said. "The place got so close and stuffy, and I found them in the pantry with the provisions. As a matter of fact, it was a silly thing to do, because we had the place full of smoke. It's gone now, though. Monty, you do these crazy things when you're locked up," she said seriously. "I don't think I can go back again."

"Go back to-morrow," he almost pleaded. "It's only for two or three days, and it means a lot to me. Especially now that Oberzohn has ideas."

"You're not going to think any more about—about marrying her, are you?"

"We'll talk of it to-night at dinner. I thought you'd like the idea of the graft," he added untruthfully.

Joan had to return to her prison to collect some of her belongings. She found the girl lying on the bed, reading, and Mirabelle greeted her with a smile.

"Well, is your term of imprisonment ended?"

Joan hesitated.

"Not exactly. Do you mind if I'm not here to-night?"

Mirabelle shook her head. If the truth be told, she was glad to be alone. All that day she had been forced to listen to the plaints and weepings of this transfigured girl, and she felt that she could not well stand another twenty-four hours.

"You're sure you won't mind being alone?

"No, of course not. I shall miss you," added Mirabelle, more in truth than in compliment. "When will you return?"

The girl made a little grimace.

"To-morrow."

"You don't want to come back, naturally? Have you succeeded in persuading your—your friend to let me out too?"

Joan shook her head.

"He'll never do that, my dear, not till . . ." She looked at the girl. "You're not engaged, are you?"

"I? No. Is that another story they've heard?" Mirabelle got up from the bed, laughing. "An heiress, and engaged?"

"No, they don't say you were engaged." Joan hastened to correct the wrong impression. There was genuine admiration in her voice, when she said: "You're wonderful, kid! If I were in your shoes I'd be quaking. You're just as cheerful as though you were going to the funeral of a rich aunt!"

She did not know how near to a breakdown her companion had been that day, and Mirabelle, who felt stronger and saner now, had no desire to tell her.

"You're rather splendid." Joan nodded. "I wish I had your pluck."

And then, impulsively, she came forward and kissed the girl.

"Don't feel too sore at me," she said, and was gone before Mirabelle could make a reply.

The doctor was waiting for her in the factory.

"The spy has walked up to the canal bridge. We can go forward," he said. "Besides,"—he had satisfaction out of this—"he cannot see over high walls."

"What is this story about marrying Mirabelle Leicester?"

"So he has told you? Also did he tell you that—that *he* is going to marry her?"

"Yes, and I'll tell you something, doctor. I'd rather he married her than you."

"So!" said the doctor.

"I'd rather anybody else married her, except that snake of yours."

Oberzohn looked round sharply. She had used the word quite innocently, without any thought of its application, and uttered an "Oh!" of dismay when she realized her mistake.

"I meant Gurther," she said.

"Well, I know you meant Gurther, young miss," he said stiffly.

To get back to the house they had to make a half-circle of the factory and pass between the canal wall and the building itself. The direct route would have taken them into a deep hollow into which the debris of years had been thrown, and which now Nature, in her kindness, had hidden under a green mantle of wild convolvulus. It was typical of the place that the only beautiful picture in the grounds was out of sight.

They were just turning the corner of the factory when the doctor stopped and looked up at the high wall, which was protected by a *cheval de frise* of broken glass. All except in one spot, about two feet wide, where not only the glass but the mortar which held it in place had been chipped off. There were fragments of the glass, and, on the inside of the wall, marks of some implement on the hard surface of the mortar.

"So!" said the doctor.

He was examining the scratches on the wall.

"Wait," he ordered, and hurried back into the factory, to return, carrying in each hand two large rusty contraptions which he put on the ground.

One by one he forced open the jagged rusty teeth until they were wide apart and held by a spring catch. She had seen things like that in a museum. They were man-traps—relics of the barbarous days when trespass was not only a sin but a crime.

He fixed the second of the traps on the path between the factory and the wall.

"Now we shall see," he said. "Forward!"

Monty was waiting for her impatiently. The Rolls had been turned out in her honour, and the sulky-looking driver was already in his place at the wheel.

"What is the matter with that chauffeur?" she asked, as they bumped up the lane towards easier going. "He looks so happy that I shouldn't be surprised to hear that his mother was hanged this morning."

"He's sore with the old man," explained Monty. "Oberzohn has two drivers. They do a little looking round in the morning. The other fellow was supposed to come back to take over duty at three o'clock, and he hasn't turned up. He was the better driver of the two."

The chauffeur was apparently seeking every pothole in the ground, and in the next five minutes she was alternately clutching the support of the arm-strap and Monty. They were relieved when at last the car found a metal road and began its noiseless way towards The Lights. And then her hand sought his, and for the moment this beautiful flower which had grown in such foul soil, bloomed in the radiance of a love common to every woman, high and low, good and bad.

# Chapter XXVIII                    At Frater's

MANFRED suggested an early dinner at the Lasky, where the soup was to his fastidious taste. Leon, who had eaten many crumpets for tea—he had a weakness for this indigestible article of diet—was prepared to dispense with the dinner, and Poiccart had views, being a man of steady habits. They dined at the Lasky, and Leon ordered a baked onion, and expatiated upon the two wasted years of Poiccart's life, employing a wealth of imagery and a beauty of diction worthy of a better subject.

Manfred looked at his watch.

"Where are they dining?" he asked.

"I don't know yet," said Leon. "Our friend will be here in a few minutes; when we go out he will tell us. You don't want to see her?"

Manfred shook his head.

"No," he said.

"I'm going to be bored," complained Poiccart.

"Then you should have let me bring Alma," said Leon promptly.

"Exactly." Raymond nodded his sober head. "I have the feeling that I am saving a lady from an unutterably dreary evening."

There was a man waiting for them when they came out of the restaurant—a very uninteresting-looking man who had three sentences to say *sotto voce* as they stood near him, but apparently in ignorance of his presence.

"I did not wish to go to Mero's," said Manfred, "but as we have the time, I think it would be advisable to stroll in that direction. I am curious to discover whether this is really Oberzohn's little treat, or whether the idea emanated from the unadmirable Mr. Newton."

"And how will you know, George?" asked Gonsalez.

"By the car. If Oberzohn is master of the ceremonies, we shall find his machine parked somewhere in the neighbourhood. If it is Newton's idea, then Oberzohn's limousine, which brought them from South London, will have returned, and Newton's car will be in its place."

Mero's was one of the most fashionable of dining clubs, patronized not only by the elite of society, but having on its books the cream of the theatrical world. It was situated in one of those quiet, old-world squares which are to be found in the very heart of London, enjoying, for some mysterious reason, immunity from the hands of the speculative property owner. The square retained the appearance it had in the days of the Georges; and though some of the fine mansions had been given over to commerce and the professions, and the lawyer and the manufacturer's agent occupied the drawing-rooms and bedrooms sacred to the bucks and beauties of other days, quite a large number of the houses remained in private occupation.

There was nothing in the fascia of Mero's to advertise its character. The club premises consisted of three of these fine old dwellings. The uninitiated might not even suspect that there was communication between the three houses, for the old doorways and doorsteps remained untouched, though only one was used.

They strolled along two sides of the square before, amidst the phalanx of cars that stood wheel to wheel, their backs to the railings of the centre gardens, they saw Oberzohn's car.

The driver sat with his arms folded on the wheel, in earnest conversation with a pale-faced man, slightly and neatly bearded, and dressed in faultless evening dress. He was evidently a cripple: one shoulder was higher than the other; and when he moved, he walked painfully with the aid of a stick.

Manfred saw the driver point up the line of cars, and the lame gentleman limped in the direction the chauffeur had indicated and stopped to speak to another man in livery. As they came abreast of him, they saw that one of his boots had a thick sole, and the limp was explained.

"The gentleman has lost his car," said Manfred, for now he was peering short-sightedly at the number-plates.

The theft of cars was a daily occurrence. Leon had something to say on the potentialities of that branch of crime. He owned to an encyclopædic knowledge of the current fashions in wrongdoing, and in a few brief sentences indicated the extent of these thefts.

"Fifty a week are shipped to India and the Colonies, after their numbers are erased and another substituted. In some cases the 'knockers off,' as they call the thieves, drive them straight away into the packing-cases which are prepared for every make of car; the ends are nailed up, and they are waiting shipment at the docks before the owner is certain of his loss. There are almost as many stolen cars in India, South Africa and Australia as there are honest ones!"

They walked slowly past the decorous portals of Mero's, and caught a glimpse, through the curtained windows, of soft table lamps burning, of bare-armed women and white-shirted men, and heard faintly the strains of an orchestra playing a Viennese waltz.

"I should like to see our Jane," said Gonsalez. "She never came to you, did she?"

"She came, but I didn't see her," said Manfred. "From the moment she leaves the theatre she must not be left."

Leon nodded.

"I have already made that arrangement," he said. "Digby——"

"Digby takes up his duty at midnight," said Manfred. "He has been down to Oberzohn's place to get the lie of the land: he thought it advisable that he should study the topography in daylight, and I agreed. He might get himself into an awkward tangle if he started exploring the canal bank in the dark hours. Summer or winter, there is usually a mist on the water."

They reached Frater's theatre so early that the queues at the pit door were still unadmitted, and Leon suggested that they make a circuit of this rambling house of entertainment. It stood in Shaftesbury Avenue and occupied an island site. On either side two narrow streets flanked the building, whilst the rear formed the third side of a small square, one of which was taken up by a County Council dwelling, mainly occupied by artisans. From the square a long passage-way led to Cranbourn Street; whilst, in addition to the alley which opened just at the back of the theatre, a street ran parallel to Shaftesbury Avenue from Charing Cross Road to Rupert Street.

The theatre itself was one of the best in London, and although it had had a succession of failures, its luck had turned, and the new mystery play was drawing all London.

"That is the stage door," said Leon—they had reached the square—"and those are emergency exits"—he pointed back the way they had come—"which are utilized at the end of a performance to empty the theatre."

"Why are you taking such an interest in the theatre itself?" asked Poiccart.

"Because," said Gonsalez slowly, "I am in agreement with George. We should have found Newton's car parked in Fitzreeve Gardens—not Oberzohn's. And the circumstances are a little suspicious."

The doors of the pit and gallery were open now; the queues were moving slowly to the entrances; and they watched the great building swallow up the devotees of the drama, before they returned to the front of the house.

Cars were beginning to arrive, at first at intervals, but, as the hour of the play's beginning approached, in a ceaseless line that made a congestion and rendered the traffic police articulate and occasionally unkind. It was short of the half-hour after eight when Manfred saw Oberzohn's glistening car in the block, and presently it pulled up before the entrance of the theatre. First Joan and then Monty Newton alighted and passed out of view.

Gonsalez thought he had never seen the girl looking quite as radiantly pretty. She had the colouring and the shape of youth, and though the more fastidious might object to her daring toilette, the most cantankerous could not cavil at the pleasing effect.

"It is a great pity,"—Leon spoke in Spanish—"a thousand pities! I have the same feeling when I see a perfect block of marble placed in the hands of a tombstone-maker to be mangled into ugliness!"

Manfred put out his hand and drew him back into the shadow. A cab was dropping the lame man. He got out with the aid of a linkman, paid the driver, and limped into the vestibule. It was not a remarkable coincidence: the gentleman had evidently come from Mero's, and as all London was flocking to the drama, there was little that was odd in finding him here. They saw that he went up into the dress-circle, and later, when they took their places in the stalls, Leon, glancing up, saw the pale, bearded face and noted that he occupied the end seat of the front row.

"I've met that man somewhere," he said, irritated. "Nothing annoys me worse than to forget, not a face, but where I have seen it!"

Did Gurther but know, he had achieved the height of his ambition: he had twice passed under the keen scrutiny of the cleverest detectives in the world, and had remained unrecognized.

# Chapter XXIX

# Work for Gurther

GURTHER was sleeping when he was called for duty, but presented himself before his director as bright and alert as though he had not spent a sleepless night, nor yet had endured the strain of a midnight train jump.

"Once more, my Gurther, I send you forth." Dr. Oberzohn was almost gay. "This time to save us all from the Judas treachery of one we thought was our friend. To-night the snake must bite, and bite hard, Gurther. And out into the dark goes the so-called Trusted! And after that, my brave boy, there shall be nothing to fear."

He paused for approval, and got it in a snapped agreement.

"To-night we desire from you a *chef d'œuvre*, the supreme employment of your great art, Gurther; the highest expression of genius! The gentleman-club manner will not do. They may look for you and find you. Better it should be, this time, that you——"

"Herr Doktor, will you graciously permit me to offer a humble suggestion?" said Gurther eagerly.

The doctor nodded his head slowly.

"You may speak, Gurther," he said. "You are a man of intelligence; I would not presume to dictate to an artist."

"Let me go for an hour, perhaps two hours, and I will return to you with a manner that is unique. Is it graciously permitted, Herr Doktor?"

"March!" said the doctor graciously, waving his hand to the door.

Nearly an hour and a half passed before the door opened and a gentleman came in who for even a moment even the doctor thought was a stranger. The face had an unearthly ivory pallor; the black brows, the faint shadows beneath the eyes that suggested a recent illness, the close-cropped black beard in which grey showed—these might not have deceived him. But the man was obviously the victim of some appalling accident of the past. One shoulder was hunched, the hand that held the stick was distorted out of shape, and as he moved, the clump of his club foot advertised his lameness.

"Sir, you desire to see me——?" began the doctor, and then stared openmouthed. "It is not . . . !"

Gurther smiled.

"Herr Doktor, are you condescendingly pleased?"

"Colossal!" murmured Oberzohn, gazing in amazement. "Of all accomplishments this is supreme! Gurther, you are an artist. Some day we shall buy a theatre for you in Unter den Linden, and you shall thrill large audiences."

"Herr Doktor, this is my own idea; this I have planned for many months. The boots I made myself; even the coat I altered"—he patted his deformed shoulder proudly.

"An eyeglass?"

"I have it," said Gurther promptly.

"The cravat—is it not too proper?"

Gurther fingered his tie.

"For the grand habit I respectfully claim that the proper tie is desirable, if you will graciously permit."

The Herr Doktor nodded.

"You shall go with God, Gurther," he said piously, took a golden cigarette-case from his pocket and handed it to the man. "Sit down, my dear friend."

He rose and pointed to the chair he had vacated.

"In my own chair, Gurther. Nothing is too good for you. Now here is the arrangement . . ."

Step by step he unfolded the time-table, for chronology was almost as great a passion with this strange and wicked man as it was with Aunt Alma.

So confident was Gurther of his disguise that he had gone in the open to speak to Oberzohn's chauffeur, and out of the tail of his eye he had seen Manfred and Gonsalez approaching. It was the supreme test and was passed with credit to himself.

He did not dine at Mero's; Gurther never ate or drank when he was wearing a disguise, knowing just how fatal that occupation could be. Instead, he had called a taxi, and had killed time by being driven slowly round and round the Outer Circle of Regent's Park.

Gurther was doing a great deal of thinking in these days, and at the cost of much physical discomfort had curtailed his pernicious practices, that his head might be clear all the time. For if he were to live, that clear head of his was necessary. The prisoner in the cellar occupied his thoughts. She had an importance for two reasons: she was a friend of the men whom he hated with a cold and deadly malignity beyond description; she represented wealth untold, and the Herr Doktor had even gone to the length of planning a marriage with her. She was not to be killed, not to be hurt; she was so important that the old man would take the risks attendant upon a marriage. There must be an excellent reason for that, because Dr. Oberzohn had not a very delicate mind.

He seemed to remember that, by the English law, a wife could not give evidence against her husband. He was not sure, but he had a dim notion that Pfeiffer had told him this: Pfeiffer was an educated man and had taken high honours at the gymnasium.

Gurther was not well read. His education had been of a scrappy character, and once upon a time he had been refused a leading part because of his provincial accent. That fault he had corrected in prison, under the tuition of a professor who was serving a life sentence for killing two women; but by the time Gurther had been released, he was a marked man, and the stage was a career lost to him for ever.

Oberzohn possessed advantages which were not his. He was the master; Gurther was the servant. Oberzohn could determine events by reason of his vast authority, and the strings which he pulled in every part of the world. Even Gurther had accepted this position of blind, obedient servant, but now his angle had shifted, even as Oberzohn's had moved in relation to Montague Newton. Perhaps because of this. The doctor, in curtailing one confidence, was enlarging another, and in the enlargement his prestige suffered.

Gurther was now the confidant, therefore the equal; and logically, the equal can always become the superior. He had dreamed dreams of a life of ease, a gratification of his sense of luxury without the sobering thought that somewhere round the corner was waiting a man ready to tap him on the shoulder . . . a white palace in a flowery land, with blue swimming pools, and supple girls who called him Master. Gurther began to see the light.

Until he had taken his seat in the theatre, he had not so much as glimpsed the man and the woman in the end box.

Joan was happy—happier than she remembered having been. Perhaps it was the reaction from her voluntary imprisonment. Certainly it was Monty's reluctant agreement to a change of plans which so exalted her. Monty had dropped the thin pretence of an accommodation marriage; and once he was persuaded to this, the last hindrance to enjoyment was dissipated. Let Oberzohn take the girl if he wanted her; take, too, such heavy responsibility as followed. Monty Newton would get all that he wanted without the risk. Having arrived at this decision, he had ordered another bottle of champagne to seal the bargain, and they left Mero's club a much happier couple than they had been when they entered.

"As soon as we've carved up this money, we'll get away out of England," he told her as they were driving to the theatre. "What about Buenos Ayres for the winter, old girl?"

She did not know where Buenos Ayres was, but she gurgled her delight at the suggestion, and Monty expatiated upon the joys of the South American summer, the beauties of B.A., its gaieties and amusements.

"I don't suppose there'll be any kick coming," he said, "but it wouldn't be a bad scheme if we took a trip round the world, and came back in about eighteen months' time to settle down in London. My hectic past would have been forgotten by then—why, I might even get into Parliament."

"How wonderful!" she breathed, and then: "What is this play about, Monty?"

"It's a bit of a thrill, the very play for you—a detective story that will make your hair stand on end."

She had all the gamin's morbid interest in murder and crime, and she settled down in the box with a pleasant feeling of anticipation, and watched the development of the first act.

The scene was laid in a club, a low-down resort where the least desirable members of society met, and she drank in every word, because she knew the life, had seen that type of expensively dressed woman who swaggered on to the stage and was addressed familiarly by the club proprietor. She knew that steady-eyed detective when he made his embarrassing appearance. The woman was herself. She even knew the cadaverous wanderer who approached stealthily at the door: a human wolf that fled at the sight of the police officer.

The three who sat in the front row of the stalls—how Leon Gonsalez secured these tickets was one of the minor mysteries of the day—saw her, and one at least felt his heart ache.

Monty beamed his geniality. He had taken sufficient wine to give him a rosy view of the world, and he was even mildly interested in the play, though his chief pleasure was in the girl's enchantment. He ordered ices for her after the first interval.

"You're getting quite a theatre fan, kiddie," he said. "I must take you to some other shows. I had no idea you liked this sort of thing."

She drew a long breath and smiled at him.

"I like anything when I'm with you," she said, and they held hands foolishly, till the house lights dimmed and the curtain rose upon a lawyer's office.

The lawyer was of the underworld: a man everlastingly on the verge of being struck off the rolls. He had betrayed a client with whom he had had dealings, and the man had gone to prison for a long term, but had escaped. Now the news had come that he had left Australia and was in London, waiting his opportunity to destroy the man whose treachery was responsible for his capture.

Here was a note to which the heart of the girl responded. Even Monty found himself leaning forward, as the old familiar cant terms of his trade came across the footlights.

"It is quite all right," he said at the second interval, "only"—he hesitated—"isn't it a bit too near the real thing? After all, one doesn't come to the theatre to see . . ."

He stopped, realizing that conditions and situations familiar to him were novel enough to a fashionable audience which was learning for the first time that a "busy" was a detective, and that a police informer went by the title of "nose."

The lights up, he glanced round the house, and suddenly he started and caught her arm.

"Don't look for a moment," he said, averting his eyes, "then take a glance at the front row. Do you see anybody you know?"

Presently she looked.

"Yes, that is the fellow you hate so much, isn't it—Gonsalez?"

"They're all there—the three of them," said Monty. "I wonder,"—he was troubled at the thought—"I wonder if they're looking for you?"

"For me? They've nothing on me, Monty."

He was silent.

"I'm glad you're not going back to that place to-night. They'll trail you sure—sure!"

He thought later that it was probably a coincidence that they were there at all. They seemed to show no interest in the box, but were chattering and talking and laughing to one another. Not once did their eyes come up to his level, and after a while he gained in confidence, though he was glad enough when the play was resumed.

There were two scenes in the act: the first was a police station, the second the lawyer's room. The man was drunk, and the detective had come to warn him that The Ringer was after him. And then suddenly the lights on the stage were extinguished and the whole house was in the dark. It was part of the plot. In this darkness, and in the very presence of the police, the threatened man was to be murdered. They listened in tense silence, the girl craning her head forward, trying to pierce the dark, listening to the lines of intense dialogue that were coming from the blackness of the stage. Somebody was in the room—a woman, and they had found her. She slipped from the stage detective's grasp and vanished, and when the lights went up she was gone.

"What has happened, Monty?" she whispered.

He did not answer.

"Do you think——"

She looked round at him. His head was resting on the plush-covered ledge of the box. His face, turned towards her, was grey; the eyes were closed, and his teeth showed in a hideous grin.

She screamed.

"Monty! Monty!"

She shook him. Again her scream rang through the house. At first the audience thought that it was a woman driven hysterical by the tenseness of the stage situation, and then one or two people rose from their stalls and looked up.

"Monty! Speak to me! He's dead, he's dead!"

Three seats in the front row had emptied. The screams of the hysterical girl made it impossible for the scene to proceed, and the curtain came down quickly.

The house was seething with excitement. Every face was turned towards the box where she knelt by the side of the dead man, clasping him in her arms, and the shrill agony in her voice was unnerving.

The door of the box swung open, and Manfred dashed in. One glance he gave at Monty Newton, and he needed no other.

"Get the girl out," he said curtly.

Leon tried to draw her from the box, but she was a shrieking fury.

"You did it, you did it! . . . Let me go to him!"

Leon lifted her from her feet, and, clawing wildly at his face, she was carried from the box.

The manager was running along the passage, and Leon sent him on with a jerk of his head. And then a woman in evening dress came from somewhere.

"May I take her?" she said, and the exhausted girl collapsed into her arms.

Gonsalez flew back to the box. The man was lying on the floor, and the manager, standing at the edge of the box, was addressing the audience.

"The gentleman has fainted, and I'm afraid his friend has become a little hysterical. I must apologize to you, ladies and gentlemen, for this interruption. If you will allow us a minute to clear the box, the play will be resumed. If there is a doctor in the house, I should be glad if he would come."

There were two doctors within reach, and in the passage, which was now guarded by a commissionaire, a hasty examination was made. They examined the punctured wound at the back of the neck and then looked at one another.

"This is The Snake," said one.

"The house mustn't know," said Manfred. "He's dead, of course?"

The doctor nodded.

Out in the passage was a big emergency exit door, and this the manager pushed open, and, running out into the street, found a cab, into which all that was mortal of Monty Newton was lifted.

Whilst this was being done, Poiccart returned.

"His car has just driven off," he said. "I saw the number-plate as it turned into Lisle Street."

"How long ago?" asked Gonsalez quickly.

"At this very moment."

Leon pinched his lip thoughtfully.

"Why didn't he wait, I wonder?"

He went back through the emergency door, which was being closed, and passed up the passage towards the entrance. The box was on the dress-circle level, and the end of a short passage brought him into the circle itself.

And then the thought of the lame man occurred to him, and his eyes sought the first seat in the front row, which was also the seat nearest to the boxes. The man had gone.

As he made this discovery, George emerged from the passage.

"Gurther!" said Leon. "What a fool I am! But how clever!"

"Gurther?" said Manfred in amazement. "Do you mean the man with the club foot?"

Leon nodded.

"He was not alone, of course," said Gonsalez. "There must have been two or three of the gang here, men and women—Oberzohn works these schemes out with the care and thoroughness of a general. I wonder where the management have taken the girl?"

He found the manager discussing the tragedy with two other men, one of whom was obviously associated with the production, and he signalled him aside.

"The lady? I suppose she's gone home. She's left the theatre."

"Which way did she go?" asked Gonsalez, in a sudden panic.

The manager called a linkman, who had seen a middle-aged woman come out of the theatre with a weeping girl, and they had gone down the side-street towards the little square at the back of the playhouse.

"She may have taken her home to Chester Square," said Manfred. His voice belied the assumption of confidence.

Leon had not brought his own machine, and they drove to Chester Square in a taxi. Fred, the footman, had neither heard nor seen the girl, and nearly fainted when he learned of the tragic ending to his master's career.

"Oh, my God!" he groaned. "And he only left here this afternoon . . . dead, you say?"

Gonsalez nodded.

"Not—not The Snake?" faltered the man.

"What do you know about the snake?" demanded Manfred sternly.

"Nothing, except—well, the snake made him nervous, I know. He told me to-day that he hoped he'd get through the week without a snake-bite."

He was questioned closely, but although it was clear that he knew something of his master's illicit transactions, and that he was connected in business with Oberzohn, the footman had no connection with the doctor's gang. He drew a large wage and a percentage of profits from the gaming side of the business, and confessed that it was part of his duties to prepare stacks of cards and pass them to his master under cover of bringing in the drinks. But of anything more sinister he knew nothing.

"The woman, of course, was a confederate, who had been planted to take charge of the girl the moment the snake struck. I was in such a state of mind," confessed Leon, "that I do not even remember what she looked like. I am a fool—a double-distilled idiot! I think I must be getting old. There's only one thing for us to do, and that is to get back to Curzon Street—something may have turned up."

"Did you leave anybody in the house?"

Leon nodded.

"Yes, I left one of our men, to take any 'phone messages that came through."

They paid off the taxi before the house, and Leon sprinted to the garage to get the car. The man who opened the door to them was he who had been tied up by the pedlar at Heavytree Farm, and his first words came as a shock to Manfred:

"Digby's here, sir."

"Digby?" said the other in surprise. "I thought he was on duty?"

"He's been here since just after you left, sir. If I'd known where you had gone, I'd have sent him to you."

Digby came out of the waiting-room at that moment, ready to apologize.

"I had to see you, sir, and I'm sorry I'm away from my post."

"You may not be missing much," said Manfred unsmilingly. "Come upstairs and tell me all about it."

Digby's story was a strange one. He had gone down that afternoon to the canal bank to make a reconnaissance of ground which was new to him.

"I'm glad I did too, because the walls have got broken glass on top. I went up into the Old Kent Road and bought a garden hoe, and prised the mortar loose, so that if I wanted, I could get over. And then I climbed round the water-gate and had a look at that barge of his. There was nobody about, though I think they spotted me afterwards. It is a fairly big barge, and, of course, in a terrible state, but the hold is full of cargo—you know that, sir?"

"You mean there is something in the barge?"

Digby nodded.

"Yes, it has a load of some kind. The after part, where the bargee's sleeping quarters are, is full of rats and water, but the fore part of the vessel is watertight, and it holds something heavy too. That is why the barge is down by its head in the mud. I was in the Thames police and I know a lot about river craft."

"Is that what you came to tell me?"

"No, sir, it was something queerer than that. After I'd given the barge a look over and tried to pull up some of the boards—which I didn't manage to do— I went along and had a look at the factory. It's not so easy to get in, because the entrance faces the house, but to get to it you have to go half round the building, and that gives you a certain amount of cover. There was nothing I could see in the factory itself. It was in a terrible mess, full of old iron and burnt-out boxes. I was coming round the back of the building," he went on impressively, "when I smelt a peculiar scent."

"A perfume?"

"Yes, sir, it was perfume, but stronger—more like incense. I thought at first it might be an old bale of stuff that had been thrown out, or else I was deceiving myself. I began poking about in the rubbish heaps—but *they* didn't smell of scent! Then I went back into the building again, but there was no smell at all. It was very strong when I returned to the back of the factory, and then I saw a little waft of smoke come out of a ventilator close to the ground. My first idea was that the place was on fire, but when I knelt down, it was this scent."

"Joss-sticks?" said Poiccart quickly.

"That's what it was!" said the detective. "Like incense, yet not like it. I knelt down and listened at the grating, and I'll swear that I heard voices. They were very faint."

"Men's?"

"No, women's."

"Could you see anything?"

"No, sir, it was a blind ventilator; there was probably a shaft there—in fact, I'm sure there was, because I pushed a stone through one of the holes and heard it drop some distance down."

"There may be an underground room there," said Poiccart, "and somebody's burnt joss-sticks to sweeten the atmosphere."

"Under the factory? It's not in the plans of the building. I've had them from the surveyor's office and examined them," said George, "although surveyors' plans aren't infallible. A man like Oberzohn would not hesitate to break so unimportant a thing as a building law!"

Leon came in at that moment, heard the story and was in complete agreement with Poiccart's theory.

"I wondered at the time we saw the plans whether we ought to accept that as conclusive," he said. "The store was built at the end of 1914, when architects and builders took great liberties and pleaded the exigencies of the war."

Digby went on with his story.

"I was going back to the barge to get past the water-gate, but I saw the old man coming down the steps of the house, so I climbed the wall, and very glad I was that I'd shifted that broken glass, or I should never have got over."

Manfred pulled his watch from his pocket with a frown. They had lost nearly an hour of precious time with their inquiries in Chester Square.

"I hope we're not too late," he said ominously. "Now, Leon . . ."

But Leon had gone down the stairs in three strides.

# Chapter XXX        Joan a Prisoner

DAZED with grief, not knowing, not seeing, not caring, not daring to think, Joan suffered herself to be led quickly into the obscurity of the side-street, and did not even realize that Oberzohn's big limousine had drawn up by the sidewalk.

"Get in," said the woman harshly.

Joan was pushed through the door and guided to a seat by somebody who was already in the machine.

She collapsed in a corner moaning as the door slammed and the car began to move.

"Where are we going? Let me get back to him!"

"The gracious lady will please restrain her grief," said a hateful voice, and she swung round and stared unseeingly to the place whence the voice had come.

The curtains of the car had been drawn; the interior was as black as pitch.

"You—you beast!" she gasped. "It's you, is it? . . . Gurther! You murdering beast!"

She struck at him feebly, but he caught her wrist.

"The gracious lady will most kindly restrain her grief," he said suavely. "The Herr Newton is not dead. It was a little trick in order to baffle certain interferers."

"You're lying, you're lying!" she screamed, struggling to escape from those hands of steel. "He's dead! You know he's dead, and you killed him! You snake-man!"

"The gracious lady must believe me," said Gurther earnestly. They were passing through a public part of the town and at any moment a policeman might hear her shrieks. "If Herr Newton had not pretended to be hurt, he would have been arrested . . . he follows in the next car."

"You're trying to quieten me," she said, "but I won't be quiet."

And then a hand came over her mouth and pressed her head back against the cushions. She struggled desperately, but two fingers slid up her face and compressed her nostrils. She was being suffocated. She struggled to free herself from the tentacle hold of him, and then slipped into unconsciousness. Gurther felt the straining figure go limp and removed his hands. She did not feel the prick of the needle on her wrist, though the drugging was clumsily performed in the darkness and in a car that was swaying from side to side. He felt her pulse, his long fingers pressed her throat and felt the throb of the carotid artery; propping her so that she could not fall, Herr Gurther sank back luxuriously into a corner of the limousine and lit a cigar.

The journey was soon over. In a very short time they were bumping down Hangman's Lane and turned so abruptly into the factory grounds that one of the mudguards buckled to the impact of the gate-post.

---

It must have been two hours after the departure of her companion, when Mirabelle, lying on her bed, half dozing, was wakened by her book slipping to the floor, and sat up quickly to meet the apprising stare of the man whom, of all men in the world, she disliked most cordially. Dr. Oberzohn had come noiselessly into the room and under his arm was a pile of books.

"I have brought these for you," he said, in his booming voice, and stacked them neatly on the table.

She did not answer.

"Novels of a frivolous kind, such as you will enjoy," he said, unconscious of offence. "I desired the seller of the books to pick them for me. Fiction stories of adventure and of amorous exchanges. These will occupy your mind, though to me they would be the merest rubbish and nonsense."

She stood silently, her hands clasped behind her, watching him. He was neater than usual, had resumed the frock-coat he wore the day she had first met him—how long ago that seemed!—his collar was stiffly white, and if his cravat was more gorgeous than is usually seen in a man correctly arrayed, it had the complementary value of being new.

He held in his hand a small bouquet of flowers tightly packed, their stems enclosed in silver foil, a white paper frill supplying an additional expression of gentility.

"These are for you." He jerked out his hand towards her.

Mirabelle looked at the flowers, but did not take them. He seemed in no way disconcerted, either by her silence, or by the antagonism which her attitude implied, but, laying the flowers on top of the books, he clasped his hands before him and addressed her. He was nervous, for some reason; the skin of his forehead was furrowing and smoothing with grotesque rapidity. She watched the contortions, fascinated.

"To every man," he began, "there comes a moment of domestic allurement. Even to the scientific mind, absorbed in its colossal problems, there is this desire for family life and for the haven of rest which is called marriage."

He paused, as though he expected her to offer some comment upon his platitude.

"Man alone," he went on, when she did not speak, "has established an artificial and unnatural convention that, at a certain age, a man should marry a woman of that same age. Yet it has been proved by history that happy marriages are often between a man who is in the eyes of the world old, and a lady who is youthful."

She was gazing at him in dismay. Was he proposing to her? The idea was incredible, almost revolting. He must have read in her face the thoughts that were uppermost in her mind, the loathing, the sense of repulsion which filled her, yet he went on, unabashed:

"I am a man of great riches. You are a girl of considerable poverty. But because I saw you one day in your poor house, looking, gracious lady, like a lily growing amidst foul weeds, my heart went out to you, and for this reason I brought you to London, spending many thousands of pounds in order to give myself the pleasure of your company."

"I don't think you need go any farther, Dr. Oberzohn," she said quietly, "if you're proposing marriage, as I think you are."

He nodded emphatically.

"Such is my honourable intention," he said.

"I would never marry you in any circumstances," she said. "Not even if I had met you under the happiest conditions. The question of your age"—she nearly added "and of your appearance," but her natural kindness prevented that cruel thrust, though it would not have hurt him in the slightest degree— "has nothing whatever to do with my decision. I do not even like you, and have never liked you, Mr. Oberzohn."

"Doctor," he corrected, and in spite of her woeful plight she could have laughed at this insistence upon the ceremonial title.

"Young miss, I cannot woo you in the way of my dear and sainted brother, who was all for ladies and had a beautiful manner."

She was amazed to hear that he had a brother at all—and it was almost a relief to know that he was dead.

"Martyred, at the hands of wicked and cunning murderers, slain in his prime by the assassin's pistol . . ." His voice trembled and broke. "For that sainted life I will some day take vengeance."

It was not wholly curiosity that impelled her to ask who killed him.

"Leon Gonsalez." The words in his lips became the grating of a file. "Killed . . . murdered! And even his beautiful picture destroyed in that terrible fire. Had he saved that, my heart would have been soft towards him." He checked himself, evidently realizing that he was getting away from the object of his call. "Think over this matter, young lady. Read the romantic books and the amorous books, and then perhaps you will not think it is so terrible a fate to drift at moonlight through the canals of Venice, with the moon above and the gondoliers."

He wagged his head sentimentally.

"There is no book which will change my view, doctor," she said. "I cannot understand why you propose such an extraordinary course, but I would rather die than marry you."

His cold eyes filled her with a quick terror.

"There are worse things than death, which is but sleep—many worse things, young miss. To-morrow I shall come for you, and we will go into the country, where you will say 'yes' and 'no' according to my desire. I have many—what is the word?—certificates for marriage, for I am too clever a man to leave myself without alternatives."

(This was true; he had residential qualifications in at least four counties, and at each he had given legal notice of his intended marriage.)

"Not to-morrow or any other day. Nothing would induce me."

His eyebrows went almost to the top of his head.

"So!" he said, with such significance that her blood ran cold. "There are worse men than the Herr Doktor,"—he raised a long finger warningly,—"terrible men with terrible minds. You have met Gurther?"

She did not answer this.

"Yes, yes, you danced with him. A nice man, is he not, to ladies? Yet this same Gurther . . . I will tell you something."

He seated himself on a corner of the table and began talking, until she covered her ears with her hands and hid her white face from him.

"They would have killed him for that," he said, when her hands came down, "but Gurther was too clever, and the poor German peasants too stupid. You shall remember that, shall you not?"

He did not wait for her answer. With a stiff bow he strutted out of the room and up the stairs. There came the thud of the trap falling and the inevitable rumble of the concrete barrel.

He had some work to do, heavy work for a man who found himself panting when he climbed stairs. And though four of his best and most desperate men were waiting in his parlour drinking his whisky and filling the little room with their rank cigar smoke, he preferred to tackle this task which he had already begun as soon as night fell, without their assistance or knowledge.

On the edge of the deep hole in his grounds, where the wild convolvulus grew amidst the rusty corners of discarded tins and oil barrels, was a patch of earth that yielded easily to the spade. When the factory had been built, the depression had been bigger, but the builders had filled in half the hole with the light soil that they had dug out of the factory's foundations.

He took his spade, which he had left in the factory, and, skirting the saucer-shaped depression, he reached a spot where a long trench had already been dug. Taking off his fine coat and waistcoat, unfastening cravat and collar and carefully depositing them upon the folded coat, he continued his work, stopping now and again to wipe his streaming brow.

He had to labour in the dark, but this was no disadvantage; he could feel the edges of the pit. In an hour the top of the trench was level with his chin, and, stooping to clear the bottom of loose soil, he climbed up with greater difficulty than he had anticipated, and it was only after the third attempt that he managed to reach the top, out of breath and short of temper.

He dressed again, and with his electric torch surveyed the pit he had made and grunted his satisfaction.

He was keenly sensitive to certain atmospheres, and needed no information about the change which had come over his subordinates. In their last consultation Gurther had been less obsequious, had even smoked in his presence without permission—absent-mindedly, perhaps, but the offence was there. And Dr. Oberzohn, on the point of smacking his face for his insolence, heard a warning voice within himself which had made his hand drop back at his side. Or was it the look he saw on Gurther's face? The man was beyond the point where he could discipline him in the old Junker way. For although Dr. Oberzohn contemned all things Teutonic, he had a sneaking reverence for the military caste of that nation.

He left the spade sticking in a heap of turned earth. He would need that again, and shortly. Unless Gurther failed. Somehow he did not anticipate a failure in this instance. Mr. Monty Newton had not yet grown suspicious, would not be on his guard. His easy acceptance of the theatre ticket showed his mind in this respect.

The four men in his room rose respectfully as he came in. The air was blue with smoke, and Lew Cuccini offered a rough apology. He had been released that morning from detention, for Meadows had found it difficult to frame a charge which did not expose the full activities of the police, and the part they were playing in relation to Mirabelle Leicester. Evidently Cuccini had been reproaching, in his own peculiar way and in his own unprincipled language, the cowardice of his three companions, for the atmosphere seemed tense when the doctor returned. Yet, as was subsequently proved, the appearance of discord was deceptive; might indeed have been staged for their host's benefit.

"I've just been telling these birds——" began Cuccini.

"Oh, shut up, Lew!" growled one of his friends. "If that crazy man hadn't been shouting your name, we should not have gone back! He'd have wakened the dead. And our orders were to retire at the first serious sign of an alarm. That's right, doctor, isn't it?"

"Sure it's right," said the doctor blandly. "Never be caught—that is a good motto. Cuccini was caught."

"And I'd give a year of my life to meet that Dago again," said Cuccini, between his teeth.

He was delightfully inconsistent, for he came into the category, having been born in Milan, and had had his early education in the Italian quarter of Hartford, Connecticut.

"He'd have tortured me too . . . he was going to put lighted wax matches between my fingers——"

"And then you spilled it!" accused one of the three hotly. "You talk about us bolting!"

"Silence!" roared the doctor. "This is unseemly! I have forgiven everything. That shall be enough for you all. I will hear no other word."

"Where is Gurther?" Cuccini asked the question.

"He has gone away. To-night he leaves for America. He may return—who knows? But that is the intention."

"Snaking?" asked somebody, and there was a little titter of laughter.

"Say, doctor, how do you work that stunt?" Cuccini leaned forward, his cigar between his fingers, greatly intrigued. "I saw no snakes down at Rath Hall, and yet he was bitten, just as that Yankee was bitten—Washington."

"He will die," said the doctor complacently. He was absurdly jealous for the efficacy of his method.

"He was alive yesterday, anyway. We shadowed him to the station."

"Then he was not bitten—no, that is impossible. When the snake-bites,"— Oberzohn raised his palms and gazed piously at the ceiling—"after that there is nothing. No, no, my friend, you are mistaken."

"I tell you I'm not making any mistake," said the other doggedly. "I was in the room, I tell you, soon after they brought him in, and I heard one of the busies say that his face was all wet."

"So!" said Oberzohn dully. "That is very bad."

"But how do you do it, doctor? Do you shoot or sump'n'?"

"Let us talk about eventual wealth and happiness," said the doctor. "To-night is a night of great joy for me. I will sing you a song."

Then, to the amazement of the men and to their great unhappiness, he sang, in a thin, reedy old voice, the story of a young peasant who had been thwarted in love and had thrown himself from a cliff into a seething waterfall. It was a lengthy song, intensely sentimental, and his voice held few of the qualities of music. The gang had never been set a more difficult job than to keep straight faces until he had finished.

"Gee! You're some artist, doctor!" said the sycophantic Cuccini, and managed to get a simulation of envy into his voice.

"In my student days I was a great singer," said the doctor modestly.

Over the mantelpiece was a big, old clock, with a face so faded that only a portion of the letters remained. Its noisy ticking had usually a sedative effect on the doctor. But its main purpose and value was its accuracy. Every day it was corrected by a message from Greenwich, and as Oberzohn's success as an organizer depended upon exact timing, it was one of his most valuable assets.

He glanced up at the clock now, and that gave Cuccini his excuse.

"We'll be getting along, doctor," he said. "You don't want anything to-night? I'd like to get a cut at that Gonsalez man. You won't leave me out if there's anything doing?"

Oberzohn rose and went out of the room without another word, for he knew that the rising of Cuccini was a signal that not only was the business of the day finished, but also that the gang needed its pay.

Every gang-leader attended upon Mr. Oberzohn once a week with his pay-roll, and it was usually the custom for the Herr Doktor to bring his cash-box into the room and extract sufficient to liquidate his indebtedness to the leader. It was a big box, and on pay-day, as this was, filled to the top with bank-notes and Treasury bills. He brought it back now, put it on the table, consulted the little slip that Cuccini offered to him, and, taking out a pad of notes, fastened about by a rubber band, he wetted his finger and thumb.

"You needn't count them," said Cuccini. "We'll take the lot."

The doctor turned to see that Cuccini was carelessly holding a gun in his hand.

"The fact is, doctor," said Cuccini coolly, "we've seen the red light, and if we don't skip now, while the skipping's good, there's going to be no place we can stay comfortable in this little island, and I guess we'll follow Gurther."

One glance the doctor gave at the pistol and then he resumed his counting, as though nothing had happened.

"Twenty, thirty, forty, fifty . . ."

"Now quit that," said Cuccini roughly. "I tell you, you needn't count."

"My friend, I prefer to know what I am going to lose. It is a pardonable piece of curiosity."

He raised his hand to the wall, where a length of cord hung, and pulled at it gently, without taking his eyes from the bank-notes.

"What are you doing? Put up your hands!" hissed Cuccini.

"Shoot, I beg." Oberzohn threw a pad of notes on the table. "There is your pay." He slammed down the lid of the box. "Now you shall go, if you *can* go! Do you hear them?" He raised his hand, and to the strained ears of the men came a gentle rustling sound from the passage outside as though somebody were dragging a piece of parchment along the floor. "Do you hear? You shall go if you can," said the doctor again, with amazing calmness.

"The snakes!" breathed Cuccini, going white, and the hand that held the pistol shook.

"Shoot them, my friend," sneered Oberzohn. "If you see them, shoot them. But you will not see them, my brave man. They will be—where? No eyes shall see them come or go. They may lie behind a picture, they may wait until the door is opened, and then . . . !"

Cuccini's mouth was dry.

"Call 'em off, doctor," he said tremulously.

"Your gun—on the table."

Still the rustling sound was audible. Cuccini hesitated for a second, then obeyed, and took up the notes.

The other three men were huddled together by the fire-place, the picture of fear.

"Don't open the door, doc," said Cuccini, but Oberzohn had already gripped the handle and turned it.

They heard another door open and the click of the passage light as it had come on. Then he returned.

"If you go now, I shall not wish to see you again. Am I not a man to whom all secrets are known? You are well aware!"

Cuccini looked from the doctor to the door.

"Want us to go?" he asked, troubled.

Oberzohn shrugged.

"As you wish! It was my desire that you should stay with me to-night—there is big work and big money for all of you."

The men were looking at one another uneasily.

"How long do you want us to stay?" asked Cuccini.

"To-night only; if you would not prefer . . ."

To-night would come the crisis. Oberzohn had realized this since the day dawned for him.

"We'll stay—where do we sleep?"

For answer Oberzohn beckoned them from the room and they followed him into the laboratory. In the wall that faced them was a heavy iron door that opened into a concrete storehouse, where he kept various odds and ends of equipment, oil and spirit for his cars, and the little gas engine that worked a small dynamo in the laboratory and gave him, if necessary, a lighting plant independent of outside current.

There were three long windows heavily barred and placed just under the ceiling.

"Looks like the condemned cell to me," grumbled Cuccini suspiciously.

"Are the bolts on the inside of a condemned cell?" asked Oberzohn. "Does the good warden give you the key as I give you?"

Cuccini took the key.

"All right," he said ungraciously, "there are plenty of blankets here, boys—I guess you want us where the police won't look, eh?"

"That is my intention," replied the doctor.

Dr. Oberzohn closed the door on them and re-entered his study, his big mouth twitching with amusement. He pulled the cord again and closed the ventilator he had opened. It was only a few days before that he had discovered that there were dried leaves in the ventilator shaft, and that the opening of the inlet made them rustle, disturbingly for a man who was engaged in a profound study of the lesser known, and therefore the more highly cultured, philosophers.

# Chapter XXXI                    The Things in the Box

HE heard the soft purr of engines, and, looking through the hall window, saw the dim lights of the car approaching the house, and turned out the hall lamp. There he waited in the darkness, till the door of the limousine opened and Gurther jumped out.

"I respectfully report that it is done, Herr Doktor," he said.

Oberzohn nodded.

"The woman of Newton—where is she?"

"She is inside. Is it your wish that I should bring her? She was very troublesome, Herr Doktor, and I had to use the needle."

"Bring her in—you!" He barked to the chauffeur. "Help our friend."

Together they lifted the unconscious girl, but carried her no farther than the steps. At this point Oberzohn decided that she must return to the prison. First they sent the chauffeur away; the car was garaged at New Cross (it was one of Oberzohn's three London depots), where the man also lived. After he had gone, they carried Joan between them to the factory, taking what, to Gurther, seemed an unnecessarily circuitous route. If it was unnecessary, it was at least expedient, for the nearest way to the factory led past the yawning hole that the doctor had dug with such labour.

There was no mistaking Oberzohn's arrival this time. The trap went up with a thud, and Mirabelle listened, with a quickly beating heart, to the sound of feet coming down the stone stairs. There were two people, and they were walking heavily. Somehow she knew before she saw their burden that it was Joan. She was in evening dress, her face as white as chalk and her eyes closed; the girl thought she was dead when she saw them lay her on the bed.

"You have given her too much, Gurther," said Oberzohn.

Gurther?

She had not recognized him. It was almost impossible to believe that this was the dapper young man who had danced with her at the Arts Ball.

"I had to guess in the dark, Herr Doktor," said Gurther.

They were talking in German, and Mirabelle's acquaintance with that language was very slight. She saw Gurther produce a small flat case from his pocket, take out a little phial, and shake into the palm of his hand a small brown capsule. This he dissolved in a tiny tube which, with the water he used, was also extracted from the case. Half filling a minute syringe, he sent the needle into Joan's arm. A pause, and then:

"Soon she will wake, with your kind permission, Herr Doktor," said Gurther.

Mirabelle was not looking at him, but she knew that his hot eyes were fixed on her, that all the time except the second he was operating, he was looking at her; and now she knew that this was the man to be feared. A cold hand seemed to grip at her heart.

"That will do, Gurther." Oberzohn's voice was sharp. He, too, had interpreted the stare. "You need not wait."

Gurther obediently stalked from the room, and the doctor followed. Almost before the trap had fastened down she was by the girl's side, with a basin of water and a wet towel. The second the water touched her face, Joan opened her eyes and gazed wildly up at the vaulted ceiling, then rolling over from the bed to her knees, she struggled to her feet, swayed and would have fallen, had not Mirabelle steadied her.

"They've got him! They've got my boy . . . killed him like a dog!"

"What—Mr.—Mr. Newton?" gasped Mirabelle, horrified.

"Killed him—Monty—Monty!"

And then she began to scream and run up and down the room like a thing demented. Mirabelle, sick at heart, almost physically sick at the sight, caught her and tried to calm her, but she was distracted, half mad. The drug and its antidote seemed to have combined to take away the last vestige of restraint. It was not until she fell, exhausted, that Mirabelle was able to drag her again to the bed and lay her upon it.

Montague Newton was dead! Who had killed him? Who were the "they"? Then she thought of Gurther in his strange attire; white dress-front crumpled, even his beard disarranged in the struggle he had had with the overwrought woman.

In sheer desperation she ran up the steps and tried the trap, but it was fast. She must get away from here—must get away at once. Joan was moaning pitiably, and the girl sat by her side, striving to calm her. She seemed to have passed into a state of semi-consciousness; except for her sobs, she made no sound and uttered no intelligible word. Half an hour passed—the longest and most dreadful half-hour in Mirabelle Leicester's life. And then she heard a sound. It had penetrated even to the brain of this half-mad girl, for she opened her eyes wide, and, gripping Mirabelle, drew herself up.

"He's coming," she said, white to the lips, "coming . . . the Killer is coming!"

"For God's sake don't talk like that!" said Mirabelle, beside herself with fear.

There it was, in the outer room; a stealthy shuffle of feet. She stared at the closed door, and the strain of the suspense almost made her faint. And then she saw the steel door move, slowly, and first a hand came through, the edge of a face . . . Gurther was leering at her. His beard was gone, and his wig; he was collarless, and had over his white shirt the stained jacket that was his everyday wear.

"I want you." He was talking to Mirabelle.

Her tongue clave to the roof of her mouth, but she did not speak.

"My pretty little lady——" he began, and then, with a shriek, Joan leapt at him.

"Murderer, murderer . . . ! Beast!" she cried, striking wildly at his face. With a curse, he tried to throw her off, but she was clinging to him; a bestial lunatic thing, hardly human.

He flung her aside at last, and then he put up his hand to guard his face as she leapt at him again. This time she went under his arm and was through the door in a flash. He heard the swift patter of her feet on the stairs, and turned in pursuit. The trap was open. He stumbled and tripped in the dark across the floor of the gaunt factory. Just as she reached the open, he grabbed at her and missed. Like a deer she sped, but he was fleeter-footed behind her; and suddenly his hand closed about her throat.

"You had better go out, my friend," he said, and tightened his grip.

As she twisted to avoid him, he put out his foot. There was a grating snap, something gripped his legs, and the excruciating pain of it was agonizing. He loosened his hold of her throat, but held her arm tightly. With all his strength he threw her against the wall and she fell in a heap. Then, leaning down, he forced apart the cruel jagged teeth of the man-trap on to which he had put his foot, and drew his leg clear. He was bleeding; his trouser leg was torn to ribbons. He stopped only long enough to drag the girl to her feet, and, throwing her across his shoulder as though she were a sack, he went back into the factory, down the stairs, and threw her on to the bed with such violence that the spring supports broke. It had a strange effect upon the dazed woman, but this he did not see, for he had turned to Mirabelle.

"My little lady, I want you!" he breathed.

Blood was trickling down from his wounded calf, but he did not feel the pain any more; felt nothing, save the desire to hurt those who hunted him; wanted nothing but the materialization of crude and horrid dreams.

She stood, frozen, paralysed, incapable of movement. And then his hand came under her chin and he lifted her face; and she saw the bright, hungry eyes devouring her, saw the thin lips come closer and closer, could not move; had lost all sentient impressions, and could only stare into the eyes of this man-snake, hypnotized by the horror of the moment.

And then a raging fury descended upon him. Narrow fingers tore at his face, almost blinding him. He turned with a howl of rage, but the white-faced Joan had flown to the furnace and taken up a short iron bar that had been used to rake the burning coals together. She struck at him and missed. He dodged past her and she flung the bar at him, and again missed him. The iron struck the green box, behind the furnace, there was a sound of smashing glass. He did not notice this, intent only upon the girl, and Mirabelle closed her eyes and heard only the blow as he struck her.

When she looked again, Joan was lying on the bed and he was tying one of her hands to the bed-rail with a strap which he had taken from his waist. Then Mirabelle saw a sight that released her pent speech. He heard her scream and grinned round at her . . . saw where she was looking and looked too.

Something was coming from the broken green box! A black, spade-shaped head, with bright, hard eyes that seemed to survey the scene in a malignant stare. And then, inch by inch, a thick shining thing, like a rubber rope, wriggled slowly to the floor, coiled about upon itself, and raised its flat head.

"Oh, God, look!"

He turned about at the sight, that immovable grin of his upon his face, and said something in a guttural tongue. The snake was motionless, its baleful gaze first upon the sinking girl, then upon the man.

Gurther's surprise was tragic; it was as though he had been confronted with some apparition from another world. And then his hand went to his hip pocket; there was a flash of light and a deafening explosion that stunned her. The pistol dropped from his hand and fell with a clatter to the floor, and she saw his arm was stiffly extended, and protruding from the cuff of his coat a black tail that wound round and round his wrist. It had struck up his sleeve. The cloth about his biceps was bumping up and down erratically.

He stood straightly erect, grinning, the arm still outflung, his astonished eyes upon the coil about his wrist. And then, slowly his other hand came round, gripped the tail and pulled it savagely forth. The snake turned with an angry hiss and tried to bite back at him; but raising his hand, he brought the head crashing down against the furnace. There was a convulsive wriggle as the reptile fell among the ashes.

"Gott in himmel!" whispered Gurther, and his free hand went up to his arm and felt gingerly. "He is dead, gracious lady. Perhaps there is another?"

He went, swaying as he walked, to the green box, and put in his hand without hesitation. There was another—a bigger snake, roused from its sleep and angry. He bit twice at the man's wrist, but Gurther laughed, a gurgling laugh of pure enjoyment. For already he was a dead man; that he knew. And it had come to him, at the moment and second of his dissolution, when the dread gates of judgment were already ajar, that he should go to his Maker with this clean space in the smudge of his life.

"Go, little one," he said, grinning into the spade-face. "You have no more poison; that is finished!"

He put the writhing head under his heel, and Mirabelle shut her eyes and put her hands to her ears. When she looked again, the man was standing by the door, clinging to the post and slipping with every frantic effort to keep himself erect.

He grinned at her again; this man of murder, who had made his last kill.

"Pardon, gracious lady," he said thickly, and went down on his knees, his head against the door, his body swaying slowly from side to side, and finally tumbled over.

She heard Oberzohn's harsh voice from the floor above. He was calling Gurther, and presently he appeared in the doorway, and there was a pistol in his hand.

"So!" he said, looking down at the dying man.

And then he saw the snake, and his face wrinkled. He looked from Mirabelle to the girl on the bed, went over and examined her, but did not attempt to release the strap. It was Mirabelle who did that; Mirabelle who sponged the bruised face and loosened the dress.

So doing, she felt a hand on her shoulder.

"Come," said Oberzohn.

"I'm staying here with Joan, until——"

"You come at once, or I will give you to my pretty little friends." He pointed to the two snakes on the floor who still moved spasmodically.

She had to step past Gurther, but that seemed easier than passing those wriggling, shining black ropes; and, her hand in his, she stumbled up the dark steps and eventually into the clean, sweet air of the night.

He was dressed for a journey; she had noticed that when he appeared. A heavy cloth cap was on his curious-shaped head, and he looked less repulsive with so much of his forehead hidden. Though the night was warm, he wore an overcoat.

They were passing between the wall and the factory when he stopped and put his hand before her mouth. He had heard voices, low voices on the other side of the wall, and presently the scrape of something. Without removing his hand from her face, he half dragged, half pushed her until they were clear of the factory.

She thought they were going back to the house, which was in darkness, but instead, he led her straight along the wall, and presently she saw the bulk of the barge.

"Stay, and do not speak," he said, and began to turn a rusty wheel. With a squeak and a groan the water-gates opened inwards.

What did he intend doing? There was no sign of a boat, only this old dilapidated barge. She was presently to know.

"Come," he said again.

She was on the deck of the barge, moving forward to its bow, which pointed towards the open gate and the canal beyond.

She heard him puff and groan as he strained at a rope he had found, and then, looking down, she saw the front of the barge open, like the two water-gates of a lock. Displaying remarkable agility, he lowered himself over the edge; he seemed to be standing on something solid, for again he ordered her to join him.

"I will not go," she said breathlessly, and turning, would have fled, but his hand caught her dress and dragged at her.

"I will drown you here, woman," he said, and she knew that the threat would have a sequel.

Tremblingly she lowered herself over the edge until her foot touched something hard and yet yielding. He was pushing at the barge with all his might, and the platform beneath her grew in space. First the sharp nose and then the covered half-deck of the fastest motor-boat that Mr. Oberzohn's money could buy, or the ingenuity of builders could devise. The old barge was a boat-house, and this means of escape had always been to his hand. It was for this reason that he lived in a seemingly inaccessible spot.

The men who had been on the canal bank were gone. The propellers revolving slowly, the boat stole down the dark waters, after a short time slipped under a bridge over which street-cars were passing, and headed for Deptford and the river.

Dr. Oberzohn took off his overcoat and laid it tenderly inside the shelter of the open cabin, tenderly because every pocket was packed tight with money.

To Mirabelle Leicester, crouching in the darkness of that sheltered space, the time that passed had no dimension. Once an authoritative voice hailed them from the bank. It was a policeman; she saw him after the boat had passed. A gas-lamp showed the glitter of his metal buttons. But soon he was far behind.

Deptford was near when they reached a barrier which neither ingenuity nor money could pass; a ragged nightbird peered down curiously at the motor-boat.

"You can't get through here, guv'nor," he said simply. "The lock doesn't open until high tide."

"When is this high tide?" asked Oberzohn breathlessly.

"Six o'clock to-morrow morning," said the voice.

For a long time he saw, stricken to inactivity by the news, and then he sent his engines into reverse and began circling round.

"There is one refuge for us, young miss," he said. "Soon we shall see it. Now I will tell you something. I desire so much to live. Do you also?"

She did not answer.

"If you cry out, if you will make noises, I will kill you—that is all," he said; and the very simplicity of his words, the lack of all emphasis behind the deadly earnestness, told her that he would keep his word.

# Chapter XXXII          The Search

" 'WARE man-traps," said Gonsalez.

The white beam of his lamp had detected the ugly thing. He struck at it with his stick, and with a vicious snap it closed.

"Here's one that's been sprung," he said, and examined the teeth. "And, what's more, it has made a catch! There's blood here."

Manfred and Digby were searching the ground cautiously. Then Manfred heard the quick intake of his breath, and he stooped again, picked up a strip of braided cloth.

"A man's," he said, and his relief betrayed his fear. "Somebody in evening dress, and quite recent." He looked at his finger. "The blood is still wet."

Digby showed him the ventilator grating through which he had smelt the incense, and when Leon stooped, the faint aroma still remained.

"We will try the factory first. If that draws blank, we'll ask Dr. Oberzohn's guidance, and if it is not willingly given I shall persuade him." And in the reflected light of the lamp George Manfred saw the hard Leon he knew of old. "This time I shall not promise: my threat will be infinitely milder than my performance."

They came to the dark entry of the factory, and Manfred splashed his light inside.

"You'll have to walk warily here," he said.

Progress was slow, for they did not know that a definite path existed between the jagged ends of broken iron and debris. Once or twice Leon stopped to stamp on the floor; it gave back a hollow sound.

The search was long and painfully slow: a quarter of an hour passed before Leon's lamp focussed the upturned flagstone and the yawning entrance of the vault. He was the first to descend, and, as he reached the floor, he saw, silhouetted in the light that flowed from the inner room, a man, as he thought, crouching in the doorway, and covered him.

"Put up your hands!" he said.

The figure made no response, and Manfred ran to the shape. The face was in the shadow, but he brought his own lamp down and recognized the set grin of the dead man.

Gurther!

So thus he had died, in a last effort to climb out for help.

"The Snake," said Manfred briefly. "There are no marks on his face, so far as I can see."

"Do you notice his wrist, George?"

Then, looking past the figure, Gonsalez saw the girl lying on the bed, and recognized Joan before he saw her face. Half-way across the room he slipped on something. Instinctively he knew it was a snake and leapt around, his pistol balanced.

"Merciful heaven! Look at this!"

He stared from the one reptile to the other.

"Dead!" he said. "That explains Gurther."

Quickly he unstrapped Joan's wrists and lifted up her head, listening, his ear pressed to the faintly fluttering heart. The basin and the sponge told its own story. Where was Mirabelle?

There was another room, and a row of big cupboards, but the girl was in no place that he searched.

"She's gone, of course," said Manfred quietly. "Otherwise, the trap would not have been open. We'd better get this poor girl out of the way and search the grounds. Digby, go to——"

He stopped.

If Oberzohn were in the house, they must not take the risk of alarming him.

But the girl's needs were urgent. Manfred picked her up and carried her out into the open, and, with Leon guiding them, they came, after a trek which almost ended in a broken neck for Leon, to within a few yards of the house.

"I presume," said Gonsalez, "that the hole into which I nearly dived was dug for a purpose, and I shouldn't be surprised to learn it was intended that the late Mr. Gurther should find a permanent home there. Shall I take her?"

"No, no," said Manfred, "go on into the lane. Poiccart should be there with the car by now."

"Poiccart knows more about growing onions than driving motor-cars." The gibe was mechanical; the man's heart and mind were on Mirabelle Leicester.

They had to make a circuit of the stiff copper-wire fence which surrounded the house, and eventually reached Hangman's Lane just as the head-lamps of the Spanz came into view.

"I will take her to the hospital and get in touch with the police," said Manfred. "I suppose there isn't a near-by telephone?"

"I shall probably telephone from the house," said Leon gravely.

From where he stood he could not tell whether the door was open or closed. There was no transom above the door, so that it was impossible to tell whether there were lights in the passage or not. The house was in complete darkness.

He was so depressed that he did not even give instructions to Poiccart, who was frankly embarrassed by the duty which had been imposed upon him, and gladly surrendered the wheel to George.

They lifted the girl into the tonneau, and, backing into the gate, went cautiously up the lane—Leon did not wait to see their departure, but returned to the front of the house.

The place was in darkness. He opened the wire gate and went silently up the steps. He had not reached the top before he saw that the door was wide open. Was it a trap? His lamp showed him the switch: he turned on the light and closed the door behind him, and, bending his head, listened.

The first door on the right was Oberzohn's room. The door was ajar, but the lamps were burning inside. He pushed it open with the toe of his boot, but the room was empty.

The next two doors he tried on that floor were locked. He went carefully down to the kitchens and searched them both. They were tenantless. He knew there was a servant or two on the premises, but one thing he did not know, and this he discovered in the course of his tour, was that Oberzohn had no bedroom. One of the two rooms above had evidently been occupied by the servants. The door was open, the room was empty and in some confusion; a coarse night-dress had been hastily discarded and left on the tumbled bedclothes. Oberzohn had sent his servants away in a hurry—why?

There was a half-smoked cigarette on the edge of a deal wash-stand. The ash lay on the floor. In a bureau every drawer was open and empty, except one, a half-drawer filled with odd scraps of cloth. Probably the cook or the maid smoked. He found a packet of cigarettes under one pillow to confirm this view, and guessed they had gone to bed leisurely with no idea that they would be turned into the night.

He learned later that Oberzohn had bundled off his servants at ten minutes' notice, paying them six months' salary as some salve for the indignity.

Pfeiffer's room was locked; but now, satisfied that the house was empty, he broke the flimsy catch, made a search but found nothing. Gurther's apartment was in indescribable disorder. He had evidently changed in a hurry. His powder puffs and beards, crepe hair and spirit bottles, littered the dressing-table. He remembered, with a pang of contrition, that he had promised to telephone the police, but when he tried to get the exchange he found the line was dead: a strange circumstance, till he discovered that late that evening Meadows had decided to cut the house from all telephonic communication, and had given orders accordingly.

It was a queerly built house: he had never realized its remarkable character until he had examined it at these close quarters. The walls were of immense thickness: that fact was brought home to him when he had opened the window of the maid's room to see if Digby was in sight. The stairs were of concrete, the shutters which covered the windows of Oberzohn's study were steel-faced. He decided, pending the arrival of the police, to make an examination of the two locked rooms. The first of these he had no difficulty in opening. It was a large room on the actual ground level, and was reached by going down six steps. A rough bench ran round three sides of this bare apartment, except where its continuity broke to allow entrance to a further room. The door was of steel and was fastened.

The room was dusty but not untidy. Everything was in order. The various apparatus was separated by a clear space. In one corner he saw a gas engine and dynamo covered with dust. There was nothing to be gained here. The machine which interested him most was one he knew all about, only he had not guessed the graphite moulds. The contents of a small blue bottle, tightly corked, and seemingly filled with discoloured swabs of cotton-wool, however, revived his interest. With a glance round the laboratory, he went out and tried the second of the locked doors.

This room, however, was well protected, both in the matter of stoutness of door and complication of locks. Leon tried all his keys, and then used his final argument. This he carried in a small leather pouch in his hip pocket; three steel pieces that screwed together and ended in a bright claw. Hammering the end of the jemmy with his fist, he forced the claw between door and lintel, and in less than a minute the lock had broken, and he was in the presence of the strangest company that had ever been housed.

Four electric radiators were burning. The room was hot and heavy, and the taint of it caught his throat, as it had caught the throat of the Danish servant. He put on all the lights—and they were many—and then began his tour.

There were two lines of shelves, wide apart, and each supporting a number of boxes, some of which were wrapped in baize, some of which, however, were open to view. All had glass fronts, all had steel tops with tiny air-holes, and in each there coiled, in its bed of wool or straw, according to its requirements, one or two snakes. There were cobras, puff-adders, two rattlesnakes, seemingly dead, but, as he guessed, asleep; there was a South American *fer-de-lance*, that most unpleasant representative of his species; there were little coral snakes, and, in one long box, a whole nest of queer little things that looked like tiny yellow lobsters, but which he knew as scorpions.

He was lifting a baize cover when:

"Don't move, my friend! I think I can promise you more intimate knowledge of our little family."

Leon turned slowly, his hands extended. Death was behind him, remorseless, unhesitating. To drop his hand to his pocket would have been the end for him—he had that peculiar instinct which senses sincerity, and when Dr. Oberzohn gave him his instructions he had no doubt whatever that his threat was backed by the will to execute.

Oberzohn stood there, a little behind him, white-faced, open-eyed with fear, Mirabelle Leicester.

Digby—where was he? He had left him in the grounds.

The doctor was examining the broken door and grunted his annoyance.

"I fear my plan will not be good," he said, "which was to lock you in this room and break all those glasses, so that you might become better acquainted with the Quiet People. That is not to be. Instead, march!"

What did he intend? Leon strolled out nonchalantly, but Oberzohn kept his distance, his eyes glued upon those sensitive hands that could move so quickly and jerk and fire a gun in one motion.

"Stop!"

Leon halted, facing the open front door and the steps.

"You will remember my sainted brother, Señor Gonsalez, and of the great loss which the world suffered when he was so vilely murdered?"

Leon stood without a quiver. Presently the man would shoot. At any second a bullet might come crashing on its fatal errand. This was a queer way to finish so full a life. He knew it was coming, had only one regret; that this shaken girl should be called upon to witness such a brutal thing. He wanted to say good-bye to her, but was afraid of frightening her.

"You remember that so sainted brother?" Oberzohn's voice was raucous with fury. Ahead of him the light fell upon a face.

"Digby! Stay where you are!" shouted Leon.

The sound of the explosion made him jump. He saw the brickwork above the doorway splinter, heard a little scuffle, and turned, gun in hand.

Oberzohn had pulled the girl in front of him so that she afforded a complete cover: under her arm he held his pistol.

"Run!" she screamed.

He hesitated a second. Again the pistol exploded and a bullet ricochetted from the door. Leon could not fire. Oberzohn so crouched that nothing but a trick shot could miss the girl and hit him. And then, as the doctor shook free the hand that gripped his wrist, he leapt down the steps and into the darkness. Another second and the door slammed. He heard the thrust of the bolts and a clang as the great iron bar fell into its place. Somehow he had a feeling as of a citadel door being closed against him.

Dr. Oberzohn had returned unobserved, though the night was clear. Passing through the open water-gate he had tied up to the little quay and landed his unwilling passenger. Digby, according to instructions, had been making a careful circuit of the property, and at the moment was as far away from the barge as it was humanly possible to be. Unchallenged, the doctor had worked his way back to the house. The light in the hall warned him that somebody was there. How many? He could not guess.

"Take off your shoes," he growled in Mirabelle's ear, and she obeyed.

Whatever happened, he must not lose touch of her, or give her an opportunity of escape. Still grasping her arm with one hand and his long Mauser pistol in the other, he went softly up the steps, got into the hall and listened, locating the intruder instantly.

It all happened so quickly that Mirabelle could remember nothing except the desperate lunge she made to knock up the pistol that had covered the spine of Leon Gonsalez. She stood dumbly by, watching this horrible old man fasten the heavy door, and obediently preceded him from room to room. She saw the long cases in the hot room and shrank back. And then began a complete tour of the house. There were still shutters to be fastened, peep-holes to be opened up. He screwed up the shutters of the servants' room, and then, with a hammer, broke the thumb-piece short.

"You will stay here," he said. "I do not know what they will do. Perhaps they will shoot. I also am a shooter!"

Not satisfied with the lock that fastened her door, he went into his workshop, found a staple, hook and padlock, and spent the greater part of an hour fixing this additional security. At last he had finished, and could put the situation in front of four very interested men.

He unlocked the door of the concrete annexe and called the crestfallen gunmen forth, and in a very few words explained the situation and their danger.

"For every one of you the English police hold warrants," he said. "I do not bluff, I know. This afternoon I was visited by the police. I tell you I do not bluff you—me they cannot touch, because they know nothing, can prove nothing. At most I shall go to prison for a few years, but with you it is different."

"Are they waiting outside?" asked one suspiciously. "Because, if they are, we'd better move quick."

"You do not move, quick or slow," said Oberzohn. "To go out from here means certain imprisonment for you all. To stay, if you follow my plan, means that every one of you may go free and with money."

"What's the idea?" asked Cuccini. "Are you going to fight them?"

"Sure I am going to fight them," nodded Oberzohn. "That is my scheme. I have the young miss upstairs; they will not wish to do her any harm. I intend to defend this house."

"Do you mean you're going to hold it?" asked one of the staggered men.

"I will hold it until they are tired, and make terms."

Cuccini was biting his nails nervously.

"Might as well be hung for a sheep as a lamb, boss," he growled. "I've got an idea you've roped us into this."

"You may rope yourself out of it!" snapped Oberzohn. "There is the door— go if you wish. There are police there; make terms with them. A few days ago you were in trouble, my friend. Who saved you? The doctor Oberzohn. There is life imprisonment for every one of you, and I can hold this house myself. Stay with me, and I will give you a fortune greater than any you have dreamt about. And, more than this, at the end you shall be free."

"Where's Gurther?"

"He has been killed—by accident." Oberzohn's face was working furiously. "By accident he died," he said, and told the truth unconvincingly. "There is nothing now to do but to make a decision."

Cuccini and his friends consulted in a whisper.

"What do we get for our share?" he asked, and Oberzohn mentioned a sum which staggered them.

"I speak the truth," he said. "In two days I shall have a gold-mine worth millions."

The habit of frankness was on him, and he told them the story of the golden hill without reservations. His agents at Lisbon had already obtained from the

Ministry an option upon the land and its mineral rights. As the clock struck twelve on June 14, the goldfield of Biskara automatically passed into his possession.

"On one side you have certain imprisonment, on the other you have great monies and happiness."

"How long will we have to stay here?" asked Cuccini.

"I have food for a month, even milk. They will not cut the water because of the girl. For the same reason they will not blow in the door."

Again they had a hasty consultation and made their decision.

"All right, boss, we'll stay. But we want that share-out put into writing."

"To my study," said Oberzohn promptly, "march!"

He was half-way through writing the document when there came a thunderous knock on the door and he got up, signalling for silence. Tiptoeing along the passage, he came to the door.

"Yes—who is that?" he asked.

"Open, in the name of the law!" said a voice, and he recognized Meadows. "I have a warrant for your arrest, and if necessary the door will be broken in."

"So!" said Oberzohn, dropped the muzzle of his pistol until it rested on the edge of the little letter-slit and fired twice.

# Chapter XXXIII                    The Siege

BUT Meadows had already been warned to keep clear of the letter-box, and the bullets eventually reached one of the railway viaducts, to the embarrassment of a road ganger who happened to be almost in the line of fire.

Meadows slipped down the steps to cover. Inside the wire fence a dozen policemen were waiting.

"Sergeant, go back to the station in the police car and bring arms," he said. "This is going to be a long job."

Gonsalez had made a very careful reconnaissance of the ground, and from the first had recognized the difficulties which lay ahead of the attacking party. The wall rose sheer without any break; such windows as were within reach were heavily shuttered; and even the higher windows, he guessed, had been covered. The important problem in his mind was to locate the room in which the girl was imprisoned, and, making a mental review of the house, he decided that she was either in the servants' apartment or in that which had held Gurther. By the light of the lantern he made a rapid sketch plan of the floors he had visited.

Meadows had gone away to telephone to police head-quarters. He had decided to re-establish telephone connection with the doctor, and when this was done, he called the house and Oberzohn's voice answered him.

The colloquy was short and unsatisfactory. The terms which the doctor offered were such as no self-respecting government could accept. Immunity for himself and his companions (he insisted so strongly upon this latter offer that Meadows guessed, accurately, that the gang were standing around the instrument).

"I don't want your men at all. So far as I am concerned, they can go free," said Meadows. "Ask one of them to speak on the 'phone."

"Oh, indeed, no," said Oberzohn. "It is ridiculous to ask me that."

He hung up at this point and explained to the listening men that the police had offered him freedom if he would surrender the gang.

"As I already told you," he said in conclusion, "that is not the way of Dr. Oberzohn. I will gain nothing at the expense of my friends."

A little later, when Cuccini crept into the room to call police head-quarters and confirm this story of the doctor, he found that not only had the wire been cut, but a yard of the flex had been removed. Dr. Oberzohn was taking no risks.

The night passed without any further incident. Police reserves were pouring into the neighbourhood; the grounds had been isolated, and even the traffic of barges up and down the canal prohibited. The late editions of the morning newspapers had a heavily head-lined paragraph about the siege of a house in the New Cross area, and when the first reporters arrived a fringe of sightseers had already gathered at every police barrier. Later, special editions, with fuller details, began to roll out of Fleet Street; the crowd grew in density, and a high official from Scotland Yard, arriving soon after nine, ordered a further area to be cleared, and with some difficulty the solid wedge of humanity at the end of Hangman's Lane was slowly pushed back until the house was invisible to them. Even here, a passage-way was kept for police cars and only holders of passes were allowed to come within the prohibited area.

The three men, with the police chief, had taken up their head-quarters in the factory, from which the body of Gurther had been removed in the night. The Deputy Commissioner, who came on the spot at nine, and examined the dead snakes, was something of a herpetologist, and pronounced them to be veritable *fers-de-lance*, a view from which Poiccart differed.

"They are a species of African tree snakes that the natives call *mamba*. There are two, a black and a green. Both of these are the black type."

"The Zoo mamba?" said the official, remembering the sensational disappearance of a deadly snake which had preceded the first of the snake mysteries.

"You will probably find the bones of the Zoo mamba in some mole run in Regent's Park—he must have been frozen to death the night of his escape," said Poiccart. "It was absolutely impossible that at that temperature he could live. I have made a very careful inspection of the land, and adjacent to the Zoological Gardens is a big stretch of earth which is honeycombed by moles. No, this was imported, and the rest of his menagerie was imported."

The police chief shook his head.

"Still, I'm not convinced that a snake could have been responsible for these deaths," he said, and went over the ground so often covered.

The three listened in polite silence, and offered no suggestion.

The morning brought news of Washington's arrival in Lisbon. He had left the train at Irun, Leon's agent in Madrid having secured a relay of aeroplanes, and the journey from Irun to Lisbon had been completed in a few hours. He was now on his way back.

"If he makes the connections he will be here to-night," he told Manfred. "I rather think he will be a very useful recruit to our forces."

"You're thinking of the snakes in the house?"

Leon nodded.

"I know Oberzohn," he said simply, and George Manfred thought of the girl, and knew the unspoken fears of his friend were justified.

The night had not been an idle one for Oberzohn and his companions. With the first light of dawn they had mounted to the roof, and, under his direction, the gunmen had dismantled the four sheds which stood at each corner of the parapet. Unused to the handling of such heavy metal, the remnants of the Old Guard gazed in awe upon the tarnished jackets of the Maxim guns that were revealed.

Oberzohn understood the mechanism of the machines so thoroughly that in half an hour he had taught his crew the method of handling and sighting. In the larger shed was a collapsible tripod, which was put together, and on this he mounted a small but powerful searchlight and connected it up with one of the plugs in the roof.

He pointed to them the three approaches to the house: the open railway arches and the long lane, at the end of which the crowd at that moment was beginning to gather.

"From only these places can the ground be approached," he said, "and my little quick-firers cover them!"

Just before eleven there came down Hangman's Lane, drawn by a motor tractor, a long tree-trunk, suspended about the middle by chains, and Oberzohn, examining it carefully through his field-glasses, realized that no door in the world could stand against the attack of that battering-ram. He took up one of the dozen rifles that lay on the floor, sighted it carefully, resting his elbow on the parapet, and fired.

He saw the helmet of a policeman shoot away from the head of the astonished man, and fired again. This time he was more successful, for a policeman who was directing the course of the tractor crumpled up and fell in a heap.

A shrill whistle blew; the policemen ran to cover, leaving the machine unattended. Again he fired, this time at the driver of the tractor. He saw the man scramble down from his seat and run for the shelter of the fence.

A quarter of an hour passed without any sign of activity on the part of his enemies, and then eight men, armed with rifles, came racing across the ground towards the wire barrier. Oberzohn dropped his rifle, and, taking a grip of the first machine-gun in his hand, sighted it quickly. The staccato patter of the Maxim awakened the echoes. One man dropped; the line wavered. Again the shrill whistle, and they broke for cover, dragging their wounded companion with them.

"I was afraid of that," said Leon, biting his knuckles—sure evidence of his perturbation.

He had put a ladder against the wall of the factory, and now he climbed up on to the shaky roof and focussed his glasses.

"There's another Maxim on this side," he shouted down. And then, as he saw a man's head moving above the parapet, he jerked up his pistol and fired. He saw the stone splinters fly up and knew that it was not bad practice at four hundred yards. The shot had a double effect; it made the defenders cautious and aroused in them the necessary quantity of resentment.

He was hardly down before there was a splutter from the roof, and the whine and snap of machine-gun bullets; one slate tile shivered and its splinters leapt high in the air and dropped beside his hand.

The presence of the girl was the only complication. Without her, the end of Oberzohn and his companions was inevitable. Nobody realized this better than the doctor, eating a huge ham sandwich in the shelter of the parapet— an unusual luxury, for he ate few solids.

"This will be very shocking for our friends of Curzon Street," he said. "At this moment they bite their hands in despair." (He was nearly right here.)

He peeped over the parapet. There was no policeman in sight. Even the trains that had roared at regular intervals along the viaduct had ceased to run, traffic being diverted to another route.

At half-past twelve, looking through a peep-hole, he saw a long yellow line of men coming down Hangman's Lane, keeping to the shelter of the fence.

"Soldiers," he said, and for a second his voice quavered.

Soldiers they were. Presently they began to trickle into the grounds, one by one, each man finding his own cover. Simultaneously there came a flash and a crack from the nearest viaduct. A bullet smacked against the parapet and the sound of the ricochet was like the hum of a bee.

Another menace had appeared simultaneously; a great, lumbering, awkward vehicle, that kept to the middle of the lane and turned its ungainly nose into the field. It was a tank, and Oberzohn knew that only the girl's safety stood between him and the dangling noose.

He went down to see her, unlocked the door, and found her, to his amazement, fast asleep. She got up at the sound of the key in the lock, and accepted the bread and meat and water he brought her without a word.

"What time is it?"

Oberzohn stared at her.

"That you should ask the time at such a moment!" he said.

The room was in darkness but for the light he had switched on.

"It is noon, and our friends have brought soldiers. Ach! how important a woman you are, that the whole army should come out for you!"

Sarcasm was wasted on Mirabelle.

"What is going to happen—now?"

"I do not know." He shrugged his shoulders. "They have brought a diabolical instrument into the grounds. They may use it, to give them cover, so that the door may be blown in. At that moment I place you in the snake-room. This I shall tell our friends very quickly."

She gazed at him in horror.

"You wouldn't do anything so wicked, Mr. Oberzohn!"

Up and down went the skin of his forehead.

"That I shall tell them and that I shall do," he said, and locked her in with this comfortless assurance.

He went into his study and, fastening the door, took two strands of wire from his pocket and repaired the broken telephone connections.

"I wish to speak to Meadows," he said to the man who answered him—a police officer who had been stationed at the exchange to answer any call from this connection.

"I will put you through to him," was the reply.

For a moment the doctor was surprised that Meadows was not at the exchange. He did not know then that a field telephone line had been organized, and that the factory head-quarters of the directing staff was in communication with the world.

It was not Meadows, but another man who answered him, and by his tone of authority Oberzohn guessed that some higher police official than Meadows was on the spot.

"I am the doctor Oberzohn," he barked. "You have brought a tank machine to attack me. If this approaches beyond the wire fence, I shall place the woman Leicester in the home of the snakes, and there I will bind her and release my little friends to avenge me."

"Look here——" began the officer, but Oberzohn hung up on him.

He went out and locked the door, putting the key in his pocket. His one doubt was of the loyalty of his companions. But here, strangely enough, he underrated their faith in him. The very mildness of the attack, the seeming reluctance of the soldiers to fire, had raised their hopes and spirits; and when, a quarter of an hour later, they saw the tank turn about and go out into Hangman's Lane, they were almost jubilant.

"You're sure that he will carry out his threat?" asked the police chief.

"Certain," said Leon emphatically. "There is nothing on earth that will stop Oberzohn. You will force the house to find a man who has died by his own hand, and——" He shuddered at the thought. "The only thing to be done is to wait for the night. If Washington arrives on time, I think we can save Miss Leicester."

From the roof Dr. Oberzohn saw that the soldiers were digging a line of trenches, and sent a spatter of machine-gun bullets in their direction. They stopped their work for a moment to look round, and then went on digging, as though nothing had happened.

The supply of ammunition was not inexhaustible, and he determined to reserve any further fire until the attack grew more active.

Looking over the top of the parapet to examine the ground immediately below, something hot and vicious snicked his ear. He saw the brickwork of the chimney behind him crumble and scatter, and, putting up his hand, felt blood.

"You'd better keep down, Oberzohn," said Cuccini, crouching in the shelter of the parapet. "They nearly got you then. They're firing from that railway embankment. Have you had a talk with the boss of these birds?"

"They are weakening," said Oberzohn promptly. "Always they are asking me if I will surrender the men; always I reply, 'Never will I do anything so dishonourable.'"

Cuccini grunted, having his own views of the doctor's altruism.

Late in the afternoon, a flight of aeroplanes appeared in the west: five machines flying in V formation. None of the men on the roof recognized the danger, standing rather in the attitude and spirit of sightseers. The machines were flying low; with the naked eye Cuccini could read their numbers long before they came within a hundred yards of the house. Suddenly the roof began to spout little fountains of asphalt. Oberzohn screamed a warning and darted to the stairway, and three men followed him out. Cuccini lay spread-eagled where he fell, two machine-gun bullets through his head.

The fighting machines mounted, turned and came back. Standing on the floor below, Oberzohn heard the roar of their engines as they passed, and went incautiously to the roof, to discover that the guns of flying machines fire equally well from the tail. He was nearer to death then than he had ever been. One bullet hit the tip of his finger and sliced it off neatly. With a scream of pain he half fell, half staggered to safety, spluttering strange oaths in German.

The aeroplanes did not return. He waited until their noise had died away before he again ventured to the roof, to find the sky clear. Cuccini was dead, and it was characteristic of his three friends that they should make a thorough search of his pockets before they heaved the body over the parapet.

Oberzohn left the three on the roof, with strict instructions that they were to dive to cover at the first glint of white wings, and went down into his study. The death of Cuccini was in some ways a blessing. The man was full of suspicion; his heart was not in the fight, and the aeroplane gunner had merely anticipated the doctor's own plan.

Cuccini was a Latin, who spoke English well and wrote it badly. He had a characteristic hand, which it amused Oberzohn to copy, for the doctor was skilful with his pen. All through the next three hours he wrote, breaking off his labours at intervals to visit the guard on the roof. At last he had finished, and Cuccini's sprawling signature was affixed to the bottom of the third page. Oberzohn called down one of the men.

"This is the statement of Cuccini which he left. Will you put your name to his signature?"

"What is it?" asked the man surlily.

"It is a letter which the good Cuccini made—what generosity! In this he says that he alone was to blame for bringing you here, and nobody else. Also that he kept you by threats."

"And you?" asked the man.

"Also me," said Oberzohn, unabashed. "What does it matter? Cuccini is dead. May he not in his death save us all? Come, come, my good friend, you are a fool if you do not sign. After that, send down our friends that they may also sign."

A reluctant signature was fixed, and the other men came one by one, and one by one signed their names, content to stand by the graft which the doctor indicated, exculpating themselves from all responsibility in the defence.

Dusk fell and night came blackly, with clouds sweeping up from the west and a chill rain falling. Gonsalez, moodily apart from his companions, watched the dark bulk of the house fade into the background with an ever-increasing misery. What these men did after did not matter—to them. A policeman had been killed, and they stood equally guilty of murder in the eyes of the law. They could now pile horror upon horror, for the worst had happened. His only hope was that they did not know the inevitability of their punishment.

No orders for attack had been given. The soldiers were standing by, and even the attack by the aeroplanes had been due to a misapprehension of orders. He had seen Cuccini's body fall, and as soon as night came he determined to approach the house to discover if there was any other way in than the entrance by the front door.

The aeroplanes had done something more than sweep the roof with their guns. Late in the evening there arrived by special messenger telescopic photographs of the building, which the military commander and the police chief examined with interest.

Leon was watching the house when he saw a white beam of light shoot out and begin a circular sweep of the grounds. He expected this; the meaning of the connections in the wall was clear. He knew, too, how long that experiment would last. A quarter of an hour after the searchlight began its erratic survey of the ground, the lamp went out, the police having disconnected the current. But it was only for a little while, and in less than an hour the light was showing again.

"He has power in the house—a dynamo and a gas engine," explained Gonsalez.

Poiccart had been to town and had returned with a long and heavy steel cylinder, which Leon and Manfred carried between them into the open and left. They were sniped vigorously from the roof, and although the firing was rather wild, the officer in charge of the operations forbade any further movement in daylight.

At midnight came the blessed Washington. They had been waiting for him with eagerness, for he, of all men, knew something that they did not know. Briefly, Leon described the snake-room and its contents. He was not absolutely certain of some of the species, but his description was near enough to give the snake expert an idea of the species.

"Yes, sir, they're all deadly," said Washington, shaking his head. "I guess there isn't a thing there, bar the scorps, who wouldn't put a grown man to sleep in five minutes—ten minutes at the most."

They showed him the remains of the dead snake and he instantly recognized the kind, as the zoological expert had done in the afternoon.

"That's mamba. He's nearly the deadliest of all. You didn't see a fellow with a long bill-shaped head? You did? Well, that's fer-de-lance, and he's almost as bad. The little red fellows were corals. . . ."

Leon questioned him more closely.

"No, sir, they don't leap—that's not their way. A tree snake will hang on to something overhead and get you as you pass, and they'll swing from the floor, but their head's got to touch the floor first. The poor little fellow that killed Gurther was scared, and when they're scared they'll lash up at you—I've known a man to be bitten in the throat by a snake that whipped up from the ground. But usually they're satisfied to get your leg."

Leon told him his plan.

"I'll come along with you," said Washington without hesitation.

But this offer neither of the three would accept. Leon had only wanted the expert's opinion. There were scores of scientists in London, curators of museums and keepers of snakes, who could have told him everything there was to be known about the habits of the reptile in captivity. He needed somebody who had met the snake in his native environment.

An hour before daylight showed in the sky, there was a council of war, Leon put his scheme before the authorities, and the plan was approved. He did not wait for the necessary orders to be given, but, with Poiccart and Manfred, went to the place where they had left the cylinder, and, lifting it, made their slow way towards the house. In addition, Leon carried a light ladder and a small bag full of tools.

The rays of the searchlight were moving erratically, and for a long time did not come in their direction. Suddenly they found themselves in a circle of dazzling light and fell flat on their faces. The machine-gun spat viciously, the earth was churned up under the torrent of bullets, but none of the men was hit; and, more important, the cylinder was not touched.

Then suddenly, from every part of the ground, firing started. The target was the searchlight, and the shooting had not gone on for more than a minute before the light went out, so jerkily that it was obvious that one bullet at least had got home.

"Now," said Manfred, and, lifting up the cylinder, they ran.

Poiccart put his hand on the fence wire and was hurled back. The top wire was alive, but evidently the doctor's dynamo was not capable of generating a current that would be fatal. Leon produced an insulated wire cutter and snipped off a six-foot length, earthing the broken ends of the wire. They were now under the shadow of the wall of the house, and out of danger so far as bullets were concerned.

Leon planted his ladder against the window under which they stopped, and in a second had broken the glass, turned the catch and sent up the sash. From his bag he produced a small diamond drill and began to work through the thick steel plate. It was a terribly arduous job, and after ten minutes' labour he handed over the work to Manfred, who mounted in his place.

Whatever damage had been done to the searchlight had now been repaired, and its beam had concentrated on the spot where they had been last seen. This time no fusillade greeted its appearance, and Oberzohn was surprised and troubled by the inaction.

The light came into the sky, the walls grew grey and all objects sharply visible, when he saw the tank move out of the lane where it had been standing all the previous day, turn into the field, and slowly move towards the house. He set his teeth in a grin and, darting down the stairs, flung himself against the door of the girl's room, and his agitation was such that for a time he could not find the keyhole of the two locks that held the door secure.

It opened with a crash, and he almost fell into the room in his eagerness. Mirabelle Leicester was standing by the bed, her face white as death. Yet her voice was steady, almost unconcerned, when she asked:

"What do you want?"

"You!" he hissed. "You, my fine little lady—you are for the snakes!"

He flung himself upon her, though she offered no resistance, threw her back on the bed and snapped a pair of rusty handcuffs on her wrists. Pulling her to her feet, he dragged her from the room and down the stairs. He had some difficulty in opening the door of the snake-room, for he had wedged it close. The door was pushed open at last: the radiators were no longer burning. He could not afford the power. But the room was stiflingly hot, and when he turned on the lights, and she saw the long line of boxes, her knees gave way under her, and she would have fallen had he not put his arm about her waist. Dragging a heavy chair to the centre of the room, he pushed her down into it.

"Here you wait, my friend!" he yelled. "You shall wait . . . but not long!"

On the wall there were three long straps which were used for fastening the boxes when it was necessary to travel with them. In a second one thong was about her and buckled tight to the back of the chair. The second he put under the seat and fastened across her knees.

"Good-bye, gracious lady!"

The rumble of the tank came to him in that room. But he had work to do. There was no time to open the boxes. The glass fronts might easily be broken. He ran along the line, hitting the glass with the barrel of his Mauser. The girl, staring in horror, saw a green head come into view through one opening; saw a sinuous shape slide gently to the floor. And then he turned out the lights, the door was slammed, and she was left alone in the room of terror.

Oberzohn was no sooner in the passage than the first bomb exploded at the door. Splinters of wood flew past him, as he turned and raced up the stairs, feeling in his pocket as he went for the precious document which might yet clear him.

*Boom!*

He had not locked the door of the snake-room; Leon had broken the hasp. Let them go in, if they wished. The front door was not down yet. From the landing above he listened over the balustrade. And then a greater explosion than ever shook the house, and after an interval of silence he heard somebody running along the passage and shake at the snake-room door.

Too late now! He grinned his joy, went up the last flight to the roof, to find his three men in a state of mutiny, the quelling of which was not left to him. The glitter of a bayonet came through the door opening, a khaki figure slipped on to the roof, finger on trigger.

"Hands up, you!" he said, in a raucous Cockney voice.

Four pairs of hands went upward.

Manfred followed the second soldier and caught the doctor by the arm.

"I want you, my friend," he said, and Oberzohn went obediently down the stairs.

They had to pass Gurther's room: the door was open, and Manfred pushed his prisoner inside, as Poiccart and Leon ran up the stairs.

"The girl's all right. The gas killed the snakes the moment they touched the floor, and Brother Washington is dealing with the live ones," said Leon rapidly.

He shut the door quickly. The doctor was alone for the first time in his life with the three men he hated and feared.

"Oberzohn, this is the end," said Manfred.

That queer grimace that passed for a smile flitted across the puckered face of the doctor.

"I think not, my friends," he said. "Here is a statement by Cuccini. I am but the innocent victim, as you will see. Cuccini has confessed to all and has implicated his friends. I would not resist—why should I? I am an honest, respectable man, and a citizen of a great and friendly country. Behold!"

He showed the paper. Manfred took it from his hand but did not read it.

"Also, whatever happens, your lady loses her beautiful hill of gold." He found joy in this reflection. "For to-morrow is the last day——"

"Stand over there, Oberzohn," said Manfred, and pushed him against the wall. "You are judged. Though your confession may cheat the law, you will not cheat us."

And then the doctor saw something and he screamed his fear. Leon Gonsalez was fixing a cigarette to the long black holder he had found in Gurther's room.

"You hold it thus," said Leon, "do you not?" He dipped the cigarette down and pressed the small spring that was concealed in the black ebonite. "The holder is an insulated chamber that holds two small icy splinters—I found the mould in your laboratory, Herr Doktor. They drop into the cigarette, which is a metal one, and then . . ."

He lifted it to his lips and blew. None saw the two tiny icicles fly. Only Oberzohn put his hand to his cheek with a strangled scream, glared for a second, and then went down like a heap of rags.

Leon met Inspector Meadows on his way up.

"I'm afraid our friend has gone," he said. "He has cheated the hangman of ten pounds."

"Dead?" said Meadows. "Suicide?"

"It looks like a snake-bite to me," said Leon carelessly, as he went down to find Mirabelle Leicester, half laughing, half crying, whilst an earnest Elijah Washington was explaining to her the admirable domestic qualities of snakes.

"There's five thousand dollars' worth dead," he said, in despair, "but there's enough left to start a circus!"

# Chapter XXXIV               The Death Tube

LATER, Manfred explained to an interested police chief.

"Oberzohn secured the poison by taking a snake and extracting his venom—a simple process: you have but to make him angry, and he will bite on anything. The doctor discovered a way of blending these venoms to bring out the most deadly qualities of them all—it sounds fantastic, and, from the scientist's point of view, unlikely. But it is nevertheless the fact. The venom was slightly diluted with water and enough to kill a dozen people was poured into a tiny mould and frozen."

"Frozen?" said the chief, in astonishment.

Manfred nodded.

"There is no doubt about it," he said. "Snake venom does not lose its potency by being frozen, and this method of moulding their darts was a very sane one, from their point of view. It was only necessary for a microscopic portion of the splinter to pierce the flesh. Sufficient instantly melted to cause death, and if the victim rubbed the place where he had been struck, it was more certain that he would rub some of the venom, which had melted on his cheek, into the wound. Usually they died instantly. The cigarette holders that were carried by Gurther and the other assassin, Pfeiffer, were blowpipes, the cigarette a hollow metal fake. By the time they blew their little ice darts, it was in a half-molten condition and carried sufficient liquid poison to kill, even if the skin was only punctured. And, of course, all that did not enter the skin melted before there could be any examination by the police. That is why you never found darts such as the bushmen use, slithers of bamboo, thorns from trees. Oberzohn had the simplest method of dealing with all opposition: he sent out his snake-men to intercept them, and only once did they fail—when they aimed at Leon and caught that snake-proof man, Elijah Washington!"

"What about Miss Leicester's claim to the goldfields of Biskara?"

Manfred smiled.

"The renewal has already been applied for and granted. Leon found at Heavytree Farm some blank sheets of note-paper signed with the girl's name.

He stole one during the aunt's absence and filled up the blank with a formal request for renewal. I have just had a wire to say that the lease is extended."

He and Poiccart had to walk the best part of the way to New Cross before they could find a taxicab. Leon had gone on with the girl. Poiccart was worried about something, and did not speak his mind until the providential cab appeared on the scene and they were trundling along the New Cross Road.

"My dear George, I am a little troubled about Leon," he said at last. "It seems almost impossible to believe, but——"

"But what?" asked Manfred good-humouredly, and knowing what was coming.

"You don't believe," said Poiccart in a hushed voice, as though he were discussing the advent of some world cataclysm—"you don't believe that Leon is in love, do you?"

Manfred considered for a moment.

"Such things happen, even to just men," he said, and Poiccart shook his head sadly.

"I have never contemplated such an unhappy contingency," he said, and Manfred was laughing to himself all the way back to town.

## THE END

9 789357 933452